"...and thoroughly satisfying."
All About Romance, Desert Isle Keeper

"A blissful read."
USA Today

I ADORED A LORD

"A riotous good time . . . Delicious."
Publishers Weekly

I MARRIED THE DUKE
*Historical Romance of the Year
Reviewers' Choice Award Nominee 2014*

KISSES, SHE WROTE

"Smoldering."
Library Journal (★Starred Review★)

"Finished it with tears in my eyes.
Yes, it was that good."
Elizabeth Boyle, *New York Times* bestselling author

MY LADY, MY LORD
*RITA® Award Finalist 2015
Romance Writers of America*

HOW TO MARRY A HIGHLANDER
*RITA® Award Finalist 2014
Romance Writers of America*

HOW TO BE A PROPER LADY
Amazon Editors' Choice 10 Best Books of 2012

WHEN A SCOT LOVES A LADY

"Lushly intense romance . . . radiant prose."
Library Journal (★Starred Review★)

"Sensationally intelligent writing and
a true, weak-in-the-knees love story."
Barnes & Noble "Heart to Heart" Recommended Read!

IN THE ARMS OF A MARQUESS

"Every woman who ever dreamed of having a
titled lord at her feet will love this novel."
Eloisa James, *New York Times* bestselling author

"Immersive and lush . . . Ashe is that rare author
who chooses to risk unexpected elements within
an established genre, and whose skill and magic
with the pen lifts her tales above the rest."
Fresh Fiction

CAPTURED BY A ROGUE LORD
*Best Historical Romantic Adventure
Reviewers' Choice Award Winner 2011*

SWEPT AWAY BY A KISS

"A breathtaking romance filled with sensuality
and driven by a brisk and thrilling plot."
Lisa Kleypas, #1 *New York Times* bestselling author

Romances by **Katharine Ashe**

The Devil's Duke
THE EARL
THE ROGUE

The Prince Catchers
I LOVED A ROGUE
I ADORED A LORD
I MARRIED THE DUKE

The Falcon Club
HOW A LADY WEDS A ROGUE
HOW TO BE A PROPER LADY
WHEN A SCOT LOVES A LADY

Rogues of the Sea
IN THE ARMS OF A MARQUESS
CAPTURED BY A ROGUE LORD
SWEPT AWAY BY A KISS

And from Avon Impulse

KISSES, SHE WROTE
HOW TO MARRY A HIGHLANDER
A LADY'S WISH

The
EARL

A Devil's Duke Novel

Katharine
Ashe

AVONBOOKS

An Imprint of HarperCollinsPublishers

THE EARL. Copyright © 2016 by Katharine Brophy Dubois. All rights reserved. Printed in the United States of America. No part of this book may be used or reproduced in any manner whatsoever without written permission except in the case of brief quotations embodied in critical articles and reviews. For information, address HarperCollins Publishers, 195 Broadway, New York, NY 10007.

First Avon Books mass market printing: November 2016

ISBN 978-0-06-241275-1

Avon Trademark Reg. U.S. Pat. Off. and in Other Countries, Marca Registrada, Hecho en U.S.A.
Avon, Avon Books, and the Avon logo are trademarks of HarperCollins Publishers.
HarperCollins® is a registered trademark of HarperCollins Publishers.

16 17 18 19 20   QGM   10 9 8 7 6 5 4 3 2 1

To my dear readers—
To those of you who wrote to me years ago
when my Falcon Club series first begun,
already begging for Peregrine and
Lady Justice's love story,

and to my readers who recently discovered
the Falcon Club and have asked me
if I would ever write this romance,
this book is especially for you.

"The exercise of the natural rights of woman has no other limits than those that the perpetual tyranny of man opposes to them; these limits must be reformed according to the laws of nature and reason."

—OLYMPE DE GOUGES, *The Declaration of the Rights of Woman* (1791)

"The marriage relation as constituted by [English] law . . . confers upon one of the parties to the contract, legal power & control over the person, property, and freedom of action of the other party, independent of her own wishes and will."

—JOHN STUART MILL, in protest against the laws governing marriage (19th century)

THE FALCON CLUB

THE MISSION
To find missing persons and bring them home

The Director
Anonymous

The Agents
Colin Gray, Earl of Egremoor—Peregrine,
Secretary of the Club (recently retired)

Lady Constance Read—Sparrow (retired)

Leam, Earl of Blackwood, heir to the
Duke of Read—Eagle (retired)

Captain Jinan Seton—Sea Hawk (retired)

Wyn Yale—Raven (retired)

Their Nemesis
Lady Justice, pamphleteer (as active as ever)

A Note from the Author

Two hundred years ago upon the heels of the European Enlightenment, Edinburgh, Scotland, glittered with style, wealth, and sophistication to rival the glamour of London and Paris. But as the city gloried in rebirth, the Scottish countryside remained spectacularly unchanged. Dark woodlands climbed the mountainsides, gleaming lochs reflected skies that knew no coal smog, and endless emerald hills and valleys boasted plentiful sheep and the occasional turret of mighty fortresses built in earlier, belligerent eras. It was a landscape of sublime contrasts, of delicate wildflowers and towering crags, silent mists and violent storms, cozy cottages tucked into safe crevices and miles upon miles of untamed wilderness. To step off the main road in this land was to enter another world, a world in which anything could happen, even the transformation of enemies into lovers and the breaking open of two locked hearts . . .

Prologue

The Silent Boy

October 1801
Maryport Court
Cumbria, England

*S*pine stiff and shoulders squared, the boy sat in the chair by the window with his palms on his knees and the soles of his feet pressed to the floor. He did not move. Not even his shallow breaths stirred his frame that was bony like an ascetic's, nor his face that was without expression, as though an artist had drawn the features at rest but forgot to invest humanity into them.

"You must allow me to see him," his mother said on the other side of the door with a voice that made the boy's insides sick.

The door handle rattled. But the panel was solid, fashioned centuries ago from some ancient tree that had grown in Gray Forest. In the past, with his inadequate fists the boy had pounded at that door. It still bore the pockmarks of a toy soldier he had once enlisted to carve a breach in that fortress, unsuccessfully. He had been too weak then.

Now he must be strong. Her sobs twisted in his belly, but he remained immobile, staring out the window into the park. Beyond the bare branches of the oak that scratched at the windowpanes like fingernails on slate, along the path to the sea two saplings battled the chill wind, tucked closely together in a nook of the hill. The gardener had said they were planted unwisely, that when they grew they would crowd each other out, and one or both would die. But his mother had insisted.

He barely remembered; he'd been only five at the time. She liked to tell the story, though, and he liked to listen to her tell it.

Now, leaves of vibrant red clung to the spindly branches of one of the saplings, the golden fronds of the other cavorting close by. In the blistered world of early winter, his eyes fixed on them hungrily.

"Come away now, Amelia," the earl said on the other side of the door, not ungently, but the Irish curl of his tongue was especially pronounced.

"I will not." The handle rattled again. "You *must* allow it, Eirnin. For a moment only. I beg of you."

"It will be to neither of your benefits."

"It will! I know what he wishes to say. I *understand* him. You do not. I—"

That a firm hand across a soft cheek could *clack* so cleanly, so neatly, was strange and painful and made the boy feel that he might disgrace himself now.

His mother's gasp gurgled into thicker sobs.

"Do not contravene me," the earl said firmly. "And do not beg. It is beneath my wife."

"Eirnin," she whispered. Now her words were muffled. *"I pray you."*

"The boy will speak for himself, or not at all."

"You *must* give him time. For pity's sake, he is only a boy."

"He is my heir. He will be a man sooner than either of us anticipate."

"He will be a good man," she insisted. "And he will be a great lord, whether he ever speaks a word or not."

The boy's pulse throbbed in his throat. He opened his mouth wide. He moistened his lips with a thick tongue. But nothing came forth. Nothing ever came forth.

"I have had enough." The earl was graver now. "You have made him dependent upon you, Amelia. I did not wish it to come to this again, but—"

"*No*, Eirnin. You cannot." Dread and disbelief threaded through her whisper. "You must not."

"Colin." The earl spoke through the closed door. "Your mother is going away. If you wish to speak, do so now and I will allow her to remain."

His body cramped. A fuzzy haze invaded his head, hot and dark and suffocating. He could feel his nostrils flare, his eyes prickle, his chest break from its frozen hold and jerk as the air swept into and out of his lungs.

No sound came from his mouth.

"So be it," the earl said.

"Colin!" his mother cried, muted, as though her lips were pressed against the panel. "I will return. Do not be anxious. We will see each other again soon, I promise." There were tears in her voice. "Be a good boy. Do what your father asks of you, and listen to Mr. Gunter. No, Eirnin! No, *please*." She was farther away suddenly. "Colin," she called, "remember what I told you. You are perfect as you are. Perfect, my darling son."

And then they were gone, their footsteps receding down the staircase, her sobs fading.

He sat for a long time in the room with only the single chair, so long that the light of day faded and he could not see the saplings on the hill. With no candle, he eventually came to be in darkness and the cold crept around him. But he remained immobile, despite the creaking somewhere that made him shiver and the sea wind that battered the windowpanes and sounded like ghosts. The earl admired courage and strength.

In the morning when the housekeeper came and unlocked the door, he would do his lessons with Mr. Gunter, who would tell the earl how disciplined he was, and how intelligent, despite his inability to recite. Then, pleased, the earl would allow her to come home, as he had those times before.

And perhaps this time when she returned, perhaps if he tried very hard, he would speak to her.

He could do it. He *would*. This time he would say, "Welcome home, Mama."

Then she would enfold him in her arms and together they would laugh with joy.

Chapter 1

The Lady

London, 1822

FROM the <u>London Weekly</u>:

> London's beloved pamphleteer,
> Lady Justice, has struck again!

To date Lady Justice has successfully influenced
members of Parliament to put their energies toward Reforms intended to aid the urban poor, coal
miners, cloth factory laborers, wounded veterans of war, aliens, deserving vagrants, chimney
sweeps, dock workers, and boys impressed into
the Royal Navy. Now, to the delight of women
throughout Britain, she has turned her attention
to the rights of wives. This week, Domestic Felicity was on the table—quite literally. At an event
dubbed "The Wives' Tea," no fewer than thirty-six
spouses of prominent politicians erected tea tables

before the Palace of Westminster, each laid with linens embroidered with the statement from Lady Justice's proposed bill: <u>Women should enjoy equal rights in marriage to men</u>.

Whether any MP will respond by introducing her bill and engaging in Sensible Debate is doubtful; some claim that allowing wives autonomy within marriage would undermine the Masculine Gravitas that makes this kingdom great. The Viscount Gray, heir to the Earl of Egremoor, the bill's most ardent detractor, spoke for many lords when he stated, "The proposal is utter rubbish." Lord Gray is unmarried as yet. Lucky he! For this columnist has no doubt whatsoever that there were at least three dozen frosty breakfast tables in London this morning.

(Lady Fitzwarren, widow of Lord Fitzwarren, whose heroic service to the Admiralty is well known, dropped by The Wives' Tea to lend her support and was overheard to remark, "If a man cannot manage to raise his mast for a wife who demands that he recognize her as his equal, he may as well chop the damn thing off.")

Lady Justice
Brittle & Sons, Printers
London

Dear Madam,

For five years you have publicly lambasted me and the other members of my club. You have published my letters to you, which asked you to cease plaguing us, alongside your responses to these letters. You have cast false accusations and willfully misunderstood our purpose. Among the cries of revolution you shout to any fool with a penny to trade for a broadsheet, you have insulted me, my friends, and the men who govern us all. You have been a thorn in my paw.

Now, when the Falcon Club is finally disbanded, you write to me—privately—begging my help.

How am I to respond? The brazen Lady Justice on her knees begging a bored, profligate member of the pampered class for aid? I can hardly countenance it. Shall I publish your desperate plea for the world to read and judge, just as you have published my every letter to you?

I will not. Instead, I will now make demands of my own. Tell me how you discovered the true mission of the club and the reason that you did not disclose it to the public. Then show me that your courage is at least as great as your bravado: meet me face-to-face. Only then will I consider your request for aid.

In anticipation of your acquiescence,
Peregrine, formerly Secretary of the Falcon Club

Peregrine
14½ Dover Street
London

Dear Sir,

For years you have taunted and teased and flirted with me through your correspondence when all I seek—all I have ever sought—is the betterment of this realm for the benefit of the majority of its people, those people you call "fools," so that everybody might enjoy its riches and prosperity, not only the privileged, wealthy few that hoard power. That you continue to claim you are the wronged party astonishes me. You say I am a thorn? I am happy to have caused you discomfort! For it is when a man feels the greatest pain that his true character is revealed—coward or hero.

I cannot tell you how I discovered the purpose of the Falcon Club. I began to suspect it in the months following my discovery of the true identity of the member of your cabal called Raven. If you possessed any intelligence, you would have noted the change in my correspondence at that time: I ceased making accusations against your club. My comments thereafter were directed solely at you, and at the injustices and inequalities suffered by countless subjects of the crown, of which men like you are entirely ignorant at best, or shrug away at worst.

As to your second demand, I will never meet you in person. To do so would be to endanger those with whom I work. I will not jeopardize the safety of the people I love in order to satisfy your vanity. Desperation, however, compels me to renew the plea from my previous letter. Allow me to put my case before you in writing, and help me.

Sincerely,
Lady Justice

P.S. Take care whom you call fools. The wrongful tax that Government exacts on pamphlets of the sort that I publish prohibits all but persons of some means from purchasing them. That is you and your friends, Mr. Peregrine.

Dear Lady,

I am awed by your tenacity. In truth, I am moved. Your loyalty to your friends and your determination to maintain their safety despite your need is commendable. It alters my opinion of you dramatically. Not only that; it makes me hopeful as never before.

Can the tender feminine heart that beats so sincerely for those friends and the people of England spare a space for one more soul?

We have been intimates in public ink for sufficient

years now that I feel I know you. I want you to know me too, but honestly. Allow me to claim your friendship in person so that you can see with your eyes the admiration in mine, and, in hearing the esteem in my voice, know me—finally—a changed man because of you.

Meet me, and I vow to respect your request for aid.

With hope,

Peregrine, formerly Secretary of the Falcon Club

Dear Sir,

From condemnation to seduction in so few lines! You have given me whiplash. Your flatteries do not, however, entice me. I will not be made love to via post and fall breathlessly into idiocy. That you imagine my submission so easily won through such transparent duplicity makes me wonder whether you have read a word of what I have written these past five years.

I repeat: I will not meet you.

But in one matter you have forced my hand. I will now divulge the substance of my request to you in the hope that your humanity will overcome your obstinacy and you will come to the aid of one who is in danger.

A young woman of my acquaintance is missing. For several years she wrote to me from the West Indies with perfect regularity, yet I have not received a letter from her in months. I have reason to believe she was pursuing a mystery, and that she traveled to Scotland seeking answers.

I haven't the resources to investigate her disappearance as I wish I could. Will you prove my original opinion: that you are an idle aristocrat with nothing but petty amusements to inspire you? Or, Mr. Peregrine—who until recently were the leader of a secret agency devoted to finding lost people—will you help me?

Impatiently,

Lady Justice

Chapter 2

The Lord

September 1822
Maryport Court
Cumbria, England

*W*ind cut across the hillside, layering salt upon lips and cheeks and ruffling the tails of the Friesians pulling the bier upon which the ninth Earl of Egremoor lay enshrouded in cloth. The mourners drew their coats and cloaks tighter about them, pressing toward the mausoleum against the gale that rushed off the ocean like a lustful god intent upon ravishing the land.

Rather, all but one mourner struggled as they climbed. Colin Gray, for a sennight now the tenth Earl of Egremoor and lord of this vast stretch of wind-raped northern coast, walked steadily as though it were the mildest spring day. Severity marked his features, which were regular, strong, and handsome, with hard, fine lines about the sides of his mouth that suggested he rarely found occasion for laughter, and eyes that were both an unlikely shade of dark, dark blue and bereft of emotion.

The new earl was neither pensive over the loss of his only remaining parent nor rejoicing in the old earl's passing. His grief was new, acute, and dark. He would not soon recover from this. But it was beneath him to reveal it.

That, and at present he was, in fact, thinking about smoking. Specifically, his mind had been occupied for many minutes now in conjuring the memory of the flavor of a particular tobacco he had not had occasion to enjoy in some time, not since returning to his ancestral estate months earlier.

And he was thinking about the flavor of woman.

Years ago the earl had taught him that the two went in tandem: a good smoke and a good woman were best enjoyed in succession, the smoke always after the woman, to cleanse the senses of inordinate carnal appetite.

Concerning the latter, Colin could not agree. He rather enjoyed the flavor of woman.

He had never mentioned that to the earl, of course. The ninth Earl of Egremoor had not approved of the weakness some men showed toward women. He had never approved of weakness in any form.

At the mausoleum, Colin followed the priest and youths garbed in vestments of lacy exuberance down the steps. One swung a censor, clinking the metal globe against the long chain in *chink-chink* rhythm, and smoke the color of rain rose to fill the crypt with sacred scent. It was a papish ritual, but the earl had been Irish, and a great man. His only son would not forsake him these last elaborate rites.

As the bearers rested the bier upon its pedestal, Colin gave no outward sign that his heartbeats had grown shallow. He had not entered this mausoleum in two decades. Five feet away lay his mother's bones.

When the ceremony concluded, he descended the hill before the silent mourners, all of them from Egremoor and the surrounding villages, except two guests: Leam Blackwood and Jinan Seton. Within the house he accepted the condolences of the farmers and gentry who were now his tenants, and the subdued sympathies of the local gentry. The earl had been an aloof man, but a just and generous neighbor and overlord. No one had reason to believe his heir would be any different. In hushed voices they wished him well.

Finally the stream of mourners came to an end and his guests were enjoying the bounteous repast his staff had prepared, and drinking liberally. Leam and Jin had disappeared. Withdrawing, Colin went to his study.

Leam Blackwood, lord of a sizeable domain fifty miles from Edinburgh and sometime poet, clasped a tumbler of brandy in his oversized palm. A rawboned Scot whose hair was shot through with a white streak that revealed the tragedy in his past, Leam had long been his closest friend. Yet now the Scot's brow was surly.

"Are you still holding a grudge?" Colin said, strolling forward.

Leam came to shake his hand. "Isn't the time for recriminations now, of course. Kitty would've come if it weren't for the wee one."

Colin turned to the other man. "Jinan."

Jin Seton's crystalline eyes assessed him with the mute wisdom of a king painted upon an Egyptian sarcophagus. Colin and the ex-pirate had never gotten on easily. But Seton's character was nobler than most men of aristocratic lineage and august titles whom Colin knew. He had not always approved of Seton's methods for accomplishing his Falcon Club missions. But he trusted him.

Of all the men in the world, indeed, he trusted these two the most. The other man he had trusted, the club's director, had recently thrown that trust to the dogs.

For more than a decade Colin had acted at the behest of the crown and the director. He had collected a small group of friends—three intelligent, courageous men and one extraordinary woman—and sent them on journeys, given them missions, entrusting to them the safety and welfare of countless others. During the war their work had helped protect the kingdom, and after the treaty the members of the club had done great good for England. But the director's last maneuver with the sole woman in the club had left a bitter taste in Colin's mouth.

"Constance has not written to you, I expect?" Jin said by way of greeting.

"She hasn't forgiven you." Leam swallowed the remainder of his brandy.

"No, she has not." He didn't blame her. For years he had kept the secret of the identity of the Falcon Club's anonymous director from Constance, Leam, Jin, and their fifth, Wyn Yale. Then in the spring the director had revealed himself to Constance—without warning or even tact—cruelly, in order to control her in a manner Colin had never imagined possible.

And him.

He went to the sideboard, unstoppered a crystal decanter, and gestured to his friend. "Another?"

"She's hurt," Leam said, offering his glass to be refilled. "Sincerely hurt to discover that you did not trust her enough to tell her. And Yale—for all that he pretends it is a fantastic jest—he doesn't like it either, mostly for Constance's sake, I suspect. But for him that is enough. Damn it, I don't like it either." He gestured to the former pirate. "And Jin risked his life in that ship of his more than once for the club. We *all* risked our lives for him, when he was right under our noses the whole time. We could have—"

"Quit?" Colin offered a glass of brandy to Jin. "Recall that you did. All of you. And he released you, just as you wished."

"You might have told us the truth," Jin said mildly.

Leam scoffed. "Constance would have been angry no matter when she learned it." He drank a healthy mouthful. "A man is only as noble as his honesty, Gray."

Colin went to the sideboard, took up an empty glass, and let the candlelight blur in his vision.

"When she created that public scandal with Sterling," he said, feeling the pattern of the crystal against his hand as though it were the first time he had ever felt such a thing—*anything.* Texture, sensation, scent, flavor; it all seemed so alien. "He instructed her to marry me."

Leam choked. "The devil he did!"

Colin poured brandy into the tumbler. "He told her that she had ruined herself for his plans, and that to save her reputation and his project she must have a husband of wealth and position, which of course Sterling was not. He said that I would do as he wished." As he always had. Until the director had broken his friends' trust in him and demanded that he give his entire future to a crusade he was not even allowed to understand.

Leam's eyes showed outrage. Jinan's mouth was a hard line.

"Too mercenary for even you, Jin?" Colin said.

"Machiavellian," the man who had once been a slave replied. "Son of a bitch."

Colin lifted a brow. "Him, or me?"

"What reply did you give him?"

"It never came to that," he said, remembering the fury in Constance's letter to him before her wedding. "She declined to acquiesce to his wishes."

"We're all better rid of him," Leam growled, then his brow knit. "You are rid of him now, aren't you, Colin? Rid of the club finally?"

"Yes." Rid of the yoke he had willingly taken on when he had been overly eager to leave this house. Rid of doing his mentor's bidding. *Any* other man's bidding. He lifted his glass to his friends and they returned the salute. "The Falcon Club is finished."

Now only one final mission awaited him: the mission he had assigned to himself.

He set down his empty glass, wanting more, wanting flavor. But he had another caller, and news to hear.

"I saw Grimm ride in," Leam said, as though hearing his thoughts.

"The club's office in town is to be let," Colin said. "He has come to finalize that." Even now he withheld the entire truth from them.

"Then we should allow you to see to your responsibilities," Jin said, finally moving to him and extending his hand. "Godspeed, Colin."

"Give my best to Viola."

Now the sailor smiled. "I will."

Leam grasped his elbow and held him tight and close. "I am sorry for your loss, lad. Your father was a cold son of a bitch. But he was a fine man." Leam released him and gave him a thoroughly Scottish grin. "Welcome to the peerage, old friend."

"Thank you for coming," he said, his throat hard against a surge of emptiness.

They departed. Colin opened a box of cigars atop the desk and the aroma curled into his nostrils with piquant tang. It was a palliative only, just as the brandy. He needed a woman. He needed the silken softness of a feminine body against his, the sweetness of a woman's mouth to taste, the lush strawberry musk of a woman's scent on his skin. But Egremoor was his now, and a man who took pleasure with women of the common class under his protection was not worthy of his rank or blood.

The door opened and Grimm filled it entirely.

"Milord." The giant bowed like a mountain bending over. The Falcon Club had disbanded, but its man-of-all-tasks still lived in the flat above the club's meeting place in London. His appearance here meant one thing only.

Colin offered him a cigar. "Have a smoke with me."

Grimm lit it from the hearth fire as Colin replaced the box on the desk.

"Have you a letter for me, Joseph?"

Grimm reached into his coat and produced an envelope. Colin knew that the hand within it was bold and firm and barely like a woman's.

"Arrived yesterday," Grimm said, blowing a cloud of smoke. "Knew you've been waiting for it."

"Thank you for bringing it to me so swiftly."

"You know I'd do anything for you, milord."

He did know it. The earl had trained him well how to command the respect and loyalty of his subordinates as well as his equals. And he was successful at it with everyone.

Everyone except his four closest friends now, who wished him to the devil, and the author of the letter in his hand.

"I am grateful for your loyalty, Joseph."

Grimm bowed his hulking frame and went out, trailing fragrant smoke behind him in tendrils of temptation.

Setting the letter down, Colin withdrew another envelope from his breast pocket, this one already opened, and laid it before him. Lord Vale had not waited even an hour after hearing of the Earl of Egremoor's death to send it. And yet, five days later, Colin had not replied.

For some time now he had believed himself free of this responsibility. Vale had attempted more than once to marry off his eldest daughter to other men. None of those attempts had come to fruition; she had rejected every suitor. Now Lord Vale seemed to believe he could force her marriage through the pact that two companions at arms had made decades earlier. This morning, at the reading of the will, Colin finally understood the reason for Vale's confidence that his old friend's son would oblige.

He would not, of course. Emily did not want it. He did not want it. For years they had both evaded it. There was no reason to alter that now.

Seeing her at Constance's wedding in April had been a shock. Distracted by the earl's illness, he had not anticipated it. Coming face-to-face with her had taken him off guard.

He did not care for being taken off guard. And he did not care for what seeing her did to him—unexpectedly or not.

Now he must deal with it, of course.

Dropping Vale's letter onto the desk, he took up the envelope that Grimm had brought from London, snapped open the seal, and read it. The bows and junctures of the final words seemed more urgently penned, and he studied them. Lady Justice had grown desperate.

Mr. Peregrine—who until recently were the leader of a secret government agency devoted to finding lost people—will you help me?

One more task, not for the club or its director. For himself.

He withdrew a sheet of paper and a pen and wrote three words in reply. Sealing the letter, he pulled the bell for his manservant. Waiting, he walked to the window.

"Inform Mr. Grimm that he will be returning to London immediately with this," he said when Cooper entered. "And prepare for my departure tomorrow."

He looked out to the hill, to the pair of trees alongside the path. They had grown up entwined, their branches entangled, the gray bark of one and the brown of the other almost indistinguishable in their embrace. Just as the gardener had foretold years ago. Just as his mother had foolishly designed.

"And, Mr. Cooper," he said. "Tell the gardener I wish to see him."

London, England

Zenobia, born Emily Anne Vale, but lately self-styled after the third-century queen of the Palmyrenes of Syria who rebelled against the oppressive regime of the Roman Empire—and known more widely to Londoners as the anonymous pamphleteer Lady Justice, champion of the poor and powerless, and disparager of the aristocracy for its wanton disregard of everybody else's welfare—was not a gossip. She needn't be. Her superior maid and longtime lady's companion both were, and she heard all the sordid details of the lives of the rich and wellborn through them.

"That one sneaks into the butler's pantry after her servants are asleep and drinks all the cooking sherry," her maid, Shauna, said about a woman walking along the path. "And that one wears cucumbers to bed every night because she thinks it'll mend the wrinkles, poor lass. And that one has illicit trysts with her first footman."

"*Ooh*. That seems not so bad a habit," Clarice responded, tossing a shawl of black fringe over her shoulder for dramatic effect. A Frenchwoman of fifty years and great style, Clarice Roche adored dramatic effect.

"If you even consider making Franklin your fourth husband, Clarice, I will turn you out of the house." Zenobia did not lift her eyes from her book. The sun was warm and the park still sparsely populated at this hour. And Dante's *Monarchy* was almost interesting enough to distract her mind from where it strayed lately. Seven months without a letter from her sister Amarantha were six and a half too many.

"How droll you are, *ma petite*."

"That man wears stays," Shauna said as a gentleman rode by.

"Many men wear stays." Zenobia flipped a page. "Gluttony drives the necessity, and vanity makes the discomfort endurable."

"You see, milady," Shauna said, grinning, "plenty of people have secrets that everybody else knows about."

"High society would disintegrate without its secrets to give it structure, Shauna. Dissipation and excess flow from one drawing room to the next, whitewashed in fashionable attire and glittering jewels to hide the stink of empty souls underneath. The British aristocracy is a seething morass of secrets and lies."

"You should tell everybody your secret."

"I would appreciate quiet to read."

"*Sauf* the Lord Gray," Clarice said. "He does not."

Zenobia refused to twitch. She had forbidden the name to be spoken in her house. But they were not now in the house. Clever Clarice.

"He doesn't have a secret?" Shauna asked.

"He does not *wear stays*," Clarice clarified.

"He doesn't need to," Shauna said a bit wispily. "He's the finest man I've seen in a month of feast days."

"*Tout à fait*," Clarice cooed. "With the broad shoulders to make the heart flutter, and the eyes of such sublime midnight that seem to look into a woman's soul."

"And he's half Irish." Shauna sighed.

"To run one's fingers through the hair of such a man," Clarice murmured. "So dark and satiny."

"And that jaw! It's nibbleable."

"*Nibbleable* is not a word." Zenobia pushed her spectacles farther up her nose and read the sentence at the top of the page for the fourth time.

"*Ah, oui!*" Clarice said. "Square and noble and clean-shaven for the fingertips to stroke."

"He's even got a dimple," Shauna exclaimed. "But only in the one cheek."

Clarice clucked her tongue. "It is suitably subdued for a man of his rank and fortune, *non*?"

"So true."

"Enough." Zenobia stood and tucked the book under her arm. "You have effectively ruined the park for me today. Betrayers, the both of you. And cease staring at me now like I am a little lost lamb, will you? It is entirely inappropriate."

Her maid tilted her head. "We only want what's best for you, milady."

"I hear enough of that in my mother's letters. I needn't endure it from you as well."

"You should marry him."

"You almost make me regret my egalitarian stance on the suitable relationship between employers and employees," she said quite sincerely.

Shauna's eyes twinkled. "But you *should* marry him."

"You mustn't let dimples and broad shoulders fool you, Shauna. All of that noble virtue and sober responsibility that he and men like him pretend are mere smoke screens to hide the idle pointlessness of their obsolete aristocratic existence."

"You're a member of the aristocracy."

"Other than that unfortunate fact, we have nothing in common. He is pretense and privilege in expensive wrapping. I am a lover of knowledge. I spend my days seeking truth and sharing it with others who seek the truth too. Why on earth should I marry a man like that?"

"*Ma petite* should not marry the Lord Gray." Clarice's crimson lips settled into a bow. "She *must* marry him."

"He is in favor of Corn Laws, and among those virulently opposed to reforming the House of Commons." She ticked off on her fingers. "He has no wife or children, yet he owns at least three carriages and no fewer than four saddle horses, the worst sort of conspicuous consumption of the privileged elite." And he had barely spoken to her in eighteen years. "And he has a stick up his arse."

"You admire him."

"In fact I dislike him. Quite a lot."

"*Ma chère*, the Earl of Egremoor is dead."

Zenobia blinked.

"It was only"—she recited aloud words she had recited silently to herself for years—"an informal agreement."

"It's what the old earl wanted most, milady."

She peered at Shauna. "How on earth do you know that?"

"Your mother—"

"Fine." Zenobia removed her spectacles and tucked them into a pocket in her pelisse. "I am walking home now. If you care to accompany me, I will welcome your companionship. But if either of you speak of this again, *I* will cease speaking to you. Permanently."

Neither responded. Silence was entirely unlike both of them.

"What?" she demanded. "Tell me."

"Don't you want a family, milady?"

A sinking sensation filled her belly.

"Do you wish to leave me?" She looked from one to the other. "Is that at the root of this? Are you weary of living with an odd duck and wish to cast me off in favor of more fashionable company?"

"No!"

"*Non!*"

"I have thought us happy—we three with Franklin and Jonah. And Mrs. Curly too. I thought *we* were a family. An unconventional one, to be sure, but content."

"We are, milady!" Shauna's freckled face crinkled as she glanced at Clarice.

"*Ma chère*, this marriage, it would be good for you."

"Marriage is good for no woman, Clarice. It binds her as securely to a master as chains, and silences her voice as surely as if she had a gag stuffed between her lips. Why should I want that? I have been blessed with an affectionate, negligent father and am free to do mostly as I wish, with the resources to do it. I have no desire to subject myself to a potentially harsher overlord. I have work yet to do—so much work that I haven't time to stand here and argue this with you."

"But, *ma petite*, there is the romance."

"Flowers and poetry and grand gestures," Shauna added. "You deserve them as well as any woman."

"Romance is a pretense to lull women into submitting to men's authority."

"But what about the *love*?" Clarice said.

"See what happened to my sister when she fell in love! She gave up her family and England to follow a man across an ocean, and now she is missing."

"*Ma chère*," Clarice said. "Marriage to a good man is not like that."

"Amarantha's husband was a good man, but she is still gone." More importantly, Colin Gray was not a good man. The trouble was that no one else knew it. Even her dear friends Kitty Blackwood and Constance Sterling cared for him. But they did not know him like she had once upon a time. "Clarice, I am not close-minded. Show me some actual good in forcing a woman to relinquish her life—her *legal autonomy*—for a man to the exclusion of all else, and I might begin to rethink my stance on marriage."

"Pfft!" Clarice scowled prettily. "You speak always of the thinking! What of the *feeling*? *Ma petite*, you must allow yourself to experience the tumult of the heart before you shut yourself away in a turret for the rest of your life."

"And it wouldn't do you any harm to try nibbling a fine square jaw either," Shauna offered.

"*C'est ça!* The delights of the flesh are to be tasted while one is young. Ah, the passion of the young love, it is sublime." Clarice sighed. "You must not deny yourself this, *ma petite.*"

They did not, of course, know that she had in fact already tasted the delights of the flesh. Curiosity had driven her to it. But the mere notion of such a thing alongside thoughts of Colin Gray made her feel ill, in the manner of lungs that have accidentally sucked up water and afterward must struggle to take in air.

"Cease this," she said. "Please. I have no intention of ever shackling myself to a man."

"But the late earl—"

"And I assure you, even if my *feelings* were to alter about the institution, the new Earl of Egremoor is the last man on earth I would ever marry."

Chapter 3

A Meeting, At Long Last

*Z*enobia was at her writing desk, quill between fingers more accustomed to pen than sewing needle, spectacles perched on the bridge of her nose, and head bent to her latest pamphlet when, in an ominous voice, Franklin announced, "The Earl of Egremoor."

Twitching a blank sheet over her work, she arose.

There in her parlor doorway he stood, dwarfing her footman. Color from the brisk day without dusted his cheekbones, but otherwise he was exactly as he had been in Edinburgh months earlier: elegant, understated, and utterly perfect. From his cravat carved of Italian marble to his boots that shone like the blade of a sword, there was no hue that jarred or angle that displeased. Motionless and severe and entirely focused on her, he was a strong, magnificent creature of impeccable noble blood surveying her like a hawk hunting from far above and judging her paltry prey.

An unnerving silence stretched across the room. That he

did not speak at once buoyed her courage; he must be at least as unhappy as she with this meeting.

"You needn't have come," she finally said. "I would have been content with a letter from your secretary."

It could not be a smile causing the slight shadow about his mouth. This man did not smile. He bowed gorgeously, however, without excess or flourish but with glorious control. The hat and riding crop still in his grasp were props to reveal the sinews and long fingers of his hands, and they made it clear that he did not intend a lengthy call.

"Good day, my lady." His voice was as smooth and deep as it had been in Scotland in the spring when he had barely spoken to her despite their attendance at the same wedding. "I trust you are well?"

"Oh, please," she said crisply. "You don't care if I am well or not. And I don't care for empty social conventions, so let us dispense with small talk. I have heard about your father's death and I am very sorry. You have my sincere sympathy."

"Do I?" He moved into the parlor and she had the most disturbing impulse to seize a fireplace poker and brandish it. But he halted in the middle of the room.

"Yes, you do," she said. "So now you may go."

Something sharp flashed in his eyes and she felt it in her stomach like a little shock.

"I have only just arrived," he said.

"And that is really about all of this call I can bear," she said. "Good day, my lord."

"Emily."

He said it unremarkably. But the sound of her name upon his tongue did something horrible to her insides: it twisted them into a knot of very old and unwanted pain.

"I go by Zenobia," she said before he could continue. "For several months now."

"I see." He advanced another step.

"Halt." She thrust out her palm. His eyes were the most beautiful shade of blue, so dark, and so familiar. At one time she had thought that the warmest smile in the world rested in those eyes. "I have offered my sympathies and said good-day, and truly I meant both." She was not, after all, a woman to fall to pieces over a pair of dark eyes. "Please go."

"I cannot yet." His jaw was just as Clarice and Shauna rhapsodized: taut and handsome and at this moment engaged in an intriguing little dance of muscular tension. "I must say something first."

She frowned and tried not to stare at the flexing muscle. "Say it, and then leave."

His shoulders seemed to set even more firmly in place.

"My lady," he said in quite a fearsome voice, "will you do me the honor of becoming my bride?"

For all of his experience in cowing people he wished to cow, Colin had never actually seen the color drain from a person's face as swiftly and entirely as it now did from Emily's. If he needed confirmation that she had dreaded this moment, here it was in the parchment white of her cheeks and brow. Even her lips paled—admirable lips, pink and shapely and formed to suggest laughter rather than the astonishment that parted them now. Her eyes widened too, brilliant emerald behind lenses of gold-rimmed spectacles. Her chin was a pixie's, not soft and rounded but slightly sharp, and her features fine. Her hair had not changed in twenty years, except that now the pale wisps were confined in a simple queue rather than tangled with pine needles and mismatched ribbons. Dressed soberly in muted blue, she was the portrait of a reclusive maiden and clearly astonished, and he had never so powerfully wanted an interview to end quickly.

"You have got to be jesting," she said into the thick silence.

"I do not jest."

"Well then, you have gone mad."

"On the contrary."

"Oh." A delicate V darted the bridge of her nose above the gold wire. "You are required to offer for me, aren't you? By the terms of your father's will."

She was intelligent and perceptive, and forthright in a

manner that would embarrass most other women. She hadn't a care for what others thought of her. She never had.

"I am," he said because he had always been honest with her. Except once.

"You needn't have come here. You might have written to my father at Willows Hall."

"The will specified the manner in which I was to make the offer."

"Did it? How loathsome of your father."

"I am—" He found the unprecedented need to clear his throat. "I am also required to await your response."

"This could not be more idiotic, could it? No, I won't marry you. Now you can leave." She turned to her desk, then looked over her shoulder, her lashes spread wide. "You are not actually required to *marry* me in order to inherit Maryport Court, are you? That could not possibly be legal. The estate is entailed."

He actually *felt* his spine stiffen, the vertebrae aligning in a perfect column.

"Why?" He should leave. Immediately. Before he said something he would regret. "If I were, would your answer differ?"

"Of course not." She paused and alarm sparked in the candid emeralds. "*Is* it the case?"

"No." But the requirement that he marry her in order to maintain control of extensive unentailed properties in the West Country, as well as his mother's jewels, was. "You are correct. The estate is bound to the title."

"That must be a relief for you," she said, turning her back to him again and sitting before a small writing table. "I would not have wished you to be separated from all you hold dear." She reached for a pen. "I imagine the stipulation, even as it is, could not be held up to law. You might have contested it."

"I chose not to." To protect the privacy of their parents' agreement. To protect his privacy. And hers.

"Well, now your devotion to duty is satisfied." She dipped the pen in ink. "Good day."

A hard, hot discomfort settled between his ribs. He was unaccustomed to being dismissed. And, for all that he had not looked forward to this meeting, he had not wanted it to go quite like this.

"Good-bye, Emily," he said to her straight shoulders and glossy hair.

She did not reply or even lift her head. He turned to the door and for the last time walked away from the girl who had once been his best—*his only*—friend.

THROUGH THE WINDOW she watched him receive his horse from Jonah, mount with the ease of a man well suited to everything he did, and ride away. He had a gorgeous seat and straight, broad shoulders and the uncomfortable heat in her belly now must not disconcert her. Any woman would find those masculine attributes alluring, and she had long since reconciled herself to the unfortunate fact that she was not unique in that regard—not regarding him.

"And that is that," she said. It was not out of the ordinary for her to talk to herself. It was, however, unprecedented for her to stare after a man. But this was Colin. He had always been her exception.

No more. Now, finally, he was no one to her.

Time spent pondering the peculiarly conflicting appeal and cruelties of men—especially this man—however, was certainly time wasted. Her latest pamphlet required her attention. Yet again it would urge Parliament to bring to the floor for debate the Domestic Felicity Act, which demanded a wife's legal right to control her own property and income, to hold equal authority over her children as her husband, and to be allowed to escape him if he abused any of them. The bill was her most ambitious endeavor yet and the culmination of years of research and drafting. Through Brittle & Sons, Printers, she had sent a draft of it to every member of Parliament. Not one of them had taken it up, which drove her pen even more furiously now. This exhortation would spare no censure.

But when her footman appeared again at the parlor door, a silver salver in his gloved hand, she discovered she had not written a word. That a pair of broad shoulders and a handsome jaw should distract a woman from her purpose so thoroughly made her momentarily despair of her sex.

"My lady," Franklin said, "a letter has just arrived from Brittle & Sons."

She whipped around in her chair. "From *him*?"

Franklin's head did quick little bobs. She leaped up. Her footman stood on tiptoes expectantly as she tore open the envelope that, as always, bore no return address and had been delivered to her publisher's office by anonymous messenger. Upon the page were three words only, written in Peregrine's firm, clean, aristocratic hand: *On one condition.*

Air hissed from between her clenched teeth. "He is still insisting that I meet him."

"The knave." Her footman shook his head. "We will be better served to find Lady Amarantha ourselves," he said for the hundredth time in a month.

Her household was split: her groom and Clarice had been urging her for weeks to seek help from the man who had been the Falcon Club's secretary, while Shauna and Franklin stood firmly against it. Her housekeeper, Mrs. Curly, held no opinion, claiming that she was far too busy with her responsibilities to pronounce judgment on matters that her ladyship should decide herself. But she was of an older generation and did not fully appreciate what she called her mistress's "radical notions."

"I am a reformer, not a spy," she said to Franklin now. "We haven't the connections or the skills to find my sister." She crumpled the paper and moved to her desk. "Remember what happened when I hired that investigator from Bow Street to track Raven across the countryside. He was bedridden for months."

"But you succeeded in discovering Mr. Yale's part in the club." Pride swelled Franklin's voice.

"I did," she mumbled. Her staff was so pleased with that

little victory. Through it, and through clues unwittingly revealed by Wyn Yale's companion on that journey, Diantha Lucas, as well as rumors and bits of information the members of her household had heard over the years, she had learned the fact about the Falcon Club that perplexed her: its handful of elite members amused themselves by finding lost people and returning them to their homes—apparently whether they wished to be returned home or not. Diantha Lucas certainly had not wanted to go home, and yet Wyn Yale, whose name in the club was Raven, had found the runaway and reunited her with her family. Whether the club's members did this from ennui with their regular amusements, or for the satisfaction of interfering in the lives of others, it hardly mattered at present.

She needed their skills now.

"If I could ask Mr. Yale to help me find Amarantha without revealing that I know he was a member of the club, I would."

"You *cannot*," Franklin said darkly. "If Lady Justice alone knows that he is Raven, it would expose you."

"I must do this, Franklin."

"Must do what?" Her groom, Jonah, stood in the doorway. Long limbs dressed in comfortable leathers were a contrast to Franklin's squat, soft frame garbed in the livery of her father's household that he insisted on wearing.

"She intends to finally meet that blackguard," Franklin grumbled.

"S'about time," Jonah said around a stick caught between his lips. "I'll be there to protect you, of course."

Franklin sniffed archly. "Fat lot of good that'll do if he's a bigger man than you, skin-shanks."

"Or you could take along tub-o'-lard here, milady," Jonah said cheerily. "He could sit on Mr. Peregrine and subdue him right quick."

"Peregrine?" Shauna said as she entered. "Has he replied to your last letter?"

The missive passed into her maid's hands.

"Oh, milady," Shauna said in a horrified hush. "You can't be thinkin' of doin' this."

"She *is*, although I have of course begged her not to," Franklin said primly.

"If he is like most of the men," Clarice said, sweeping into the parlor, "the moment he has gotten that which he wishes, he will—*pfft!*—lose interest. I commend you on the courage, *ma petite.*"

"Throwing oneself before a hungry lion is not courage, Madame Roche," Franklin said. "It is an act of desperation."

Clarice peered down at Zenobia's writing.

"*Ce soir!* Ah, *ma petite* has the bravery beyond every other woman!" she exclaimed to the others. "She writes to him that she will meet him tonight."

Shauna gasped. "Tonight! Oh, milady, you—"

"Stop." Zenobia swiveled around in her chair. "To find my sister I must do this. I have made my decision."

"But tonight? So soon?"

"If I am to be exposed to the world as Lady Justice, then it may as well happen now than later. But I am hoping that will not be necessary. Please, now, leave me to do this."

In heavy silence, they filed out of the parlor.

"Thank you," she said to their backs. "Thank you, my friends. If it all ends tonight, I want you to know that I am grateful for everything you have done for Lady Justice, but mostly for the people of Britain. Whatever happens now, I will not allow you to suffer for having supported me."

"You know each of us would go to the gallows for you, my lady!" Franklin declared. "But if we do, I should like to choose your ensemble for the trip there," he added with a disapproving glance at her gown.

"Let us trust it shan't come to the gallows."

Jonah, Franklin, and Shauna departed and Clarice draped herself over a chair.

"Now, *ma petite*," the Frenchwoman said with a sigh worthy of the stage, "it is time we have the conversation."

Zenobia reached for sealing wax. "About what?"

"About the male desire."

"Clarice."

"You know nothing, *ma chère*, of what truly inspires the men. This man that has written to Lady Justice for years, he is infatuated with her. *Non, non.* He is *obsessed* with her."

"No. He wants to silence her. He wants to stop her from advocating for the rights of people he believes are fools. He is intelligent and manipulative and he thinks that because she is a woman flattery will make her silly and behave incautiously."

"*Oui*, he wishes to silence her. But he is also intrigued by her. Stimulated. He wants to control her. He wants to *have* her. To the men, you see, these are the same."

"I daresay." That was, after all, what the Domestic Felicity Act would inhibit: men's desire to control women.

"A woman is a fool if she does not use a man's desire to her advantage. And you, *Emilie*, are not a fool." Clarice pursed her lips. "Now, *ma chère*, you must decide: Are you prepared to do what you must to obtain your goal?"

THE MOON HAD ceded the night to the stars when Zenobia arrived at the meeting place they had agreed upon via letter: a small ancient cemetery surrounded by a fence and hedges on a street still busy with carriages and horse traffic. A long black cloak and veil aided the dark in disguising her.

Jonah walked beside her, a hood drawn around his face as well, but he would not accompany her to the meeting. For all his taunting, Peregrine did not frighten her. A man who dedicated his leisure time to rescuing strays was unlikely to harm a lone woman.

The cobbles shimmered with an earlier rain as she gestured for Jonah to remain across the street. Lamps lit this part of London irregularly, and the break in the wall was in shadow. Beside the gate stood an enormous man.

"Ma'am." The behemoth bowed. "He awaits you within."

It was immediately clear why he had suggested this place. The thick hedge within the walls created a bower of privacy and the gravestones scattered unevenly throughout made swift escape impossible.

He had staged the situation to his advantage too. He stood among the stones not four yards away, a lamp on the ground behind him casting him in silhouette. He was tall, and the breadth of his shoulders and solid stance suggested a man of fine physical conditioning. The night was mild and he wore no hat or overcoat—nothing to disguise him.

He was entirely willing for her to know his true identity.

The gate creaked closed behind her.

"Good evening, madam," he said into the darkness. "It is a pleasure to finally make your acquaintance. I have looked forward to this moment for years. But, of course, you already know that." His voice was smooth and low, far from menacing, rather intimate, and shockingly, unbelievably, horribly familiar.

Only hours earlier this elegant voice had proposed marriage to her.

"I am Gray," he said. "Now remove that veil and tell me your name."

Chapter 4

The Promise

The pavement was falling away beneath her feet, one slab of stone at a time. And he was moving toward her.

"Come no closer," she said in French. She had practiced pitching her voice low in the language she spoke every day with Clarice. She had depended upon street traffic tonight to disguise her voice even further, but now only the sound of his steps on the path disturbed the cemetery's silence. As he advanced she could manage no more words. Her mind could not seem to wrap itself around the truth.

This man. It could not be.

She backed up, but in three steps she was at the gate.

"You are French," he replied in the language she had used, and then he was so close that through the veil she could see the sculpted angles of his face and the dull glimmer of night in his eyes.

"I might have expected it," he continued in French. "I have a gift for you."

"You are too close." The foreign words fell off her tongue. "Back away."

"This gift is not a surprise. I have told you twice that I would bring it to you when finally we met." His hand clamped around hers so swiftly that she gasped. She tugged but he enclosed her fingers entirely, forcing her to make a fist. Points of pain shot through her palm.

"I promised you a red rose." His words rumbled. "And I am a man who keeps my promises."

"Release me," she continued in French, "or the knife I am now pointing at your hip will swiftly make its way into a sensitive part of your anatomy."

His fingers clenched harder around hers, driving the thorns deeper into her flesh. It was all she needed to be certain that he had come so far from the boy she had known that she needn't have scruples about lying to him now.

"I will release you," he said, "when you have told me your master's name and where to find him."

"My master?"

"The author of Lady Justice's pamphlets."

This she had not anticipated.

"I am the author of her pamphlets." She wrenched her hand free and lurched to the side, putting space between them.

"Don't lie to me." His tone was hard now. "Only a man could play this game so successfully for so long without detection. Now take me to him, and I will see that you are not punished."

She could only laugh. "This is absurd. Although I suppose I should have anticipated it." Panic now crawled over her astonishment. He had been her last hope. Now she must take what little skill she possessed and set off to find her sister alone. "I have come here for naught. You will not help me, will you?"

There was a long silence. "Are you actually French?"

"Yes," she lied.

"Are you his mistress?"

"Pig."

"His daughter?"

"I *am* Lady Justice. And you are an even greater disappointment than I expected." It was crashing in on her now, the tragedy of it. In another life she might have been able to simply ask him for help finding Amarantha—as herself.

But regrets were for people without purpose.

He still stood between her and the gate.

"Move aside," she said.

"I will find her," he said. "To show my good faith to your master, I will find this girl he wishes found. And then I will expect him to meet me in person."

Air crowded into her lungs. "What information do you need?"

"Your master's best guess at her location in Scotland, her ports of embarkation and disembarkation, the names of her closest associates in the West Indies and here, and a physical description."

"You will have them tomorrow. Now allow me to pass."

He stepped to the side, but as she passed he grasped her arm. Her breath caught. His grip was tight, powerful.

"Unhand me."

"Give me your price," he said, "and I will pay it if you give me his name now."

"There is no price that can make the truth into a lie." It had been years, another lifetime, when he had last touched her, and this—*this* brutal touch—was a travesty. "You cannot bear to believe that a woman has bested you all these years. Can you?"

"Lady Justice needs my help." He bent his head close to hers and spoke like the slide of a whetstone across a blade. "How do you imagine that means I am bested?"

"Unhand me *now*."

"I am threatening you, but I feel no trembling in you."

"You do not frighten me."

"Courage in a woman so slight? He chooses his associates well, it seems." His voice was a soft, deep caress. It stroked the core of her desire like a fingertip.

And cleared her mind entirely.

"You *are* trying to seduce me."

"Is that what I am doing?" Amusement threaded through his murmur.

"You will not succeed. All of those letters you wrote to her—the flirtation—it was to lure her into false confidence. To make her believe she had you under her boot. Wasn't it?"

"Did he imagine me naïve?"

"You are more naïve than you realize." She yanked free. "Yet still I must depend on you, which certainly makes me the greater idiot between the two of us." She reached for the gate.

"Say that again," he said sharply. "Call me an idiot."

Sweeping her cloak more closely about her, she slipped through the gate.

IN THE SPRING, Zenobia's sister, Amarantha, had written home that she was worried about her friend Penny Baker, who had disappeared without warning on a ship bound for Scotland. With Amarantha's husband gone to fever, nothing remained for her in Jamaica, and she intended to go after Penny. It was the last anyone heard from her.

Zenobia could not reveal to her nemesis that Lady Justice knew Amarantha. But if he found Penny, she hoped Amarantha would not be far away.

Nor could she reveal to her household that the man who had plagued Lady Justice for five years was the same man who had pretended Emily Vale did not exist for eighteen. She knew how they would react, and the prospect was too humiliating.

She wrote the details she knew of Penny and sent it to her publisher, to be passed along to 14½ Dover Street in the usual manner. She was tucking the draft of her latest commentary on the Domestic Felicity Act into a portfolio when Franklin entered the parlor.

"This arrived with the post." He hurried forward. "From Scotland!"

The hand on the front was unfamiliar. She sliced it open.

My lady,

> *Your sister is in Scotland and in need of your help. At dawn on the morning of All Saints' Day, come to the south gate of Castle Kallin and you will be re-united with her.*

—*A Friend*

"Franklin." Her hands shook. "Instruct Shauna to pack the trunks for a lengthy journey, and bid Jonah ready the chaise. Mrs. Curly must prepare ample traveling food. Tell everyone I wish to depart as soon as possible. Then return here quickly. I must send a message to Peregrine at once."

"Peregrine?"

"My sister is alive," she said upon a rush of relief. "I know where to find her. I needn't depend upon him now."

"Did you read the other part of the letter?" Franklin said in hushed horror.

She flipped over the sheet. It was blank. "What other part?"

"The part that says, 'P.S. This is a trap.'"

"A *trap*? Whatever for?"

"To exact from your parents the very same thing this villain wishes to exact from you."

"Villain? Franklin, please—"

"Your sister would never have intended for you to travel to—"

"*Franklin.*" She faced him. "If anything in this letter is to be believed, I have a limited time now to ensure that I find my sister. Please now, go and instruct the others as I wish."

"You must at least tell your father"

"He would only tell Mama, and she would fret endlessly that I am traveling without the escort of a gentleman."

His nose quivered. "The only bright spot in this is that you will not be beholden to *him*."

"I agree." She almost regretted having asked Peregrine for assistance. But if she had not, she would never have known who he was.

Franklin left and swiftly she penned a final note to the former secretary of the Falcon Club, retracting her request for assistance. Two hours later, she received a reply, only three words: *As you wish.*

She set his message on the grate, ignoring the heat of mingled desire and fury and grief that flared inside her again as the flames blazed for an instant, consuming, erasing the past.

Now it was truly the end. Finally. Nothing more connected her and Colin Gray.

FOR SIX YEARS Zenobia had adored the close companionship of Clarice Roche. But six days in a carriage with the Frenchwoman—even for the sake of Amarantha—was enough to drive a sane person to murder. In the absence of their maid, who liked carriage travel even less than Zenobia and could not have endured the haste of this journey, Clarice doubled her remonstrations regarding the new Earl of Egremoor's suit, as though arguing for Shauna as well. That his suit had already been firmly rejected, she brushed away.

"The powerful men, they do not cede *la bataille* so easily."

Zenobia suspected that the powerful man in question was thanking his lucky stars this particular *bataille* was over.

When after a sennight they halted at the Laird's Leed Inn on the southernmost shore of Loch Lomond to take luncheon, with her joints stiff and ears full of the inestimable attractions of the new Lord Egremoor, Zenobia stumbled from the carriage into the freedom of crisp Scottish air and blessed silence. She asked the innkeeper to direct her to a comfortable walking path.

He gave her a thoughtful perusal, and then studied Clarice, who was debating with Jonah over whether to unload the traveling trunk for this short pause.

"There be a path to the loch there." The innkeeper paused. "Milady." He pointed to a gate shaded by a thicket of trees.

"We are so close to Loch Lomond?"

"Aye." Casting another narrowed glance at Clarice and Jonah, he went into the taproom.

So close. Castle Kallin was tucked in the mountains beyond the lake's northern end. If the weather held, in mere days they would arrive.

Tugging her cloak tight against the chill wind, she followed the path to the lake. Reflecting the azure of a sky strewn with dramatic clouds, Loch Lomond stretched in miles of sparkling glory, mountainous hills rising on either shore. A few fishing boats floated upon the shimmery surface, and the banks were lashed thickly with trees. It was just the sort of place Amarantha would adore, wild and thoroughly untamed.

Filling her lungs with crystal air, she walked briskly back to the inn, buoyed by hope.

Where her carriage had stood thirty minutes earlier, a horse was tethered, a tall, thick muscled black with a gleaming saddle and traveling pack strapped to its rear. Moving around it, she threw open the door and stumbled to a halt.

And cursed herself for a fool.

She should have known not to trust him. As she had been telling herself for eighteen years, she should have known.

Chapter 5

A Not-So-Happenstance Encounter

Colin was removing his gloves and saying to the innkeeper, "Only tonight," when the inn's door swung open to admit a woman wrapped in a cloak the color of a forest. She threw back her hood, and his next words to the innkeeper simply vanished.

Lengthy, awkward silences were apparently becoming rote for them.

"How do you do, madam?" he finally managed and, belatedly, bowed.

She said nothing, only stared like she had when he asked for her hand.

"I must know," he said. "Do you treat all men to this visage of horrified shock, or only me?"

"Only you."

"I suppose that's as fine a 'good day' as any. I should no doubt politely inquire now as to your purpose traveling in this part of Scotland."

"I am visiting friends." Roses sat upon her cheeks, deposited there by the trek she had taken outdoors, which was obvious from the quantity of mud on her boots and hem. Her pretty lips were parted and her eyes brilliant, and her hair was every which way. It had to be the surprise of this moment, or the taxing fortnight he had spent traveling between pubs and taverns from Newcastle to Glasgow interviewing tradesmen and laborers, or the frequency with which his thoughts had been going to that conversation in her parlor weeks earlier—whatever the reason for it, suddenly he could not make his tongue function.

Alarm gripped his chest like a hand squeezing.

The paralysis spread to his throat, darkness coating his thoughts, tangling them.

Not now.

Drawing air slowly into his lungs, he looked straight into her eyes and forced words through his lips.

"Lady Blackwood at Alvamoor or Lady Sterling in Edinburgh?" he said.

"Neither. I am traveling north. To Castle Kallin," she added, a bit rushed.

Kallin?

"Ah. You are acquainted with its master, the Duke of Loch Irvine, it seems." The words came less haltingly.

"Slightly. Are you?"

Not in the manner she would imagine. "He and I have never been introduced."

"You are staying here? Tonight?"

The innkeeper was watching them closely.

"Yes," Colin said, and to the man: "I haven't any luggage."

He gave him a heavy-browed frown. "Travelin' on horseback, are ye, sir?"

"I am."

"Without a manservant?"

"Not at present." He was accustomed to this sort of questioning when he traveled alone without using his titles. But this fellow seemed oddly suspicious.

"Will ye be takin' meals here, sir?"

"I will." He looked at her. "Unless you object?"

"No."

For years, all she had done was talk, ceaselessly, about everything and anything that seized her interest. This taciturn woman was a world apart from that girl.

"The key to my room?" he said when the innkeeper remained silently staring at Emily and him both.

"Aye, sir. Dinner's at sundown." He stomped on heavy feet from the foyer. Emily remained, the brisk morning clinging to her cloak and cheeks and in her vibrant eyes. Just as always she was disconcertingly pretty, and now staring at him as though he were a monster that had crawled from the loch.

"If my presence here makes you uncomfortable," he said, "I will remove to another inn."

"He called you sir. He does not know who you are."

She was nonsensical. "No."

"Why didn't you tell him your name?"

"I saw no need."

"But you used your earl's voice with him."

"My what?"

"Your earl's voice. The voice you use to assert your authority."

"I have only one voice, madam," he said and it was the oddest, most uncomfortable thing to say *to this woman*. "And I rarely find the need to assert my authority, as it is generally acknowledged without the use of force. Now, pray excuse me. I have been riding through half the night and the morning, and on the other side of that door is a pint of ale." He bowed and went into the taproom.

"HE IS HERE," she said as she closed the door to the bedchamber the innkeeper had offered them in which to freshen up. She leaned back against it and squeezed her eyes shut. "In this inn."

Clarice gasped. *"Le Duc Diable?"*

Zenobia opened her eyes. "Who?"

"The duke to whose castle we travel, of course! The one who is the abductor of maidens, they say."

"*Abductor of maidens?* The Duke of Loch Irvine? Clarice, no. Don't be silly."

Her companion waved her hand about. "Then who is here that gives you distress?"

"Lord Egremoor."

"*Mon dieu!*" Clarice's lips split into a marvelous smile. "It is the fate, *ma chère*. You seek to toss him away, but the destiny, it throws you together with him in this remote land."

"Fate hasn't anything to do with it." Rather, Lady Justice's pleas for help. A coincidence was unthinkable. That he had tracked Penny to this part of Scotland already astonished her. But finding missing people was, after all, his favorite pastime.

"*Ma petite,*" her companion said. "You must not reject this man so firmly. And now that he is here, you must ask him to help us find your sister."

"No."

"*Mais—*"

"No. Clarice, I absolutely cannot." He would know her as Lady Justice instantly. "He seemed to accept our destination as unremarkable." Perhaps he had not yet traced Penny to Castle Kallin. "He intends to remain here the night. After luncheon we will continue onward. There it will end." If he did not catch up with them.

"*Emilie,*" Clarice said firmly. "You must cease this foolish running away. Especially from this man who hurt you."

"Running away? Clarice, I am going to find my—"

"Bah!" She waved her hand dismissively. "You tell the tales always to yourself and to everybody! No wonder it is so simple for you to be someone else." Slinging her shawl around her neck, she came forward. "I go now to enjoy the luncheon with the handsome young lord. Perhaps I will convince him to take an aged Frenchwoman as a bride, *eh*?" Her brows peaked, and then she was gone.

Zenobia pressed her forehead into her palms.

A *Frenchwoman*.

She could still feel him gripping her arm, and hear him asking if she were his archrival's mistress. He could not believe that a woman was capable of the things she had accomplished. Everything she was proud of having done he credited *to a man*.

She hated him for it.

And yet, for the briefest moment in the foyer below, as she had watched his throat work and his beautiful eyes flicker with terror, and waited for him to speak, her entire body had filled with the most dreadful ache. Still it remained like a fever.

This was a nightmare.

For years she had avoided him. Now to be thrown together . . .

Straightening her shoulders she went to the door. She was ravenous and she would enjoy luncheon, even if she must sit in the same room with him to do so. She was, after all, no longer Emily Vale, the peculiar girl who preferred books and frogs to gossip and pretty dresses; whom no one ever listened to; whom no one petted or rhapsodized over, or missed from tea or the picnic or Christmas dinner; whom no one except one boy ever sought out—*until he didn't*. She had not been that girl in years.

She was Lady Justice now, the voice of Britain's oppressed and downtrodden. This minor dip in the road meant nothing.

FROM THE AGE of seventeen, Colin had served powerful men in one way or another. In much the way medieval lords had sent their sons out to apprentice to other magnates, the Earl of Egremoor had sent his heir to London to learn the craft of government and diplomacy from other great lords. The following year Colin proceeded to Oxford where he continued to learn statecraft from philosophers.

After university, he made the acquaintance of another

nobleman—the man who soon became his mentor. Rarely venturing from his estate, that lord had heard fine things of Colin and he had a task he needed accomplished, but quietly, carefully. A young man of science whose work on avionics was far ahead of his time had recently blundered into debt, and in a panic had fled to Amsterdam. Such talent was not meant to be lost to brothels abroad. Would Colin— intelligent, exceedingly well bred, and trustworthy—go and retrieve the lad?

At the time Colin had had a pressing wish to be away from both Maryport Court and London, and he accepted. Traveling through the tumult of war, using social connections and his quiet manner of putting men at ease through a careful play of instinct, natural authority, and easy companionship, he found the scientist in an opium den. With some gold and much diplomacy, he extracted him.

Returning to England, he received a request from the same nobleman asking for another favor. The wife of a diplomat had disappeared with sensitive documents tucked in her jewels case. Following hard-won clues, Colin found her in a smugglers' cave on the coast of Cornwall, trussed and bound and near death. In order to free her he allied himself briefly with a sailor, Jinan Seton, who spoke like a gentleman but knew the secrets of thieves.

Shortly after that, the same nobleman invited him to travel to the East Indies in pursuit of a disaffected Highlander suspected of selling military secrets to the French. Colin had never wanted to be a spy, and he was sole heir to Egremoor; he declined the invitation. But a friend, Leam Blackwood, had recently lost both his brother and his wife to unspeakable tragedy and needed distraction from his grief, and Colin suggested that this was a task for a Scotsman anyway. When Leam agreed to it, Colin wrote to Wyn Yale, a young Welshman seething with intelligence and anger that cried to be put to good use. He invited Wyn to join Leam in Bengal.

And the Falcon Club was born.

In his years as a member of the club, Colin had traveled

the length and breadth of Britain, from Dover to the Isle of Skye, Caernarfon to Ipswich, and through every drawing room and alleyway in London. At no time and in no place during his years performing odd tasks for the crown had he encountered locals who stared at him like the farmers and laborers in the taproom at the Laird's Leed Inn. It had been an unusual journey already, to be sure. Either Scots had become markedly more suspicious of strangers since his trip to Edinburgh in April, or a recent spate of armed robberies on the lowlands roads were making the locals edgy.

But this attention was extreme by any measure. Beneath hat brims, and some openly, the denizens of this inn watched him with suspicion verging on hostility.

Emily ignored him entirely.

Her companion nodded graciously but said nothing to him.

Finishing his repast, he went to see to his horse. In the stable, the stallion hung his head, and his coat was slick where the blanket and saddle had lain for too many hours of the long night. He had pressed the creature hard for many days. But he felt an urgency about this mission he had never before known. The quicker he found Penny Baker, the quicker he could discover why Lady Justice had retracted the request for help.

That his nemesis had sent a woman to their meeting in London had surprised Colin. For two years now he had thought marginally better of the rabble-rouser. The honor he had displayed when he discovered Yale's identity—in not revealing to the public Diantha Lucas's scandalous part in it—had impressed Colin.

Hiding behind a woman, however, was neither honorable nor impressive.

"G'day, milord." Emily's groom stood in the stable doorway, a straw caught between his lips.

"How are you, Jonah?"

"Happy to be servin' at milady's pleasure. My sympathies, milord. Your father was a great man."

"Thank you." He put his hand to his horse's bridle to unfasten it. "Hasn't this establishment a groom?"

"Ostler's gone down the road to Dumbarton. Said he'd a word for the constable there. Been up to the taproom yet, milord?"

"Just now."

"Seen anything . . . *peculiar*?"

He had known Jonah Crowe since he was in leading strings, twice a year when his family had visited Willows Hall. "*Peculiar*?"

Jonah chewed slowly.

Emily Vale was odd, but she was not a woman to surround herself with fools.

"Yes," Colin said. "What have you seen?"

Jonah drew the straw from between his teeth. "Before he left, the fellow here was askin' some mighty poky questions about milady, and *you* after you came ridin' in."

"What sort of questions?"

"Like he'd somethin' on his mind. Somethin' weighty."

"Jonah, what exactly did the ostler ask about Lady Emily?"

"Well, milord, he asked if she'd ever worn trousers."

"IT IS THE most extraordinary thing, Clarice," Zenobia said, buttoning her cloak as she walked into the little chamber.

"Oh?" Clarice dabbed perfume from a crystal bottle onto the insides of her wrists. Even traveling without a maid, she remained elegantly, adamantly French.

"The innkeeper's wife just asked me if I have ever worn breeches."

"*Les paysans ignorants*, they do not know how to speak to the lady."

"Clarice. It is I, the girl to whom you read the *Declaration of the Rights of Man and of the Citizen* while my sisters were reading fashion magazines. You do not believe peasants are ignorant any more than I do."

"*Là*," she cooed and waved a hand. "I am deep in the role."

For the sake of the nobleman below. Her entire household pretended anything it must in order to keep Lady Justice's identity safe.

"And I think someone rifled through my traveling case while we were in the taproom. The books are all disarranged. But nothing is missing, not even my cameo pin, and that is worth at least ten pounds. It was either a very stupid thief or someone was looking for something and did not find it." She refused to imagine it was Colin. He could not possibly know that the woman in the cemetery had been she. If he did, she was certain he would confront her, not search her belongings. His grave English rectitude would allow for nothing else.

But he was not what he seemed on the surface either.

"*Peut-être* it was the maid straightening." Clarice capped the perfume bottle and rose languidly to touch a single fingertip to Zenobia's chin. "Now, *ma petite*, I have instructed Jonah to remove the horses from the carriage and I have commanded two bedchambers for tonight."

"Uncommand them. We are departing now."

"There are many days still before *Toussaint*," her companion said. "And I must rest today. For you see"—she laid a flaccid hand upon her brow—"I have the most wretched megrim."

"You are making a mistake."

Her companion smiled sweetly. "You must only allow the time to come to know him again. A *petit* delay at this charming inn, it will force you to speak to him."

"Clarice, allow me to be clear: you could lock me in a room with him for an entire sennight and I would not speak a single word to him."

"*Mais, bien sûr!* One has no need to speak, *ma petite*, when one is locked in a room with a handsome man."

"*Clarice.*"

She lifted imperious brows. "I refuse to depart this quaint little house until tomorrow. You must simply accustom yourself to remaining here this night, *ma chère*."

"I could leave without you—oh, no. Have you bribed Jonah? Not with money, of course. No. You threatened him, didn't you? What would he—"

"*Pfft!* I did nothing but give him the suggestion. He is ever so fond of the young Lord Egremoor."

If they were aligned against her, it was useless to fight. Affection and familiarity had made her employees into a family, and families were exasperatingly good at believing they knew what was right for a person.

Stuffing her hands into her cloak pockets, she went outside. Several men stood before the entrance to the path to the loch, their rolling brogue raised in dispute. One of them swiveled to her and made a sound in his throat like a growl. They all fell silent and stared.

"Good day," she said.

The growler lunged at her.

With a gasp, she fell back as another man restrained him.

"No, Aillig! The constable's comin'. "

"Constable?" she said. "Has there been trouble?"

"Aye, there be trouble," Aillig said with a dark brow. "*Sir.*"

"I beg your pardon?" She looked over her shoulder but the yard was empty except for her. "Are you speaking to me?"

"I'll see ye hanged, ye villain," he snarled. "If the law dinna do it, I'll fetch a rope myself."

"Gentlemen," she said more shakily than she liked, "I suggest that you find a pot of coffee for your friend. And when he is recovered, recommend to him that drinking excessive spirits does not suit him."

"Ye're as smooth a talker as ye be a crack shot," another of the men said. "Ye've had everybody fooled."

"Till now," the drunken man spat out.

"Come, Aillig. We'll wait for Gibbs inside." He tugged Aillig into the inn and the others followed, casting her dark glares.

Alone, she stood trembling. She had been luckier than most women never to be the victim of a man's violence—not until three weeks earlier when a man had forced the thorns of a rose into her palm. But, as alarmed as she had been at that moment, she had known Colin would not seriously harm her.

She wanted to return to Clarice. But instinct told her that going inside where the drunken Scotsman and his friends gathered was not the best idea.

She would take a brisk walk and cast off the frustration and now fear jittering through her limbs. A field bordered by woodlands sloped away from the road. The day was unusually warm for October, and the sun glorious. She would climb the hill and perhaps have a glimpse of the lake from above.

Beyond sight of the road, she untied the ribbons of her hat and removed it. If Clarice saw her expose her face like this to the sun, she would blanch. But the appearance of Colin Gray in her world again had awakened memories of a childhood in which no one cared if she ran about in the sunshine without a bonnet, and in which her mother had been far too busy dressing up infant after infant as pretty little dolls to pay any heed to her eldest daughter's peculiarities—a daughter who was peculiar because she liked books and frogs and hollow trees and a boy who never said a word.

BEYOND THE STABLE door, a commotion was sounding. Jonah narrowed his eyes. Leaving him, Colin went out into the yard.

"'Tis the earl!" a man shouted from among the five standing in the yard by a cart drawn by a draft horse in which two other men sat. Among the group was the innkeeper and a man Colin had spoken to two nights earlier at a pub in Glasgow. He had known nothing of Penny Baker, nor had anybody else there, and Colin had continued on north where other clues suggested she had traveled.

"That's the one," the fellow said. "Bought me a pint."

"With my appreciation," Colin said.

"Dinna play games with us, sir," another man said. "We know who ye be."

She had told them, clearly.

"I see. Good day, then," he said, and moved forward.

Every man backed up a pace.

Colin halted. A musket lay across the knees of one of the men in the cart.

"Gentlemen," he said, "it would no doubt be to all of our advantages if you told me what it is you wish to tell me, straight away. Mr. . . . ?" He looked to the innkeeper.

"Brady," the innkeeper said warily.

"Mr. Brady, do explain."

"These men"—he gestured to four of the men—"be up from Dumbarton. They're saying ye be the Earl of Egremoor."

"I am." He had not stopped in Dumbarton last night on his route here to Balloch. No information indicated that Penny Baker had been in that village.

"He's admittin' it, the blaggard!" one of the other men said.

"Ye certain 'tis the name'?"

"Certain as death, Brady."

"If you have a grievance with me, I advise you to address me as though you actually wish me to consider it," Colin said, and it was the outside of insanity that he recognized he was speaking in his earl's voice. Their trouble, whatever it was, was certainly with their own lord—Mar or Argyll or even Loch Irvine—the nearest magnates to Loch Lomond. This aggression toward him, a stranger, was irrational.

But he understood the true root of this sort of outrageous belligerence toward titled men. He had met the man's puppet in a London cemetery three weeks earlier.

In the pub in Glasgow he had seen one of the rabble-rouser's broadsheets posted to the wall. And at a tavern a sennight earlier a trio of laborers had been spouting Lady Justice's insurrectionist nonsense over a bottle of whiskey to anybody who would listen. The Scots were uncomfortable under English rule; men still lived who remembered the bloody finale of that centuries-long battle. And Scots did like a good story. Lady Justice's message of disrespect toward the aristocracy had poisoned even this little village.

None of the group before him said a word. An axe in one man's fist caught the afternoon sunlight.

"P'raps, sir," the innkeeper said, "ye'll tell us a word about yer travelin' companion."

"I am traveling alone. Now, I have swiftly grown weary of this—"

"The thief that shot and killed poor Aillig Kendrick's wife on the road," another man said.

"I am grieved to hear this." His throat filled with lead. "But I still haven't any idea what it has to do with me."

"Drove in just afore ye," the innkeeper said with lowered brows.

"Who?"

"The *lady* friend o' yers," one of the Dumbarton men said. "The one that murdered Betsy Kendrick."

Ice slipped through Colin's veins. "Explain this accusation at once."

"We know ye're him, the highwayman callin' himself the Earl o' Egremoor."

Madame Roche stepped out of the inn's front door. "*Mon dieu! Is not the drunkenness of les paysans* tiresome?" She sighed and then seemed to notice the crowd.

"Am I to understand," Colin said to the innkeeper, "that these men believe I am a thief claiming to be the Earl of Egremoor?"

"But of course he is the Earl of Egremoor!" Madame Roche exclaimed. "He is the very image of his handsome father. *Mais*, handsomer."

The innkeeper said to the men from Dumbarton, "No one's said a Frenchwoman's travelin' with the robbers."

"They bribe folks to help them," one said. "First they talk sweet, pretendin' to be a gentleman and a lady, sometimes a gentleman and his manservant, and they've had trouble with their carriage—"

"Now there are three thieves?" Colin said. "Two men and a woman?"

"Yer friend, the little one, dresses up. Sometimes he's a grand lady, other times a young gentleman or a valet. Then ye threaten folk into pretendin' ye're whoever ye say."

"This is absurd," Colin said. "I needn't threaten anyone to do anything." Except a woman in a cemetery three weeks earlier.

"Where's the other?" one of the Dumbarton men asked Madame Roche.

"The other?" she asked with Gallic imperiousness.

"The *person* that came here with ye."

"Lady Emily has gone upon a stroll to the lake—over there." She gestured airily. "*Une bonne idée, certainement.* The company here, it is less than ideal." She flipped her shawl around her shoulders then smiled at Colin. "*Sauf vous,* your lordship." She glided into the inn.

"I have had enough of this foolishness." Striding toward the stable, Colin felt their anger like a fire lapping at his back. Inside the stable, he saddled Goliath and withdrew the pistol from his traveling pack. Then he located Jonah.

Exiting the building mounted, he found the men of Balloch and Dumbarton standing in a line across the yard. Another three men had joined them.

"Aye, that be him," one of the newcomers growled, his face a mottled mess of tears and fury. "'Tis the one that shot my Betsy."

Two men moved swiftly to either side, circling behind Colin.

"Sir," Brady said tightly, "the constable at Dumbarton's on the road now. If ye're no' the thief these men say ye be, ye've no cause to worry."

Behind him, a man was running a length of rope through his hands, his eyes shining with drink.

Whiskey, anger, and grief: a dangerous combination. The pricking tension of madness filled the yard.

He could await the constable of Dumbarton and hope that he had not been drinking of the same insanity as these men. Or he could ride away now and save himself the trouble of a lengthy interview with a provincial official and probably a journey to the nearest magistrate's home.

And leave Emily in danger.

"Mr. Brady, I advise you and these men to clear a path for my horse, or I assure you that he will take no notice of them when I instruct him to run them down."

"Ye'll no slip away, villain," Kendrick slurred. "I'll see ye hanged."

Goliath twitched his ears. He was a magnificent beast, powerful, tender-mouthed, intelligent. Under normal circumstances, no man would injure such a creature.

Behind the innkeeper, a man lifted a shotgun to his shoulder.

Reaching for his pistol, Colin gave Goliath the rein.

Chapter 6

The Flight

*Z*enobia climbed the slope toward the copse. Here within the verdant splendor of the Scottish hills, it seemed almost as if Amarantha could appear at any moment, her fiery hair gleaming in the sunshine and generous smile wide. Of her six younger sisters, Amarantha was her favorite. When they had grown to what their father called a conversant age, he had liked to take his two eldest daughters on strolls through the gardens at Willows Hall, settle on chairs set by footmen near one of the life-sized nude sculptures of ancient gods and nymphs, and tell them stories of his youth. Sometimes he would read to them. The Earl of Vale was a pleasure-loving man, a fashionable socialite but a person of intelligence and thoughtful ponderings when he was not busy doing everything he could to please his wife.

On the other side of the field, a sheep trail wended around a hillock through a gate in a stone fence. Perusing the open hillside for sign of a bull or rams, she saw only sheep afar off. She let herself through and closed the gate behind her.

Hoof beats pounded the earth at a distance. Not a bull.

A horse. Galloping across the field toward her on his big black horse was the man she had left the inn to escape. He did not ride to the gate but directly toward the wall that stretched between them. Nor did he slow for the wall, and she watched the bunching of the animal's massive muscles then the glorious trajectory from ground into air and over the stone barricade.

Colin pulled his mount to a halt just before her.

"You are in danger." He leaned down. "Take my hand."

"What?"

"We must go. Swiftly. Take my hand."

"*Go?* What are you talking about?"

"Men have come up from Dumbarton where a pair of highwaymen have killed a woman. They believe us to be those highwaymen and are ignoring the counsel of those among them who wish to wait for the constable to arrive. They are out for blood. Take my hand."

"Highwaymen? *Us?* You and *I?*"

"Apparently we strongly resemble the pair. One of them is calling himself"—he seemed to recoil a bit—"by my name. As we happened to arrive at the inn close upon each other, the men from Dumbarton have rushed to conclusions."

"But—I—have you been drinking spirits?"

"I wish I could say that I had."

"But this is unbelievable."

"Yet it must be believed."

"Did you tell them that other man is *lying*?"

"Yes, of course. They chose not to believe me. Emily, please. There isn't time for this. I must get you to safety."

"But I cannot just *run away*. Clarice is at the inn! And Jonah."

"I don't believe they will harm them. They are convinced we tricked them into assisting us. Apparently the pair has used chicanery and lies to obtain assistance from unwitting accomplices before."

"How do you know all of this? What did you do, take tea with them before jumping onto your horse?"

"No. They came at me with shotguns and axes and I pointed a pistol at them while they cursed me until I was out of sight. Now *take my hand*."

She grasped his fingers and her shoulder wrenched violently as he pulled her up behind him, his hands gripping her as she struggled with her skirts and cloak and heard tearing. But she got her legs to either side.

"Are you ready?" he said.

She tightened her legs to the horse's sides. "Yes."

The animal sprang away. The ground that was mossy and soft underfoot was uneven and rough under hoof, but the creature was powerful and Colin controlled it with ease. As the ground barreled by, she held tight and tried to ignore the jostling of her breasts against his back and the disturbing sensation of her inner thighs about his hips, and to not think about where he had held her to get her settled behind him. Where her fingers clung to his coat he was gloriously firm, and she had the impression of clinging to one of the statues in her father's garden, only he was made of real male flesh rather than stone.

"Mistaken for thieves," she said near his shoulder. "It is utterly incredible." Not least because of the irony of two people with hidden identities being mistaken for two other people entirely.

"It did not seem incredible when they were threatening to put a noose around my neck." The growl of his voice rumbled beneath her palms, and a thrill of something entirely unfamiliar went through her. Years ago, when she had adored him, she had never heard his voice. Now, when they disliked each other, she could *feel* it. It was strange, confusing, and silenced her for a time.

"Where are we going?"

"Far enough into that wood that they will not see us."

Halfway up the slope the forest began abruptly, rising in dark command beneath the vibrant blue sky swept with clouds. She hadn't any fear of woodlands. She had spent her childhood seeking quiet in the forest—the first half of that childhood with this very man.

"And then?" she said.

"Then I will decide what to do."

As they entered the wood, she swept her eyes across the slopes behind them. "No one is pursuing. Not that I can see."

"Your vision is not impaired at a distance?"

"Only in poor light. I use my spectacles for reading."

"That is helpful." He sounded deadly sober, as though he were assessing their advantages and disadvantages. And his voice had changed. It had grown quiet, pensive. It was a voice she had never heard before.

Within the trees the shadows thickened and the air was cool on her cheeks and stockinged legs. She tried to tug her cloak around her knees and managed to cover one.

"Do you think they are truly pursuing us?"

"Me. At present they are only pursuing me." He clipped each syllable.

"What—"

"When they were demanding to interrogate you, your companion appeared and announced that you had gone for a stroll to the lake. Her blithe disregard for your safety was impressive."

It would be like Clarice to hint broadly to him that he should join her on her stroll. "If she had sensed a real threat, she would not have."

"I am hoping they chose to seek you at the loch rather than ride after me."

"How did you know I wasn't at the loch?"

He was silent as his horse picked its way swiftly through the trees. There was no path or trail, only a bed of needles and bracken, and the hoof falls were muffled.

"I had watched you walk away from the inn," he finally said.

The spaces between trees abruptly grew wider and he urged the horse into a canter, and they made their way between pines and fir and towering elms. After some time the trees thinned and they emerged from the forest on a slope that descended to a rift in the valley below that was bordered by trees. A creek, probably. No house or barn marred the emerald landscape, not even a single sheep. Behind woolly clouds the sun was close to touching the apex of the opposite hill and shadows lay thick across the valley.

He drew the horse to a halt. "I am unfamiliar with this countryside. I haven't any idea where the local magistrate is to be found."

"We must be nearly two miles from Balloch. Perhaps the highwaymen have not been in this part of the country yet and we can find a rational farmer who will not mistake us for them."

Running a palm over his face, he uttered, "This is *fantastical*."

"It is," she said, feeling quite acutely the strained tension in his body.

"Emily, I claim that we are being chased by murderous men and I swept you onto my horse, and you are simply going along with it?"

"I haven't any other choice, have I? If you are telling me the truth then it is to my advantage to go along with it, especially if it will ensure Clarice and Jonah's safety. On the other hand, if you are not telling the truth and have simply absconded with me on a whim or by some devious design, then you are either mad or a villain and I haven't much say in the matter. And what would you expect me to do anyway? Flail about in a swoon?"

He turned his head a bit, revealing the marked dent in his cheek.

Abruptly, she lost the easy use of rational thought.

Eighteen years. In eighteen years she had not seen that dimple. But eighteen years ago it had not shown above a man's hard jaw and it had not turned the very core of her to hot liquid.

"A villain?" The scratch of his voice had become a low rumble. "Really?"

"It isn't so far a stretch. If we are in grave danger why on earth are you smiling? And my name is Zenobia."

Both of his hands settled around the reins again. "Will you introduce yourself to your imaginary rational farmer by that name?"

"I think if you introduce yourself as the actual Earl of Egremoor it won't matter to the rational farmer what my name is. Why do you carry a pistol?"

"On occasion it proves useful."

"On what occasions?"

"On occasions when a woman gripping my chest like it is a life raft asks questions that are none of her business."

She snatched her hands away. "Hold the horse still. I am dismounting." She threw her leg over the animal's rear and slid to the ground. Shaking out her skirts she moved several paces away, stepping carefully on her wobbly legs.

"Do you plan to walk to the rational farmer's cottage?" he said almost conversationally.

"Of course not. But I am not accustomed to this and I need a moment."

"You are not accustomed to riding?" He was watching her; she could sense his attention as she had always been able to years ago. "Does the bookish Lady Emily only go about town in her barouche-landau?"

"You are a toad. I am not accustomed to riding *straddling a man*."

A slow smile curved his lips. It was at odds with everything she had known of him, a devastating smile, confident and handsome and thoroughly sensual.

"So, am I a toad or a man?" he said. "I should like to know whether to croak or speak henceforth."

"I liked you better when you didn't make any sound at all."

The dimple deepened. "You chose to mount the horse as you did."

"And sitting in your lap would have made swift flight much more effective, of course." She wished he would look away from her. "This is *insanity*. What are we doing here? Do you have any ideas, or was flight your only plan?"

The smile disappeared. "Removing you from danger was my first concern. Now we must find shelter before the light is gone and hope that whomever we encounter will not draw the same conclusions about us that the men from Dumbarton and Balloch have."

"It is unusual, I believe—a woman highwayman."

"It seems that both are actually men. One occasionally disguises himself as a lady. It is the other who calls himself by my name."

"But how do people know the thieves aren't actually a man and a woman, and the woman occasionally disguises herself as a man?"

"Perhaps they do not imagine a woman capable of succeeding at such a ruse."

Of course he would presume that.

"Yet a thief is capable of making people believe he is an earl?" she said.

"Apparently he strongly resembles me." He glanced across the valley at the sun touching the opposite peak. "We must continue on. How would you like to ride?"

"As I did before." Sitting within his arms was *not* viable. "Give me your boot to mount."

He did so, and waited for her to untangle her skirts and drape her cloak over her thighs.

"I haven't an idea how anyone could mistake you for a man," he said. "One glance at your legs and they would know otherwise."

Her hands reaching for his waist halted. "You cannot possibly be flirting with me."

"Of course not." He urged the horse into motion and she grabbed his coat. "But perhaps you should sit before me, after all. If anyone were to see us they would know you were a woman simply by the strain upon my face."

Heat rushed into her cheeks and thighs and hands and everywhere. But she knew this man would never, ever say such a thing to a woman—not to a woman of his own class.

"That was not meant as I heard it," she said. "Was it?"

"It certainly was. If you are unaccustomed to riding straddling a man, I am equally unaccustomed to riding with a woman's thighs about my hips."

"Cease this." Every inch of her body where she was pressed to him felt horribly hot and uncomfortable. "I know why you are saying this and I don't like it."

"Why am I saying it?"

"Because you think I am insulted that anyone would mistake me for a man, and you wish to soften that."

"Not at all."

"Then you are trying to heal my wounded feelings over that dreadful proposal of marriage."

"I am not."

"I haven't any wounded feelings from it, so you needn't."

"Emily, I find you distractingly attractive, even before I saw your legs. This situation is not any easier for me than it is for you."

Not possible. "Halt this horse. I will walk."

"We haven't time. There is lamplight."

Peeking from behind a spray of conifers in a crevice carved by the creek below was a building. As the opposite peak cast shadows over it, a wisp of chimney smoke caught the lamp's light rising above the treetops.

"A house," she said.

"A tavern. There is a marquee at the door."

"A tavern in a deserted valley?"

"There might be houses we cannot see. Centuries of warfare have made Scots clever at concealing their homes. And see, beyond that wall."

"Sheep. Then there is at least one farm in this valley."

"We are not far enough from Balloch to be at ease here," he said. "But Goliath is weary, and I suspect you would like dinner."

"Aren't you hungry too?"

"I told you: I am *distracted*."

She was not a beautiful woman. Her friends Kitty and Constance were beauties, and she understood what drew men to them. She did not understand this man now, and the knowledge that he was proficient at pretense jarred with the simple sincerity in his voice.

She liked his voice. It was deep and resonant and easy, as though he hadn't the need to hurry or demand. Even when he had been ordering her to take his hand to flee, he had not shouted.

But as Peregrine he had threatened her. And he had pretended seduction.

As the horse made its way carefully down the hill, the angle pressed her more closely to her companion's body.

"Goliath is an awful name for a horse," she said. "It speaks to man's insatiable desire to dominate others, even great noble beasts like this one."

"The biblical Goliath was not noble. He was a murderer. And I did not name this horse."

"You might rename him," she said.

"Might I, *Emily*?" She could hear his smile. "What trouble do you have with your given name?"

"That name means nothing."

"Your parents gave it to their eldest child. It must have meant something to them."

"My parents were wont to make poor decisions then."

He did not reply and she could only imagine he was thinking the same of his parents, when they had agreed to the betrothal of their five-year-old son to their dear friends' infant daughter.

He needn't have called on her in London. He might have written to her, informed her of the stipulation in his father's will, and received in reply the response he must have known she would give: that she was as happy to end the foolishness as he, and they could both pretend it had been done in person, that no one else need know it hadn't. But he had gone through with the charade. While she defied her parents whenever it suited her, he had always done what his father expected of him.

Near the base of the hill a wall paralleled the creek and

ended in a gate. On its other side, a path ran directly to the tavern, the lamps at its door glimmering warmly in the failing light.

Colin dismounted and gave her the reins.

"Are you comfortable riding this misnamed beast alone the remainder of the distance?"

"Yes." As he unlatched the gate she pulled herself forward on the saddle and slipped her feet into the stirrups that were far too low for her, then urged the horse forward. A stable with a roof falling in on one side and a single lantern before it sat apart from the tavern.

"Colin?"

He glanced back. She sat his horse well, with a straight back, confident hands that had clutched his waist, and strong thighs he could still feel gripping his hips. Another hour of that and he would not have been distracted. He would have been insane.

"Emily?"

"Ze-no-bia," she enunciated. "What about your valet?"

"My valet?"

"Your valet. The man who presses your linens and shaves you and brushes tiny specs of lint from your coats."

"Yes, I know what a valet is, Emily."

Her lips pursed. "Did you leave him at the Laird's Leed too?"

"I am traveling alone. I was traveling alone, that is."

He moved to Goliath's side and she looked down at him again in the swiftly changing light of evening, when the eye is sometimes confused into blindness and at other times certain of visions that are not actually present. Her gaze upon him was focused, thoughtful. She had a look about her as though she was always thinking. He imagined her pale hair unbound and tousled about her brow and shoulders, the silky length slipping through his fingers, and those dark emeralds alive with pleasure.

And adamantly shoved the image from his mind.

"We are not traveling together," she said. "This is momentary."

He laid his hand on the horse's neck. "I do not yet know what danger we truly face. But I regret that my presence in this country at this time has put you in this situation."

"You cannot be blamed for this. But why are you in this country, actually?"

"I am doing a favor for a friend."

Abruptly the emeralds seemed to glitter. She swung her leg over the horse's rear and he reached to assist her.

"No, *don't.*" She jerked away from him.

"Wait here." He took the reins and drew the horse into the ramshackle stable. No groom or boy greeted him. The place was empty except for one dozing mule. Colin ran his hand along the horse's coat and shut the stall door. He would care for the animal after he had seen to the woman's needs.

She had drawn her hood up around her shining hair and was a mere shadow waiting for him now. She had removed herself from the light of the lantern's glow. He was unsurprised. She was intelligent. She always had been.

But her eyes were full of care.

"Do you believe Clarice and Jonah will be safe?" she said.

"Are they loyal to you?"

"Unquestionably."

"I spoke with Jonah earlier."

"Spoke with him? About what?"

"About the possibility of danger. He had noticed something odd in the welcome they gave you at the inn. I told him that if trouble should come to you or Madame Roche after I traveled on, he should send word immediately to a man of mine at Maryport Court who would know what to do, then he should seek the help of the local constable."

Her features, fashioned as though with a fine-tipped pencil, opened in perfect astonishment.

"Your thoughts are so clear on your face," he said. "You've no idea how to dissemble, do you?"

The little dart appeared above the wire rim of her spectacles. "Jonah said nothing to me of his worries."

"I suspect he wished to spare you unnecessary alarm."

"Necessary, as it happened. We might have departed immediately and spared ourselves rushed flight."

"Perhaps. But it might have been too late already. Now, let us hope we find food here, and directions to the nearest gentleman's house."

Within the tavern two rooms let off of the foyer, one partially obscured from the doorway. Two men of dark complexion and rough garb nursed ales at a far table, a backgammon board between two. Two other men stood at the bar, and a man with whiskers to his chest snored in an armchair by a hearth. The tavernkeep looked up from pulling ale and nodded.

"Evenin' to ye, sir, ma'am. What'll ye have?"

"Whiskey. And dinner."

"Tea, please," she said.

The fellow nodded and moved into the kitchen. Colin caught the eye of one of the men at the bar, but the Scot turned away quickly.

Emily's gaze was fixed across the room. He touched her elbow and she started and jerked away from him. He gestured her to a table in the rear room from which he could see straight through a window to the stable.

When the tavernkeep came with the whiskey and a pot of tea, she accepted it with thanks but her eyes strayed again.

"Travelin' through, sir?" the proprietor asked.

"Yes. I have put my horse in the stable, but I'm afraid my companion's mount came up lame a half mile back and we were obliged to leave it there. I don't suppose there is an inn or a gentleman's house nearby?"

"There be the Laird's Leed Inn in Balloch. And there's Landry's farm th'ither side o' Dumbarton. That be the only gentlemanly abode in these parts, save Sir Cheadle's down at Paisley."

"And here I'd thought Scots were all gentlemen farmers these days." Flattery was a tool he had often used to put men at ease.

"We've no need o' *gentlemen* here, sir," one of the

laborers said, jutting his chin in the air. "No' with the lady on our side."

"Another word o' that, Cletus"—the tavernkeep scowled—"and I'll no' be lettin' ye hammer nails into my wall." He gestured to a broadsheet attached to the wall beside the bar. "Fiery young hearts," he said to Colin with a shake of his head. "Always thinkin' the world can change overnight."

"The lady?" Emily said.

"Lady Justice, ma'am," the tavernkeep said. "Writes a load o' good sense, though young louts like Cletus here can take it wrongly. My missus'll have yer dinner in a jiffy." He ambled off into the kitchen.

One of the men at the bar bade the others good-night and went out.

Emily's eyes were very bright, and a flush of pink sat upon each clear cheek.

"Are you all right?" he said quietly.

She nodded. She wore no hat or bonnet, and her hair had escaped its bow and draped over her brow.

Movement through the window caught his eye.

One of Emily's hands rested on the edge of the table. He reached over, grasped it tightly, and whispered, "Go. *Now*." He stood swiftly and she came to her feet.

"My wife is ill," he said aloud, guiding her around the table as she thrust her other wrist against her mouth and seemed to choke. Wrapping his arm around her waist, he propelled her toward the kitchen, through the little room, and past their wide-eyed hosts to a door at its rear. Flinging the door open, he said close to her ear, "Can you run?"

"Yes." She pulled free of his hold.

Into the darkness she ran ahead of him precisely in the direction he would have told her: toward a stand of hedges leading to trees. The shadows were already deeper there. Her dark skirts and cloak were lost to the night, but he followed her by the wintry gleam of her hair revealed by moonlight. They broke into the tree cover and she paused.

Tugging the hood up around her head, he said, "How far can you run?"

"As far as necessary," she panted. "Up the opposite hill on its northern ridge?"

His eyes shone with a spark of pleasure. "You took note of the landscape? When we were approaching."

"Of course. But the creek must be ten feet wide."

"There is a footbridge on the other side of this copse. Come, quickly."

"But Goliath—"

"On foot."

"You will leave your *horse*?"

"I have other horses, Emily. There is only one of you."

This statement she had never heard from another person in her life, coming on the heels of her own broadsheet posted to a tavern wall in the Scottish countryside, stole her every word. Without comment, she followed him closely through the trees. The activity of regular riding and walking in London kept her mind fresh and fruitful. But she was stiff from riding astride, and her skirts were unwieldy. The footbridge was close, though. They paused by the hedge before crossing, and listened. The sounds of the night were all around them: the quick burble of the creek from recent rain, the chirping of a few crickets who did not yet realize the summer had gone, the bleating of a sheep from far up the mountain, and the murmur of conversation slipping easily along the waterbed to them from the little tavern upwind.

No lanterns or torches came through the trees after them. No footsteps or voices either.

"Go," he whispered.

She made her footfalls light on the boards of the bridge, her pulse hard in her throat. He met her in the trees on the other side. But he did not start off immediately. Instead he drew her hood back a bit and looked down into her face.

"Were they armed?" she whispered.

"Two men from the Laird's Leed, both with shotguns."

"This cannot be happening. Can it?"

"Do you understand what it means to run now?"

"That we will not be shot and killed and buried as thieves in a remote Scottish valley? Yes."

Now he smiled slightly. "Let's go."

She pulled her hood tight around her face again and they set off.

The climb was horrendous, the ground mossy and thick where it was not rocky. Her boots she had thought so suitable for travel proved disappointingly thin, and the darkness concealed rabbit holes and tussocks of hard grass that cut her ankles. But she refused to stumble. He insisted on following her, and he had a pistol. By the time they reached the summit she was heaving in air.

"All right?" he said, glancing at her only briefly before turning to look out over the valley from which they had climbed. The hills here were almost mountains.

"Yes." She could not complain. Field laborers, factory workers and miners, chimney sweeps, common soldiers, dockworkers, and prostitutes suffered much worse every day of their lives. "A stroll in the park."

Moonlight lit his curious smile as he turned to her. It was not the sensual smile of earlier, and it did not heat her in telling places; it sank softly beneath her ribs beside her thudding heart.

"I did not know you knew how to smile," she heard herself say. "Lately."

"You are taking this rather more in stride than I would have expected."

"On the contrary. I am terrified. Do you think they will come after us?"

"I think the men of this countryside have been primed to resent their inferior station. It is difficult to know what they might do to criminals whom they believe are taking advantage of the deference owed to gentlemen."

It was on her tongue to retort that the men of this countryside had been subjected to war for hundreds of years because so-called *gentlemen* had stolen their lands and liberties, and that they were well justified in their resentment. But those were Lady Justice's words.

In the silence of the deepening night she could hear nothing but the sounds of nature, the crackling of the damp earth, the swish of wind through tree branches, and at a distance an owl's cry.

"Why aren't they pursuing us?"

"Because, I suspect, they believe we would try to kill them."

"We must wait them out, and then return to that tavern for your horse."

"No."

"Colin—"

He grasped her shoulders and dragged her around to face him. "We will not return anywhere that there are men with weapons intended to point at you," he said harshly, moonlight like ice in his eyes. "Under no circumstances will I take that chance."

She pulled out of his grasp. "Then what should we do?"

"Continue on to a place of safety. Castle Kallin was your intended destination, was it not?"

"It was. By *carriage*. It is almost fifty miles."

"Then we will hope to encounter your imaginary rational farmer en route." His voice had changed entirely.

"En route where? To where were you traveling before being mistaken for a highwayman?"

"In that direction as well."

In pursuit of Penny.

He had not even blinked when the tavernkeeper mentioned Lady Justice. He was in control of himself, entirely self-possessed, even now, even in anger and desperation. That he could be thinking one thing and saying another altogether made the tiny hairs all over her body prickle.

"Speak to me now of practicalities," she said, "of food and sleep and the potential that righteously angry men will decide to follow us despite your pistol."

"My hope is that when we are far enough away from

Balloch, the pursuit will cease. And we must trust that Madame Roche and Jonah will convince a person in authority of our true identities before those angry men catch up with us. With that object in mind, let us continue on now." He started down the hill into shadows striped with moonlight. She followed. She hadn't any choice. She hadn't any experience running away from angry men or any method of defending herself should they appear. She was now dependent upon this man. In his control.

Like women were trapped in marriage.

Like the wife he had pretended she was at the tavern, without even blinking an eye.

Chapter 7

The Unbuttoning of a Bookish Lady

"How do you know in which direction to go?" They had been walking for hours. The moon had disappeared, and the darkness deepened across the hill they climbed now along a stone barrier.

"I am using the stars to navigate." He went two yards before her, keeping to a steady pace, as though he were accustomed to hiking across farmland in the middle of the night. She supposed he might be. Her mother had told her frequently that he lived principally in his Grosvenor Square house. But his estate was on land that she had once loved for its rugged wildness.

What an unlikely caretaker the severe former Earl of Egremoor had been over such a country. Zenobia could not imagine the old earl trekking to the bluffs on the coast or through the wild darkness of Gray Forest, where his son and the eldest daughter of his closest friend had spent so many days.

"Have you been a sailor lately, then?" she said.

"No." His voice revealed no hint of weariness. It was strong and clear and plain and perfect. He was perfect, even to his neckcloth still in its neat folds, while her hem was soaked in mud and her hair clung to her brow with sweat, as would be the case with anyone who marched across Scotland of a fine late-autumn night. Except him, apparently. Never him. Never the serious, sober, righteous Colin Gray.

"Would that the stars produced a cozy little inn just over that rise," she said.

He did not reply, and when they came to the apex there was no cozy little inn, only broad stretches of hills steeped in midnight, and entirely deserted. No stone walls snaked over the landscape to inhibit sheep from wandering, not even wooden fences or hedges. It was a barren place, and spectacularly beautiful beneath the light of the stars.

"No shelters," he said.

"It will have to be pine bedding and a fir canopy, then. For I cannot walk another mile."

"There," he said. "That wood will do."

"As the setting for a medieval fairytale? I daresay you are correct."

For the first time in hours he looked over his shoulder at her.

"Well," she said. "It is dark and vast and undoubtedly chock-full of crones in questionable cottages luring children with gaily colored sweets in order to cook them for dinner. I'm sure we will find room and board there. If they demand payment I will offer you as barter."

"I am not a child."

"Given my limited resources at present, I suspect the crones will nevertheless be satisfied." She passed by him and started down the hill. "As long as they don't imagine you a prince intent upon their destruction, of course. Then they surely would not make the trade."

"Are you the damsel in distress in this scenario?" he said behind her.

"Of course not. I am not in any of those old tales."

"Yet I am?"

"Those tales were *made* with men like you in mind."

After some time he said, "Men like me."

"Handsome, wealthy, unhesitatingly certain of your purpose, courageous, and lucky enough to outwit a poor crone attempting to eke out a living isolated from the society which has rejected her because she is old and unbeautiful. You, my lord, are the epitome of a fairytale hero."

"You say that as though it were a bad thing."

"Oh," she said, "it is."

"You prefer outlaws?"

"Not when I am being mistaken for one, it's true."

They had arrived at the top of the treeline and she continued forward, but he came beside her.

"I will go first," he said.

"You needn't," she said. "I spent the large part of my childhood hiding in forests to escape my sisters."

He looked down at her and the starlight made his eyes glimmer.

"Yes," he said. Then he lifted a hand and stroked three fingertips across her cheek, dislodging hair adhering to her skin. "I know."

The shock of his caress, the intimacy and tenderness of it, went through her like something hot and wild. She backed away a step.

Heading toward the trees, she sought relief in the dark coolness of the forest. He followed. When she had gone some distance into the wood, her footsteps illumined only by the barest glow of starlight peeking between the trees, he said, "This is far enough."

She collapsed. Dried leaves and moss blanketed the woods floor, enough to cushion her shoulder as she hitched her arm beneath her head, tugged her cloak closer about her, and let her eyes drop closed.

THE CREVICE IN the rock had no overhanging roof and the hail pelted her from the black sky, each drop a tiny biting

*fury upon her exposed skin. She wiggled to press closer to
the cliffside, struggling to hide from the deluge, but it kept
coming.*

She awoke with a groan to points of vicious pain across
her body, the dream dissipating swiftly. Groggily she knew
she was in the wood, lying on soft pine needles, and that she
was under attack but not by hail. Along her legs, on her belly
and prickling between her breasts, tiny jolts of fury rocked
through her.

She batted at the pain with frantic hands, her legs tan
gling in her cloak as she struggled to stand, and the agony
spread.

"What is it?" His voice came to her from nearby, clear
and awake. "Are you—"

"Ants," she gasped.

"Ants?"

"Inside my—*ouch*. Biting me. I must have lain down on a
nest. They are *legion*." She dug into her bodice, thankful for
the darkness and for nothing else at the moment.

"You would be best served to remove the garments and
clean them away that way."

"I am managing—*ohh!*"

"Let me—"

"No! Stay away from me."

"I have removed ants from you before."

"That was—" She gasped and her hands could not move
fast enough. "That was rather a different circumstance."

"Not really."

"I was *five*."

"You hopped and screamed then dove into that lake like
the grass was on fire."

The lake where he had tried to teach her how to fish and
she had made a hash of it. The woods where they climbed to
the tops of trees to see across the entire world. The cliffside
from her dream . . .

She shoved away the memories and smothered her cries
of pain. "This is *intolerable*."

"Remove your clothing."

"Be quiet."

"It's dark. Your modesty is safe."

"I can see *you*." As a silhouette only. Still.

"I will turn away."

It was *excruciating*. "Do you promise?"

"Upon my honor."

"Your honor couldn't fill a thimble."

"My back is to you already. Would you like me to cover my eyes with my hands as well? Or perhaps employ a blindfold?"

"I am laughing uncontrollably. *Ergh . . .*"

"What is it?"

"The buttons of my gown—" A groan of pain wrenched forth. "I cannot unfasten—"

"Let me help you." She heard the dry underbed crunch as he moved toward her.

"No."

"I cannot bear your whining." His voice was closer.

"I am not whining," she bit out. "I am in actual pain."

"You must—"

"Do *not* come closer."

Then his hands were upon her, strong and certain, twisting her around so her back was to him, and he was unfastening the buttons swiftly and with great ease in the dark, which suggested he had done this any number of times. She was at once furiously angry and breathlessly aware of the maddening pain, the scents of gentle autumnal decay but also something delicious and entirely male, cologne mingled with sweat, and the cool air upon her skin as her gown and petticoat sagged away from her shoulders and her stays loosened.

An ant bit the underside of her breast.

"Oh, *dear God*," she moaned, needing to swipe her hands over every inch of her skin. "Go now."

He did not move.

"Turn away," she said.

She heard nothing but the swish of breeze in the treetops.

"Turn *away*. Haven't I enough to suffer now without you enjoying my misery?"

With a sudden rustle of underbrush, his footsteps moved away and faded. Dashing her hands over her flesh she listened to the night around her, nearly silent but for a tiny scuffling several yards away.

"Next I will find mice in my shoes," she mumbled, swiping off her shift. Standing in only stockings and boots she shook out the shift then ran her palms over every inch of linen, removing ants until she felt no more on it. She slipped it over her head, found her stays, and repeated the action.

She was fastening the only buttons of her gown that she could reach when she heard him return.

"You know," she said, her chin tucked under, her fingers shaking on the buttons, "I would not believe any detail of this day and night if someone told me the tale. It is unendurably horrible." And he didn't even know the half of it.

"Allow me to assist you," he said as though he sat across a table offering to pour tea.

"Thank you." She steadied her senses against the brush of his fingertips against her back. He said nothing and the silence was intimate and even more excruciating than the biting had been. "It cannot be long after midnight, can it?"

"It is still several hours until dawn."

"I am loath to lie down again. There might be more nests."

"You will sleep where I was sleeping. Ant-free."

"Oh? Do you wish to try your luck at insect invasion tonight?"

"You are remarkable, Emily."

An exhale seeped out between her lips. "It is Zenobia."

"You haven't wept or caviled or fallen apart—"

"You accused me of whining."

"Have you done this before?"

"Stood in a forest at midnight while a man buttoned up my gown? What if I said yes?"

"Have you been in real danger before?" His voice was quieter but firm.

"Only the once," she said, and naturally he would know what she meant by that. "I lead a quiet life."

"Yet now you are fearless."

"Why shouldn't I be? You are."

His hands left her and she turned to look at him. The darkness was nearly complete now, nearly silent, and soft. She felt the heat of his body so close, the unwanted warmth in her own body, and she wondered what it would be like to kiss him—to lean forward and press onto her toes and feel his lips with her own.

Which was sufficient proof that this misadventure had made her stark raving mad.

"Have you been in danger like this before?" she said.

"Not with a woman in my care."

"You were already awake when the ants woke me, weren't you?"

"I was."

"Yet you must be as exhausted as I. You were keeping watch."

"I cannot allow you to come to harm, Emily."

"Zenobia. You won't be particularly useful in defending either of us if you don't sleep." She fastened the clasp on her cloak. "If you refuse to sleep, we may as well continue on. Perhaps just over the next hill we will find that cozy inn I am dreaming of, or at least the rational farmer's cottage."

"You have slept only four hours."

Four more hours than girls were allowed who worked on their backs all night through. Four more than servants in wealthy households, ever responsive to their masters' demands at all moments. Four more than miners who did not see daylight for weeks, sometimes months, but whose clocks were set by the rapacious greed of the mine owners.

"I will not sleep if you refuse to," she said.

There was a silence in which the breeze rustling through the treetops far above was the only sound.

"You have not changed," he said. "Not in the least."

Abruptly the wood seemed too close a space to contain her heartbeats. "What do you mean?"

"You were nearly five years younger, yet you always had to prove that you could match me at anything."

"I did not have to prove anything. I simply did what I wished." This hurt. Too much. She knew it should not, that it was a wound far too old and scarred over to give her such pain. "Now I wish to continue on." She stepped away, but he grasped her arm and moved close.

"Emily—"

"*Zenobia*." She yanked free of his hold. "And do *not* touch me again."

"Again?"

"Today you have taken my hand, touched my face, and grasped my arm and waist and shoulders, all without my consent. This unbelievable situation in which we have found ourselves does not give you free rein to do whatever you wish."

"I took your hand to pull you onto the horse."

"You took my hand in the tavern. Don't do it again." She started toward the edge of the wood.

"Are you afraid of being touched by a man?" His words came like velvet through the still woods.

"I have no fear of being touched by a man." Only by him, who weeks earlier in a dark cemetery had touched her to harm her, yet whose touch now tangled her into confusion. That her body betrayed her so acutely filled her with frustration.

"Is it that you prefer a woman's touch?" he said.

Her footsteps fumbled. She swung around. "Do you think that the darkness makes this questioning acceptable? That if you cannot see the astonishment on my face now that it mustn't be there? Is that it? Or is it your arrogance? You may ask any question you wish, however intimate and inappropriate, because by dint of your noble blood and position you are above reproach?"

"No. I want to know why for years you have made it clear that you did not wish me to offer for you."

The air shot from her lungs. For a moment, she could not breathe.

"Go to hell, Colin."

SHE WALKED AHEAD of him through the small hours, keeping to a steady pace over the uneven ground. When the dawn arose in mists over mountains that were as green as her eyes, she paused on the apex of a hill and stood there, wavering, wind capturing her skirts and canting them to the side.

Colin reached the summit. Before them, at the base of the hill, Loch Lomond spread in pale, sparkling magnificence to the opposite bank. All around it the trees were dressed for autumn in red and amber and ochre. In an hour when the mists dissipated the lake would reflect the blue sky, and the scene would be breathtaking.

But it was as easy to turn his gaze from Scotland's natural beauty to the woman's profile as it always had been to ignore the rest of the world when Emily Vale was near.

"I beg your pardon," he said.

"For what? For making the assumption most men do when a woman rejects them: that she must be deviant in some manner?"

"For asking you what it is not my right to know."

Her shoulders rose upon a hard inhalation.

"It is a beautiful lake," she said. "But I wish it were an enormous bowl of porridge. Or a rasher of bacon, a plate of muffins, and a vat of tea."

"You truly are extraordinary."

"And yet for all the superlative adjectives you apply to me, I cannot manage to make breakfast magically appear before us now. Several hills ago I saw sheep. I wonder how mutton tartar tastes. I suspect Clarice knows. The French are so adventuresome with their cuisine." She chewed upon her lips. "I should not have left them."

"They are not under suspicion. They will be well."

"I wish we could use your pistol to shoot breakfast. But you must save those bullets to threaten angry men, of course." She turned fully to him. "Why don't we turn ourselves over to them? How difficult could it be to convince a mob infuriated by theft and murder of our actual identities?"

"That is your hunger speaking."

Her face abruptly flushed with pink. "Then clearly I must not let my hungers rule me." She gathered up her skirts and moved down the hill. "Loch Lomond stretches almost due north," she called back to him. "We have most certainly bypassed Luss. The next village of any size along the bank should be Tarbet."

"How do you know that? I'd thought your Scottish travels only took you to Edinburgh and Blackwood's estate."

"I studied maps of this region before making this journey. The terrain continues mountainous. If we follow the edge of the lake it will require less climbing and we will move more swiftly north, and we are more likely to come upon houses. This is not the only path from Stirling to the western isles, but it is less mountainous and shorter than the journey around Loch Lomond's northern end. It should be peppered with habitations. Indeed, I depend upon it. It is ten miles at least to Tarbet from Luss, and another five to the port at Ardlui, and I truly don't think I can walk that far without a meal or a change of clothing. How intrepid world travelers must be."

As intrepid as this woman, apparently. But her plan suited him. Every piece of information he had collected on Penny Baker's movement from the eastern Port of Leith west across the country, showed her traveling west. A peddler he had shared ales with in Stirling believed he had seen Miss Baker near Tarbet in the winter. Another traveler had put her at Arrochar. He hadn't been surprised at the long memory of these men: a woman with dark skin and a West Indies accent was easily noticeable in the Scottish countryside.

But in Balloch, the trail had gone cold. If anyone there had remembered her, they had been too intent upon studying his likeness to a highwayman to share the news.

Once Emily was safe and he had cleared up this dangerous case of mistaken identity, he would find Penny Baker's trail again, and find her.

The rabble-rouser's influence had spread, even to a tiny tavern in a remote valley of rural Scotland, stirring up the anger of ignorant men against their superiors. Lady Justice must be stopped. The men and women of Britain had suffered enough from war abroad in the past decades. It did not need war between countrymen on its own soil now. He would publicly expose Lady Justice for a fame-seeking anarchist, and bring him down before any more people were seduced by his lies.

The day had arisen fully in autumnal splendor, sun illumining the severe landscape and sky into rich magnificence. The woman amidst it all—plainly dressed, spectacle-wearing, reclusive—seemed as at home in this rugged wilderness as she had years ago in the vast park at Willows Hall and in the forests and cliffs of Egremoor.

Fifty yards ahead of him, sunlight caught in her hair as she moved beyond a stand of trees, and Colin paused to watch her. Years ago, when the Earl of Vale's family had come north for holidays, the mere sound of her voice as she burst through the doors of Maryport Court and called his name had soothed away his every anxiety.

Then, overnight, the opposite had become true.

That now he hoped to sow peace among Britain's rulers and subjects when he could barely avoid quarreling with a woman he had known his entire life did not bode particularly well for his chance of success. But Emily was an exception to every rule.

And she had the softest, smoothest skin of any woman he had ever touched.

And beneath her subdued dark gown she wore a silk petticoat, with satin ribbons binding her stays.

And her shift of gossamer linen clung to her buttocks like no modest maiden gentlewoman's undergarment should.

And her legs were lithe and strong and clasped a man's hips as though she spent every day in the saddle astride.

And he should not know any of that. But he did. And he could not get it out of his head. Or the scent of her hair, an intoxicating medley of sage and honey. Or the brilliance of her eyes when she smiled. Or her courage in the face of this fantastical threat.

Ahead a narrow path ran into the hills from the banks of the lake below. A dilapidated lean-to stacked halfway to the rickety roof with bales of straw marked where the path turned abruptly toward the apex. She halted before it, turned to him with her forefinger over her lips, and lifted her hand, palm toward him. He shook his head. Her eyes flared with displeasure and he nearly laughed. But he remained still and silent, all about him bird chatter and the rustle of the lake below.

Then she was gone, beyond the corner of the lean-to, and his muscles bunched to spring after her.

Protect her whether she liked it or not? Or trust in her intelligence and courage?

He reached into his pocket for his pistol and stood his ground. It was the most difficult thing he had done in years.

Chapter 8

An Unfortunate Misjudgment

"I do not feel guilty, Colin."

"Are you saying this to convince me or yourself?"

"The universe." She took another bite of the pie and filled her mouth with the buttery pastry and savory meat stolen from the carriage parked in the shade of the lean-to. "In general, I disapprove of theft."

"In general? Except when you are hungry and a picnic basket is left unprotected?"

He was sitting with his back against a stone fence and his dimple was flirting with his cheek. A day's growth of whiskers shadowed his jaw and she was having trouble not staring again. She had never seen him anything but perfectly groomed—not since he had become a man. Now he was straying dangerously far from that. The day had grown warm and he had removed his neckcloth and unbuttoned his coat. His boots were understandably dusty, and his hair was a bit tousled, and in his dark, wonderful eyes resting upon her was the warmth of extraordinary charity.

"What of the poor farmer," he said, "who will now go without his midday meal because of your clever theft?"

"Or his poor wife, whom he will no doubt blame for forgetting to pack his basket with pie," she said, wiping her fingers on a kerchief.

"Will he blame her?" he said.

"Yes. Husbands commonly blame their wives for wrongs they have not actually committed." He of all people should understand that. But she could not say that aloud. And something in his eyes changed. Or perhaps the fascinating muscles in his whisker-shadowed jaw had shifted. Or perhaps the rigidity of his shoulders had loosened. Whatever caused it, suddenly he looked different.

"Until yesterday, you had not called me Colin in eighteen years," he said.

A flake of pastry caught in her throat. "What did I call you?"

"My lord. Mockingly."

She could say nothing to that. He was probably right.

"In any case," she said, "I do not feel guilt when the owner of the picnic basket can so obviously provide herself with more of its contents. She was a lady of material comforts. You should have seen her jewels. Can you imagine driving about the Scottish countryside wearing diamonds?"

"Diamonds?" he said. "You did not steal this food from a farmer?"

"No. I would think she had been sent by the men of Balloch as a decoy to lure the thieves out into the open, but I am acquainted with her and I don't believe she is intelligent enough for subterfuge."

The charity disappeared from his eyes.

"Emily, this is a detail that you should have mentioned to me immediately."

"I wanted you to enjoy your pie." She smiled. He did not. "I doubt you have ever made her acquaintance. She is a very silly woman."

"Did you perhaps consider that this silly woman *who knows your real name* might have vouched for your identity to the locals before she drove away?"

"Of course not. Why should I have considered such a thing?" She batted her lashes.

This time she was certain his jaw clenched.

"Don't you dare tell me you wanted me to enjoy my pie first." He stood up.

"I won't." She dusted off her skirt. "Though I did want to enjoy mine as swiftly as possible, to be sure. But that is not why I decided not to speak to her at the moment. And I am certain she hasn't driven away yet."

"*Yet?* You mean, you did not *see* her drive away?" His gaze snapped across the sloping terrain toward the lean-to. "How are you certain she is still there?"

"When I happened upon her carriage behind that lean-to, she was busy disrespecting her marriage vows. With her coachman, I believe. I don't know what sort of social encounters you are accustomed to having, *my lord*, but mine do not typically include interrupting two people in flagrante delicto."

Lips parted slightly, he stared at her. But his surprise was nothing to the shock she had felt the moment she had realized what was happening behind those piles of straw.

"I was dizzy from hunger," she added. "And I thought it wouldn't hurt to wait until they had finished before making our presence known."

Again he looked across the hill toward the lean-to, then at her swiftly.

Then he took off at a run.

She followed him, reaching the lean-to with strained lungs and tangled skirts to find him standing on its opposite side entirely immobile. Wheel tracks marked the place in the soft ground where the traveling chaise had been parked.

"They are gone already?" she exclaimed, running past him and down the narrow track twenty yards before turning around. He had begun walking back the way they had come.

She hurried to catch up with him.

"I am sorry," she said. "I never imagined. It has only been a quarter of an hour."

"Your naïveté would be charming if it weren't to our disadvantage at present."

"And you have extensive experience pausing for lightning-fast tups by roadside lean-tos, do you? How delightfully convenient you must find that."

"I seem to recall not twelve hours ago someone demanding a halt to inappropriate intimate questioning." His stride did not falter. "Your moral high ground, madam, has plummeted into a valley."

"Well, I am angry. And disappointed. And I feel like a fool."

He halted and turned to her.

"Forgive me," he said without trace of anger, and his gaze seemed to move over her face with care. "You cannot have known."

She knew much better than he imagined. She simply hadn't thought clearly in the moment. She had seen the pair and her entire body had flushed with heat. Then she had not been able to resist studying them.

It was not the first time she had glimpsed a woman and man in the throes of passion; stealing away from crowds at parties had its accidental disadvantages. But the particulars of the couple's pose had entirely robbed her of discretion. Instead, she had stared, watching as, standing before the kneeling woman, the man had put his hands around her head and the woman had put her mouth where Zenobia had not known a woman's mouth could go. Not only her mouth, but also her hands. And then her mouth and hands got busy. Eventually the man grunted, rolled his head back, and his hips jerked forward as his partner moaned. Releasing her lover, the woman had then sprawled onto her back, knees wide as she wrenched up her skirts, and he sprawled atop her. It was at that moment that Sybil Charney's face had become clear.

The fervency with which Mrs. Charney and her coachman then copulated in the grass had paralyzed Zenobia's body while her mind had gone directly to the man she had left on the other side of the lean-to. And instantly she had not been imagining kissing only his lips but rather more of him.

"No," she said. "It was foolish of me, so I deserve to feel like a fool. Perhaps if we hurry we will encounter her along the road. They cannot be traveling on trails like this the entire journey." Merely in order to have sex unnoticed by anybody—*except her.* She went around him and began walking again in the opposite direction.

"I suspect that road circles around to the other side of that peak before continuing north, if it continues north at all," he said. "Following it will take us far from the loch, and the likelihood of overtaking the carriage on foot is slim in any case. We must continue directly north along the loch."

"Perhaps that lean-to belongs to a farmer nearby."

"Also possibly on the other side of that peak. And we cannot trust a farmer." His eyes were troubled. "We must find a church."

"What makes you imagine that a churchman will believe us any more than anyone else?"

"His education."

The hill swept dramatically down to the loch that was bordered here by trees and shrubbery, and her legs ached descending as fervently as they had ascending. Her feet ached too. Now that her hunger was satisfied, she felt all of the aches of hours riding astride yesterday and many more hours walking.

"Education does not automatically make a man rational or compassionate," she said, "only powerful."

For a lengthy series of moments, he was silent behind her. Finally she looked over her shoulder. The Scottish sky framed him in azure and his dark gaze upon her was unreadable.

"Why do you look at me like that?"

"Just then, those words," he said. "You sounded like someone else of my acquaintance."

"Oh. Who?" she asked, carefully nonchalant.

He shook his head. "No one important."

She set off down the hill again.

"Emily—"

"Zenobia."

"Thank you for acquiring lunch."

He sounded sincere. The vividness of her shame dulled somewhat.

"There was no one inside the carriage. I wonder where her maid had gone off to? Perhaps she was in the woods with the footman, hm? I know I am scandalizing you. Spinsters must be at least sixty-five years of age before they can jest in this manner without rousing public disapprobation."

"Is that so?"

"To be sure."

The slope was vast. Finally wending through trees at the steep base of the hill, they stepped out from among them onto the road. Following the bank, it was a poor specimen of a road, strewn with puddles and rutted with wagon wheels. But the lake was spectacular, endless to either side north and south, its tranquil beauty reflecting the peaked hills on the opposite bank. She wondered if he still fished in the river at the Court, into which she had once dived after an encounter with an anthill, and into which he had followed her on that occasion, despite the cold. She wanted to ask him.

"There must be a church somewhere ahead," she said. And perhaps safety. And relief from this strange adventure that made her fantasize and remember and feel his gaze upon her like she had once upon a very faraway time.

HER STEPS HAD slowed and Colin eased his pace as well to remain several yards behind her. When hoof beats sounded at a distance behind them, rhythmic like the hard beats of his heart, they were walking along a straight stretch of bank, entirely exposed from both north and south. He went to her side and she looked around. A lone rider cantered along the road toward them.

"It is too late to run into those trees," she said. "And I

don't think I can run up that slope anyway. It is too steep and my legs are too tired. I believe I would collapse."

"It is only one man."

"One man who could ride away and tell many men that he saw us."

"Then let us hope he's not looking for us."

As the rider neared he slowed, and then drew up beside them. By his dress he seemed more townsman than farmer. Colin did not recognize him from the group at the Laird's Leed. Stepping between the horse and Emily, he nodded.

"Good day, sir," the rider said with a nod. "Ma'am."

"Good day," Colin said.

"I don't suppose ye've seen a pair o' gentlemen travelin' this way, one about yer height, sir, an' the other a fair little lad." He glanced at Emily.

"We have not."

The rider peered at him for another long moment. Then he reached into his coat.

In the next instant two pistol barrels faced each other.

"Return that to your pocket and I will not shoot you," Colin said.

The Scot's brow glistened with sweat. "What be yer business in this county, sir?"

"My business is none of yours. But I assure you, I am neither thief nor murderer." He took a step toward the mounted man. "Yet."

Emily burst into tears.

The rider glanced at her and Colin dove forward and smashed the butt of his weapon across his knee. The man howled. Colin knocked his pistol away. The horse shied. Colin grabbed the reins. Kicking out, the Scot scrabbled for the leathers.

"Halt!" Emily's voice rang clear out across the lake. "Or I *will* shoot you."

She stood on the horse's other side, pointing the Scot's pistol dead at his head with one sublimely steady hand.

The man went motionless.

"As perhaps you are already aware, sir, I am a crack shot,"

she said. "I recommend that you do exactly as his lordship requires now. And do not even consider spurring this horse onward or I will shoot you in the back of the head as you ride away."

The Scot's nostrils flared. But his lips pinched closed.

"Lean forward and wrap your arms around its neck," Colin said.

The fellow did so swiftly. Colin removed the bridle from the animal's head and used the reins to bind the man's arms. Then, turning the horse to face the direction from which they had come, with a shout he slapped its haunch and it hared off at a canter.

Emily stood immobile, the pistol pointed at the retreating horse and rider. When they disappeared around a bend, her arms finally dropped. Pistol dangling from her fingers, she wavered.

"Good heavens," she said airily.

He snatched the weapon from her limp fingers, tossed it away, and caught her up in his arms as she collapsed.

WITH THE SNAPPING open of her eyes and a gasp, she awoke abruptly.

"I cannot believe that I swooned," she said thickly.

"How do you feel?"

"I've a vile headache." She flinched as her eyes swiveled about the little enclosure open on one side to the mountain's slope. "Where have you brought me? Presumably you brought me. I don't suppose helpful Scottish elves whisked me up and deposited me here."

He had no wish to smile. "We are in a shepherd's retreat, I believe."

"At the top of the hill? You carried me all the way up?"

"You are very light." He leaned forward and set his elbows on his knees and folded his hands together. "I beg your pardon for disobeying your order."

"About touching me?" She sat up. "I forgive you this time, of course."

He rubbed his hands over his face and drew in a long

breath to fill the place where anxiety was now dissipating. She had remained unconscious for too long.

"I hope there will not be a next time," he said.

"You and I both." Her perfectly shaped lips, which he had been staring at for a quarter of an hour, twisted as she tucked her hair behind her ear without any grace whatsoever and very obviously avoided looking directly at him. Climbing the mountain he had had ample time to bemuse himself on the scent of her hair before he had found this hiding spot. She despised him, and she had more courage than every man he knew except perhaps Jin Seton, and she was an even match with Wyn Yale for sheer gumption. But she was a lady and a town dweller; her physical abilities did not match her natural bravery.

"Stop staring at me," she said. "I won't perish, except perhaps of mortification."

"I am not staring at you because I am concerned you will perish." He was remembering the first time he had held her. His mother had insisted, saying that it would be his responsibility to care for her someday, and the sooner he learned how to do so, the better. Standing before God and their families in the chapel at Willows Hall, he had accepted into his arms a warm, surprisingly heavy little bundle of cloth, and for the first time ever had held another person's life in his hands. As he held her, the priest had anointed her with holy water and chrism. He had been five. "You forgot to breathe."

She blinked. "I think I did. But that does not explain why I was unconscious long enough for you to ascend a mountain."

"Shock, perhaps. And exhaustion. Hunger, of course."

"You have a lot of experience with this, it seems?"

"Some. Are you actually a good shot?"

"I am competent. But apparently the thief who resembles me is an extraordinarily good shot. The men who spoke to me at the Laird's Leed suggested it."

"Those men spoke to *you*?" He shook his head. "Why didn't you tell me this before?"

"It was not necessary."

"Emily—"

"Did you imagine that I agreed to flee with you on the basis of your justifications alone?" She laughed. "You really don't know anything about women, do you?"

Pain fanned out from the muscles in his jaw that had been bunched for an hour. He could actually feel his anger rising, hot and urgent. *Alien.*

Yet peculiarly good.

It felt good to *feel.*

He inhaled slowly through his nose, and even that— even the stream of cool, clear air—felt good. Smelled good. Tasted good on the back of his tongue.

"Am I to understand," he said not entirely steadily, "that they confronted you?"

"They threatened me." She tilted her head. "Now I have threatened one of them, and I did not enjoy it. Did you?"

"One does not take pleasure in threatening another person."

"One?" She smiled. "Oh, Colin, you sound like a pompous idiot." Abruptly, she bit her lips together.

"Be that as it may . . ." he mumbled.

Her eyes popped wide. "Have you just made a self-deprecating comment?"

"I will not honor that question with a response." He lifted a brow. "There. Pompous enough for you?"

A grin tugged at her lips.

"You held the pistol correctly and with a steady aim," he said. "How is that so?"

"My father had no son. I wished to learn. He was an indulgent parent. And he wanted me to be safe. I was alone on the estate quite a lot before I removed to London permanently."

"Were you?"

"Well, I never came to like dolls and fashion like my mother and sisters did." She stretched her legs and made a choking sound.

He started to rise. "Are you—"

"It is only my feet." She lifted her skirts a bit and swiveled her ankles.

"You acted bravely," he said, staring at her ankles, knowing he should not but who the hell would know?

Her. She would know. She could glance at him any moment and see him staring.

Yet he could not look away.

"And wisely," he added.

"There was no wisdom about it. That man was terrified of us. My instinct was to use his fear against him."

"It was a good instinct."

"I have never fully comprehended it before, but I think I finally understand how men eagerly use other men's fear to control them. I think it is because they fear for themselves. They prey upon the fear of others to assure their own safety." In her emerald eyes was a brittle gleam, like the despair of the last breaths of autumn before winter. "It is despicable," she said.

"It saved our lives today. You did."

"Yet I feel besmirched."

"No," he said. "You feel besmirched because you acted falsely."

Her brow wrinkled up. "That is what I just said."

"Not because you pretended to be a crack shot," he said. "You feel besmirched because you pretended to cry."

Her beautiful lips split into pleasure. "How do you know I pretended that?"

He smiled.

She slid her gaze away. She studied the straw-strewn ground then sat down again. "Where is his pistol?"

"I left it."

"Left it?"

He shrugged. "Something about carrying both you and a loaded firearm at once did not sit right with me."

"Oh?" Both brows canted above the gold wire. "You gave it that much thought at the moment?"

"The occasion required a swift decision."

"Colin," she said, her voice subdued, "do you think it likely that we will be murdered before we reach safety?"

"I think it likely that you will not allow that to happen," he said with another smile he could not dampen.

All expression slid away from her face and she simply stared at him.

He leaned his shoulders and head back against the embankment and closed his eyes. They were too close to the location in which they had been seen, and not safe in this spot. But her eyes swam with exhaustion and she needed sleep.

"We will travel by night," he said.

Fighting the weariness that dragged at him, he resisted sleep. But she dozed off swiftly. He moved to the edge of the shelter and sat facing outward as the day receded.

IN THE DARKNESS beyond the mouth of the enclosure she could see only the silvery black of deep night beneath a sky cluttered with stars. One upon another, each star seemed to fight its neighbors for dominance. An infinite universe, and yet the battle raged. Just like men.

She crawled out of the shelter and walked across the mottled grass to the man sitting on a stone outcropping several yards down the hill.

"You did not sleep, did you?" she said, surveying the loch far below glittering with starlight. "You are very foolish."

"Good morning to you too." He came to his feet as gracefully as he might in the Queen's drawing room. As he looked down at her she did not feel small. He had carried her up a mountain, stood nearly a head taller than her, his shoulders marvelously broad, and yet the starlight in his eyes seemed to reach out and caress the strength within her. The power.

"This plan is also very foolish," she said before she could say something else—something *unwise*.

"If you've another, do share," he said equably.

"Lord Egremoor," she said, "it may come as a vast surprise to you, but I am entirely out of my element here."

"You slept six hours on the ground in a shepherd's retreat.

I don't believe such a talent is typical for daughters of earls who usually reside in London."

"I am not out of my element in *nature*. Rather, in *intrigue*."

"Come. We need water." He started down the hill. "At dusk I saw smoke rising beyond that copse."

"A village?" She went after him.

"A farm, probably. Worth investigating."

"You intend for us to call upon the farmer?"

"I will go alone."

"But—"

He halted and faced her. "Emily, it is not my fondest wish to be obliged to travel to Willows Hall with the purpose of informing your parents of your death."

"You could write them a letter instead."

He stared at her, his gorgeously whiskered jaw hard, his beautiful eyes reflecting the nighttime in which they were the lone souls upon a mountainside.

She offered him a grin.

He moved away again.

"Colin," she said to his back. "You are not in any humor to convince anybody of our innocence. I don't think—"

"It doesn't matter what you think."

It was the last he said to her until they neared the farm.

MISTS WERE LIFTING off the ground, making ghosts everywhere in the steely predawn. He ordered her to await him concealed in a nearby copse. Astonishingly, she obeyed. Her father was a weak-willed man more interested in fashion and light amusements than ruling his family, and Colin suspected she was as unaccustomed to taking orders as she was to walking great distances. That she acquiesced to his demand now was nothing less than a miracle. But she was as eager as he to hasten their journey.

Not for the same reason, he was quite certain.

He was having trouble not staring at her lips.

She was disheveled and insolent and quick-witted and he was having fantasies of laying her down on a bed of soft white linens and kissing her, of coaxing her tempting lips open and tasting her heat, of caressing her tongue with his until she wrapped her arms about his neck and moaned into his mouth.

Given their present circumstances and his entire lack of sleep, this fantasy did not alarm him. He wanted a cigar rather desperately too. And brandy. Creature comforts—woman, cigar, brandy—in that order.

But by far the greatest of his cravings at present was woman.

Not any woman. *Emily*. Her scent in his nostrils, her skin beneath his hands, her flavor upon his tongue. His senses craved *her*.

How disappointed the earl would be if, from the realm of the afterlife, he could discern his son's unwieldy appetites now. But the earl was not here, and Colin found that he liked fantasizing about kissing Emily.

Situated on a broad flatland between the hill to the west of the bank, the farm was comprised of two buildings of stone and a wooden slat barn, and two fenced pastures containing about a hundred head of sheep. No torches or lanterns dimmed the unearthly starlight illumining it all. As he walked along a wooden crossbar fence toward the barn, one after another the sheep lifted their heads from grazing and stared at him. No one stirred in the clearing between the dwellings, and not a lamp or candle flickered in a window.

Silently he drew open the barn door. Its walls muted sound from without, but in the loft a bird chirped already. Hooves shuffled in a stall. Passing a pen containing a goat and three pigs, he went toward the shuffling sound.

The animal was enormous, a creamy-coated draft horse certainly used for fieldwork. It watched him with placid eyes and allowed him to slip a halter over its head and lead it from the stall, its hooves falling heavily on the packed dirt floor.

"Be ye a smithy, sir?"

From the loft above, a tiny face covered with freckles and surrounded by matted black hair stared through the darkness at him with eyes the size of the horse's hooves.

"I am not a blacksmith. I am an earl. Who are you?"

"Pip." The urchin crawled to the edge of the loft and sat up, its knees catching in the skirts of a shabby brown skirt. "If yer no' a smithy, what do ye be wantin' with Charlie?"

"I want to ride him to the castle of the Duke of Loch Irvine, after which I intend to return him here, unscathed."

"Ye're to see the *Devil*?" The eyes popped wide again. "'Tis brave ye be."

"Rather, I am desperate." He bowed. "Good day, Miss Pip." He led the horse toward the door.

Behind him a light thump signaled her dismount from the loft.

"I'll be comin' with ye." Before he could speak, she leaped from a stack of straw onto the massive animal's back and wrapped her hands in its mane.

He halted the horse. "You cannot come with me. Now jump down and go back up into your loft and finish your night's sleep."

Her eyes burned into his. "But I've been waitin' for ye."

"Have you?"

"My mither said an angel'd come save me," she said.

"Save you from what?"

"Tom."

"And who is this Tom?"

"My cousin. Before she passed to heaven Mama said ye'd come wring Tom's neck an' rescue me."

Through the door that stood ajar he could see the pale glimmer of dawn. Where there were sheep there would be dogs. Unless he bothered the sheep, the dogs would probably not bother him. But they might bark.

"Pip, I do not intend to wring anyone' neck. And I cannot take you with me."

Her tiny face wrinkled into a scowl. "Ye've got to. 'Tis what angels do."

It was on his tongue to say that he was not an angel. Far from it. But the light in her eyes reminded him of another little girl's eyes years ago, bright and defiant.

"When the door opened," she said, "I thought ye were Tom. He always comes afore dawn so nobody else knows it."

Colin regarded her little face a moment longer.

"What is your cousin's age, Pip?"

"Seventeen this shearing past."

He pulled the horse and its tiny rider out the door.

Chapter 9

The Prospect of a Bed

$\mathscr{P}$ip was silent, her eyes darting about as he drew the horse toward the fence, climbed it, and mounted behind her. She clung naturally to the animal's mane and he did not need to tell her to remain silent; she did so without command, entirely unlike another little girl he had known years ago, who had rarely ever kept still.

What that girl-turned-woman would now say when he arrived at their rendezvous place with an urchin, he could not anticipate. Perhaps she did not wish to marry because she did not like children.

He liked children. He always had. He had liked her six younger sisters with whom he was forced to spend every holiday and many weeks besides those, at either Maryport Court or Willows Hall. And he had liked her, especially her, despite the five years' difference in age. He had liked her more than any other person in the world.

"Pip," he said as they entered the copse. "Have you lived on your cousins' farm your entire life?"

"No, sir. Only since Christmas last," she chirped, all

strain vanished from her high voice. "Mama and I came after the fever took Mattie to heaven. We weren't supposed to stay. But she fell sick and God took her up to Mattie."

"I see. Since then did you, by chance, make the acquaintance of a traveler named Penny? She has hair quite like yours, very black and curly, and dark skin. She would have passed by your farm before the lambs dropped." The peddler in Stirling had seen Penny Baker just south of Tarbet.

"No, sir." She shook her head. "After the drovers, only the one leddy came through. But her hair was fiery like Mama's."

Not Miss Baker.

They broke from the tree cover into a small clearing where Emily should have been waiting, but was not.

"Why're we stoppin'?" Pip kicked her heels into the horse's sides and it stepped forward. "The Devil's days' ride away."

He tugged on the rein and the animal halted again as he scanned the wood all about and his heartbeats raced.

"My traveling companion is to meet me here."

"Is he an angel too?"

"You know that I am not an angel, Pip. How old are you?"

"Eight come Epiphany."

"Seven is old enough for you to be using your intelligence. Think. Would an angel steal a horse?"

Her freckled nose wrinkled up. "I dinna ken why he couldna."

Nothing stirred the trees around the clearing and sickness was growing in the pit of his stomach. But she was capable. He had watched her carefully avoid ditches and nimbly cross streams for a day and a half now. She could hold her own in this wilderness. Yet his pulse would not slow.

"Pip."

She craned her neck to look up at him.

"What will your cousin do when he discovers you missing from the barn?" he asked the urchin.

Her freckles puckered.

"I will not return you there," he said. "But I must know how much time I have before they come looking for you."

She peered at him as though he had lost his mind. "'Tis *Charlie* they'll be lookin' for."

"Understood."

A moment's silence became two, then three, then many more as the birds around them grew accustomed to their presence and the woodland awoke to full dawn.

"When'll we be movin' on?" Pip finally whispered.

"Not until my companion returns." His hands clutched the reins hard. She might have gone in any direction, or been taken in any direction. He'd heard no gunshots, but he had been inside a barn, and the trees might have also muffled the sound of a small pistol's discharge.

He scanned the trees again.

A rustling in the underbrush caught both their attentions at once. A shape appeared among the trees, making no sound. *Her shape.* Relief clamored into his throat. At the edge of the clearing she paused.

"They gave you a horse at the farm?" she said. "It seems I was entirely misguided in my worries."

"They did not give it to me."

"I see." She tilted her head. "Did you steal the child as well?"

He swallowed thoroughly inappropriate laughter and nudged the horse into movement toward her.

"We must go," he said. "Swiftly."

"How do you do?" she said to the urchin. "My name is Zenobia. What is yours?"

"Pip," the child said with eyes so wide now they seemed to consume her face. "*She* be the angel," she said wonderingly.

He smiled. "Perhaps."

Emily studied them both, carefully it seemed, but said nothing.

"My lady." He extended his hand. "Haste is in order."

Without complaint she clasped his hand, set her foot onto his boot, and they hauled her up onto the animal's broad, bare back behind him.

"That direction," she said at his shoulder and pointed. Then he felt her hands lodge in his coat at his waist. "I believe that is the church at Tarbet."

It was not far to the tree that she had climbed to the top, where she had glimpsed the squat stone bell tower poking up at the edge of the loch in the distance like a bolt sticking out of a wheel. Miles away, it sat atop its own little hillock at the water's edge a quarter mile before the town. As much as she hated to admit it, Colin was correct: a vicar was more likely to give them haven than anybody else. She wanted a hot cup of tea so desperately that she barely felt a twinge of conscience at the obvious worth of the horse she straddled now, stolen from hardworking people by a lord who could afford many such animals.

The child was another matter altogether.

"Do you know that church, Pip?" he said to the girl now.

"'Tis Saint Andrew's. Uncle drove us there at Easter."

Unlike in their flight two days ago, they did not trot or run, but walked. She wondered at his choice to go so slowly, but suspected it had to do with the child clinging to the animal in the circle of his arms. Pip looked as exhausted as Zenobia felt. And when she had gazed up at Colin and pronounced her an angel, Pip's round eyes had been saturated with relief.

Lulled by the horse's steady gait, Zenobia resisted the urge to lean into him and lay her cheek upon his broad back, to wrap her arms entirely around his waist, and to enjoy the rhythmic friction of her thighs against his while wondering if he was *distracted* by it again. By her.

She had not ridden astride since she was a child younger than Pip. Then, of course, she had ridden with him too. She wondered if he remembered and hoped he did not. She remembered complaining that he would not allow her to hold the reins, boasting at age five that she was a superb rider, and begging him to make it go faster. Now the memory did not fill her with discomfort. Now it was peculiarly comforting and she clung to it instead of to his back.

The big horse went at a steady pace. They encountered no one, and by the time they came within sight of the church's outer wall of thick stone, the sun had not yet reached its apex.

"Down you go, Pip," he said, and the child slid off the horse. Before Zenobia could do the same, he dismounted and reached up for her.

She hesitated.

"You are eighteen hands up," he said. "Imagine your sore feet hitting the ground from that height."

She threw her leg over the horse's broad back and put her palms on his shoulders. He lifted her down easily and for an instant every betraying mote of starved femininity inside her cried out. He held her only a moment, then he released her and she ducked her head, making a pretense of smoothing her skirts and adjusting her cloak. Her cheeks were too hot.

"Do we have a plan?" she said and chanced a glance at him. He was staring in what seemed bemusement at the church beyond the iron gate that sat with quiet ease above the water amidst dark-needled pines and birches bare of leaves. As though her words surprised him, he glanced at her. His jaw was dark with whiskers and his eyes swam with a sort of reverie.

"Colin," she whispered so the little girl waiting with her fingers curled around the gate could not hear. "You must sleep."

His brow creased and he blinked. Then he drew the horse to the gate and bound it there. Opening it, they went within.

THE VICAR OF the parish of Saint Andrew's-on-the-Cross that served the town of Tarbet was a year or two shy of ancient, with the brow of a thinking man and the eyes of a praying man. His wife, at least two decades his junior and clearly English, had a curious face and a brisk manner. In a small, plainly furnished parlor, the vicar sat with a book open on his lap in a slant of sunshine. As he rose to his feet, he actually creaked.

"Good day, Reverend. I am Colin Gray, the Earl of Egremoor. Allow me to introduce to you Lady Emily Vale, daughter of the Earl of Vale. And this is Pip."

"Well, isn't this a surprise?" the vicar's wife exclaimed.

"Welcome," her husband said with the mildest brogue, and offered a bow. "Ma'am." His eyes crinkled into crescents. "Miss Pip, the lady of the house baked cakes this morning. Alas, my dyspepsia won't allow me to sample them. Mrs. Archer," he said to his wife, "I believe I've found a cake taster for you."

She held out her hand for Pip. "Come along, child. You will help me prepare the tea tray."

Pip turned a questioning face up to the earl. He nodded. She put her hand into Mrs. Archer's and the door closed behind them.

"Do have a seat," the vicar said.

Flames danced in the fireplace. Zenobia took a chair before it, but Colin remained standing.

"Our horse requires tending," he said.

"Of course," Reverend Archer said, pushing himself from his chair again. "My manservant, Griffin, has gone to town upon an errand. But I'll see to—"

"Do not trouble yourself, sir," Colin said. "I will return in a moment." He left the room.

"Now, that's a sight I never would have thought to see," the vicar said thoughtfully, regarding her with careful eyes. "A great lord tending to his own horse."

"You don't believe us, do you? A ragamuffin pair arrives upon your stoop claiming to be an earl and an earl's daughter, and you cannot possibly accept that."

"It is my duty to give you hospitality," Reverend Archer said kindly.

"Have you heard news of a pair of highwaymen, one of whom is calling himself the Earl of Egremoor?"

"I received a careful description of them only this morning. The messenger of the news had been through a dreadful ordeal. It seems the pair tied him to his horse."

"That was actually us. But he was about to shoot Lord Egremoor, so I pretended to be the highwayman. The lie was necessary, but I feel poorly about it."

"I can see you are a person of strong conscience." He folded his knobby hands together. "It is clear to me that whoever you claim to be, you are in need of help. How might I assist you and your traveling companions?"

"You could make it known to the people of this region that we are not the highwaymen they seek to apprehend. No one believes us. They have come at us with curses and fire-arms, and we have been forced into hiding and flight."

"Astonishing. These thieves must have a remarkable facility for aping their betters."

"I have sympathy for our pursuers, Reverend Archer. They are suffering from thefts and murders. But it is proving inconvenient for me and Lord Egremoor."

His eyes upon her were grave. "And what of the child? Pip."

"We became acquainted with her this morning. She lives at the farm not far to the south where Lord Egremoor stole the horse. But you mustn't worry about that. I am certain he means to return it or at the least compensate the owner of it when this is all over. He is wealthy and exceedingly moralistic."

"I see," he said thoughtfully. "Is she . . . the child . . . the gentleman's?"

"The gentleman's? Oh, Lord Egremoor's." Her stomach did a tight somersault. "No. That is, I don't believe so. I do not actually know why he brought her along when he borrowed the horse. I am so tired I'm not thinking particularly acutely about anything."

Colin entered the room.

"Did you find everything to your needs in the stable?" the vicar asked.

"I did." He took a seat across from the vicar. "Reverend Archer, Lady Emily and I are in need of your assistance."

"He knew about the thieves," she said.

"When Griffin returns, I will send him for the constable," the vicar said. "What else may I do for you?"

"I would like to send a message to my estate, as well as to His Grace of Argyll's castle in Inveraray and acquaintances of mine in Edinburgh. Is there a man who could ride swiftly with these letters? A man you trust?"

The vicar's brow wrinkled. "Only Griffin."

"My second request is for the loan of your carriage. We were obliged to leave behind our transportation abruptly. Our destination is Castle Kallin. The more swiftly we can travel there the better."

"Of course. You are welcome to the gig and old Maggie. She is as rickety as I, nearly, but she should be able to take you to Ardlui at least, where you might find a better horse."

"We cannot take them," she said to Colin. "It will leave Reverend Archer without a means to visit his parishioners in an emergency."

The vicar smiled. "I am not averse to riding. You can leave me with the horse you have taken from the MacLeods and I will see that it finds its owner."

"Lady Emily, will you allow me a moment alone with Reverend Archer?" Colin said.

"Why? What can you not speak of with me here?"

"The particulars of Pip's presence with us."

That the child could be his was not impossible. Her eyes were precisely the color of his, and she shared his hair color.

"I would like to hear those particulars," she said.

Finally he shifted his attention back to the vicar.

"When I found the child she was hiding from her cousin, whose treatment of her is unacceptable. She was eager to escape him, and I could not leave her in that situation. She is an orphan and has lived with her uncle and aunt only a year. Can you find a safe home for her away from that family?"

"This is troublesome," Reverend Archer said, placing his palms on his knees. "I remember now a little girl in church at Easter with Roger MacLeod's family. His three sons are much older than the child."

Colin nodded. "So I understood from her."

"What sort of treatment?" she asked.

"The sort that no man should inflict upon a child," Colin said tightly. "Nor upon anyone else."

The vicar nodded. "She may remain with me and Mrs. Archer for now, of course, until a situation for her can be arranged. But Roger MacLeod will come looking for the child. Every spare hand in a sheep farmer's household is a working hand."

"I will see to it that does not happen," Colin said.

As Mrs. Archer entered with Pip, bearing trays laden with tea and cakes, Zenobia's stomach gave off a spectacular growl. The tension about Colin's mouth loosened, and he offered her the slightest smile.

She could not look away. There was such tenderness in his eyes, the sort she had not seen there in years.

Pip proved adept at pouring tea, careful and deliberate. After they ate, the vicar asked her if she would like a tour of the church. She leaped from her chair with her wonderful eyes quite wide, demanding to see the bones of the saint. The vicar responded that the relic was not Saint Andrew's bone, only a fragment of the cross upon which he had been martyred, which made her mouth pop open as wide as her eyes.

But before taking the vicar's outstretched hand, she looked again to Colin for confirmation. He nodded.

The vicar invited them all to come.

"If you cannot see that Miss Emily is asleep where she sits, Mr. Archer," his wife said, "then it is time to send away for new spectacles." She took up the tea tray. "I'll clean this up, miss, then show you to a bedchamber." She went out with firm efficiency, the vicar and Pip following.

Colin sat with his hands resting on the arms of the chair and his eyes closed.

"You are her hero." There was a thickness in the back of her throat.

Slowly he opened his eyes.

"It seems that you have not left off rescuing little girls," she said. "Despite becoming a mighty lord."

"You imagined otherwise?" he said with a calm assurance which only days earlier she would have thought arrogance. It was not. Rather, *discomfort*.

"Well, I did not imagine that you had taken her hostage to ensure our safety. I don't think you quite that heartless."

A hint of amusement graced his very fine lips. "Thank you."

"But, yes," she said. "I am surprised."

He leaned forward to rest his elbows on his knees and folded his hands.

"Admittedly, it was not the wisest decision I have made lately," he said. "I did it—" He paused. "I did it on impulse."

"Impulse?" The calculating, carefully manipulative Peregrine who had played games with her and everybody else in England for years? "That is unusual for you, I suppose."

He lifted his eyes to her and there was an odd light in them. "It seems that this country is having a singular effect on me. And, perhaps, being with you."

"I do not act on impulse." Except in meeting her nemesis in a dark cemetery after insisting for years that she would never meet him anywhere. And hurrying north to find her sister.

"What, then, was climbing a tree in search of church steeples?" he said.

"That was not impulse. It was desperation for hot tea and a bed. And I wasn't any more impulsive than children typically are. Children except you, of course. You were always so deliberate about everything. So careful."

He did not reply. She stood and crossed the little room to the window.

"The Reverend and Mrs. Archer are likely to have a boat," she said.

"A boat?"

"They live on a lake. He is quite elderly, it's true. So perhaps they do not keep a boat themselves." She traced the windowsill with a fingertip. "Reverend Archer asked me if Pip was yours."

"My what?"

"Your child."

"*My* child?"

"Why are you looking at me disapprovingly? It was his assumption, not mine. And Pip does have your eye color, which is unique. Her hair is similar in color to yours too. He was merely trying to comprehend our peculiar circumstances. And of course he does not believe we are who we say we are. I cannot blame him."

"How good of you to defend his prying," he said dryly.

"Do you have children?"

He peered at her. "No."

"Are you certain?"

Beneath the two-day whisker growth that made him look rather fierce, his jaw abruptly became stone again. "Quite certain."

"Why don't you?"

"Because I do not have a *wife*."

"One does not require the other, of course. Half the titled men in England have illegitimate children."

"A man of my rank who fathers bastards is a scoundrel," he said. "Worse, he is foolishly careless, irresponsible, and heedless of the respect due his ancestors."

"But why don't you have a wife, Colin? You are nearly thirty-two, well past the age you might have married. All of your friends are married." She could not resist adding, "And, of course, if you had married before your father's will became relevant, you would never have been obliged to propose to me. That should have given you reason enough to rush to the altar with some lovely young maiden of impeccable birth and a vast dowry years ago."

"For God's sake, Emily." His chest expanded upon a hard breath. Then he stood up and walked out of the room.

Chapter 10

A Buttoning Up

The bedframe was as narrow as a penknife, but Zenobia leaned toward it, ready to collapse in mingled gratitude and delirium.

"Miss," the vicar's wife said. "I hope you won't imagine me overstepping my bounds to ask a delicate question."

"I am not attached to notions of delicacy, Mrs. Archer, or to those sorts of boundaries, really." Her voice was slurring. "Ask me whatever you wish."

Mrs. Archer clasped her hands together. "Are you altogether comfortable with this?"

"In fact I don't think I have ever seen a more comfortable bed." Her body swayed toward it again.

"What I'm asking . . . Is your situation with the gentleman entirely to your liking?"

"Not at all! It is unquestionably the most desperate straits I have ever been in, save perhaps one other desperate strait, but that was many years ago. However, this situation cannot be helped, except to put as much road as possible between us and the men who mistake us for criminals."

"But, the gentleman?"

"He feels quite the same way I do about avoiding the noose."

"He is a fine-looking man," she said with tight lips. "But I know something of young men, and I am anxious to know whether you feel cause for concern from *him*." Her gaze was at once entirely expressive and intriguingly evasive.

"Oh, I see. You don't believe us either." She blinked to keep her eyes open. "Well, I don't suppose you would. Both of us are ashambles. Usually he is as starched and severe and elegant a man as you will ever see, and entirely lordly. I am, admittedly, not at all the usual run of things for a nobleman's daughter, not even on my good days. But Lord Egremoor is most certainly exactly as an earl should be, usually."

"Some men will say anything if they fancy a girl. And some girls will believe any sort of nonsense if they fancy him too."

"I am fortunately not one of those girls. Just as significantly, if Lord Egremoor could have been trapped in this situation with any woman on earth he would certainly not have chosen me. I daresay I would be at the dead bottom of his list. Of thousands. Millions." She could not wrest her attention from the mattress.

Mrs. Archer shook her head. "From the moment the two of you came through the door, I imagined the worst."

"*Is* there anything worse than being mistaken for thieves and murderers and pursued by angry men?"

"A man doesn't look at a girl as he looks at you without certain intentions."

"No, truly. He has no such intentions toward me. Trust me. But more importantly, Mrs. Archer, I fear that if I do not lie down in the next instant I will probably fall down."

"Poor dear. I'll leave you to rest now."

Dropping to the mattress, she gathered up the blanket and closed her eyes. Contrarily, sleep did not come swiftly. She had angered him, or perhaps frustrated him. This time, rather than hiding it, he had revealed it to her. Exhaustion was affecting him poorly. Or perhaps it was as he had said: this country, wild and beautiful and dangerous all at once, was having an effect on him. As it was on her.

"EMILY."

His voice came to her through dreams.

"Emily, wake up."

She cracked open her eyes to darkness illumined by a single candle. A man loomed beside the bed. Colin. His broad shoulders. His strong arms. His powerful presence. *Beside her bed.*

She was certainly still dreaming.

She shifted onto her side, away from the apparition.

"Emily."

She peered over her shoulder. The apparition stood too rigidly to be anything but actually him. "You're real," she mumbled.

"Wake up."

"'M awake. Is it morning?" It could not be. Even her bone marrow throbbed.

"It is time to go."

The warmth of sleep dragged her down again. Her dream had been so much more agreeable than this. "Mm-hm."

"Get. Up."

Slowly she forced her eyelids to rise again. "What is the time?"

"An hour before dawn." He flipped the bedclothes aside. She crawled off the mattress and he filled her hands with her own clothing.

She reached for her spectacles. "I am assuming this haste is necessary," she whispered.

"It is."

"You must button me up again, unless you've brought Mrs. Archer, who would not be pleased you are here witnessing me wearing only my shift and stockings."

"Quickly."

In the wavering candlelight he fastened her stays again

and then her gown, and she bore it because she was still mostly asleep and she hadn't any choice anyway. She would write her next pamphlet about the evils of clothing that required a woman to have assistance to dress, rendering her dependent upon another person to even leave the house. But certainly that was the whole idea of haute couture: the more delicate fabrics and unreachable fasteners, the more servants one required to prepare one's gowns and then to dress, therefore the more obvious wealth one displayed in the simple act of wearing clothes. His fingers strafed the curve of her buttock and instantly she was composing the pamphlet in her head—anything to distract from the wild image from her dream of his hands circling her waist and pulling her back against him.

It did not happen.

Dressed, she crept behind him down the stairs. The night was still unseasonably warm, and in a thicket by the wall a lonely cricket chirped at the stars. But Colin did not walk toward the stable. Instead he gestured her toward the church. In the darkness she followed him, her feet sinking into mossy earth as they passed the door and went around the exterior curve of the apse. Glittering black and broad beneath the moon, the loch lapped against the bank, rhythmically slapping a modest dock.

Tied to the end of the dock was a rowboat.

"What are we doing?" she whispered.

"Slipping away in the dark of night," he replied, unlashing the rope that bound the boat to the dock. "I should think that obvious." He extended his hand.

"But, why? The Archers are willing to help us."

"I am not entirely certain of that. But if they are prepared to help, they are to be thanked rather than dragged into danger."

"You want to preserve them from trouble, don't you? He is so old and infirm."

"Why must I continually demand that you get onto transportation?" he said impatiently.

"If you hoped for a docile female with whom to share this horrible adventure, you hoped in vain." But she took his hand and stepped gingerly into the boat. Sliding onto a bench, she pulled her skirts tight around her and peered at the massive silhouette of the church on the bank above.

"I cannot like leaving Pip in the middle of the night," she said. "Not even with churchy people."

He pointed to a pile of blankets on the floor between them, then pushed the vessel away from the dock and took up the oars. She twitched the blanket up at the corner to reveal a little foot. Replacing the blanket, she looked up at him.

He shook his head and plied the oars. She understood. Sound carried swiftly and clearly over the lake's surface. Even the light *slap-slap* of the oars cut the silence disturbed only by water sloshing at the bank and the chirping of birds waking in the trees.

"When you tire, I will take a turn rowing," she whispered.

He responded with a thoroughly expressive stare.

Swiveling around on the bench to face the front, she tugged her cloak more closely about her. The sky was awakening in folds of gray over the opposite bank, and the hills rose in rolling peaks, layered with dark conifers and blue mist.

"It is stunning," she sighed, but of course he did not reply. He was exceedingly disciplined. He always had been.

Keeping close to the uneven bank, concealed by the mottled trunks of the birches, they went swiftly up the loch. Moving around a stand of trees jutting out into the lake, they came upon the fishing boats suddenly. Colin drove the oars into the water portside and the boat jerked abruptly toward the shore. Zenobia grabbed the sides and from beneath the blankets came a whimper. Freeing one hand, she leaned down and touched the blankets. They wiggled and Pip's little freckled nose that reminded her so much of her sister Amarantha poked out.

"Miss—?"

Squeezing Pip's hand, she held a finger up to her lips.

Pip crawled out of the blankets and to the bench. Zenobia put her arm around the tiny girl, her eyes on the backs of the three fishermen. Their bow bumped the bank. Colin set the oars silently into the boat and handed both of them out before climbing onto land himself. In a close file, they poked through the loosely spaced trees, feet snagging on roots and underbrush until they climbed onto the road.

It was deserted. True daylight was still an hour or more away. Colin nodded to her and she caught up with him, Pip at their heels.

"We are not to trust fishermen either?" she said.

"Mr. Griffin returned to the vicarage last night after you went to sleep. The imposters shot a man at Inverberg."

"No."

"The man is still alive. But the hunt has intensified."

"Then why are we headed north?"

"I am hoping they will not have reached Ardlui."

"Hoping?"

"If you prefer praying, be my guest. We made good time on the water. I guess we've another mile or two only to walk. The road is the most direct route, and I asked the Archers and Mr. Griffin to deny that they had encountered us if anyone should ask."

"You hope to hire horses or a vehicle in Ardlui. It is a drover's village."

"So Griffin and Archer told me." He offered her not quite a smile. "Clearly I might have simply consulted you."

"I told you, I studied the route." And every possible hill, village, and byway her sister might have traveled at one time. "I am *bookish*, recall."

"Admittedly, I am having a difficult time keeping that in mind."

Pip came up between them. "Are we comin' to the Devil's castle?"

"Not yet." Zenobia took her hand. Stifling her cringes from the pain in her feet, she quickened her pace. "Come now. We must make haste."

"Aye, miss," Pip declared and, breaking from her hold, ran ahead.

But when Pip's little steps began to drag, Zenobia welcomed the slowed pace.

"We must move more quickly," Colin said. "The road is too narrow here to tarry."

She imagined Pip's terrified, sleepless nights until yesterday. "She is sleeping even as she walks."

Then she stared, astonished, as Colin bent and lifted the little girl up as though she weighed a feather. Pip slung her arms around his neck, laid her head on his shoulder, and promptly fell asleep. He started off again.

When a few minutes had passed he said quietly, "We could not leave her there."

"Yes." The Reverend and his wife had good intentions. But Pip belonged to her uncle's family, and four strong farmers versus one aged man of the cloth was no fair contest.

"Why have we left Charlie at the vicarage?"

He glanced at her. The ghost of a smile dented his cheek and a responding twirl of nerves went through her stomach.

"Why do you look at me so?" she said.

"Why did you wait so long to ask me about the horse?"

"I was still mostly asleep." And any conversation that reminded her of straddling his hips made her hot. She dragged her attention to the fog now hovering over the sparkling gray mass of lake. "Tell me."

"I returned him to the MacLeods' farm."

"To the—last *night*? But that must have taken you hours!" And potential danger on the road. The thought made an abrupt, odd weakness wash over her. "Did you not sleep?"

"A horse like that comes dear. Pip would have been blamed for the theft. Why were you traveling with only Madame Roche and Jonah? Without a maid and outrider? Does your father know how you travel?"

"How long have *you* been waiting to ask me that?"

He did not respond.

"My father has very little concern over my life these days."

"I beg to differ." There was a quality of certainty in his voice.

"Why do you say that?"

"When did you last receive an offer of marriage?" He glanced at her over the fuzzy top of Pip's head. "From a man other than me, that is."

She could only blink in surprise.

"You needn't tell me, actually," he said. "I know that Lord Willis offered for you last Christmas."

Her blistered feet stumbled and halted. The shadows beneath the canopy of gray trunks and branches encrusted with green lichen swallowed him swiftly.

"Papa told you?" she called ahead.

"Each time. Each suitor. Each offer," he said without breaking stride or raising his voice. "So you see, your father does remain concerned with your life. My compliments to you on the number of impressive offers you have received, by the by, despite your reputation for turning down admirable suitors."

"Sarcasm now?" she said with suddenly numb lips. The lake lapped close at their right, not four yards below where they walked, nor thirty feet away. If it wished, it could swell up a gentle, probing wave and swallow them whole, unsuspecting, helpless against the sheer slope of the mountainside to their left. But she watched him walk before her and doubted a mere lake, even mammoth Loch Lomond, would dare to swallow the Earl of Egremoor. After a night sleeping in a wood and another not sleeping at all, and despite a scruff of dark whiskers that made him look more like an actual highwayman every hour, he was still elegant, still severe, still in perfect control.

"The suitors were not my idea," she said. "My dowry is grotesquely enormous, of course."

He swung around and came to her. Before she knew what he was about, his hand wrapped around her chin and he jerked her face up.

"Cease this," he said upon a growl. "Cease pretending you've nothing to attract a man."

The child stirred in his embrace, then sighed and tucked her chin more snugly into his chest.

"Remove your hand from me."

He released her and she stepped back. His eyes burned peculiarly bright in the pale glow of dawn.

"I cannot believe you are as naïve as you pretend to be," he said.

"I am far from naïve. I know what attracts men of wealth and status: more of the same, and beauty if it can be gotten too. But I have no beauty, nor even gentle feminine airs. I don't care for simpering or flirtation, and I don't understand half of the quips that pass for sophisticated conversation among gentlemen and ladies in London. Rather, I do understand them but I think them inane. I am shy in company, and when I do speak most gentlemen look at me like I am a simpleton or as if I have grown a second head. But that is not really even at issue, for neither Lord Willis nor any of the other men who offered marriage had spoken even fifty words to me before asking my father permission to pay their addresses."

"I had," he said stonily.

"You did not need to ask him, did you? He invited you. And your father demanded it from the grave. So I think we can safely discount that little exercise in filial duty. But to return to the issue, my decisions—whether to marry or travel with a bevy of servants—are my own, not my father's."

"Why does he continue to allow you to live alone, and give you an allowance? Why hasn't he forced you to wed by threatening the removal of those privileges?"

The weight of his words emptied her lungs.

"Is *that* your solution to women who do not do what their male relatives wish them to do? Withhold money from them until they capitulate?"

"I have only wondered why," he said, "when he obviously wishes you to marry, that he—"

"That he does not threaten me with poverty if I don't do his bidding?" Her stomach was a knotted pit of vipers striking at her. "I suspect it is because he *cares* for me, Colin. As a person. And he knows me well enough to understand that marriage to the men who have offered for me would kill me."

A complete transformation came over his face, the anger melting into an entirely different arrangement of his features. Shock, but something else too. There was such emotion in his eyes now, she felt as though her insides were pressing on her ribcage and twisting in her middle. For years she had thought him a stranger. Now, here, on this road by uncertain light she saw again such acute feeling in the beautiful eyes of the boy she had once adored. She let herself look at his arm so firmly about the little girl, a child he barely knew yet felt the responsibility to protect, and something hard and encrusted inside her shattered.

It was too much for her—too much, and she did not understand it. She dragged her gaze from him and passed by him, and her blisters and aching muscles were nothing now that she was desperate to get away.

She was lying to him again.

Her father did not withhold funds from her to force her to wed, because he knew it would not matter if he did. For years he had known that she had an independent income. When she had earned her first few pounds from the sale of her pamphlets, she had requested that her father sponsor a bank account in her name. As Lady Justice's popularity soared and her income had grown beyond the needs of her household, she began donating the ample allowance her father gave her to charities. Yet he never questioned it. Instead, he complimented her on her choices: Serena Savege's charity for war widows and orphans, Lady Ashford's program at the docks, and the modest school Diantha Lucas had recently established to educate children working in the Welsh mines.

Her father knew about her income. But he had never asked its source. She only knew that he wanted her happiness, unlike this man—this man who was twisting her inside out.

"Shall I quiz you about your travel arrangements too?" she said. "I was not aware that great lords typically take to the road alone on horseback."

"You say *great lords* as though the words have a bad flavor."

She squeezed her eyes shut and her feet carried her along the road swiftly. He knew Lady Justice too well for her to be so careless.

It was some time again before he spoke. His voice came from several yards behind her.

"Before you voiced your concern over it earlier," he finally said, "I had not considered the inconvenience to the vicar and his parishioners that a lack of transportation would cause him."

"I suspect you rarely find yourself without multiple carriages and horses at your immediate beckon."

"Never, of course."

"Nor did you consider the wrong in demanding that three blameless people lie for us."

"I did not demand. I asked."

"When an earl requires a poor vicar and his wife to lie for him, the difference between demanding and asking is slim."

"As you note, none of them believed I am an earl. And I thought only of taking you to safety as swiftly as possible."

She halted and waited as he walked toward her. There was a peculiar wariness in his step now, his shoulders rigid and face severe and unreadable.

"Thank you," she forced past the lump in her throat.

"For what are you thanking me?"

"For finding me and taking me away from danger at the Laird's Leed. For carrying me up that hill after I swooned." She looked at the child in his arms. "For rescuing Pip from evil. For not sleeping."

"I slept three hours before I went out tonight. Are you satisfied?"

"Will you accept my thanks or not?"

"If you insist."

"And I apologize for asking you about illegitimate children and marriage. Clarice often tells me that I speak without first thinking. Like you, she believes me impulsive. That is not entirely true. But I have difficulty curbing my tongue. She insists if I do not mend my ways that someday I will be like the Duchess of Hammershire, saying whatever I wish to whomever without any notion of anybody's feelings."

"You don't wish to be mistaken for a duchess?"

"I don't wish to hurt other people. And yet sometimes I do, as I think I did when I questioned you about children. I should not have spoken of that with you."

"Yet here you are speaking of it again." Miraculously, a hint of lightness had entered his voice, like the first stirrings of dawn upon the lake beside them.

"I should not have spoken of your father's will so blithely either. It must be difficult for you."

"You have always spoken blithely to me," he said. "You have always said anything that occurred to you."

"When we were children," she added, because there was so much she was not saying to him now. She started walking again. "I did not take to my mother's lessons in feminine reticence. I believed my opinions were as worthy as anybody else's."

"Everyone else spoke to me in a whisper."

Behind her, his words fell into silence. But she heard the sound of his footsteps on the pebble-strewn road.

"They did," she said. "I had forgotten that."

"All of them did. Servants, tenants, villagers, guests—they all spoke to me as though my silence required theirs as well. My tutor, Mr. Gunter, whispered every lesson he gave to me. There were times I wished I had a metal pot to bang over his head, simply to wrest some volume from him."

She smiled. "He was a mouse. And he steadfastly refused to lend me your books, which put him on my permanent list of least favorite people in the world."

"He was a brilliant scholar," he said easily enough. "Those who did not whisper to me shouted, as though I could not hear regular speech."

"How irrational."

"Except you. You did not. You neither whispered nor shouted. And you never held your tongue. You spoke to me as though I actually spoke back to you."

"I'm certain I was not the only person. There must have been others who—"

"No. Only you." A moment passed. "You did not hear my silence."

In truth, she barely recalled his silence. She remembered only that he had listened to her as no one else did, not distractedly or impatiently, but with his full attention. Years older than she, he might have ignored her or played tricks on her. But he had not. He had treated her with great kindness—until the day he changed.

"Your father spoke rationally to you," she said.

"He believed that if he pretended my impairment did not exist, then it would not."

She had nothing to say to that. The old earl had never hidden his disapproval of her. Never blaming her father, he had believed that her deficient character was due to her mother's poor training of her eldest daughter.

"His death has not affected me as I expected it would." Colin looked at her very clearly, as though there were nothing hidden behind his words. "I am not in grief. I was, but I believe that was more due to his suffering while he was ill than my loss of him. The strongest feeling I have now is . . . relief. I am relieved he is gone. There. I have admitted an unflattering truth to you."

"Have you admitted it to anyone else?"

"No."

"Why not?"

He hesitated a moment.

"Because no one else would understand, I think," he finally said.

Her stomach was a tangle of confusion.

"I know," she said. "I am also surprised by a sort of familiarity with you that encourages me to say things I should not." She wrapped her cloak more closely about her. "It is a false familiarity, of course. But I suppose it is the effect of knowing a person when one is young. It tricks me into imagining that I know you now, and perhaps it has had the same effect on you." Perhaps that was what Mrs. Archer had seen, that false familiarity.

"Emily, consider our current circumstances." A smile lurked at his lips again. "Familiarity is inevitable."

Around them the earth crackled with life—birds in the trees hanging over them waking, and wind stirring the branches, and the constant swoosh of water against the bank yards away.

"You have buttoned up my gown twice, after all," she conceded.

"Just so."

She bit back her smile. "And you may call me Zenobia."

He seemed to be studying her face now, particularly her lips. "But I think you underestimate the effect you speak of," he said. "It is not a trick."

"It is. Two decades stand between then and now." And two secret identities. "We are not the same people we were then. That is very clear to me. For instance, you dislike me now, which you did not then."

"I do not dislike you now."

"Of course you do. The stiffness of your spine and chill in your eyes have declared it every time we have met for years."

Looking up into the trees, he lifted a hand and ran it over his face. On his shoulder, Pip's fuzzy head turned.

"'R we there yet?" she mumbled around the little thumb stuffed into her mouth.

"Not yet," he said, then looked over her head again. "It will be daylight soon and the road is too narrow here for us to escape it if a rider overtakes us. Do you see the fire ahead, near the bank?"

Zenobia peered until it came into focus. "The bank juts out there. It is a cove, perhaps Ardlui."

"Let us hope so."

"I think I now understand why you have not yet married," she said, forcing her sore feet to ignore the stones and depressions in the road.

"Do you?"

"Your duty to your father was to offer for me yet you could not bear the idea of it. But you could never deny his wishes. So you waited to do your duty until you could wait no longer. What an awful burden your devotion to him was in this case. How horrid it must have been to have that hanging over your head all these years. Now, happily, you are free to do as you wish. Marry at will, my lord! For I have given you leave."

After some time he said in a low voice, "You are a baggage."

"I am at least to be handled as one, it seems," she said, feeling the memory of his hand so firmly about her face. "Despite my wishes."

He did not reply, did not seek to justify himself. It was for the best. When he touched her as though he had the right to do so, it infuriated her. But when he looked at her lips she wanted to forget that he was an arrogant, manipulative, lying stranger, and she no longer knew herself. She wanted to remember a time when they had understood each other. When they had been each other's exception.

Best instead to encourage his stony silences.

Best to remember that he had changed.

"WHAT IS OUR plan now?" Her eyes were dim and her skin pale, but her voice was clear, unlike the morning rising around them. Clouds thick and dark with rain were rolling across the sky. The wind had picked up. Sweeping across the surface of the earth, it curled off the loch in cold bursts. Colin watched as a blast hit her and she wavered to the side, then pressed her shoulder into it. She lifted a hand and brushed loose strands of hair from her cheek.

"To find horses or a carriage as swiftly as possible and drive to Loch Irvine's castle today," he said. "Unless you have another wish."

"We are within twenty miles," she said.

"If we maintain this pace we should reach the duke's castle by the Christmas after next."

"Do not say so," she said with a crease in her brow.

"That was meant to make you smile, you know."

"I cannot."

"Because you are still angry with me for handling you roughly?"

"Nothing has changed in the past several minutes, has it? But in fact blisters, not you, are currently preventing my mirth."

"Does the duke expect you?" he said.

She was chewing on her lower lip. It was a peculiar sight—this woman confused in thought.

"Emily?" he prodded.

"Zenobia."

"Are you expected at Castle Kallin?"

"Am I to quiz you on your travel plans as well?" she replied shortly, tugging her cloak more tightly about her. "Your original travel plans, that is."

"If you wish," he said.

Her gaze shot to his. "What were they?"

"I came to Scotland in search of a young woman who has not been heard from in several months. Her friends are concerned for her safety yet unable to make this journey."

"I see," she said quietly. "When you were forced to flee Balloch, had you yet found her?"

"Traces of her only. Some months ago she traveled in this direction, it seems."

"She might be anywhere now."

"Yes," he said.

"When we are safe again—if we are safe again—will you continue your search for her?"

"Until I have found her."

"Who are these friends of hers, that you would go to such lengths for them?"

"Only one of them requested it of me. And of course I did

not anticipate losing my horse or being obliged to flee angry Scots. It was to be an unremarkable task to accomplish."

"But you must have many other responsibilities that demand your attention, and plenty of servants to do this instead. You have only just succeeded to your father's title, and Parliament is in session."

"Parliament can wait."

The emeralds were wide. "For one person's request? You must hold this person in very high esteem."

"Rather the opposite. But I made a bargain with him." A bargain Lady Justice had canceled. It mattered little. The pamphleteer had been desperate to find Penny Baker and Colin knew that if he did so, Lady Justice would meet him. "I intend to keep it."

Red spots shone livid on Emily's cheeks in stark contrast to the rest of her pale face, and the wind battered her skirts and whipped her hair about her face. Her palms were pressed to her stomach. She had lovely hands, supple and lithe. Seeing her now, here, in this wilderness, tousled by the wind, with her gaze set upon him so fixedly, shifted something in his chest—something sharp and painful.

She despised him. Since Constance and the others had learned of the director's true identity, Colin had been enduring the anger of his closest friends. Someday they would come to understand why he had kept that secret from them. They would forgive him.

But Emily hated him.

He shouldn't care. He had stopped caring years ago. Yet with each hour he spent in her company, it angered him more. *Acute* anger. Anger he felt like a scald inside him.

A raindrop fell heavily between them. Then another. But she did not speak or move.

"We must find shelter," he said, remembering another rain, another wind-battered night. The darkness crawled into his throat. "Come," he pressed out between his teeth, then readjusted the child on his shoulder and increased his pace.

Ahead in the gray shroud that was now lake, trees, and sky combined, a plume of smoke arose from the bank. To the right the trees thinned abruptly, and they were looking out upon a tiny crescent cove with no more than a half dozen fishing boats. A long, wide platform extended from the bank into the water. On the bank, a broad barn stood with its doors wide open to the loch.

"The drovers' dock," he said.

"More chimney smoke."

"Several chimneys. Look for food. I will find transportation. Meet me beyond the farthest building in a quarter of an hour."

"I haven't a watch."

"Emily."

"What?"

"Estimate."

"You are clearly trained to this sort of thing, while I am not." Her voice rang with peculiar reticence.

He went to her. "Are you too anxious to proceed separately?"

"No. I am accustomed to facing the perils of the world alone, of course. I will take Pip." She reached up and stroked the little girl's cheek, and Pip roused from slumber. Blinking big eyes, she yawned. He set her on the ground.

"Time to see the Devil, miss?" she said.

"Not quite yet. We are to find breakfast while his lordship finds horses." She took the little girl's hand, cast him a quick glance, and went toward the buildings.

In the fog rolling along the cold lake and spilling onto the land, as the gray silhouettes of the bedraggled woman walking hand in hand with the bedraggled urchin nearly disappeared, the same furious ache he had felt the night before at the vicarage assailed him again. Dragging his eyes from them, he went in search of horses.

THE SCENT OF bread led them to the bakery, Pip's stride brightening with each step.

"Now," Zenobia said to the little girl, "not a word, do you understand?"

Pip's matted head jerked up and down.

"Good day," Zenobia said to the woman behind the counter, aromas besetting her with all the rich, warm, delicious glory of fresh baking. With shaking fingers, she placed several coins on the counter. "One of everything, if you please."

"Aye, miss." The baker wrapped up a collection of cakes, rolls, and two pies. "Where be ye headin' today?" She counted out change.

"North. Do you happen to know of an inn nearby?"

"The Drover's Inn, other side o' the cove. Be ye travelin' far?"

"Yes. But I am afraid my traveling companion and I have run into some trouble with our lead carriage horse." It was not *entirely* untrue. Behind the baker, a broadsheet was nailed to the wall, yellowed with age and plain. It was one of hers, Lady Justice's call for Parliament to allot special funds for a program to reintegrate wounded war veterans into the labor force. Above it was pinned a tartan emblem, the sort that Scottish soldiers wore into battle.

"Are ye with the lady that just came through the village, then?" the baker said.

"A lady?"

"A grand lady, travelin' with only a coachman. Came by no' an hour ago." The woman gestured toward the street.

If Sybil Charney were on the road just ahead of them now, they could hurry and catch her. If the lady and her coachmen were the imposters, however, the thieves, *Colin could be in danger.*

"How lovely for her that she is able to enjoy your baked delights too," she said swiftly, gathered up the package, and grabbed Pip's hand. "Good day."

Pip ran alongside her up the path between the buildings. They turned a corner, and Colin was walking toward them, the hulking mass of the drovers' barns dark against the lightening lake behind him. Relief flooded her.

"There are no horses to be had here," he said. "But there is an inn on the other side of the cove at which a pair of hacks are stabled." His gaze was all over her, on her face and hands holding the bakery package, and everywhere.

"The baker told us that a lady and her coachman in a grand carriage passed through here not an hour ago. It could be them. Or—"

Then she saw it, driving around the bend in the road directly toward them. Not Sybil Charney's carriage.

Hers.

Her own carriage.

"Colin, we are saved."

"Damn it," he said. *"No."*

Chapter 11

The Price

*J*onah pulled them to a halt and Madame Roche threw open the door.

"Ma petite!" She clasped Emily's hands and threw kisses onto her cheeks. "We have found you!"

"Oh, Clarice, Jonah! I am so happy to see you well and safe."

Colin looked to the coachman on the box. "Why didn't you go for help, as I instructed?"

"Respectfully, milord, I tried," Jonah replied. "Madame Roche insisted we come searchin' for her ladyship."

"If you had done as I wished, my people would be here now and her ladyship would no longer be in danger."

"There is no more of the danger now that we are together," the Frenchwoman exclaimed.

"Clarice, this is Pip. She is traveling with us." Emily drew the child forward. "Pip, this is my dear friend Madame Roche."

"Enchantée," the Frenchwoman said with a curious glance at the child, then at Colin. Pip's little brows leaped up and she looked to him.

Emily bent to her and pressed the bakery package into her hands. "Now pop up into the carriage and eat your breakfast."

Pip climbed into the coach.

"*Ma chère*, come!" Madame Roche grasped Emily's arm and drew her to the carriage door. "You must not remain in these filthy clothings another moment! Jonah, the trunk of *ma petite*, untie it, *tout de suite*. You will change the gown *immédiatement* at the *auberge*. It is a wretched place, but one must endure the hardships when one is traveling always, *non*? And then you will tell me of all the running away. *Quelle aventure romantique!*"

Emily cast Colin a discomfited glance and took her coachman's hand to climb into the carriage.

ALE SLID DOWN Colin's throat with the welcome caress of a lover's hand. He would have preferred brandy but this inn, whose other patrons all appeared to be laborers, offered only ale and whiskey. Standing at the bar as he swallowed the last drops, he understood enough of the men's heavy brogue to know that none of them suspected the travelers of villainy. But they would not be safe here for long. A delivery of grain was due by north-traveling boat this very day. That boat would surely carry with it news of the imposter earl and his accomplice.

At a table nearby, the women and girl waited for the barkeep to return with the steak pie he claimed was the best in Scotland. Pip gnawed at her rolls while Madame Roche chattered without pause in half French and half English and with her hands, and Emily stared at the other patrons' food. There was a quality of hunger in her eyes that he had never seen before.

Then, suddenly, her gaze alighted upon him and the bright intensity of her hunger seemed all for him alone. On his skin, his jaw, his shoulders, his chest—she looked at him as though with her eyes she meant to *feel* him as well.

Impossible.

Setting down the glass on the bar, he took up his coat and went out of the inn.

Her coachman dozed on a bench beside the carriage.

"Jonah, how far have you traveled today? Are the horses fresh?"

"They'll go all day, milord. We lodged here last night and were just settin' out in search of you. Since I heard the news from those blokes"—he pointed toward the inn—"of the price the duke's put on the highwaymen, me and Madame Roche didn't want to dillydally in findin' you."

"The *price*?"

Jonah's brow bent. "You'd not heard?"

"Loch Irvine has put a price on the thieves' heads?"

"Loch Irvine and Argyll both, milord, though they say His Grace of Argyll's down to London at present."

"Good God. What price?"

"Ten pounds."

A fortune to any man in this country. "Which of these horses is fastest?"

"That'd be Mason." Jonah patted the lead horse on the rump.

"How is he to ride?"

"Tetchy. Toby's a gentle soul. He's stronger, got more stamina, and he takes to a saddle better, but I haven't got one. What's your plan, milord?"

"We need haste. Bridle Mason." *Good God*, there was no good solution. "Once we have left, allow an hour at least, then go to the local man of authority and tell him the truth about how the Earl of Egremoor took the horse, and that you believe I am riding south. Then ride like the wind to Castle Kallin. It is my hope that one or the other of us will arrive there before Lady Emily and I have been found."

"Yes, sir." He had already begun untethering the carriage leathers.

"And damn it, Jonah, if Madame Roche complains of this plan, ignore her."

"Not much use in that. She'd steal the reins if I let her."

"You won't have a pair to drive anyway. Have you sufficient money to settle her and the child in a room at this inn for a sennight?"

Jonah nodded.

"Make it so."

"What am I to say to the law about her ladyship?"

"The truth. That I have taken a lady with me, but do not give her name. The less known about her the better."

Reentering the public house, he met Emily's wide stare trained upon the doorway. She leaped from her chair and came to him.

"Clarice has just told me that the Duke of Loch Irvine has put a price on our heads," she said quietly. "Rather, on the thieves' heads."

"Jonah spoke of it to me just now."

"Why don't we give ourselves up to the duke?"

"I fear what could befall us between giving ourselves up and being brought before him."

"We should leave now. Those men on the other side of the room have been staring at me."

Colin looked into the brilliant emeralds and thought that if he were those men he would be staring at her too. Her lips were nearly red, her cheeks stained with color, and her hair this way and that. She looked nothing like the London spinster he had called on a month earlier. Instead she looked . . . *edible*.

He wanted to taste her.

He wanted to taste her lips. He wanted to taste first her upper lip, that softly curved flesh that could pinch with consternation, and then its mate. Then he wanted to taste her tongue. Then the silky skin of her neck. Then he wanted to unbind the laces of her gown and stays that he had bound twice now, and taste the salty valley between her breasts. Then her nipples that would be tight from his caresses. Then her fingertips and the soft flesh of her belly and the hot crevice of her womanhood that would taste like sex and woman. *This* woman.

Emily.

Good God. *Emily.*

He had been wise to make himself scarce from her for years. This fantasizing was out of control. Even in the midst of hurried danger he could not stanch it.

Something had happened to him. Like coals lit beneath his ribs, the long-slumbering organ there was agitated into wakefulness. It beat far too swiftly and hard. He did not feel like the man he had worked so assiduously to become. For the first time in years—*years*—he felt like another person altogether.

He wanted to believe it was the danger, or Scotland, or anything else that caused it. *Not Emily.*

She blinked those wonderfully candid green eyes, and he knew it was she. Purpose and responsibility and rigid control had been his entire world for years. Now he wanted to lay everything he was thinking—and feeling—*everything*—before her. He wanted to cease thinking entirely. He wanted only to feel because now, with her, for the first time in years he *felt* good.

Not only good.

He felt *alive.*

It was an illusion, a lie buried in memory and distorted by distance. There was nothing in that remote past except shame and pain. Yet his heart would not cease its frantic pace.

"Colin?" She peered at him. "Are you well?"

"Fine. Yes." He spoke too swiftly. "Come outside, behind the building." Turning, he went without, and as she grabbed up her cloak he heard her speak to her companion. Then she was following him, without question.

That miracle ended instantly.

"Why is Mason unharnessed? Jonah, why have you—"

"We are riding," Colin said. "Up you go." He made his hands into a step for her.

"Again? *Now?* Why?"

"They are close behind us and the men here have already

had word of them. There is no place safe to delay on this road."

"It is as though the imposters are following us intentionally." There was a woven thread of fear and disbelief in her voice. "It is awful coincidence, is it not?"

"Does seem like more than coincidence to me," Jonah commented.

"Coincidence or not, we must leave here immediately, Emily."

"But there must be another solution. Clarice and Jonah will vouch for us. We will all plead our case."

"Is that what you wish to do?"

She stared at him as though he had spoken in a language she did not understand.

Then she shook her head. "I want to flee from danger. Every time I close my eyes, that man with the pistol is pointing it at—at us, and I do not wish to ever swoon again."

He almost laughed. "That is your principal concern?"

"I am a wretched coward, I know."

"No. You are extraordinary."

She blinked once, eloquently. "You are trying to flatter me into agreeing to it."

"I am not."

"What of Pip?" She glanced at the carriage horse. "Charlie could carry three, but Mason cannot, at least not far."

"Pip will remain at this inn with Madame Roche. Jonah will tell a convincing tale and we will collect them soon, once it is safe."

"That won't do. Consider Pip's dress and speech. No one will believe a Scottish peasant urchin is traveling intimately with a woman of Clarice's sophistication."

"She could bunk in the stable," Jonah said. "Noticed she's got a way with the horses. Truth be told," he added around the stick of straw in his teeth, "I always wanted a daughter. Might as well pretend I've got one now."

"You are as nonsensical as Lord Egremoor," she said

with a creased brow. "People will know you are lying. Pip looks nothing like you. Why, she looks more like *his* daughter than yours."

"Then she shall be mine," Colin said. "Jonah, if you or Madame Roche are asked, claim that I have left the girl in your care to go searching out her mother in the south."

"Yours?" She gaped at him. "But yesterday you said—"

He grasped her hand, only her hand, and even that was too much; he felt it everywhere. "I *cannot* allow you to come to harm."

"I—I am not your responsibility," she said brokenly, thinly.

"Of course you are."

"We must separate," she said, drawing her hand away. "If we are separated, if we were not seen together at all, no one would think that we are the thieves."

"I will not leave you unprotected. Now how many times must I tell you to *get on the horse*?"

"Only if we bring Pip with us."

He had no choice. She knew it.

"Jonah, bridle Toby instead."

Jonah found the little girl in the corner of the stable, munching happily from the package of rolls. Colin tossed both females onto the animal's bare back, Pip on the horse's rump with her arms wrapped around Emily's waist. He climbed up before the lady.

"Jonah," Emily called back as Colin urged the horse forward. "Tell Clarice we will be well, and that I am sorry to leave so abruptly. Take care of each other, I beg of you. I will see you again shortly."

The afternoon was pressing onward already, clouds heavy over the lake and darkening the wooded slope to their left. The horse was fresh and, despite its load, its gait was steady enough on the road so pitted and pocked that it was clear cattle had been its most frequent travelers. He could not take it above a trot without danger of injuring the horse's legs or Pip tumbling off.

Eventually the lapping of the lakeside to their right became the busy gurgle of a river, and they left behind Loch Lomond's shimmering gray surface and gentle green and blue hills, and the scents of moss and lichen and water.

Finally she spoke.

"We left the rest of the rolls behind," she said quietly at his shoulder, the sound almost swallowed by the river's rush.

He smiled. "That is your first concern?"

"I am preoccupied by the gaping hunger in my stomach. It has overtaken my head. This climate clears the mind of all thoughts and replaces them entirely with feelings. It makes a body ravenous. Colin, another night without food will be the end of me," she whispered. "And another night outdoors. Couldn't we find a cottager's house or some such? Any place that we can eat a meal and drink tea and sleep on a bed. Not every farm north of here will have heard of the thieves yet. And clean clothing! What I would do at this moment for a fresh shift and silk stockings. And soap and a copper tub filled with warm water."

"You have already proven yourself hardier than every other town dweller of my acquaintance." He bent his head and spoke so that his words would not reach the little girl. "But if you could refrain from mentioning your undergarments and bathtubs, that would be helpful."

"Don't be ridiculous. I am not wearing silk stockings *now*, of course. But I think you are merely trying to distract me from my hunger."

"Rather, I am expressing mine. Which I should not be."

After that she was silent for quite a long time. The landscape had broadened, the loch disappearing entirely behind them now. High hills carpeted in emerald with patches of rust and gold-colored grass bordered the road, sloping steeply from their apexes. To the west a wood of fir and birch bent its shadow toward them, dark green and black and white with a few remaining golden-brown leaves clinging to the boughs and scattering in the wind. The sun had disappeared behind a mountain and the sky was lit with striations of vivid orange below the low-hanging clouds.

"It is spectacular, this countryside," she murmured. "Every day, even when the sun is lost. Magnificent. I have only traveled to Edinburgh for Constance's wedding, and to Alvamoor to visit Kitty and Leam. The Lothians are beautiful, to be sure. But I'd no idea that this part of Scotland was so dramatic, so wild. Despite all, I cannot help noticing."

"Despite your empty stomach and blistered feet and exhaustion. And me."

"Perhaps because of them and you." Her words were slurred. He considered that she might be speaking from a half sleep. She would not say such a thing otherwise.

"It . . ." Her voice trailed away.

He waited.

"I think it is changing me," she finally said. "It has changed me."

He was glad now that her hands were not on him, so that she could not feel the quickened drum of his heartbeats. "Into what has it changed you?"

The coat fabric at his waist pulled where her fingers grasped.

"Into a woman who enjoys riding astride behind a man," she whispered.

"You mustn't admit that," he barely managed.

"Why? Because a modest female should not enjoy such a thing or because you are the only one of us allowed to make fantastical remarks?"

He hadn't any idea how to respond.

"Yes," he finally said. Then, when she did not reply: "How do you come to know how to ride bareback?"

"I don't. This is my first time. But riding a horse in this manner is really nothing in comparison to riding with you in this manner."

"Emily—"

"Colin, I don't think you should say anything more that you will regret having said when this is all over."

"I haven't yet said anything that I will regret having said when this is over." Which was entirely true, despite everything he had already said that he should not have—that he never would have said only a sennight ago. "What do you imagine I intended to say?"

"I don't know. My rational thoughts are coming and going haphazardly. I am exhausted beyond sense and I think my imagination is playing games with me, as my tongue certainly is. I will cease speaking now, for safety's sake. Pip?"

"Aye, m'ss?" came the muffled mumble.

"Are you asleep?"

"Aye."

A mile farther along, the horse stumbled over a rock and Colin drew it to a halt and dismounted. Pip followed him down, rubbing the sleep from her eyes.

"Are we stoppin', sir?"

"No, Pip. We are pressing on as far as we can before nightfall." Taking the animal's bridle, he started walking. Warm little fingers grasped his other hand and she walked along beside him, commenting on this and that, humming or occasionally whistling.

"No friendly cottager's farm in sight?" Emily said after some time. "I suppose the Clearances have destroyed them all."

"Even if there were one, it would not be safe. We are not yet three miles past Ardlui. I would press on now. The horse is capable of it. But you must sleep."

"It is astonishing that we have passed no one on this road today. But by the state of it, it seems wholly given over to cattle droving."

"We passed two others while you slept. I drew off the road behind trees and we were not seen. One, a lone rider, was moving in haste. We can only hope his errand had nothing to do with the thieves." He looked up at her. "How do you know of cattle droving and Clearances?"

"I read all the news journals." Her spectacles were askew, her hair a tangled nest, and her eyes bleary yet still brilliant. "Reclusive spinster. Barrels of leisure time." Then she pinned her fine lips together.

Ahead, the road bent around the wood-covered hill.

Beyond it the landscape extended into deepening dusk, spreading before them like a portrait. For a half mile at least there was nothing but the mountains to either side, grass, and the wood.

"No friendly farm, alas," she repeated. "Another night in the woods it must be then, like lost children in fairytales. Do you know, if we do find a witch's cottage hidden among the trees, at this time I will happily give myself up to be baked for her supper, as long as she shares some of her apples and dried plums before stuffing us with them."

"Mebbe she'd let us wait on anither traveler," Pip said. "Then we could stuff *him* an' all have a mighty feast."

"Bloodthirsty little monster," he said.

Pip showed all her teeth when she grinned.

"No," Emily said. "That won't do, Pip. We will offer his lordship to the witch, instead, and in gratitude she will allow you and me to go free."

"Why would she do that?" Pip said with perked brows.

"Oh, because she will fall hopelessly in love with him. He is very rich. He could *buy* her hapless travelers to feast upon for the rest of her life, you see."

Pip giggled and her tiny fingers squeezed his.

"I willna let miss give ye to the witch."

"Thank you, Pip. I appreciate your loyalty." It required a strange effort to lift his gaze to the woman in the saddle. "It is a relief to hear that you do not now wish the witch to eat me."

"I have decided that you are more useful alive. And I am delirious with exhaustion. Colin, after this, after we are safe, you will not tell everyone the details of what we have been through, will you? My father and mother? Anyone?"

"Why would I do that?"

"In order to force me to marry you so that you can maintain possession of the Devonshire property and your mother's jewels. Shauna discovered it," she said. "My maid. Servants talk, of course."

Not his servants. Not if they wished to remain in his employ.

"Are ye to marry him, then, miss?"

"No, Pip," she said, then looked at him with such understanding in her eyes, such honesty. "Will you?"

"If I did?"

"I would refuse you again, of course."

"On principal that a woman should not be forced to do what she does not wish to do?"

"Yes." She seemed to consider him a moment. "And also because I don't like you. And you don't like me."

"I see." He smiled. There was a smear of dirt across her cheek and her emerald eyes were pools of delirium and he hadn't felt so good in years. "All right. If we should survive this, I promise not to tell a soul."

His smile confused her. It seemed a ridiculous thing, after so many years. Certainly his smile had not confused her when she was a girl.

Now the curve of his lips and the flash of the dimple in his cheek created a dreadful, tantalizing heat inside of her. It was a heat that *wanted* something. Him, probably.

All those years ago she had wanted him too—as a friend. Her only friend. Her best friend.

Of her six sisters, she was closest to Amarantha. During childhood they had shared a great fondness for their father, and he for them. But Colin Gray's friendship had been special, unique. She had worshipped him.

Until he abandoned her.

The abandonment had come abruptly and thoroughly, just shy of her ninth birthday.

Every year, four times a year, their families visited each other up and down the length of England. Twice a year the Earl and Countess of Egremoor and their only son—after Lady Egremoor's death, only the earl and his son—traveled from Cumbria to Willows Hall in Shropshire for a visit of nearly a month, depending upon the earls' responsibilities in Parliament. And twice a year the ever-expanding Vale family traveled to Maryport Court in turn. The patriarchs, who had been companions at war in America long ago, would tell stories of those days, play an inordinate amount of chess, and drink brandy late into the night.

Consequently, the eldest daughter of the Earl and Countess of Vale had never known life without Lord Egremoor's son, who excelled at all that was put before him, but in complete silence. He never spoke. He never had, while she, from the moment she began to speak at the precocious age of twelve months, never ceased speaking. Since she never spoke of anything that her mother or sisters cared about—books and toads and maps and chimney sweeps and wheat plucked and chewed directly off the stem, and worms and more books and whatever occurred to her, rather than ribbons and dresses and dolls—they were all glad to leave her to the company of the silent boy five years her senior. Because of his peculiarity and the isolation in which he lived at Maryport Court when his father was in town for the session, he had no other companions. And she, entirely unimpressed with her glorious future as the Countess of Egremoor, was glad of company that allowed her to explore much farther afield than Nurse typically allowed. With her mother and ever-increasing stable of sisters, she was almost constantly watching her tongue. With him, she could be entirely herself. He was the ideal companion. He never criticized her and rarely disagreed with her plans, and on occasion it was wonderfully convenient to have a person of greater height and strength to depend upon.

On one summer holiday at Maryport Court, that dependence changed her world.

The weather was especially tumultuous, with tremendous storms rushing onto the bluffs overlooking the ocean then rushing back out again swiftly. Her mother, Nurse, and four little sisters at the time were baking with Lord Egremoor's cook. When she joined them, they chastised her for sculpting the dough into shapes like the statues of Greek gods in her father's garden instead of neat biscuit shapes, and eventually she had given up and gone off to read. But the house was full of servants busy with a cleaning project, and none of her quiet nooks were in fact quiet.

Accustomed to being forgotten at dinnertime, teatime, church time, and really any time when everybody gathered, she knew she would not be missed now. Before leaving the house she tucked a book into her pocket and told Colin, who was at lessons with his tutor, that she was going to the bluffs to read.

But she felt deeply unsettled. Why an earl's daughters must be relegated to baking and embroidery and flower arranging when an earl's son got to learn mathematics and Latin and history she could not understand. Her father was a fond admirer of Great Women in History and always said that a female's natural intelligence was certainly higher than an average male's. Still, when she asked him to hire a tutor for her, he deferred to his wife—as he did in all things—who found the idea disgusting. She also begged Colin to let her attend his lessons. She could read every one of his smiles, and the smile he reserved for this regular request indicated that he thought her batty in the head.

Walking along the edge of the bluffs overlooking the sea, and listening to waves smashing against the rocks below, she had watched the thunderclouds roll across the sky miles out like the inky disquiet gathering in her heart. Obviously, there was nothing to be done for it but to forget about her sisters and parents and the unfairness of it all and instead discover a new cave in the cliffside. Colin had long since shown her all the easily accessible nooks and crannies. But she knew of at least three more, situated in precarious spots, that he steadfastly refused to take her to.

She chose the closest and started her descent.

Making her way down the hard face of the bluff abraded her fingers and knees horridly, but when her feet met the ledge she crowed in triumph. It was not a cave, exactly, rather a modest depression in the side of the cliff, and not entirely covered. But the sun would not set for hours yet, and there was a comfortable little cranny to tuck herself into with her back up against the stone. She filled her nose with the salty air, opened her book, and lost herself in the story.

She only noticed the clouds when the page became too dim to read. Dark and angry and swirling with wind, they blotted out the sun and made the ocean the color of iron. Peering downward, she saw the waves and her heart did a furious leap. The tide had risen considerably.

Then the clouds split open.

The rock wall that would have been a challenge to climb up even dry proved impossible to ascend wet. Her fingers slipped and she tumbled back to the ledge again and again. All the while the tide continued to rise. And behind the storm, the sun was setting.

Clinging to the rock as the horizon darkened from gray to black, she sobbed and shouted and cried for help until her throat was raw.

Then she heard him.

She had never heard his voice before. But she knew it was Colin. No one else would come looking for her. No one else had ever cared enough to do so.

"Emily!"

It came like the howl of a wild animal across the bluff. The wind whipped at the harsh, desperate sound, whisking it away into the oncoming swells.

"Emily! *Emily!* Where are you? Emily!"

She had shouted back, shaking so hard she could barely hold on to the slick rock.

Clever Colin that he was, he had brought a rope. But he did not toss it to her, for which she teased him later, claiming that she was as strong a rope climber as he, and she might have shinnied up it herself. But he hadn't let her. He tied the rope to an outcropping above and climbed down to her.

"Come on," he said, and made her wrap her arms around his neck and hold on while he climbed. She had not cried then, not even in relief. But when they reached the top of the bluff she had not wanted to let go of him.

"You little fool," he only said.

She let him take her hand that was numb with cold and they walked back to the house like that. Her lips were frozen and she was trembling so violently she couldn't even make words, and she did not mention that he had spoken, and neither did he. He had a good voice. Rough and awkward and very unsteady. But she liked it.

When they returned to the house, he was silent again and she had to explain the whole thing to everybody through chattering teeth. Then Nurse swaddled her up and whisked her away and she did not have the opportunity to thank him. As she fell asleep, warm and cozy beneath four layers of blankets, she wondered if he would only speak to her now.

He did not. Beginning the next day, he spoke to everyone—haltingly, slowly, like a colt taking its first wobbly steps. Still, speaking. It did not occur to her until years later, but his speech seemed too clear too quickly: he must have used it before that day, only not to others. Not until he had called out for her. Or perhaps it was by sheer force of disciplined will that he made himself understandable so swiftly. He had always been a dutiful son, and in this, now, he proved himself no different.

At the time no one remarked on it—not in his presence. A physician came to Maryport Court, and after a private interview with Colin and another interview with the earl, departed with equally little fuss. Her family and the servants were all astonished. But the Earl of Egremoor behaved as though his heir had spent the first thirteen years of his life speaking too, and that this was nothing out of the ordinary.

To everybody including Colin, she mimicked Lord Egremoor's nonchalance. But each time he struggled to speak, and succeeded, her heart felt like bursting. Secretly she liked it that the first words he had ever spoken were for her, and the very first word had been her name.

A few days later, when Nurse finally allowed her entirely free of the nursery, she knocked on his bedchamber door. Gray Forest was full of mushrooms from the rain and did he want to go searching with her? Standing in the doorway that was only partially open, as though he had something to hide inside, he had frowned.

"Men," he said slowly, deliberately, "don't play with girls."

She had laughed. But there was something in his eyes at that moment, something fierce and hard, that she did not recognize.

"You are a toad," she had said breezily. "When you regret being nasty and not getting any of the mushrooms you can come find me and kiss my feet in apology. Then I *might* forgive you."

But he never came to find her and he never sought her forgiveness. The next day she found him alone again, and he brushed her off; he was going riding with his father. The following day she could not even catch his eye across a room, and he would not answer her knocks on his bedchamber door. He was always engaged after that, going off on adventures with his father or both their fathers or the gamekeeper or his tutor or the estate's steward.

A fortnight later her family departed Maryport Court. Her parents' conversation on the journey home was all about the grand time they'd had, the earl's lavish hospitality, and wasn't Colin speaking a fantastic miracle? But she did not think it was a miracle. She thought it was rot, and her throat was all clogged up with thick tears that she was continually obliged to choke back. He was a toad-wart-villain of the worst sort to cast her off so shabbily. Her best friend, *her only friend*, had turned into the most horrid bounder overnight, and her humor was as black as tar. While her father and mother and silly sisters rhapsodized, she sank into a corner of the carriage with a book before her face and felt a little like she had in that crevice in the bluff as the rain beat down and the tide rose—a little like she might die.

She did not understand why he had abandoned her. And, because she had loved him so much, she hated him for it.

Chapter 12

The Unanticipated

At the edge of the wood they went a short distance along the trees toward a stone fence that was long and solid and hemmed with shrubs and natural hedges, sufficient for keeping a herd of sheep from wandering onto another man's land. The wall made an abrupt turn up the hill to one side, creating a partially sheltered nook in the shadow of branches. She went toward it.

"I will now halt here, search this patch of ground for anthills, and immediately sleep," she said, unclasping her damp cloak, draping it over the thick grass, and dropping to her knees. "If you prefer to rush along now toward a pint of ale and a soft, dry repose, you must feel free to do so without a worry about me, though you must take Pip along with you. Having slept half the day, she is as fresh as a spring brook."

The little girl was leading Toby to a patch of green grass, deeply engaged in conversation with the horse.

"For my part," Zenobia added, tugging her cloak more closely about her—the day had grown chilly as the sun descended, "I will be content to remain here forever if it means

I needn't walk or ride again for the rest of my life." Closing her eyes, she curled up on her side and tucked her hands beneath her head.

She heard his footsteps close by. She cracked open her eyes to see him settling with his back to the trunk of a tree a few yards away, arms crossed, and eyes closed.

"Have I slept?" she mumbled.

"For half an hour or so," he replied.

"Where is Pip? And Toby?" She tried to blink but the dusk had deepened and her eyes were so weary.

"Pip is curled into a ball not three yards away, sound asleep. Toby is standing sentinel over her." He smiled and she peered at the child. Wrapped in Colin's coat, she was a lump on the ground, the carriage horse's head hung low and his nose as close to the lump as could be.

"She is a natural with horses, it seems," Colin said. "And a gleaner. She found mushrooms in the wood. Safe mushrooms," he added, and her heart did a little trip. Long ago in a wood like this one, he had taught her how to discern poisonous from edible mushrooms.

"What shall we eat for dinner?" she said.

He smiled slightly. "Whatever your vivid imagination conjures."

"The crickets are gone, finally," she said, "or I would capture and eat some if I had the energy to stand up. I wish I had captured some last night. They were still singing then. The cold today must have driven them all into hiding holes."

He must be as tired as she—more tired. And yet the smile lingered about his lips, and despite the heaviness of her eyes she could not look away from it. How wonderful that a man's lips could be so beautiful, and that studying the whiskers around those lips and on his jaw made her own lips feel peculiarly sensitive. And rather more than her lips. Beneath the layers of her clothing, her nipples were prickling.

Pushing away the feelings, she propped herself up on her elbow. "Do you remember when I collected all those crickets to feed the rat I discovered in the gardener's shed?"

"Yes," he said in a half-asleep voice.

"You do?"

"I do."

"I made you store them in your coat pocket. You didn't like it, but I insisted."

"You did."

"In a way," she said, "this adventure out of doors feels very much like then. Except for the obvious difference."

There was a beat of silence before he said, "That I speak?"

"That we are adults."

He opened his eyes and looked directly at her with startling intimacy, as though assessing the truth of her words in the swell of her breasts and curve of her hips.

"You're really not that much different now, Emily."

"And you are a toad. Still. After all these years."

He laughed, the smile in his eyes entirely uncontrite.

"You already know what I think of you now," he said easily enough.

She did. He thought that her greatest accomplishment was the work of a man.

But then his smile slipped away. "How did you always seem to know?"

She knew what this question meant, the question he had never before asked her.

"How did I know what you did not say aloud?" she said.

He nodded.

"I don't know," she said. "I certainly don't have the same skill now. For instance, I've no idea why you have spoken to me now so differently than you did this morning, why you are trying to tease me when earlier you were angry. How contrary that I did know then but that now, with speech, you have become adept at hiding your thoughts."

His gaze upon her revealed nothing. He was practiced at this sort of deception, at showing the world a face that hid the truth. She was the opposite. Clarice and Kitty had often told her that her every emotion appeared on her features. Only one deception had ever come easily for her, and that was from necessity.

But perhaps he practiced deception for the same reason. Perhaps he believed it was necessary.

With the enduring clarity of an oil painting, one stark memory from her childhood had never left her. After the countess's death, Colin had not changed outwardly; he had still been the studious, disciplined silent boy who went about the estates with a girl five years his junior, throwing himself into whatever adventure she demanded. But whenever he spoke of his mother, his eyes had shone with fierce longing. Even then, so young, she had felt his grief.

She had never heard his father speak of his deceased wife. Ever. To the Earl of Egremoor, it was as though she had not existed.

"Our fathers were such different sorts of men," she said into the darkening evening. "What rigors they must have suffered together in war to attach them so thoroughly." Like the unwelcome attachment she was feeling for this man now, a person so different from her in every way that mattered. He saw the world in terms of bloodlines, duty, and responsibilities. She saw the world as a place to improve for those who had little or nothing. They were fundamentally incompatible, no matter how well they got along when chased by furious men, and no matter the betraying sensations in her body.

"I don't understand your meaning," he said.

"Once my father told me that the battle of Yorktown altered his perspective on humanity. He said he was never the same after it. I think that must have been the case with your father too. The bond forged between them then was powerful."

"Like brothers," he said. "He rarely spoke of the past. But he said that they became brothers on that battlefield."

"Thus all of those holidays that our families spent together, and the foolish betrothal. They wanted their children to be like siblings too."

"Not quite siblings, obviously," he replied in a deep voice.

"Do you remember our trees? How whimsical of your mother to have had them planted like that, so close, side by side."

"She did not anticipate that you would someday refuse to take up her mantle," he said, his lips curving just a bit on one side. It was a smile she recognized, and all the undesirable heat returned, and an awful, acute longing.

"I don't suppose she did. But she also did not anticipate that you would someday be thrilled that I refused." Her stomach ached. It was the hunger, of course. And her exhaustion. She closed her eyes.

SHE FELL ASLEEP swiftly and hard. Colin watched her as clouds consumed what remained of the dusk. The night was bringing with it a northern wind. But if the temperature did not drop further, she would endure until they reached Castle Kallin. Pip too. He would make certain of it.

No one would search for them on this road traveled only by cattle drovers and sheepherders. Seeking valuables, the thieves preyed on coaches near towns and villages. Their pursuers would never imagine they had gone in this direction. Tomorrow they would press on toward Glen Irvine. Once safely in the duke's castle, Colin would send word to both Maryport Court and Argyll's seat in nearby Inveraray, and to faraway Read Castle for insurance. Then he would find new clothing for them both, hire a carriage and horses, and take her home. Penny Baker—and Lady Justice—must wait.

For now it seemed safe to finally sleep. Resting his head back against the trunk of the tree, he crossed his arms.

He awoke to cold and the sound of soft moans. The darkness was complete and the temperature had descended dramatically. From the muddled state of his head he knew he had slept at length. Frost was gathering in the air, settling upon his skin. Several yards away Emily released a whimper of dreaming misery.

He climbed to his feet. His joints were stiff and sore, like the mornings after those nights in his school days when the other boys would lock him out of the dormitory and he spent the dark hours on the frigid stone steps of the courtyard. The first time it had happened and he wrote home, the earl had written back that boys would be boys and he must learn to defend himself. So he had, blackening the other boys' eyes and breaking their noses and hands and an occasional rib, and being called before the headmaster for it. But he was only one and his tormentors were many, and the tortures continued.

The earl had left him in that hell for three terms while he made perfect marks in all but recitation, despite never sleeping a full night in his own bed, and despite not saying a single word to anybody, including his masters. Only when the headmaster wrote to the earl personally, recommending that he return home to private tutoring, had he been allowed reprieve. He had been nine. It was how he had spent the year immediately following his mother's death.

From where the tiny girl slept, protected by the horse, came the soft sounds of sleep. In the darkness he could see the solid silhouette of the animal and Pip, swaddled in one of his finest coats, beneath it.

Emily moaned again. Following the sound, he went to her, knelt, and felt for the edge of her cloak. It was a thin garment, suitable for travel in a closed carriage. Within its inadequate folds, she trembled. Steeling himself, he drew back the hood that covered her face and stroked his knuckles along her cheek. Her skin was soft, dry, and icy cold. In her sleep, she sobbed.

Dreaming unsettled dreams.

Stripping off his overcoat, he draped it over her and tucked it around her arms and legs. She was small, and the heavy wool covered her from boots to shoulder. Then he settled with his back against the stone and drew her into his arms, against his body. The thin fabric of his waistcoat and shirt was scant protection against the stone at his back, but it mattered little.

She did not wake. With a soft, stuttering exhale that made a frosty puff in the darkness, she tucked her cheek against his shoulder. Then she was still.

Her spectacles sat askew on the bridge of her nose, the wire bent almost comically. Carefully he drew them off of her face and straightened the frames. Pulling the kerchief from his pocket, he wiped the lenses clean. It was unusual for a young woman to wear spectacles—openly, without hesitation. But she had never been typical. When her sisters had followed their mother in feminine fashion, drawing, watercolors, and pouring tea without spilling a drop, she had rejected all of that in favor of building forts, gleaning in the woods, reading her father's books, swimming in the lake, and crawling down the sides of cliffs.

As her trembling diminished he studied her face in repose, so different than in waking when thought and spirit animated her eyes and lips. Yet still pixie-like. Still unostentatiously pretty.

Still Emily.

In the years since he had ceased spending holidays with the earl and her family, he had not wanted to know what sort of woman she had become. He had striven very hard, he now realized, *not* to know. But he had spoken the truth to her earlier: she had not changed in the essentials. She was still honest, direct, and blithely unconcerned with codes of comportment and propriety. And she still made his heart ache.

WHEN HE AWOKE to the vision of her brilliant eyes trained upon him from inches away, her spectacles were still cupped in his palm and the air was crisp with the scent of snow.

"YOU SLEPT," SHE said, and knew instantly that she did so because what else could she say upon waking to find herself draped over him like a blanket? All around her was his body, his strong arms holding her, and her thighs were lying along his. "In my bed."

His foggy gaze dropped to her lips. "You say the damnedest things," he murmured roughly, sweetly.

Then he bent his head.

Heat stole over her frozen lips. She tilted her chin upward.

"'Tis aboot time ye're up!"

They both jerked back at once.

Pip stood two yards away, Colin's coat swallowing her, its hem draped to the ground.

"Come on, then," she piped. "There be puddock-stuils aplenty! A wee bit shriveled from the chill, but they'll do!" With a bouncy wag of her head, she darted away.

Untangling herself from his arms, Zenobia clambered to her knees and then to her feet, her muscles protesting. Her clothes were stiff with frost and a horrible weakness rushed through her, jarring against her racing pulse. On the knobby ground she lost her footing. He grasped her shoulder just as she shoved his overcoat at him.

"Take care," he said, his grip firm. "You are weak from hunger."

She pulled away and saw her spectacles in his hand. He offered them to her. With frigid fingers she affixed the wire frames to her face. They were warm from his skin, but through the lenses he was still the same man who had almost just kissed her.

"Colin, I—"

"Don't make anything of it," he said.

"But—"

"Just *don't*." Tugging his greatcoat over his shoulders, he started toward the horse and girl. "Good morning, Pip." Taking up Toby's lead, he led the horse toward the road. Walking alongside, the tiny peasant girl lifted a muddy handful of mushrooms to the great lord. He paused, accepted a mushroom from her palm, said "Thank you," and they continued onward.

Feet rooted to the ground, Zenobia could not find enough air in the whole of Scotland to breathe.

BEFORE THEY HAD gone a quarter mile the rain began to fall. In thick, frigid droplets it splashed across her nose and hands and she pulled the cloak tightly about her. Within minutes it had soaked through the toes of her shoes. Puddles gathered on the pocked road and she wove between them awkwardly. That he did not now insist that she ride proved his unhappiness with that almost-kiss.

Soon her cloak was sodden and Toby's coat was dark. Pip skipped along, matted hair dripping, racing off every few moments to explore fallen logs and other mysteries. Colin had lost his hat when they fled Balloch in haste, but he walked onward now as though his hair and shoulders were not coated with sleet.

"I don't suppose the sun will make an appearance today," she said. "I do not fancy walking the remainder of the way to Castle Kallin in layers of soaking-wet clothing."

Colin found himself swallowing the recommendation rushing to his tongue that they find shelter and she remove some of the layers. She would think his suggestion practical. It was not; rather, roguish. He did not think he could bear to look into those eyes that reflected the rain-washed verdancy of the hills around them and see her thoroughly misunderstand him. Not after she had recoiled so abruptly from him.

He was a titled man of wealth with an impeccable name and reputation. He kept himself fit and his valet kept him well appointed. He knew his appeal, even at present. He did not, however, know what to do with a woman who was entirely oblivious to it.

"You are a curiosity, Emily."

"Because I don't wish to spend the day soaked through? What interesting women you must know that you find me unique in that. And it is Zenobia."

There were no women more interesting than she, or more unconsciously enticing and maddeningly elusive at once. Or more kissable. Damnably kissable. He had awoken with his head full of dreams of touching her and his body primed to make those dreams real. At that moment all sense and self-control had dissolved in the powerful need to immediately make those parted red lips his.

Unprecedented indiscipline.

Madness.

He imagined his hands gripping her hips, his chest pressed to the sweet line of her bared back, her hands splayed upon the wall, his teeth on her nape . . .

He shuddered. Groped for air. The road before his hard-blinking eyes was a flooded mess and he needed to readjust.

"Wasn't it Pocahontas not long ago?" he said.

"What's a Poca-harness?" Pip said, returning from an exploration of the river wending its way along the glen.

"Pocahontas was an American woman of the Algonquian people." Emily glanced at him. "You remember that I went by the name Pocahontas at Constance's wedding?"

He managed to nod.

"It did not suit me that she left her home to follow a man across an ocean only to die a terrible death alone after he abandoned her." She leaped over a wide puddle. He reached to offer his hand, then retracted it. She did not want his touch. She had said so in uncompromising terms, several times. And he didn't really trust any part of his body in proximity to hers at present.

"I don't recall that detail of the story," he said.

"The historical record does not lie. And why should he have been different from any other man who is faithless to a woman he has loved?"

She did not wish to marry, obviously. But this virulence was too marked. The Earl and Countess of Vale were publicly besotted with each other, even after twenty-seven years. Where their eldest daughter's cynicism originated, he hadn't an idea.

Her eagerness to call on the Duke of Loch Irvine pricked at him anew. She might have become acquainted with Loch Irvine at the time of Constance's wedding in the spring, when she had been visiting Leam and Kitty Blackwood at Alvamoor.

Some said Loch Irvine was a villain, others a smuggler, others merely a man who liked his privacy. The director of the club had tasked Constance with learning the truth about him, but she had swiftly relinquished that mission. Colin had not taken it up. By then the earl had fallen ill, and his own lands and responsibilities had stolen his entire attention.

Now, however, Loch Irvine's secrets interested him. Perhaps Emily believed that marriage to the so-called Devil's Duke would not *kill* her as marriage to him would.

Yards behind, Pip was trotting along merrily now, studying a length of branch she had found. But on the other side of the horse Emily walked with obvious discomfort, limping and occasionally tripping, yet without complaint.

"You must ride now," he said.

"On Toby's sodden back, the poor thing?" she said. "My skirts are already wet enough."

"Use my overcoat as a saddle blanket."

She darted a glance at him over the horse's neck then attached her gaze to the road ahead.

"Thank you for the loan of it last night," she said tightly.

"You are welcome." He tried for nonchalance. "Why are you in a hurry to arrive at the castle?"

"That was a non sequitur."

Not to him.

He glanced at the sky. The clouds had grown pearly gray. Shortly this frozen rain would turn to snow. He could not allow her and Pip to remain outside for much longer.

"Am I to have an answer?" he said.

"Do you know, Lord Egremoor," she said with a twist of her lips, "my private business is not automatically yours simply because we are trudging across the Scottish countryside together with a little girl, now soaking wet, while fleeing men intent upon our demise."

She had no respect whatsoever for him. He should be put off by it. At the least he should be disgusted by her defiant rejection of the gentility to which she had been raised and which her father's name demanded. He was not. It was as though they were on opposite sides of a tightly locked door. She stood firmly and proudly on the outside, a clean, fresh wind whipping about her, while he was inside the room, suffocating. Yet until now he hadn't even known he could not breathe.

His cravings for drink and smoke had gone. Entirely. Despite the rain in his boots and chill on every surface of his skin he had no desire for brandy warming his throat or the scent of tobacco in his nostrils. And that other craving—the need for a woman—had changed. Dramatically.

Rather, it had simply remembered what he had, years ago, succeeded at forgetting.

"Why on earth are you smiling?" Then her eyes widened. "Colin, look."

He followed her attention. "At what?"

She ducked around the horse and hurried toward the hillside, purpose in her steps. Through the fall of icy rain he saw nothing on the slope swathed in gray.

"Emily?"

"Zenobia," she called back.

Then she disappeared entirely.

Dropping the reins, he jolted forward. But where she had stood there was nothing now, only rain turning to snow and panic spreading through his chest and seizing his throat. And in an instant, he was back again on that cliff decades ago, with the howling wind tearing at him in the darkness lit only by bursts of lightning, his throat raw, screaming her name.

Chapter 13

A Cozy Cottage

"Why have you left Toby behind? And why are you shouting at me? You are frightening Pip."

She stood before him as though she had appeared from between raindrops, hood thrust back, hair plastered to her brow, snow melting off her nose, and everything about her wan and wet except her eyes that blazed with emerald fire.

He commanded his feet to remain rooted to the sodden ground; he wanted to lunge forward, grab her, and suck that fire inside himself. He wanted to hold her until she held him too. Until she surrendered. *Until she understood.*

"Where did you go?" His voice sounded harsh even to his own ears and she screwed up her nose.

"Around that earthen stile. We are on cultivated farm-land. Didn't you see it?"

"No," he could only utter.

"Of course not." Her lips pursed. "Colin Gray is no country squire to recognize the detailed functioning of his tenants' farms. He is an exalted lord. He has *minions* to muddy their boots for him."

"Well, for God's sake, of course I do!" he exclaimed, the frustration of his empty hands and mouth that wanted her finally overcoming his temper.

She stared at him in obvious shock. Then her gaze dropped to his feet. Dismay washed across her features.

He looked down. Sunk in slushy grass and speckled from toes to tops with dirt, his finest pair of riding boots was far beyond repair.

She burst into laughter.

The sound, like honey and whiskey and coffee all at once, washed through him, loosening his shoulders and jaw and filling his chest with pleasure.

"What is it now?" he said and it sounded like the growl of a surly dog but he could not be blamed for it. Her eyes were filled with tears and she slapped one hand over her beautiful lips as her laughter tumbled into the rain.

"Your boots," she practically shouted, then dissolved into fits again.

"'Tis an awful shame," Pip said with lips pursed exactly like Emily's could, as though she had learned it from the lady.

He glowered.

"You always were easily amused," he grumbled, then, turning around, went to retrieve the horse that had dropped its nose into the icy grass to graze. "It is, of course, a challenge to remain perfectly groomed when one has not spent above five minutes indoors for several days," he said flatly as he passed by her.

Behind him her laughter stumbled then ceased.

"Colin, I beg your pardon." She sounded entirely sober.

He looked over his shoulder. Her eyes were filled with a gorgeous, transparent sincerity. Staring into them, he wondered that he could ever endure dishonesty in anyone else's eyes. How had he learned to do so? How had he learned to pretend so successfully that he had fooled even himself? It was as though he had been asleep for years, in a strange, unfamiliar dream, and now awakening to taste, texture, scent, every splash of every raindrop and every note in the arpeggio of her laughter, every shade of every color of green and silver and pale gold.

"For laughing at my boots?" he said.

"No," she only said, and he had no idea what she meant, only that if he thought she would not swat him for it he would walk to her now, take her into his arms, and breathe her in until his lungs gave out.

"Look," she said and pointed past him.

On the other side of the bluff, at the edge of the trees, smoke rose in a white column.

"That is most certainly a hearth fire," she said, plucking her cloak up around her knees and starting off toward it. "Come on, Pip." She held out her hand and the girl grabbed it. "We will pray that they are the friendly cottagers of my dreams."

THEY WERE.

Pip whispered to her that her angel had sent a miracle. Zenobia agreed without reservation. From the moment they opened the door, Abigail and Graeme Boyd, a middle-aged pair with youthful brows and warm smiles, welcomed them into their cozy cottage tucked into the side of the hill; made them known to their five daughters, two sons, and Abigail's aged uncle, Murdo; offered them hot water and soap, clean clothing, and an ample tea of biscuits, sausage, and cheese; and saw to Toby's needs in their sturdy barn.

The solid stone house had two stories, the second merely a narrow shelf over the first in which the children's sleeping pallets were neatly arranged. But even that modest feature proved the family's prosperity. Sheep farmers for three generations, the Boyds had the advantage of a prime location within miles of both the northern crossroads and the northern end of Loch Lomond, and ideal for commerce. Their many healthy children ensured that they needn't hire men to help on their farm.

Shortly Zenobia sat by the wide fire in the main room

that served as both kitchen hearth and a heat source for the entire house. The two youngest girls, no more than six and seven years old, stood behind her, their little hands drawing combs through her hair, exclaiming at its silky shimmer compared to their own springy black curls, and plaiting it again and again. Their elder sisters, one of them a young woman, sewed and cooked as the snow fell without, and Abigail and Graeme spoke cheerfully of their family and farm. Their sons and a dry, cleaned, and combed Pip had accompanied the old uncle to the barn to rub down the horse and see to the other animals as the storm gathered energy.

"'Tis likely to snow the day through," Abigail said with a wide smile that split cheeks the shape and color of apples, which her daughters and sons all shared.

"Aye, she's a fine storm." Graeme nodded thoughtfully and tamped tobacco into the bowl of his pipe. "'Tis a bit o' luck ye found Siccar Ha'en afore the wind rose." As though to illustrate, a gust slammed against the wall of the house, rattling the windows and sending a burst of chill from the chimney into the room.

"Siccar Ha'en?" Zenobia asked.

"Safe haven," the middle daughter said, stirring a pot over the fire.

Safe haven.

Standing by the window closest the door, which looked out onto the hill sloping downward to the road, Colin was staring not outward but at the glass of whiskey in his hand. As though he felt her gaze, he lifted his.

He had insisted she use the house's single bedchamber to clean up while he waited, and he had just now come from there himself. Whiskers cast a dark shadow across his jaw and around his lips, his hair was wet and curling at his collar, and he wore Graeme's clothing, which fit him well—a shirt of rugged linen and neat trousers—and his own dark coat, now cleaned and dried and brushed free of horsehair and mud.

The borrowed clothing must be their hosts' finest; the

linen and wool were soft. Abigail had lent her a gown of excellent homespun in a mossy color and warm undergarments to wear while her own shift and petticoat dried from the washing the girls had already given them. Abigail was broad in bosom, waist, and hips, and the gown gaped even cinched twice around Zenobia's waist with a long sash. She was dry, though, with food in her stomach and a cup of tea in her palm. The simple comforts of this family suited her.

But even in farmer's clothing and with guarded relief etched in the handsome lines of his face, Colin still looked like a lord. He could look like nothing else, she thought. Natural authority had been so thoroughly bred into him that even his stance now, relaxed yet watchful, spoke of confidence of the sort that needn't be shouted from the rafters or insisted upon. And yet, when Graeme had opened the door to them an hour earlier, Colin had introduced them by their Christian names only. She wanted to ask him why. And she wanted to stroke her fingertips along the hard line of his jaw and know the texture of him there.

"Have a smoke?" their host said to Colin, pulling a second pipe from a wooden box.

With a swift glance at her, Colin said, "Thank you, Mr. Boyd. But I will pass."

"Only ever smoke after the flock's back in the glen," Graeme said, then with a quick addition: "Never at shearin', o' course. Afterward, aye, I'll enjoy a pipe or two."

"A man deserves a moment of pleasure after hard work," Colin replied, his voice a rumble of dark, rich velvet. He was exhausted, but trying to hide it. How long he had slept without his greatcoat, instead with her in his arms, she'd no idea, but it could not have been many or restful hours. She hoped the storm would not cease until nighttime so they could remain here a full night. No one would come searching for them in this weather. And with two more days until All Saints', she could afford the brief delay.

Abigail refilled her cup with steaming tea.

"There, lass," she said, clasping her fingers for an extended moment. "Now that ye're warmed up a bit, I'll be havin' the whole story, startin' at the beginnin' if ye will."

"Story?"

"Mither likes nothin' better than a fine romantic tale," her second daughter, Claire, supplied.

"Ye've up an' eloped, haven't ye?" Abigail said upon a satisfied nod. "I've heard stories o' English lads an' lasses crossin' into the borderlands to tie the knot, but I've ne'er seen it for myself, no' all the way up here. But the moment Claire said a fine young man and a pretty lass were standin' at the door with no' but a single horse, I knew the truth o' it."

"Mrs. Boyd," she said, praying that Colin had not overheard their hostess, "I can assure you, we are not eloping."

The Scotswoman's brow furrowed. "Ye're no' married to somebody else?"

"No. No, I am not married."

Abigail offered the earl a silent perusal. "And Colin?"

"He isn't either."

Her hostess nodded and patted Zenobia on the knee.

"Then ye'd best snatch him up quick, or some other lass'll beat ye to it." Relaxing back into her chair, she took up her own teacup and settled both of her hands around it. "When a fine man's sweet on a lass, she's a fool to make him wait."

"He is not—" She dipped her voice. "He is not sweet on me. We were merely traveling in the same direction and came upon some difficulties."

Abigail's eyes twinkled. "Then ye'll need to make quick work o' it, lass. But dinna be givin' him the milk till he's bought the whole cow."

"The milk? I—oh. Oh, of course."

"Nary a lad'll offer a ring when he's already got what he most wants," she added with a wink.

The front door opened and, upon a blast of snow and cold wind, admitted Abigail's uncle and sons and Pip. Abigail set down her cup and went to see to them, saving Zenobia from trying to explain why she was blushing.

DINNER WAS A hearty meal taken at the hour of the afternoon when most of London high society was barely stumbling from their feather beds. Abigail and her daughters set dish after dish of simple fare on the table: thick black sausages, salty pink bacon, oat biscuits that crumbled upon the tongue, mashed turnips, cabbage stewed to buttery softness, and tangy gravy. Abigail explained that she would have stewed beef for their guests, but she'd nothing fresh until the drovers came through. The comment set her eldest daughter to blushing fiercely and hiding her face behind her apron.

"Meghan's beau's expected with the herd from Orchy any day," Claire explained in a whisper as Uncle Murdo launched into complaints about the drovers' last journey past the farm, how part of the herd strayed and trampled a field of winter oats.

"Aye, Murdo. But they brought more gold to the mountains than trouble," Graeme said.

"If the cattle'd never come," Murdo said, "the farmers'd have five times more gold than they do now, ye fool." He had been drinking liberally from the whiskey jug.

"Five times leaner, ye mean to say," Abigail said with an eye on her uncle's belly. "The shearin' took double the price this year since the new dock got built."

"Do you mean to say," Zenobia said, "that the dock built to haul cattle across the loch is now used to ship wool elsewhere as well?"

"Aye, lass," Graeme said, pulling on his pipe. "All the way down the Awe. 'Tis a blessin'."

"Aye, Father, but only for us who've the use o' it," Claire said with a sober eye. "The Fletchers took only half o' what ours did, since they hadna the coin to pay the tax."

"'Tis a trouble," Graeme agreed with a shake of his head. "But no' a one to weigh the minds o' our guests today." He hefted the jug of whiskey toward Colin. "A dram o' Loch Lomond's finest for ye, sir?"

She wanted to ask more, to understand exactly why the Boyds could afford to pay the tax but their neighbors, the Fletchers, could not. Scottish reformers in Edinburgh claimed that the enclosures of lands for herding cattle and even sheep had pushed Highland family farmers into poverty, while MPs in London claimed that the crown's policies in all its territories were for the benefit of the entire empire. That some local farmers here could prosper like this family while others suffered proved the situation was far more complicated than either side admitted.

The mere idea of that complexity made her blood sing like it always did when she learned something new. She longed to hear everything this family knew, and when she returned to London she would write about it for her readers.

She could not. The nobleman sitting across the table, drinking whiskey with their host, made it impossible.

And perhaps she would never return to London. Perhaps they would never reach home, despite his determination to take her to safety that had him tromping through mud and sleeping outdoors and almost kissing her.

The Boyds' younger son launched into a tale about his brother and a goat that set everyone to laughing, and taxes and cattle droving were forgotten. Stealing a glance at Colin, she saw his attention not on the boys, but on their hostess. There was such affection and pride in Abigail's merry smiles for her sons. Yet Colin's face was pensive as he studied her. His eyes held an odd light.

Pain.

He mustn't realize it. He would never reveal such a thing knowingly.

When the little children began to fidget, Abigail sent them all off to chores, including Pip, who fell in happily, while the eldest daughters cleared and cleaned the table. Zenobia asked to assist, and her hostess shooed her away.

"I'll have none o' ye washin' pots and pans, miss. 'Tis my best Sunday dress ye've got on. And ye should keep those fine soft hands for pleasin' yer man," she said in a perfectly audible sotto voce.

Zenobia's cheeks flamed. Chancing a glance at Colin, she found his quiet gaze upon her.

Moving to the window, she drew the curtains aside and swiped at the condensation on the pane. Without, the snow-fall seemed lighter.

She took her cloak from beside the hearth. It was not quite dry yet, but well enough.

"I am stepping outside for a moment only," she said to Colin, and went quickly.

The world without had changed entirely. Scattered ivory clouds now sent a dusting of soft flurries onto the hillside, which had turned from emerald to white in hours. Everything smelled of fresh, damp cold, and silence blanketed the earth, broken only by the gurgling crackle of a creek running in a quick, bumpy streak down to the road.

But of course it was not the road she was seeing below, she realized; that would be covered in snow too. The dark line was a river, gleaming in the late-afternoon sun, winding the length of the valley between the mountains. They must have walked alongside it, yet she had not even heard it. A symptom of her exhaustion, she supposed, and the muddle that Colin made of her head.

Beneath the crest of the mountain opposite, a lone bird with massive wings soared, coasting toward the valley but remaining high in the sky, aloof from the snow-covered earth. An eagle, probably, in this mountainous country, searching for a last bite to eat before nightfall. A bird of prey surveying his realm, safe from the turmoil of life below— like the former secretary of the Falcon Club, who would not speak of the thread of desire that drew them together now— much as she did not like speaking of the ropes of affection that had bound them together when they were children, she supposed.

She dropped her gaze from the eagle's wide spirals to its valley kingdom. In the distance, by the river, a shape moved against the snow-blanketed earth. There were no wolves in Britain. *She thought.*

The figure moved away from the river, toward the road. Her vision often tricked her at distances in poor lighting. But when the shape suddenly became taller, she understood what she was seeing: a man mounting a horse. And he was riding toward the Boyds' farm. Swiftly.

She swung around toward the house and the door burst open. The Boyds' eldest daughter flew out of it.

"'Tis Davie!" Meghan cried, and took off down the hill in the falling snow.

Chapter 14

The Truth

avie Wallace was a youth of nineteen years with red hair, ruddy cheeks, and shoulders that must be the size of the cattle's he drove. He wore layers of clothing, all of them threadbare. He had left the herd several miles up the road with the other drovers in order to spend the night with the Boyds, as he had clearly done before. The family welcomed him warmly.

"Stuart didna mind me comin' on ahead for the night," he said, clasping Graeme's hand but his eyes slipping to Meghan again and again. "The herd's standin' shoulder to shoulder in this weather."

"Beasts like to warm up against each other's hides," Graeme said.

Davie cast another glance at the Boyds' eldest daughter, and both their cheeks grew ripe as cherries.

Graeme clapped the youth on his thick shoulder. "Ye must be cold as little Jack Frost, lad. Take a dram wi' us."

He introduced Colin and Davie, and the men settled again around the table while Abigail, Meghan, and Claire set dinner before the youth and Graeme poured whiskey. Zenobia would have liked to take a place at the table too. Instead she retreated to a chair where Pip and one of the little Boyd girls brought her ribbons to weave into their hair like they had dressed hers earlier. With six little sisters of her own, as a girl she had always tried to escape the chore. But her sisters said she was the best, adding that it was a sad curiosity she could never dress her own hair as prettily as theirs. So she had plaited and tied their golden locks and Amy's red tresses, endlessly it seemed sometimes, insisting only that someone read aloud to her while she worked.

It was a comfortable memory, but now laced with bittersweet longing. She would never have daughters to set between her knees, no heads of fine hair to twine into braids, and no husband to make her chest ache as he took their daughter's tiny hand into his own with tenderness and walked down a puddle-strewn road.

Foolishness. Nostalgia painted over the painful bits of history and made it all new-penny bright. To linger in it was to teeter too close to her mother's favored sort of sentimental silliness. She had more important matters to occupy her thoughts, such as the discontent of Scotsmen like Uncle Murdo. With a head full of whiskey, now he openly cursed the men in London who forced their greedy laws on this land a world away. Twisting Pip's thick, dark locks into tight braids, she listened with half an ear to the little girls' chatter and with the other half of her attention to the old Highlander's complaints, to Graeme's more measured comments, and to young Davie's accounts of clansmen to the north who had reluctantly sold the last of their livestock to his employer so that their families could eat come winter. And she watched Colin. He said little, his eyes sober.

Good. The more he heard of the disastrous effects of England's high-handed policies in its conquered territories, the better.

But heaviness weighed in her that had nothing to do with the dinner that warmed her now. The members of Parliament that Murdo blamed for his countrymen's woes were men of wealth and position. They would never understand what it was to labor ceaselessly for months to glean a handful of oats or a single healthy sheep, to go to bed with empty stomachs and hands calloused from working sunup to far past sundown, and to sell everything they had to ensure their children did not starve to death before the spring. They were tasked with protecting and governing for people who lived like that. And yet with few exceptions none of them wanted to hear that story—Colin among them. He had proven it again and again each time Peregrine disparaged another of Lady Justice's pamphlets.

She turned her face away and found herself wishing that she had never been forced into his company again, that he was still the severe, remote, arrogant stranger who had strode into her parlor and showed not even a hint of feeling when she refused his offer of marriage.

The last of the daylight had disappeared entirely. Graeme lit a lamp in the center of the long table, setting the men's glasses of spirits to gleaming.

"To bed, all!" Abigail called, and ushered the little children to the loft.

Claire and a younger sister sewed by the light of a single candle and talked softly. Meghan had disappeared.

Pip appeared at Colin's side and cupped her hand around his ear to whisper. His gaze shifted across the room to her, sending a flock of starlings pirouetting in Zenobia's stomach. Smiling, he nodded. With a nod of her own, Pip leaped onto the ladder and disappeared above.

Setting the remaining ribbons and hair ties aside, Zenobia drew her cloak from the peg by the door and slipped outside.

Waning in silver splendor, the moon hung low over the mountain, shrouded in the pale wisps that were all that remained of the day's clouds. By the light of that moon and infinite stars illumining the snow she could see everything: the river at the base of the hill, the little copse of snow-covered trees upon the opposite slope, the empty sheep pen, and the barn where the animals were keeping warm for the night. She breathed a lungful of cold air, willing away the foolish starlings.

She did not attract young Davie's notice when he exited the house and hurried to the barn. Closing the barn door behind him, he left the hillside in perfect stillness again.

Then she heard them: Meghan's giggles, Davie's laughter. And then deep, pleasured sighs that curled her toes in her cold boots.

Behind her the door of the house opened again, shedding golden light momentarily upon the snow. It shut, his footsteps crunched in the snow, and then Colin was beside her.

"Do you think the clouds have done with it, or that we will wake to snow again tomorrow?" she said.

"And be trapped here another day? Would you mind that?"

"If our pursuers were trapped wherever they were as well, I would not." She burrowed her hands in her cloak for warmth and made herself look at him. "Dinner. Tea. Fireplace," she explained, finding that perhaps she was after all a woman to fall to pieces over a pair of dark eyes—at least just a little bit. It was the height of ridiculousness, but his nearness now was making her stomach tight with nerves, and his gaze upon her seemed so intent. So *interested.*

"Why did we stay when Davie arrived?" she asked. "I expected you to make an excuse to allow us to exit hastily."

"We need to sleep." His attention turned to the valley below. "And I trust these people."

Like he had trusted Pip when she had told him her story.

"Not enough to tell them who we are," she said.

"They did not ask. And I did not wish to make them . . . uncomfortable," he finished with what seemed extraordinary discomfort himself.

"You like them," she said, fighting the smile tugging at her mouth. "These sheep farmers. Don't you?"

"Murdo is an old fool. But Graeme is an intelligent man, a good man. Honest. Why have you come out here and forsaken the comforts within?"

"To breathe," she said.

"You've had enough conversation of cattle herding and taxes?" he said a bit wryly.

She must step carefully. "I was not part of the conversation."

"You listened attentively to it."

"No wonder you barely said a word throughout, if your attention was on watching me braid little girls' hair."

"I would have enjoyed hearing you take old Murdo to task."

The nerves in her stomach did a turnabout. "Why would I have done that?"

"You clearly wished to say something. Your heel was drumming a pace on the floor."

"My *heel*?"

"Revealed by your jiggling knee."

"If I had known I was being studied so carefully, I would have taken greater care in my behavior." She would *now*.

"You wouldn't have." He smiled. "You have never allowed convention to rule you. Why did you refrain from speaking?"

"I did not wish to offend our hosts." The lie tasted sour.

"You might have chanced it," he said, folding his hands behind his back. "Abigail doesn't seem the sort of woman to hold her tongue if she has a piece to say."

"Perhaps. But men prefer to discuss politics with men."

"Honesty is a welcome contribution to any debate. And intelligence." His gaze traveled swiftly over her features, dipping briefly to where her hands clasped her cloak together over her breasts. "Even when their closest companions are a sharp tongue and, occasionally, exhausted delirium." The dimple creased the severe line of his cheek.

Everything inside her was confused and hot.

"There are moments . . ." she said.

"Moments when you wish to throttle me?" He nodded. "I do know this."

"Moments when it seems as though you respect me," she said.

"There is no 'as though' about it. I do respect you."

"At those moments . . ." She swallowed. "I feel something for you."

His eyes arrested, and his smile disappeared.

"Emily?" he said uncertainly.

"My name is Zenobia."

"I will call you Zenobia when hell freezes over."

"Why won't you call me the name I wish to be called?"

He turned to her fully and he was standing very close now, and she was having trouble breathing.

"Because to me you are Emily," he said. "You will always be Emily."

"A little girl?"

"A girl who did not think spoken words were necessary for friendship." The corner of his lips tilted up. "A girl who spoke enough for two people anyway."

"I only spoke like that to you. You were the only one who would listen."

"A girl who made me laugh."

"So you insist on calling me by that name because you still think I am eight?"

"Not exactly." His voice seemed much lower. "What do you feel for me at those moments? That old friendship?"

"No. I put those feelings aside years ago." She looked directly into his darkly beautiful eyes. "I find being spoken to with respect by a man arousing. Riding astride behind you makes it worse."

He coughed, or perhaps laughed. "You really are still that girl."

She turned her face away.

He touched her chin and drew her eyes back to his. "You have the courage and intelligence of a man and the desire of a woman, yet you speak with the honesty of a child who does not yet know how to lie."

She shifted away from his touch. "Courage and intelligence are not exclusively masculine traits. And honesty is not a natural characteristic of childhood. Naïveté is. And I am not naïve. But if you call me a child once more, I will behave as one and kick you in a location in which you will feel enormous pain."

This time she was certain he laughed.

"You should curb your amusement," she said. "I will make good on that threat."

"You have always made me laugh easily."

"Because I am odd."

"Because you are yourself."

No. She was living behind a façade, using a grand name, *names*, because she must. Except that he did not know that. He did not know that the Emily he once knew was gone.

"Why should I be anything other than myself?" Only her names were adopted. The rest—her speech, her causes, her writing, her life—was all real, all her.

"There is one mistake I regret," he said, bending his head a bit.

"Only one?" She did not know why her heart should beat so swiftly now, except that his voice had grown quiet and especially deep. "You have lived a blameless life, it seems."

"I am sorry for not having called upon you when your parents took you to London for the first time."

Emily's eyes opened wide. The soft, brittle crackling of wind through frozen treetops gave music to the stillness of the night, but he wanted only to hear her voice.

"My debut season?" she said, blinking once.

He nodded, not knowing what he would say next, for the first time in his memory not having planned even one of the words that came from his mouth.

"Your father was furious with me for it," he said.

"My father has never been furious a day in his life."

"He was then. He believed that my absence from town shamed you."

"You could not have shamed me. No one knew of our fathers' agreement except our families."

"He felt your embarrassment with your sisters acutely on your behalf." Lord Vale had written in uncompromising terms, berating him at length. But Colin had been well accustomed to criticism of a much more efficient and biting variety. Vale's fluid chastisements had not even pricked his conscience.

Not *then*.

"I did not intend any insult to you, Emily. I was out of the country at the time. Unable to return."

"My father's distress was unnecessary," she said. "I felt no insult, nor embarrassment. Anyway, my parents threw so many suitors at my head that my sisters had plenty of material with which to poke fun at me. I didn't care about any of it." But color had risen to her cheeks and he could see her quick, short breaths by the plumes of frosty air at her tempting lips.

"Then what did you feel when I did not come to claim you as they had all planned?"

"Nothing." The word fell cleanly into the cold night.

"Nothing?"

"I had long since known you would not offer for me." She spoke without any trace of emotion. "I never expected you to call on me that season. Or ever."

Impossible. Years of buried guilt were surging up. "You didn't?"

"Colin, you had barely spoken to me in a decade." Her brow crinkled. "Do you think me entirely witless?"

This was incredible. Unexpected. There was no making sense of it. "Marriage alliances are made on much less than that."

"Not in my family. Recall that my parents were a love match."

"But . . ." He could barely speak. "You were not angry with me?"

"I was not."

"Since then—your curtness with me when we have met accidentally in society, your incivility . . . I don't understand."

"Have you believed these past years that you disappointed me *then*? That I was devastated by your indifference to our parents' agreement, that my marital hopes were dashed when you did not offer for me when I was seventeen?"

"I—" What could he say now but the truth? "Yes."

"Then you have been wrong. For I assure you, I was neither disappointed nor devastated at that time."

She could not be telling the truth. The insult he had dealt her—then and every moment until he finally offered for her—was too great.

"I think, actually, that you know exactly how and when you hurt me," she said, "and it had nothing to do with London seasons and offers of marriage."

He frowned. "How else could I have offended you? When? We've barely seen each other in two decades."

Only then, as her lashes quivered and she drew back a step, did he see the hurt deep in her eyes. Like poison in a well, it gleamed darkly, and it twisted his gut with alarm.

"Emily," he said, "tell me what I did that hurt you."

"You don't know?"

He shook his head.

"You saved my life," she said, "and then you disappeared from it."

"I—" It required only a moment for the memory to come. "After the *cliff*? The thunderstorm?" His lungs were tightening, cinching around the air there. It was a memory he never allowed himself.

She nodded.

"But—good God," he uttered, "that was *eighteen years* ago."

She said nothing.

"I think you must remember it poorly," he said. "You were a child. Far too young to—"

"I was old enough to feel my heart break."

"Your—*what*?"

"You were my entire world, Colin. My *entire* world," she said bluntly. "You knew you were, and yet the moment you no longer needed me, you abandoned me."

Words would not come.

"Good," she said. "You do not attempt to defend yourself. At least in that I cannot fault you."

"*Fault* me?" he exclaimed. "Of course I will defend myself. I was *thirteen*. Barely more than a boy."

"A man's character is formed when he is a boy," she said with calm certainty. "With the passage of years he only becomes more firmly what he was."

"I did nothing then that any other boy my age would not have done."

Now her eyes flared. "But you *weren't* any other boy your age. You were nothing like other boys. You were *you*, unique and kind and generous and good. When you changed, there was nothing I recognized in the person you became."

He drew a steadying breath and made his voice strong.

"Boys grow up, Emily. They become men, with the cares and responsibilities of others upon their shoulders. To believe that they should not change is the misguided wish of a naïve girl."

"Blame my feminine sentimentality, if you wish. You would not be the first man to assign fault to a woman for his own misdeeds. But I know who you are, Colin Gray, better than anybody else, I suspect. And despite the flutters of lustful excitement your flatteries have inspired my vanity to produce lately, I know that this familiarity between us, born of this strange adventure, is false. It means nothing." Crossing the folds of her cloak snugly about her, she went into the house.

Chill settled around him swiftly, but he did not follow her.

She had changed after all: from a mostly sensible girl she had grown into an irrational woman. For eighteen years she had held a grudge against him for behaving as any boy would have in his circumstances. Eighteen years.

You weren't any other boy.

"Damn it." He forced his fists to unclench and he pulled in a long lungful of night air.

The barn door slid open. Davie Wallace crossed into the yard.

"Davie," he called to him. "A word?"

The youth came forward, a smile lightening his broad, honest face.

"Cold enough for ye tonight, sir? 'Tis a quick freeze, only. Come mornin' it'll warm up."

The barn door opened again, and the Boyd's eldest daughter darted out, cast them a playful smile, and hurried into the house. Evidently not every man on this farm was serving as a whipping post for the woman he wanted tonight.

Emily would relent. Her character was steady, but her humors were as changeable as the Scottish weather—frosty one moment, warm the next, and everything in between. They always had been. She was piqued over his failure to apologize for an ancient sin he hadn't known he committed. But she was too intelligent and forthright to try to make him suffer for it. By morning she would throw off her discontent with him, and the remainder of the journey to Loch Irvine's castle would be spent in the state that passed for amicability between them now.

And he believed his own musings not one bit.

Which made him furious—with her or with himself, he'd no idea. But the path that his mind now wanted to rush down led to another place than anger, another altogether, and he'd no other direction to turn.

He moved toward the Scotsman.

"Davie, I have a proposition for you."

In Abigail's capable hands, the blanket floated gracefully to the mattress.

"There now, lass," she said, sweeping a palm over the bed's surface. "Ye'll be as comfy as two souls can be."

"Thank you, Abigail. You are tremendously generous to give up your own bedchamber for us. But, I told you, we are not married."

"Ye will be after tonight." Her hostess grinned conspiratorially. "Graeme and I made five healthy daughters and two fine sons in this bed, and all seven o' them are still with us,

God be praised. Ye give that handsome lad a wee cuddle, and promise him a fine bairn once he's made ye his by law, and he'll run ye to the altar quick enough."

Hardly. On all accounts.

"Rather, give me a blanket and I will be more than comfortable in the loft with the children tonight. Colin can sleep in the barn." With the dumb animals, *where he belonged.* She grabbed a corner of the blanket.

Abigail snatched it away with a friendly scowl.

"Ach, English folk, tossin' away hospitality!" She bustled out of the bedchamber.

Uncle Murdo was pouring whiskey, and Colin and young Davie were at the door removing their overcoats.

"Come now, lass," Abigail said with a gentle hand on her back propelling her forward. "Sit and take a dram. It'll calm yer fidgets."

It was the height of idiocy that her cheeks were flames even as her palms were damp. She could feel Colin's gaze upon her and she despised it that he might think her agitated on his account.

She took a seat beside Abigail and accepted a glass of spirits. If he wished to imagine her overset by their conversation, so be it. His relationship to the truth was deeply flawed in general anyway.

"The finest peaty brew for our guests," Graeme said, pouring from a jug the size of a small pig into Colin's glass. "I wager ye canna find whiskey fine as this in England."

"You wager correctly." Colin lifted the glass. "To our hosts. For their hospitality, we are grateful."

Graeme smiled. Abigail beamed. Davie tossed back his dram. Murdo scowled.

"Will nobody be askin' the question we're all thinkin'?"

"What question, Uncle?" Abigail said.

"How many o' our throats the two o' them'll be cuttin' while we sleep?"

Chapter 15

Proof, of a Sort

The only sound in the room was the crackling whoosh of the fire in the hearth.

"I beg your pardon?" Colin said.

"'Tis us who'll be beggin' ye for our lives, more's the truth o' it," Murdo said upon another scowl.

"Why didn't you say something about this earlier, sir?" Zenobia asked.

"'Tis no' my place to tell my foolish niece and her simpleton husband how to welcome strangers, now is it, *sir*?"

"Uncle," Abigail said, laying a hand upon his arm. "Ye've drunk—"

He snatched his arm away. "I've no' drunk enough, ye daft cow, to forget the news Blaisie MacDowell told us all only yesterday." He poked the tabletop and glowered at Colin. "Aboot a pair o' bandits roamin' the byways, pretendin' to be a Sassenach gentleman and leddy. And now here we've the pair settin' at our own table, eatin' our food and drinkin' our spirits."

"'Tis no' *yer* food and whiskey, Murdo," Graeme said. "And I'll thank ye to be beggin' apology to my guests now."

"I'll apologize to the villains when I see them strung up."

"*Uncle,*" Abigail exclaimed, then said to Zenobia, "What yer business here is, lass, Graeme and I've no cause to ask."

"You may ask, if you wish. We know of the thieves. We have been mistaken for them further south. We have in fact had to leave our traveling companions and carriage behind to flee pursuers. Our destination is Castle Kallin. Colin is acquainted with its master."

"Aye," Murdo said with a nod. "'Tis only to be expected the Devil's Duke's a piece o' this villainy."

"Enough o' that, Uncle," Abigail said then laid her hand on Zenobia's. "I've no doubt, lass, yer fine gentleman knows a duke. Why, anybody can see ye're as genteel a lady as there be."

"Leddy?" Murdo snorted. "If the villain's a leddy under those skirts"—he gestured contemptuously toward her—"make him prove it."

"Ye've gone mad, old man," Graeme said with round eyes.

Davie frowned. "I've seen a picture o' the pair, Graeme, over at Tyndrum no' two days ago," he said soberly. "Somebody that'd seen them drew it, and it's gone from hand to hand. 'Tis true Colin here's a twin o' the one. But the other's nothin' like Miss Emily," Davie continued. "Aye, they say he's a wee fella, wi' silvery locks and a figure sweet as any lass's, and that he sings like a swallow. But Miss Emily here's a whole world o' bonnie compared to the picture." He offered her a blushing smile.

"'Tis as plain as the jug there that Emily and Colin here dinna like their business known, and they're no' tellin' us their whole tale," Abigail said. "But nobody'd argue she's a lady. Only see the stitchin' on her dress, Murdo." She gestured to the traveling gown hanging by the fire. "'Tis as fine as I've ever seen. No common thief'd be wearin' sich a thing."

"Stitchin' dinna make a lady," the old man grumbled. "*Or* a gentleman."

"You are correct, Murdo," Zenobia said. "Fine airs and

comfortable wealth are the most typical markers of people of the gentry. But any thief might acquire those, of course."

Murdo's scraggly brows ticked up. "Aye," he said warily.

"But if what you require to be able to rest easy tonight with us in this house is proof that I am not a man, I can furnish that proof immediately to your niece in the adjoining room."

"No," Colin said the same moment their hostess exclaimed, "Lass!"

"Why not?" Zenobia said. "If baring my breasts will convince everybody that I am not a man dressed as a woman, then I will eagerly do so. I should have thought of it before."

"I understand," Colin said with sublime calm. "But what would begin with your voluntary submission to Mrs. Boyd's inspection could swiftly become a forced public exposition to every man in this country who demands the same proof."

"Colin—"

"You are a lady. You deserve respect."

"All women deserve respect."

"Uncle, ye must stop pesterin'," Abigail said. "The poor things've had a rough time o' it."

Murdo's eyes narrowed. "Aye," he said, looking at Colin, "I'll leave off wi' it if ye do a wee deed to show me yer good faith."

Colin had never appeared more severely austere than now. His indigo eyes were forbidding.

"What deed do you wish me to perform?" he said with steely sobriety.

"If *she's* a lady, as ye claim," Murdo said with a smirking mouth, "ye willna mind kissin' her."

"I would be more than delighted to."

A zing of energy went straight through Zenobia's stomach. And abruptly the severity was gone from Colin's eyes. With a slight smile, he took up his glass and leaned back in his chair.

"Regrettably, however, I cannot oblige you."

"Aye," Murdo nodded. "Yer none too keen on kissin' a lad, I'll wager."

"Uncle." Abigail's cheeks were livid. "Lass, he's drunk as a sow. Ye mustn't take offense."

"Your uncle's request is reasonable, Mrs. Boyd," Colin said. "But you see, the lady and I recently quarreled, and she has forbidden me to touch her." Slowly, decadently, his gaze slewed to her. Zenobia felt its intimacy in the pit of her belly.

"Forbidden?" Murdo slapped the table. "Ye'd like us to believe *that*?" he cawed. "What sort o' man allows a lass to tell him what he canna do wi' her?"

"A man who prefers domestic felicity to warfare, I daresay," Colin replied, and swallowed a mouthful of whiskey. Then, glancing at her, added, "And a man who respects a woman."

Zenobia's heart was beating like thunderbolts, one quick, violent boom after another. *Respect*, as she had said outside. And *domestic felicity*, Lady Justice's pet legislative reform. She knew he did not approve of the legislation. Peregrine had written to Lady Justice on the subject, mockingly claiming that wives already controlled their husbands entirely; there was no need for laws to ensure it. And as Lord Gray he had publicly denounced it.

But perhaps she had been wrong about him. Perhaps she was influencing him. After all these years, perhaps he was finally listening to Lady Justice.

"More importantly," he said, "what sane man wants to battle a cat for a mere cuddle?"

The old Scotsman cracked a laugh and slapped the table again. "Aye, lad! Ye're right aboot that."

"Men," his niece mumbled. "He'll come around, lass. Ye're too pretty for him to be happy outta yer arms for long."

"Thank you, Mrs. Boyd." She looked at her traveling companion. "But if it will convince your uncle that I am not a man, I will allow Colin to kiss me now, before all of you."

That surprised him. She knew it only by the same twitch of the muscle in his jaw that had entranced her in London. But it was enough, and it sent a curl of deviltry through her tight stomach, the sort she used to feel every time she bested him at anything—climbing the bluffs, playing bowls, gleaning in the forest, making him smile when he was determined to be far too solemn.

"All right," he said, and slowly came to his feet, his gaze steady in hers.

And the curl of happiness became a maelstrom of panic.

"Now there's a good lad." Abigail folded her arms over her bosom. "Show my fool old uncle ye're no afraid o' his taunts."

"It is not his taunts that concern me, Mrs. Boyd," Colin said, coming to her. "My lady." He extended his hand.

She did not take it, but rose and drew her skirts around the bench. He would make it a quick demonstration, she knew. Still, her hands were not entirely steady and she'd no intention of revealing that to him.

But he did not make it a quick demonstration. Instead, he stepped close to her and cupped her jaw in his palms and she felt the heat of his hands sink beneath her skin. So large, his hands that had held her roughly before, yet now his touch was tender. He tilted her face up. His eyes seemed to study hers; they asked if she were certain. Blessedly, he did not actually ask, saving her from forcing an assurance across her dry tongue. But it occurred to her that now she could read the words in his eyes, when he wished it.

She nodded.

Finally, after too long another silent moment, his gaze dipped to her lips. He bent his head. There he paused, and her breaths that were quivering mingled with his.

He kissed her.

His lips were soft, his skin warm, his scent entirely in her nostrils and wonderful. It was whiskey and musky and heat, and she wanted to swallow it. She wanted it to fill her entirely. She returned the gentle pressure of his lips and a rush of hot, delicious nerves raced straight up her center like lightning.

Then it was over. It lasted only the briefest moment, but long enough for Abigail, Meghan, and Claire to coo in appreciation and old Murdo to declare, "Ach! Enough o' that."

Colin's hands slipped away from her face. He turned to their host.

"Are you satisfied, sir?" he said in an unremarkable voice, making it clear that his world had not also just fallen into a thunderstorm. She slid down onto the bench and took up her glass.

"Any man might kiss a bonnie lass," Murdo exclaimed. "And a lass can dress up in trousers and pretend she's a man to rob honest folk."

"I am not a thief," she said, setting down the whiskey that was jiggling in her hand. "Nor have I ever worn men's clothing."

"If ye did, lass, ye'd be as takin' as ye are now," Graeme said with a kind smile. Davie nodded his agreement.

"Indeed," Colin said, settling again at the other end of the table. "No man would ever mistake her for one of his kind—"

"No sober man," Abigail inserted.

"—even dressed in breeches." He glanced at her. "Though, to be honest, I should like to see that."

He was teasing her. She had no doubt that in the person of Peregrine or Lord Egremoor he would condemn any woman courageous enough to discard layers of cumbersome skirts in favor of comfortable clothing. The thought steadied her hands.

"Speaking of robbery, this whiskey has stolen my ability to remain awake a minute longer. Mr. and Mrs. Boyd, I thank you for your kindness, from my heart." She could not now avoid sharing the master bedchamber with Colin; to do so would be to prove to Murdo and perhaps even the others that they had something to hide. She took up the iron handle of a candleholder. "Good night."

Without a hearth of its own, the little bedchamber was dreadfully cold. She stared at the blankets longingly and told herself that being forced to share a mattress with him was no worse than riding astride behind him or waking up wrapped in his arms.

"When they've all turned in," he said at her shoulder, and she jerked her face around, "I will go to the barn."

She had been mistaken. This *was* worse. Simply standing so close to him now, with his gaze upon her and the knowledge of how his lips felt, was horrible.

"That is what you prefer, is it not?" he said, lifting a single brow. "That I find a spot in a livestock pen and remain there indefinitely. Till death, if possible?"

"Yes."

He smiled.

"But you must sleep, Colin. If we are pursued tomorrow, we must be well rested."

"I have told young Davie the truth of our situation," he said. "He knows who we are, and I have instructed him to tell Graeme and Abigail as well, once we have departed. He will ride to the border where a man in my employ will bring help."

"But Jonah and Clarice—"

"Are likely to be detained in Ardlui, given what Davie has told me about the determination of the men of Loch Lomond to bring the thieves to justice. This drawing of the thieves that seems to be circulating is more proof that our pursuers are single-minded. We cannot depend upon your friends to succeed in summoning help. I've no doubt they will be questioned, but they are unlikely to be harmed," he added. "Rest your mind on that account."

"But—Davie—how do you know he will not turn us in for the reward?"

"He will not."

"How can you be certain? Did you request it of him in your earl's voice?"

"You are nonsensical with exhaustion." He gestured to the mattress. "Go to sleep."

"*Tell* me. Do you think he will do as you wish simply because you *requested* it of him?"

"I know he will do as I wish because I offered him a farm." He moved away. "Now, I am—"

She grabbed his sleeve. "A *farm*?"

He glanced down at her fingers gripping him and she released him.

"What farm?"

"A tenant of mine recently died without heirs. The farm remains vacant. It is a sheep farm, like this, though larger. It should suit him and Meghan."

She stared at him. "You gave him a farm. An entire farm?"

"He is a poor man, Emily," he said quietly. "The girl he loves has enjoyed modest prosperity in her father's house, yet he has nothing to give her except himself. I merely offered him that which any man in his situation would sell his soul for. But I have not asked him to sell his soul. I have only asked him to ride to England as swiftly as possible with a message, and then to take a chance on making his living on an excellent piece of property. He would have been a fool to decline the offer."

"But—can he truly believe that you are who you claim to be?"

"It seems he does." He turned away, then over his shoulder offered her the slight smile. "I used my earl's voice with him."

When he had gone and she shut the door behind him, she was too cold to remove her clothing. Setting the candle on the bedside table, she untied her boots, shucked them off, and slid beneath the covers. The bed was a miracle of springy ticking over wooden boards, and she thought of how Colin had spoken of Graeme and Abby Boyd's "modest prosperity," and could not sleep. That he thought this two-room house and small flock anything more than a hovel astonished her. That he had considered Davie's prospects and hopes, and offered a youth he knew nothing about property on his own estate in order to wrest her from danger now, was too much to accept easily. She had no doubt that were he alone he would have taken the fastest horse he could find and ridden to Glasgow—Lady Justice's search for a missing girl be damned. He was doing all of this because of her, and now for Pip too, an orphan peasant child he had met only two days ago.

She stared into the candle's flame and could not stop seeing his smile, and feeling his mouth against hers, and thinking that perhaps she had not spoken the truth to him earlier when she said she knew him. Perhaps, after all, she did not.

The candle's flicker lulled her to sleep.

She awoke to lamplight and no air—suffocating panic—a huge, callous palm clamped over her mouth and nose. Flailing out, her arms and legs caught in the bedclothes. She broke free and gasped air into her mouth, and then gagged as a rag filled it, smashing against her tongue, and her head was jerked backward. A thousand pricks of pain erupted on her scalp and she choked as the cloth pushed deeper into her throat as he tied a band around her head. Then his knees were pressing into her thighs, trapping her to the mattress, his hands snatching her wrists, binding them with more cloth.

"There's a lass." Murdo's voice was raspy, and her nostrils were clogged with the scent of whiskey. The pressure left her legs. She tried to thrash, but her feet jerked back and up to her buttocks. "There nou," he huffed, and she grunted and screamed into the gagging cloth and fought as he dragged her across the mattress. "Yer a feisty lass, to be sure. Hush now, and I'll no' be forced to quiet ye. I only want the ten pounds. What they'll do to ye in Inveraray, I'll be makin' no promises, o' course."

Hauling her up from the bed into his wiry arms with the strength of a man who had labored every day of his sixty years, he lunged across the bedchamber's threshold, stumbling into the main room, unsteady from drink, she knew.

But again she knew wrongly. As she pulled her shoulder out of Murdo's hold to knock over a small wooden chair, she saw that the old man had not tripped on his own feet. He had stumbled over Colin. Lit by the glow of the dying embers in the hearth, the Earl of Egremoor was sprawled across the bedchamber threshold, deathly still.

Chapter 16

Courage

*H*is stomach rolling into his throat was nothing to the pain crashing through his skull. Gulping back the nausea, Colin grabbed the doorpost and hauled himself to his knees, then lurched to his feet. Dissonant bells clanged between his ears, and all around him was black. He reached out, banged his thigh against a table, and swallowed a curse.

But he knew where he was, and the bells in his head were fading, leaving a pounding ache at the base of his skull and sudden, acrid fear in his mouth. Gripping the bedchamber doorjamb, he fell into the little room. The candlelight by which he had been watching her sleep was gone, the room dark, save for a pale glow of moonlight leaking through the draperies. The bed was empty.

Abruptly the room got darker yet. A black cloud filled it. Air.

He needed air.

He forced himself to breathe, dragging his thoughts from terror. Swinging around, he stumbled into the main room and collided with Abigail Boyd.

"Colin? What're—"

He seized her shoulders. *"Where has he taken her?"*

"Taken?" Her voice was thick with sleep. "What do ye— oh, *no*. What's that old man done?"

He released her. "Where would he have gone with her?"

"Down to Inveraray, I expect. 'Tis the closest law this side o' Kallin."

He peered into the darkness of the main room. "Where is your husband?"

She pointed to a pallet on the other side of the hearth where Graeme's snores rose in thick rumbles from the floor where he had collapsed senseless after they'd hauled young Davie to the barn to sleep off the whiskey before taking to the road at dawn. The young Scot had been celebrating his good fortune, and his prospective father-in-law along with him. They would be no help now. He dragged his hands through his hair.

"He'll no' harm her, Colin dear," Abigail said gently. "He's a greedy old fool, but he's no' got a wicked bone in him."

"I am not as concerned about him as I am about the people to whom he intends to take her." The lump at the base of his skull throbbed. "I must leave Pip with you now." He shoved his arms into his coat. "Will you care for her until I am able to retrieve her, whenever that is?"

"Like one o' my own!"

"Tell her I will return for her. Abigail, I hope I needn't harm your uncle."

She shoved a woolen hat into his hands. "Ye've my permission to tan the hide clear off his old bones."

He went to the door.

"For her!" She threw a pair of women's shoes to him. "And take the saddle, lad. I know ye're good for it." She smiled gamely.

The moon sat upon the opposite mountain peak as he urged the carriage horse down the hill toward the road. He mustn't have been unconscious for more than an hour. But that was enough time for a man who had spent his life in this countryside to make good distance toward the nearest large town.

But Murdo had not in fact gone far. Colin caught up to the cart no more than a mile west of the farm. Plodding along the road in the dark behind the Boyds' burly draft horse, the cart was hung with a lantern bright enough to light only the old man slumped over the reins on the driver's bench, chin resting on his chest.

Colin slowed Toby and studied Murdo. In his dread he hadn't thought to ask Abigail whether her uncle was likely to be armed. Rash oversight. *Unprecedented* oversight.

Across the snowy stillness, Toby nickered a friendly greeting to the other animal. The draft horse lifted its head and whinnied in reply. Murdo did not stir.

Colin dismounted. In the bed of the cart, a bundle of blankets wiggled.

Alive.

Leaping up onto the cart's break rub, he gathered the bundle into his arms and lifted her out. The cart horse and old man continued onward without breaking stride.

The blankets fell away as her feet found the ground. A gag was cinched tight around her mouth, her hair caught in it and sticking out at all angles, and her eyes were as wide and bright as the starry sky. She grunted, made noises that must be intended as speech, and tugged against the bindings holding her arms behind her, wiggling out of his embrace and frowning.

The gag was too tight to tug free. Working at the knot at the base of her head, he got it open and pulled off the rag.

"That was exciting!" burst from her.

He started on the knots that bound her wrists together. His hands shook and he drew in lungfuls of cold air, one after another.

"Exciting?" he managed to press through his teeth.

"Well, it certainly was not *relaxing*. He tied my ankles too. I had just managed to pry the bindings loose and slip my feet out when I heard hooves." The ropes fell free and she faced him, rubbing her wrists. He put the boots into her hands and she tugged them on. "Thank you. When I heard hoof beats approaching so swiftly, I was certain all of my work had been for naught. But it was you, happily." She smiled a vibrant smile of red lips and white teeth. "Oh! Wait here." She ran toward the cart.

Heartbeats frantic, he went after her. She climbed up onto the brace and, bending over, afforded him a moonlit view of her round behind. Then she was straightening up again, the farmer's whiskey jug and a lumpy canvas sack dangling from her hands. Stepping down from the cart, she came toward him walking. He met her as the cart took a turn in the road and disappeared behind trees bordering the hill.

Then it was only the two of them, standing alone on the road in the snow. He looked into her upturned face that was splashed with color still so wildly brilliant beneath the starlight, as though every bit of light available would inevitably find its way to her.

She hoisted the jug and sack. "Breakfast."

"Emily, you were just abducted," he said as steadily as he could without any air to propel the words. His heartbeats would not slow.

"Isn't it fantastic?" Her arms dropped. "It was horrifying, and excessively uncomfortable. But after I realized he did not intend to do me lasting harm, it was a little thrilling. I hoped, of course, that I would be able to break free before we reached civilization. I did not have much of a plan after that, it's true, especially since I did not have shoes. How clever you were to bring these."

"Mrs. Boyd's idea." He wanted to grab her, feel her wellness, her wholeness, her outrageous vitality.

"Of course it would not have been fantastic if you had not come, or if Murdo had intended any unpleasantness in addition to collecting a reward for me."

"Are you . . . all right?" His eyes were as dark and wonderfully full of emotion as she had ever seen them. Full of *her.* She saw it clearly. And suddenly, safe now, with him, her body started shaking from her lips to her damp, frozen toes stuffed into strange boots.

"It was frightening," she said. "But I am well now. Are you?" She reached up toward his face but snatched her hand back. "I saw you on the floor. I—are you well?"

"Yes. Now," he said in a strange, rough voice she did not recognize.

"You aren't. You look bemused." And bright-eyed and completely tousled, thoroughly unlike *him* yet even more thoroughly perfect. "He must have hit you astonishingly hard. Tell me the truth." *To hell with not touching him.* She reached up to explore his head. "Are you injur—"

"Emily." He grasped her face between his palms. And then his mouth was upon hers, his hands encompassing her, holding her still. For the length of one long breath that neither of them took, he held her mouth against his.

He released her, his hands fell away from her face, and both of them were staring between the inches.

She saw him swallow thickly. Her lips parted, as though the surprise of touching his again, unexpectedly, had been far too much for them and now they would not function properly.

Pivoting on the road, she walked swiftly up its slushy center. Her spectacles were still on the Boyds' bedside table and she saw nothing in focus, and her hands gripped the handle of the jug and canvas sack with unwonted force, her feet scrabbling and slipping with each hasty stride. Fifteen yards distant, a trail led off the road along a crumbling stone fence wending into the hills, grass poking out to the side of the path where the wind had whisked the snow away. A sheep route. She hurried onto it.

She had imagined kissing him plenty of times. But until earlier she had not imagined the softness of his lips or the strength of his hands on her face or the violent surge of hot awakening that swept through her. For hours now she had been telling herself that he had kissed her so beautifully for the benefit of the others—that in that moment he had not felt what she had.

But perhaps he had.

Dropping the jug and sack of apples that she had watched Murdo toss into the cart after her, she swiveled around and walked back to the nobleman. Colin halted as she approached, his gaze unreadable in the waning moonlight that made everything all silvery blue. Without slowing her pace, she went straight to him. She lifted her chin and his hands came around her face to either side and he bent his head and covered her mouth with his. She parted her lips and felt him and tasted him. He was strength and tenderness at once, heat and softness and the scratch of whiskers and deep, sweet urgency. It was knee weakening, the pleasure flooding her, and she drank kisses and air from him as his hand slipped beneath her hair to her nape, and he arched her neck to make their mouths fit together even more perfectly.

Her hands rose to his shoulders. Digging her fingertips into his coat, she gripped hard. Then she flattened her palms, tore her lips from beneath his, and pushed herself away.

Spinning around, she set off on the trail anew, grabbing up the jug and sack as she went, her footsteps crunching the snow, strides quick and desperate to put distance between her and this insanity. Her blood was spinning and her head was muddled and her lips were damp and now cold from the wintry air and *what was she doing*?

Not him. Not *him*. Of all the men in the world, she should not—*must not*—

Not him.

If he only knew whom he had just kissed.

If he knew . . .

She halted and watched him walk slowly to her in the snow-lit darkness.

"He grabbed me in my sleep," she said into the resonant silence. "He has a surprisingly large hand. He covered my mouth and nose entirely with it. I was unable to call out to you but then I saw you on the floor and thought you were dead and I—I—I cannot explain how I felt. I have never felt like that before in my life."

"I think he hit me with that jug." He ran a hand over the back of his neck and his eyes were black as midnight, wary and bright. "I am sorry I did not protect you. I am sorry I allowed him to surprise me. I was distracted."

Distracted.

"I thought you intended to sleep in the barn," she said not very steadily. "What were you doing there? In the bedchamber."

"Watching you."

"Watching me?"

He nodded.

"Watching me *sleep*?"

"Yes," he said. "I was looking at you. Enjoying the vision of you. When you are awake I can barely glance at you without you assuming that you know exactly what I am thinking and that it's all rubbish. I was taking simple pleasure in a moment of liberty to study the shine of your lashes and the tilt of your nose and the belligerent point of your chin and the lushness of your lips that somehow, miraculously, you had allowed me to kiss, and I failed to notice the man sneaking up behind me with a jug of whiskey, a misstep which I now regret thoroughly because I never, ever want to see you in danger again. I have had enough of that now to last me a lifetime." His eyes looked fevered and the taut distress of the muscles in his jaw set off a shower of heat inside her.

This could not be happening.

"You are exhausted. As I am," she said, trying to pretend that he had spoken sanely. "Neither of us can be blamed."

His Adam's apple jerked. "For everything?"

"For—" Her throat caught. "That kiss."

"Which one?" he said huskily.

"It was an anomaly, of course," she said.

"Was it?"

"Wasn't it?"

"I don't know," he said. She could see his hard breaths

upon the frozen air. She was certain her eyes were far too wide, fixed on his face as he stepped toward her and every detail of his gloriously uncompromising masculinity came into complete focus.

Grazing her chin with his fingertips, he looked at her lips and bent his head as she remained entirely still.

He kissed her very softly, the sensation of him, his closeness, and the caress of shared breaths all still new and yet perfectly familiar, as though this were the most natural thing in the world—to kiss him. He lifted his lips from hers barely an inch but did not retreat. She looked into his eyes that were so close, and saw in the flecks of gray hidden in the blue the same helpless need that was inside her.

The next kiss lasted longer. As soft as the first, equally careful and deliberate, it sent warmth from her lips down into her belly and spreading through her abdomen in fine, hot tendrils of pleasure.

He drew away again, but only for an instant, only long enough for her lips to regret the lack of his. Sinking his fingers into her hair and tilting her head back with his hand, he captured her lower lip with his, and then with his teeth, and a quick gasp of delight escaped her.

Covering her lips, he slipped the tip of his tongue across the seam of her mouth and opened her to him. She let him take her into the kiss. Without hesitation, he tasted her—the curve of her lips, the sweep of her tongue, the cadence of her breaths—all of her, and she wanted it all, his mouth giving her pleasure and his hands in her hair and her fingers working beneath his coat to find his chest. She spread her palms over his ribs, met the intoxicating caress of his tongue with her own, and felt a hard constriction in his chest. Hands fanning over his waist, she sighed against his lips.

He took her mouth entirely then, completely, as though he were a starving man seeking satisfaction he must find in her lips. There seemed to be only hunger, taking and giving and wanting more with each touch. His mouth was a miracle. She felt his hand curve down her neck to her shoulder, strong and certain as it swept along her spine, and she welcomed it. It spread over the small of her back. And then he pulled her against him. A moan jerked from her throat. Chest to chest, thigh to thigh, arm wrapped around her waist, he held her to him, kissed her passionately, deeply. He was hard everywhere, his body powerful. She twined her fingers in his hair and could not have enough of his mouth, of the aching pleasure of his kiss, and of his taut, male arousal against her.

"Emily, forgive me for hurting you," he whispered. "*Emily.*" Her name upon his lips was harsh, low, beautiful. *Too beautiful.*

"No," stumbled over her tongue. "No." Dragging herself out of madness, she pushed away from him and fell back a step. Her eyes sprang open. "No," she uttered. "*No.* What are you *doing*?" She swiped the back of her hand across her lips. They were soft and raw—used—adored. "What am *I* doing?" Her feet took her another step backward. "I cannot be kissing you."

"You can," he said, his breathing as jagged as hers. "You are."

"No. This is a mistake."

"It is not a mistake." He reached out and grasped her hand. "Emily—"

"Of course it is a mistake." She wrenched free. "So, stop now. We must stop." She swung away from him and walked swiftly up the trail, the oversized boots slipping in the snow.

"Emily," he said behind her. "I am sorry that I hurt you and I am asking your forgiveness." His voice was superbly unsteady. "Why won't you give it? Do you wish to hold a grudge against me forever?"

"No. Of course not." She twisted to face him. "I will give you my forgiveness. I do. You have it. There, now it's over. In the distant past. Story closed. Conversation finished." She set off again along the wall.

"I don't understand," he called after her. "One moment you were kissing me like you were glad to be doing so— more than glad," he added so low that it made all the heat inside her constrict. "And the next moment you are running away. It's as though this is some sort of disjointed dream. I—"

"You are correct." She pivoted around. "It was a dream. You were not kissing me. You were kissing a phantasm of your imagination."

Silence fell into the moonlight between them.

"What?"

"You don't know me, Colin," she said with remarkable stability given the racketing pace of her pulse.

"I have known you since *birth*, Emily. I stood beside the font of holy water at your Christening and heard them give you to me."

The breaths swept out of her. "You don't *own* me. And you know nothing about me now. Your memories are confusing your affection, and your notion of what a woman should be is coloring your perception. You believe that because I have refused offers of marriage from rich men of impressive status that I am a reclusive eccentric with a preference for books over people."

"I believe nothing of the sort."

"Of course you do. You haven't any reason to believe otherwise. You don't have any idea who I am. For pity's sake, you cannot even call me by my *name*."

"Emily *is* your name. And what in the blazes does it matter what I call you? You are the same woman whatever name you go by. And you're doing it again, imagining you can read my thoughts."

"I am not the same woman. And I cannot have been *wrong*." A rumbling thunder of emotion was in her ears. "I cannot have been wrong all of these years, that the gratification of your wishes is all that matters to you. I cannot allow this, now, to be anything but the basest and most primitive of carnal desire, inspired by the heightened sentiments of the moment."

"Heightened sentiments? What in the blazes is that supposed to mean?"

"Don't you see?" she cried. "I cannot have been wrong that you don't have a *heart*."

He came toward her swiftly, grasped her wrist, and flattened her hand to his chest. Through his ribs, his heartbeats beneath her palm were fast and hard.

"You are denying me this?" he said close to her brow, the depth of his voice coating her rawness. "Because it has been like this since you walked through the door of that inn four days ago. It was like this when you stood across your parlor in London refusing me. And in Edinburgh in April. And each time I have seen you for longer than I can say."

"*Stop*. Do not say this."

"I don't need to kiss you to feel this," he said. "You have been turning me inside out for years."

Then she heard the thrumming beats quite clearly—not in her head or his chest but on the road not a hundred yards away. Horses. Moving swiftly.

Growing louder.

Colin was entirely still, his fingers wrapped around her wrist.

The hoof beats turned onto the sheep trail.

He pulled her to their horse. Vaulting into the saddle, he reached down and dragged her up.

"Hang on," he said and she barely had an instant to wrap her arms around his waist and tighten her legs before Toby leaped forward.

The hill rose gradually, the stone border snaking up the slope and offering a natural path for the horse to follow. Halfway up, the fence crumbled into scattered rocks and the trail abruptly became a stream cutting through snow.

"Jumping *now*," Colin said and then she was hanging on as the horse gathered beneath them and he took it over the remnants of the barrier to land with bone-rattling precision in the snow on the other side. She tightened her arms around his waist, astonished that she was still in the saddle, and tried to ignore the whipping cold wind against her bared legs as he urged the horse into a gallop.

He had always been a marvelous rider, excelling at the hunt and every other hurdle his father had erected for him to jump over. Now she clung to him, felt the power in his body commanding Toby so thoroughly that her carriage horse was racing across a mountainside like a thoroughbred, and she trained her ears for sound of pursuit. For some time she heard nothing—no one following them—but she did not wonder why Colin did not slow or halt. Dawn was creeping in a pale halo over the mountaintop far to the east, spreading swiftly and layering the snowy hillside in shimmering gray. There were no trees anywhere, only sheer snow-draped slopes. Too soon they would be entirely visible to anybody riding along the road, this hill, or the mountainside opposite.

They galloped until there was no hill left.

Slanting down the slope at a speed that made her clamp her eyes shut and pray for Toby's sturdy legs and hooves to hold out, they crossed toward the road that ran higher here above the valley. The snow was fresh on the ground, unmarked by hooves or footsteps. Their pursuers must be from the south or east. Perhaps they had encountered Murdo. Perhaps they had already visited the Boyds' farm and threatened Abby and Graeme into giving them up. And perhaps she had been so entirely wrapped up in kissing the man who had been her secret nemesis for five years that if a mob of angry Scots had borne down upon them three minutes earlier she would not have even heard them.

The hill sped away behind them, dipping to the road and giving way to the next slope rising steeply to the left. Already the snow was melting, and Toby's hooves slapped at the slushy road, making dark tracks easy for their pursuers to follow. All around them the dawn was rising, streams gurgling down the mountain to their right and the sun casting silvery-golden rays into the heavens dotted with a smattering of new white clouds. Not a sound but those of nature called across the slopes.

Colin slowed the horse to a canter, but she could not bring herself to release him. Hands spread over his waist, fingertips sunk in his coat, and the rest of her body pressed to his back, she was shaking too hard. Forcing herself to inhale slowly, she willed her hands to loosen.

Distant hoof beats came to her upon the damp wind.

"Damn it," he growled.

They sprang into a gallop again.

With only half a night's rest and carrying two people, the carriage horse labored as he barreled along the sodden road, his sides heaving beneath her knees but his steps certain and strong. She blessed Jonah for keeping a good horse, then blessed Toby himself and held on to Colin tightly.

But the animal could not run indefinitely burdened by two people. He stumbled once, jolting her aside, and Colin grabbed him up and the horse regained his footing. But his gait grew less steady, less confident, even as his pace did not slow.

Opening her eyes, she peered over her shoulder into the pale gray of morning, and her stomach rose to her throat.

Four men on horseback followed at a gallop not a hundred yards behind.

"Colin."

He leaned forward, pulling her with him, and she clamped her thighs about his hips, her calves about Toby's sides, and held on.

As though he understood, the gelding gave a mighty surge forward, and flew. It was still miles to Castle Kallin. They would be caught. And their flight would prove to their pursuers that they were guilty.

To their left, a stream cascading down the snowy hillside had become a river. Ahead it cut to the north, forcing the road to curve around it.

Wind whipping her hair across her face, she glanced back. The Scotsmen were within fifty yards.

They were beaten.

It began as a humming rumble, so faint that above the pounding of Toby's hooves and their pursuers' horses she barely heard it. Growing swiftly louder, it became a burbling, steady grumble of earth, as though the ground had at one time heard the lightning shout and wanted to attempt that sound too. Then upon the eastern slope she saw it. Down the hill they came, a dark rusty brown, shaggy horde of bobbing horns and massive shoulders, covering the mountainside like a mighty river. Churning and groaning, they descended, dozens upon dozens of cattle.

Racing down the mountain straight toward them.

Chapter 17

Pip's Angel

"Go!" she cried. "*Go!*"

Toby lunged forward, hooves skimming the ground as the herd flowed like a single creature to the base of the mountain and barreled toward the road. On the northern edge of the herd, a cattleman appeared, racing ahead and shouting, hundreds of hooves drowning out the sound. Neck straining, haunches laboring, her sweet, placid carriage horse shot forward just as the lead cattle hit the road.

Groaning and mooing, the herd fanned across the flat ground, their keeper racing by not twenty feet away, tearing off his hat and waving it at them with a jaunty grin before crushing it back onto his head and continuing on.

Zenobia craned her neck around. Cattle covered the road from mountainside to river, streaming eastward toward the rising sun. On the other side of the river, the hillside to the south, their pursuers wheeled their horses about, their shouts lost to the herd's mighty din.

Another cattleman came toward them down the hill, changing course to meet them in the empty road.

"Guid day!" he called, tipping his hat. His face was deeply whiskered, and he wore leather breeches, thick boots, and a fine blue tartan pinned to his shoulder.

"How do you do?" Colin said, slowing Toby to a trot to approach the man. "I am Gray. We are friends of a man whom I believe must be your companion, Davie Wallace."

"Are ye?" The cattleman's face broke into a wide grin. "Shane MacDougal here. Any friend o' Davie's a brother o' mine." He brought his mount close with confident disregard for safety, extended his hand, and clasped Colin's. "'Twas a near miss ye had there." He gestured to the head of the herd streaming along the roadbed.

"Although fortuitous," Colin replied. "We would like to avoid those men on the hillside."

The cattleman's attention shifted to her. He grinned.

"Been stealin' yerself a wifie down the loch, have ye? Her menfolk none too happy aboot it, aye?"

Colin glanced at her over his shoulder, and his smile turned everything inside her shaking body to jelly.

"That is precisely what I have done," he said to Shane.

The Scotsman threw back his head and roared with laughter.

"Fancy a wee bit o' adventure nou and again, do ye, lass?" he said to her.

She managed a wobbly grin. "A wee bit."

"We are en route to Castle Kallin," Colin said. "What is the distance by the road?"

"'Tis no' three miles to Glen Village on the byway. Another two to the castle."

Safety. And only one day shy of All Saints'.

"Can you help us escape those men, Mr. MacDougal?" she said.

"Aye. Glad to, lass. The herd needs water. May as well water 'em here." He grinned. "Those lads'll be hoppin' mad, but ye'll reach Kallin afore they catch ye." He tugged on his hat and turned his horse's head from them. "My compliments, Gray! Ye've nabbed yerself a bonnie lass." His mount's hooves flicked up the snow as he rode off.

The sun thrust the clouds aside and cast itself upon them. The sparkling green and white highlands smelled of heated cattle and churned snow, and her skirts were spattered with mud, her legs and arms and back screaming with exhaustion and shaking, and they had barely escaped death and everything had changed. *Everything.* She had kissed him. Really kissed him.

And then he had said the unimaginable.

"I now believe in Pip's angel," she said as Colin urged Toby forward again and she craned her neck to watch Shane enter the edge of the herd and ride toward another cattleman farther along. Settling her hands at his waist, she let her body move with the horse's exhausted ramble.

"She will be well until I can return to the farm," he said. "I spoke with Abigail."

"I knew you would not have left without first assuring her safety. She will miss you," she said close to his shoulder. "You are her hero, you know."

In response he was silent.

"And now you are mine too," she said. "Again."

"Both villain and hero," he said. "Interesting."

"More lately hero. You rescued me."

"I have no doubt that if I had not, you would have managed to free yourself and escape from Murdo. And from anybody else who came along."

"I could not have ridden Toby as you just did."

"Well." He shrugged. "You are a woman."

Her stomach crimped.

He looked down to where her hands fell away from his waist, and the dent appeared in his cheek, auguring the dimple.

"You said that only to pique me, didn't you?" she said.

"Of course not." But he smiled. "I never jest."

Urging Toby onward, he directed them north and they left the milling herd behind.

They went steadily, Toby's gait weary but strong, as suited a carriage horse. She did not know that she dozed until sudden motionlessness nudged her awake. Her arms were about her companion's waist again, and she withdrew them swiftly, which was the epitome of absurd at this point.

"Why have we—"

At the side of the road, five men moved from beneath the tree cover, watching their approach. Waiting for them.

Poorly dressed, with ragged coats and torn trousers, each had whiskers scragglier than the next. One lacked a forearm, another wore a patch over his eye beneath a tattered hat, and yet another leaned on a crutch snagged beneath his arm. Soldiers at one time, perhaps, by their injuries. Now vagabonds. Men used on the battlefield to win the wars of men of wealth and power, then sent home, their hearts clouded with death, to suffer the hellish aftermath of their own disordered minds. Lady Justice had written about such men. She had pleaded for the crown and Parliament to assist these poor souls in finding work and regaining their honor.

But these men before them had not found help. Pip's angel was nowhere in sight.

Her fingers climbed to Colin's arm. Beneath his coat, the muscle was packed hard.

"I haven't a weapon," he said. "We must turn back."

"No. We are too close to the castle."

"I cannot protect you." A strained sort of desperation colored his voice.

The man in the middle of the road held a cup in his weathered hand. Around the handle of the cup was tied a clean yellow ribbon, in a bow. In the ragged lapel of another's coat was a single fresh pink rose.

"You needn't. I don't believe I am in danger here." Throwing her leg over the horse's rump, she slid to the ground.

Colin leaped from the saddle and pulled the horse after her. But her stride was quick and confident, and the animal was wasted; he reached her just as she halted before the vagabonds.

"Good day, gentlemen," she said brightly, drawing back

her hood to reveal a thorough tangle of pale locks. "How do you do?"

"Good day, miss," the burliest said with a nod. He looked to Colin. "A penny for men who saw Waterloo, sir?"

"Waterloo?" she uttered.

"Aye, an' Quatre Bras afore that. The Forty-Second we been, miss."

"The Forty-Second—" she began. The Royal Highland foot had seen hundreds of casualties at the battle of Quatre Bras. With a subtle shifting back of her shoulders, she moved a step closer to him. "You are heroes. Thank you for your service."

The Scot screwed up his brow but he nodded.

"Of course we have a penny for you."

"We do not," Colin said.

"Colin—"

"My wallet is gone. Murdo must have taken it." And he hadn't thought to retrieve it from the old drunk because he had been shaking with relief at the time. And kissing her.

"*Oh*. That is unfortunate." She looked back at the leader. "Our money was stolen last night. I am so sorry we cannot help you. Do you"—she glanced toward the trees—"live here?"

"No, lass. Only restin' here for a bit afore we move on. Bryce canna go more'n a mile or two a'time." He gestured to the man with the crutch who lacked the bottom half of his leg. "Where be ye travelin'?"

"At this moment we are fleeing from pursuers who intend us harm. So it is probably best if we continue along. I shouldn't like to draw their unfriendly attention to you."

"'Tis kind o' ye, lass." He beckoned to one of the others. "The purse, Cal."

One of them pulled a small sack from within his coat. The chief shook two coins into his palm, took Emily's hand between both of his own thick paws, and pressed the money into it.

"Oh, goodness," she said, her eyes growing wide. "I couldn't. You—"

"We've got some, lass. Ye've got none," he said. "God be wi' ye." He stepped away from the center of the road.

"Thank you. You are very kind." She curled her fingers around the coins but her brow was troubled. "Why are you . . . here? Why aren't you home?"

"We've no home. Waterloo took all the Grady clan but us—our laird too. Returned to discover fever'd taken our women and bairns. We'd be gone too, except for the grace o' God and the Solstice."

"The Solstice?"

He gestured. "'Tis the inn up the road apace, lass."

"An inn? Close by?" She cast animated eyes at Colin. "We must be near Castle Kallin."

"The castle be juist down the glen," the Scot said.

"Do you know if the duke is in residence?"

"Aye, he's there."

She clapped her hands. "This is the best news we have had in days."

He perused her skeptically, his shrewd eyes slewing over her bedraggled peasant's clothing and disordered hair then returning to her eyes that were far too full of life for a lady's.

"Oh, I'm not—" she said. "That is to say, I am not well acquainted with the duke. But I am eager to visit his castle."

Quite obviously she was hiding something about her visit to the Duke of Loch Irvine's home. That it made Colin sick to have his suspicion thus confirmed only proved that he was also, quite obviously, hiding something.

And that name—the name of the inn—disturbed him. *Solstice.* Months ago, when Edinburgh society had accused Loch Irvine of abducting maidens for evil purposes, the girls had gone missing on the nights of solstices and equinoxes. Colin knew only fragments of the actual abductor's part in it, and the peculiar rituals that Constance and her husband had crushed.

Furious with him at the time, Constance had told him no

more. But by then the earl had fallen ill; Colin had had no attention for mysteries, only for his responsibilities to his lands, people, and Parliament, and a tenacious pamphleteer to finally track down. And he'd no interest in serving the man who had for years forced him to lie to his friends.

No. *Not forced*. He had done so willingly. He had believed in the importance of that secret—for a time. But he had believed in many things that now felt wrong to him.

Until apologizing to Emily, he had rarely apologized to anyone in his life. The earl had taught him that to apologize was to admit wrong and weakness.

Apologizing to her had not felt wrong or weak. It felt honest. With her he wanted to be honest. He wanted to remember a time when he had never hidden secrets, never pretended anything, never forgotten the sound of her laughter or the quick glimmer in her eyes.

They bade the soldiers good-day and she came to the horse's side.

"Will you toss me up?" she said, but her eyes meeting his were crisply defiant.

So be it. If she wished to remain piqued, he hadn't any particular desire to make himself a target for further irrational insults. Not at present.

She used the step he made of his hands and settled into the saddle, her skirts catching up beneath her knees. The animal was exhausted, and Colin could not bring himself to feel her so closely for another moment, not with her flavor still on his tongue and the soft strength of her body still in his hands. Taking the animal's lead, he walked ahead and they left the veterans behind. She did not speak—unprecedented—and he ignored his aching head and wildly fluctuating temper— also unprecedented—and walked as swiftly as the beast would go.

As Shane MacDougal had promised, the road came to an end as it met another. The new byway ran at the feet of a long ridge of peaks, the slopes rising to them mottled gray and green with melting snow. A hundred yards eastward on the road, a cluster of buildings were nestled at the edge of a copse of dark conifers.

He led the horse to the largest building. Painted with cheerful artistry on the marquee set dead center of the long white building was THE SOLSTICE INN. And in smaller letters, "All Are Welcome."

Tying the horse to the post before the door, he went to its side.

"I will not allow you to come to harm," he said.

"Nor I, you," she replied sincerely, as though she believed she could actually protect him if it came to that. And perhaps she could.

Courage trapped in his throat, he reached up. She allowed him to grasp her waist, and she slid down.

"All right?" he said, never wanting to remove his hands from her.

"Yes." She moved out of his grasp, but she paused before the door. "Shouldn't we continue on to the castle now that we are so close, rather than risk more unfriendly villagers?"

"Is that what you wish to do?"

"You have asked me so often what I wish—on this journey."

"Have I?"

Her throat moved in a singular roll, like a ripple on the surface of a brook created by the casting of a stone into it. But she was not a tranquil brook meandering its way along. She was a river at the height of springtime thaw, volatile and unpredictable, her moods as inconstant as the Scottish weather and her temperament at one moment sweet and the next tart.

"I would not have expected it of you," she said.

"I am full of surprises, it seems," he said, and pushed open the door to the jingle of a bell within. "Now for clean clothing, food, and sleep," he said. "In that order. Come, lady adventurer, and let us hope for sympathetic innkeepers and soft mattresses."

"If I were any other woman," she said, looking up at

him, "you know that I would be offended by your mention of mattresses. You know that." It was not a question. It was a challenge.

"If you were any other woman," he replied, every inch of his skin alive to her nearness, "I wouldn't even be thinking of mattresses."

She blinked like a curious bird. Then she went into the inn.

So much for honesty.

In the foyer lit with sunlight from a window above the door, as she removed her cloak he caught sight of her face. Her cheeks were pink. Violently pink. He wanted to cup them in his palms and feel the fire of her indignation sinking into his blood.

The entranceway was a plain wood and stucco painted space, but clean, and smelling of the sap of freshly cut evergreens. A woman appeared, an apron tied about her waist. Wise, wrinkled eyes assessed them swiftly.

"Welcome," she said. "Luncheon and a pint for you, sir, and tea, ma'am?"

"Yes," Colin said, "but rooms first, and hot water and soap."

"Aye." She nodded, and said over her shoulder, "Plum, fetch our guests' luggage up to the Sappho and the Fanny Burney, then draw baths."

The maid came into the foyer, young and dark, with sullen eyes, but pretty. She went to the door.

"We've no luggage," Emily said. "And, actually, no money either. We cannot afford baths, or even rooms."

"Whether ye've the money for baths or not, miss," the innkeeper said, planting broad fists on her hips, "ye'll be havin' them. Mary Tarry willna seat a soul in her dining room covered in mud from head to heels. Charity it'll have to be for ye."

"You are very kind. We are good for the expenses, once we have contacted our friends."

"We've a horse that has been ill used and requires

tending," Colin said. "And I wish to send word to the duke immediately."

"No money, and still making demands?" Mary Tarry said with a raised brow. "Aye, ye be quality, for sure. Plum, bid Zion give the animal a good rubbing, and oats. Then she'll ride to the castle for ye," she said with a lifted brow at him. "I'll suppose ye'll be wanting to write a message to His Grace now?"

Zenobia could practically see the battle in him between set down and amusement.

"On your finest stationery, of course." His beautiful eyes hinted at a smile.

"Colin, I think we should tell Mrs. Tarry the truth."

"As you wish."

"Mrs. Tarry, I am the daughter of the Earl of Vale, and my companion is Lord Egremoor. Villagers from Balloch and along Loch Lomond have mistaken us for a pair of thieves who have stolen his lordship's name and robbed people and committed crimes of an unspeakable nature. Apparently we resemble the thieves, and we have been forced to leave our traveling companions and flee to the nearest place of safety."

"'Tis a story, to be sure! But ye'll find no welcome at the castle, milady. His Grace dinna accept visitors."

"He will accept me," Colin said.

She gave him a careful appraisal. "Aye, perhaps he will."

"Do you believe us?" he said.

"If this lass is a thief, I'll eat my door knocker." She set warm eyes upon her. "Ye've got a bonnie soul shinin' out through those eyes. Come now." She beckoned toward the stairway. "I'll see to yer comfort myself."

"Oh, you needn't. I borrowed this gown from a woman of good sense, so I can remove it on my own." She could not stop her eyes from darting to her companion. To all appearances, he was studying the dirt on his boots.

But Mrs. Tarry would hear no refusal, and she bustled her up the steps. The Fanny Burney room was luxuriously comfortable, with a thick rug into which her blistered toes sank gratefully, clean curtains about the four-poster bed, fluffy white linens of exceptional softness, goose down pillows, a cozy chair upholstered in blue satin set before the fireplace that crackled with merry flames, and a roll-top copper tub into which the maidservant, Plum, was already pouring steaming water from a pot.

"Books!" Casting her filthy cloak aside, Zenobia went toward the bookcase and fell to her knees. "I have never seen such a bookcase in an inn before. What a wonderful place this is, Mrs. Tarry." Her fingertips slipped over the bindings, some new and silky, others old and soft. She bent close to read the titles. "Good heavens! Every one of Miss Burney's novels! And here are Eliza Heywood's as well. What a wonderful collection."

"Well, aren't ye an odd one," Mrs. Tarry said, obviously pleased.

"When we fled Balloch I was obliged to leave my luggage behind, and I haven't seen a book since—oh, except the psalmody on the bed table at the vicarage near Tarbet. But I was so exhausted I remember little from that night." Except Colin buttoning her into her gown in the darkness. "Mrs. Tarry, you do believe us, don't you?"

"Aye."

"But our story is utterly fantastical."

The innkeeper nodded. "I've heard worse. Seen worse too. Now, into the bath ye go."

Bathed, and wrapped in a dressing gown of fabric softer even than anything her mother owned, she sat before the fire enjoying the food Mrs. Tarry had brought up and paging through a book she could not read without spectacles, simply for the pleasure of touching the pages, until her eyes closed. She awoke curled up in the chair by the fireplace to sore muscles, late-afternoon sunlight, and a soft rap upon the door.

Not Colin. Of course. The knock was too tentative for the Earl of Egremoor.

That she wished it were him, that she could not stop

thinking about his lips, his kiss, and his hands on her face, his arms around her, pulling her close, making her feel him beyond anything proper, lordly, and reserved—feel him *acutely*—proved her temporary insanity.

The maid who entered was not sallow-cheeked Plum, but even younger and smiling tentatively. She carried a pile of linens that, when she spread them upon the bed, were revealed to be women's clothing—expensive woman's clothing, by the quality of the fabric and embroidery and the quantity of delicate lace and satin ribbons decorating the undergarments. Even the garters and little satin slippers were embellished.

"I'm Rebecca, mum." Her voice had the flat tones of an American. "His lordship bade me bring these to you before tea."

Zenobia's hand darted back from stroking the beautiful gown. "His lordship? But where did he find them? Is there a shop in this village?"

"Aye, milady. Miss Sophie sews a pretty frock, don't she?"

"Yes, indeed! Prettier than anything I own." Including the single ballgown her mother and Clarice insisted she keep. "His lordship, however, cannot afford this gown at present, Rebecca, nor any of the undergarments." He had unbuttoned and buttoned her into hers thrice, and yet the notion of him choosing for her these delicate linens and the stays decorated with a tiny pink satin ribbon at the top of the boning made her flush with heat. She preferred plain linen to frilly undergarments. These were not precisely frilly, rather elegant and beautiful. But ribbons and lace amounted to one thing either way: painstaking work by the fingers of women paid meager wages for hours of labor so that wealthy, foolish society ladies could feel secure that they were wearing fortunes each time they stepped out of the house.

It was despicable.

But her fingers strayed again to the soft gown of such a subtle shade of green that it was nearly white.

"Mrs. Tarry extended him credit." Rebecca's eyes were deeply brown and positively starry.

"I see." She chewed on her lip.

"Don't you like them?"

"They are exquisite." Exquisitely feminine. He saw her as *this*? "I hope you will give Miss Sophie my most sincere compliments."

"Gladly, miss. She's like a sister to me. We came over together."

"Did you? From America?"

The girl smiled again. "Mrs. Tarry will be wanting me to help with the tea." She backed toward the door. "Unless you'd like me to stay and button you in?"

She accepted the offer. The clothing she had borrowed from the Boyds was in the laundry, and she hadn't any wish to be trapped in this bedchamber until it dried. Declining hairdressing, she tied her hair in a queue and followed Rebecca downstairs.

"Well!" the innkeeper said as she set a vase of pine fronds decorated with cones on the table in the empty parlor. "Ye clean up nicely, milady."

"It is kind of you to allow us credit, Mrs. Tarry. Is Lord Egremoor still asleep?"

"Oh, no, lass. He didna sleep. After washing up, he took the saddle horse and rode out."

"Rode out?" Without her. Without telling her. Without even sleeping first. "To where?"

"To the castle, lass. Now, if ye'll be wanting tea, there's a fine little teahouse along the street. Plum's run over to tell them ye're to have whatever ye'd like."

It was as if she had stepped out of a nightmare into a dream. The inn's stoop was swept clean, the street paved along its edge so that her new slippers suffered no puddles before she came to the teahouse. The teahouse itself was a portrait of quaint style, with a post displaying a white sign painted in scrolling letters. A bell tinkled as she stepped inside. Looking around the little space arranged with tables laid with floral porcelains, pressed linens, and dishes of marmalade, her gaze followed the line of a charming brass counter upon which sat a plate of scones, and up to meet the astonished stare of her sister.

Chapter 18

Several Significant Discoveries

*T*he two eldest daughters of the earl and countess of Vale had not spent childhood concealing their less admirable escapades from their parents without learning the swift, subtle cues in each other's faces. Now it was instantly, entirely clear to Zenobia that Amarantha did not wish her to do any of the things that she wished to do: shout her name, throw her arms about her, and burst into tears of relief.

Instead she dragged her attention away from her sister and allowed the tiny mistress of the teahouse to seat her in an upholstered chair, pour tea into a cup decorated with a pattern of primroses, and place a plate of cakes before her.

For all their buttery goodness, they were dust upon her tongue. Amarantha disappeared behind a door in the back of the shop, but when she reappeared occasionally to serve customers, Zenobia struggled not to stare as she choked down the sweets with sips of tea. Waiting until the proprietor disappeared into the kitchen, she went to the counter.

"Did you enjoy the cake, ma'am? Mrs. Tarry over at the inn baked them just this morning." Amarantha's voice was all the warmth of summer and the color of every flower at once, and her eyes overflowed with affection and eagerness.

"They were delicious." Her own voice was no more than a croak, emotion thickening her throat.

"Are you passing through the village today?"

"I am remaining overnight, actually. I have been traveling for some time and came out for refreshment and to stretch my legs. Can you recommend a fine stroll? Not too lengthy, of course, given the hour."

"Oh, yes!" Amarantha ushered her toward the door. "It's the prettiest path you'll ever see. A trickle of Irvine River makes its way here. I'll show you."

The proprietress emerged from the kitchen.

"I'll return in a trice," Amarantha said to the woman, her lovely smile filling her face, and Zenobia wanted to wrap her arms around her and hug and hug and hug.

As they left the shop Amarantha whispered, "Smile. Pretend we are chatting about the cake, or the weather, or—"

"Anything except how happy I am to see you?" She blinked away tears. "Amy, I am *so* relieved."

"Emmie. *Emmie!*" And then she was opening a gate onto a path bordered by enormous shrubs, and they were clasping each other tightly.

Amarantha broke the embrace, taking Zenobia's fingers in firm hands.

"My darling sister, why are you *here*?"

"I am looking for you, of course. Where have you been? Why haven't you written?"

"Oh, Emmie, how much I want to tell you! But there isn't time. I must return to the teashop or that silly woman will wonder where I have gone, and she will tell everyone. She does not trust me. I don't know if any of them do, except perhaps Sophie. She is the seamstress here. I know for certain that Mrs. Tarry suspects me. She is far too clever—"

"*Suspect* you? Of what? Are you in trouble of some sort?"

"No." Amarantha sounded sensible. But her grip was overly tight. "I am well. I have done no wrong, and I don't believe anyone here wishes me ill."

"But why haven't you written to me? To Mama and Papa? The last word we had was that you had boarded a ship, and then nothing for months and months. And then I received a letter from someone calling herself a friend and bidding me come find you at Castle Kallin."

"A letter about me? From a *friend*? Someone here that knows who I am?"

"I came as quickly as I could, of course. We have all been sick with worry."

"I haven't been able to write. We were delayed in the crossing by storms, and then when we landed in Edinburgh I was obliged to hide for several weeks—"

"*Hide?* Whatever for? Was Penny in trouble after all?"

"It's complicated. Emmie, Penny is—" Her throat constricted. "She is gone."

"Gone? *Oh.* Amy, I am so sorry. So very sorry. Was it on the crossing?"

"No. Her ship arrived in Edinburgh two months ahead of mine. I found her, eventually. But . . . I was there when she died."

"Was she ill?"

Amarantha squeezed her hands harder. "I will tell you all. I promise. But I must return to the shop now." Her cloverleaf eyes went suddenly wide. "Emily, I've just realized—that *was* Colin I saw near the Solstice's stable earlier today, wasn't it?"

"I suspect so. Yes." Unless the imposter earl had arrived in the village.

"Colin," Amarantha said flatly. "Colin *Gray*?"

"Yes."

Astonishment paled her sister's cheeks, making the freckles leap out across her nose. "Did you travel here with *him*?"

"In a manner of speaking. But, Amy, that really isn't important now—"

"Not *important*?" She blinked long cinnamon lashes. "Emmie, you aren't planning to marry him after all, are you? Good Lord, have you *already*?"

"No. Amarantha, this is the outside of enough. Cease these questions and tell me why I cannot acknowledge you as my sister to everybody in that teashop."

"Not only the teashop. In the entire village, Emmie. Don't tell anyone, I beg of you! And for goodness' sake don't let Colin see me. He is far too righteous to lie, even for an excellent reason. It is disastrous enough that the person who wrote that letter to you knows my real name. I wish I knew who sent it, and why she has not revealed me to others. But if everybody else here discovers who I am, I won't learn a thing. And I am so close, after so many months." Her voice pleaded. "I beg of you, sister. Be assured that I am safe, and do not reveal me."

"But, Amy, what is this all about? What are you close to?"

Her eyes flared. "Emmie, I think I have uncovered the mystery of the Devil's Duke!"

COLIN HAD NEVER spoken with the Duke of Loch Irvine, only seen him across a room in London a handful of times. The duke had held his title since the war when his elder brother perished and their father shortly after. At that time Gabriel Hume had returned prematurely from his sojourn at sea for the Royal Navy to take up the dukedom. To outward appearances he managed it well. Master of extensive lowlands sown with wheat, barley, and oats, with his highland estate given principally to sheep, and owner of two castles and an impressive ship engaged in modestly successful merchant ventures, he seemed a typical enough Scottish lord—except for the accusation of kidnappings and murder that gossips had been throwing at him from London to Edinburgh for over a year.

While Loch Irvine had courted Constance months earlier, she had discovered that he traveled throughout Britain frequently, rarely remaining at any one residence for long, and that he was both more secretive and more savvy than society even imagined. Colin had always assumed he must be; a naval captain was either savvy or he was at the bottom of the ocean with ship and crew. And Loch Irvine had courted Constance even after he had learned that sharp intelligence accompanied her exquisite beauty.

That the disappearances from Edinburgh families of girls of marriageable age had been pinned to Loch Irvine had one origin: an emblem drawn on the bloodied cloak of one of the missing girls. The symbol existed in only one place in Britain, carved in stone over the portal of Haiknayes Castle, and Haiknayes belonged to Loch Irvine.

Now, as Colin crossed the duke's drawing room to greet its overlord, rumors of abduction and violent killings seemed a world away. The room was appointed as befitted a bachelor of means and taste, with subdued furniture of elegant construction, tapestries of ancient design, and a massive hearth whose chimney functioned well for an old pile of stones; no smoke tainted the cool air. Instead Colin could practically smell on his skin the soap he had used to shave at the inn, and the freshness of the fine linen shirt and neckcloth Mrs. Tarry had provided.

All scents were coming with peculiar acuteness to him now, and sounds crisper, like the snapping flames in the hearth and the duke's footsteps upon the wooden floorboards. Textures as well: the brush of smooth linen against his jaw, the caress of a lock of his own hair fallen over his brow. Colors seemed brighter too: the brilliant crimson and gold threads of the tapestries, the vibrant blue of the tartan banded about the hilt of the claymore affixed over the mantel, and the wary deep brown of Loch Irvine's eyes beneath a slant of raven hair. It was as though the world had become a festival, and he in the midst of it, experiencing it all as though he had been living in a cave until now.

"My lord," Loch Irvine said curtly. "What brings you to Kallin?"

"Your Grace," Colin replied and, without thought,

extended his hand. For God's sake, he was behaving now as the commoner he'd been pretending to be for a sennight. But Loch Irvine took it, his callous paw clasping tightly—for a moment, too tightly—before releasing him. "Thank you for admitting me."

"I've no quarrel with you," the duke said with brow drawn. "You've my sympathy on the loss o' your father."

"Thank you." Peculiar that a recluse duke should know this news so soon. "It happened quite recently, of course."

Loch Irvine's eyes narrowed. "I read it in the *Times*."

"Naturally."

Loch Irvine offered him no tea or wine or whiskey. Not even a chair.

"I've no quarrel with you, Lord Egremoor," the duke repeated in a deep, rolling brogue, "unless you've brought me one now."

"I haven't. Rather, I have come to ask a favor of you. I am in Scotland on an errand, seeking a woman who has gone missing."

The duke's lashes twitched ever so slightly. "A woman?"

"A friend of an acquaintance of mine to whom I owe a debt of sorts. Nothing terribly interesting." Colin waved a negligent hand. "In seeking the woman here, however, I have unfortunately happened upon a run of ill fortune on my journey. It seems that a thief is using my name to ingratiate himself with innkeepers and travelers from Stirling to Loch Lomond, and then robbing them. He and an accomplice have killed at least one person. It seems that since you and Argyll together put a price on the heads of these thieves, the locals are eager to collect. They have, however unfortunately, decided to direct their attentions toward me rather than the actual thief."

Loch Irvine's brow had canted down again. "I didna know the villain had borrowed your name."

"Apparently he resembles me, and I'm afraid it has caused me some difficulty. I was obliged to abandon my horse quite suddenly near Luss."

"Blast poor luck." The duke scowled. "I'll give you the loan o' one o' my own, o' course. And I'll call off the reward."

"I am much obliged. I should also be grateful for the loan of a carriage and team, only to drive to Ardlui, however."

"Found the missing girl, have you?"

"Woman," Colin corrected, and the duke's eyes sharpened. "No. Not yet. But the imposter's accomplice seems to be a small man who occasionally dresses as a lady—as a distraction to their victims, I suspect. It has put an actual lady of my acquaintance in danger down in Balloch, and she has been traveling with me—rather, fleeing danger with me—for several days now. The carriage is to return her to her own vehicle."

The duke studied him. "'Tis a strange, unlikely tale you're telling."

"No more strange or unlikely than a duke who is generally assumed to be an abductor and murderer of maidens never once speaking up to defend himself," he replied smoothly. The hairs on the back of his neck were prickling, every muscle aware of the simmering violence of the man standing before him.

"Are you threatening me?" Loch Irvine snarled.

Colin lifted a single brow. "Is there any reason that I should?"

Thoughts, then, seemed to pass behind the duke's deep eyes in rapid succession. Abruptly his massive shoulders slumped. The air about him shifted.

"A lady o' your acquaintance?" he said.

"An actual lady." Colin offered a man-to-man smile. "I've had the devil of a time of it, in fact." *An understatement.* "Will you offer me a drink finally?"

A smile flashed before the duke moved to the sideboard.

"I'll send the carriage to the inn in the morning." He poured two glasses and gave one to Colin. "Will that suit you?"

"Quite well. And you will call off the hounds?"

"Aye. I'll send word by a swift rider." Loch Irvine swallowed half the glassful in a gulp.

"I am obliged to you." Colin swiveled the whiskey, its smoky tang in his nostrils but the scent of her skin suddenly everywhere in his memory. Her mouth had tasted of whiskey when he kissed her in that sheep farmer's kitchen like a youth tasting his first girl, tentatively, carefully, so afraid she would bolt. Yet she had not.

Then, on the road, she had kissed him back.

"Which actual lady?" Loch Irvine's grumble speared through his bemusement.

"Emily Vale" fell across his tongue before he could catch it, and he was abruptly looking into deep brown eyes filled with surprise. "I trust in your discretion, Loch Irvine," he said, watching the duke's gaze shutter swiftly.

Intelligent. That was what Constance had said of Loch Irvine. Savvy. *Secretive.*

He added, "Lady Emily has suffered the worst sort of inconvenience to be trapped in this misfortune that is in no way her fault—rather the thieves', and yours, and very likely mine as well."

"Aye," Loch Irvine rumbled. "A man dinna steal another man's name without reason."

"That has been my thought as well. But I trust you not to share her part in this with anyone."

"Who do you imagine I'd be telling?" Loch Irvine drained his glass and set it on the sideboard. "Your secret's safe." He looked over his shoulder. "And hers. They'll no' be sharing her name in the village either," he said seriously, a man certain of the loyalty of his people.

"I am in your debt."

The duke went to the door. "Pike'll show you out." Then he was gone and the little footman who had given Colin entrance earlier was standing in the doorway. He followed him to the main portal.

Loch Irvine was a peculiar man. Yet Colin trusted him.

At an early age he had learned how to read people. In his

childhood, in the months between holidays with the Vale family—endless months during which he saw no one but servants—he had found diversion in filling his silence with careful observations of every sound he heard, every shifting tone of voice, every whiff of scent, every shade and color, every sensation that came to his fingertips and skin and tongue. From his corner of silence, he had grown expert at noting the minutest tick of a man's brow, the twitch of a woman's lips, the tilt of a child's head, the *tap-tapping* of a toe or *snuff-sniffing* of a whiskered nose or *scritch-scratching* of a head. Human movement and human sound became his playmates. And eventually he had learned how to interpret them.

After his mother's death the court had been a hushed place full of shadows into which he had faded. Most of the time, when the earl was in London for the session, Colin went about the house and estate unnoticed. Sometimes the servants saw him watching them while they talked or gossiped as they worked. They would lower their voices, but they never halted their conversations. It was as though they knew that the speechless heir of Egremoor would not share what he heard with anyone.

He had not. He might have written to his father about any or all of what he heard. But he had not listened with that purpose. He had listened because their worries and angers and joys and hurts and all that they felt made him feel less alone. They made him *feel*.

Pairing the silent language of their bodies with their words that he envied, from profound loneliness he had taught himself the skill of discerning in a man or woman's smallest sound or slightest action everything he needed to know to understand them.

At the time he had not known that skill was valuable.

Years later, the man who became his mentor saw the ability in him, and he had cultivated it to serve his needs. While other young men of his birth spent their days in town whoring and gaming away their income, Colin welcomed the tasks set before him, honing his skill. A man must first be able to understand others in order to control them, the earl always said. What better way to control the inferior people who would someday be his responsibility than by practicing on his unwitting peers?

He had never believed it, though—not during his childhood—that the tenant farmers and gentry of Egremoor were his inferiors in anything other than rank. How could they be when they could speak and he could not? Nor had he believed that the director of the Falcon Club was motivated wholly by honor. But he had gone along with it. In the steely gray succession of duties to the earldom and England that his life became, the alternatives of mild dissipation, inexhaustible gossip, and elegant ennui that were the life's blood of his social set had not appealed to him.

So he could read people like books. And now it was entirely clear to him that the Duke of Loch Irvine was, in fact, hiding a secret. It was equally clear that the duke himself was not villainous. As such, he was not Colin's concern.

Emily was. Again, after so many years, she was his responsibility—Emily, whose every emotion showed in her brilliant eyes and upon her mobile mouth and across her soft skin, and yet whose thoughts were nevertheless entirely a mystery to him.

Of every soul he had ever met, she alone overthrew his unique ability to see into another's mind and heart and draw out what he needed from them.

She alone.

Where she was concerned, he was blind. Deaf. *Mute.* Entirely undone. *She* was the festival, a revelry of colors and sounds and textures and scents that filled his senses until he could not breathe, could not think, could not *speak* for being sunk so deeply in sensation. With her he was on his knees in the midst of a decadent cacophony of feelings, entirely at her mercy.

And she had no idea.

SHE PACED THE parlor, her eyes not seeing the comfortable furniture or cozy fire or rug beneath her slippers, nor the hem of a gown far too fine for her tastes or even the door upon which her gaze was fixed. He had not returned from Castle Kallin, and she could not make herself sit.

No rumors suggested that the Duke of Loch Irvine abducted or murdered *men*, of course. And if it came to it she suspected that Colin could hold his own at fisticuffs; there must be a reason he maintained all of those hard muscles beneath his coat, after all.

But he was exhausted, and she could not cease imagining the worst-possible scenarios. His horse might stumble in the dark and he would tumble into a ravine. He might get trampled by cattle, or fall afoul of the imposter earl and his accomplice, or ride swiftly away sighing in relief at finally being rid of her.

Her sister was safe, healthy, full of energy, and determined to prove the duke's innocence to the world as soon as she could gain access to his castle. That Zenobia could not dissuade her from this mission was clear from the fervor in Amarantha's eyes and the firm set of her lips. They had decided she would keep the appointment at the castle the following day. In turn she had made Amy promise to write to Constance in Edinburgh if she found herself in need, and to write to her in London as soon as she could send a letter without detection. Then they had embraced, said good-bye, and she had returned to the inn to discover that Colin was still absent.

Now, with the weight of months of worry lifted, and the certainty that Peregrine would never find poor Penny Baker and demand Lady Justice's true identity as reward, she had only one wish: to collect Clarice and Jonah and return home as swiftly as possible. Few in the village seemed concerned about the thieves; their misdeeds were mere rumor this far from Loch Lomond. With the Duke of Loch Irvine's assistance, they would finally throw off the danger pursuing them. Then she would be free to set out to Ardlui where she would reunite with her friends.

And yet the more she imagined driving away from Colin,
the more swiftly her feet paced from one side of the room to
the other and back again.

Amarantha's astonishment over finding her with him
could not have been greater. Whenever her parents mentioned the hoped-for marriage, her instant dismissal of the
idea had long since led her sisters to believe that she despised him and would never agree to such a thing.

She wouldn't—still—no matter how fantastically good it
felt to kiss him. Nothing had changed in that.

But she did not despise him. She thought now that perhaps she never had and it was a rude, hard, painful awakening to her own willful prejudice to stand in the middle of
Mrs. Tarry's lovely parlor and finally understand herself.

For years she had been spinning her thoughts onto reams
of paper, sharing her feelings freely with thousands of
people, including one exasperating man. Yet she had absolutely no idea what to *do* or *say* when he told her she made
him think of mattresses. She was a wreck at flirtation and in
any case she could not quite believe he was flirting with her.
Which only meant that he truly meant what he said. Which
had nothing to do with the man she had believed him to be
for years.

If only they could return to chilly indifference in person
and vicious insults in writing. *That* she knew how to do.
This—this merely glancing at him and feeling her entire body
flush with excited anticipation—this was alien and terrifying
and she wanted to pack it into a ball of clay and cast it into
a lake, as they had done when they were children and wrote
secret magical spells that she did not want her sisters to find.

The door opened and Colin came through it.

Her cheeks flamed hot as coals.

He, however, was perfect—perfect as always, a bit tousled from riding in the cold, with color high on his cheekbones, yet nevertheless severe and handsome and strong and
utterly confident in the manner in which he merely entered a
room and seemed to command it.

Arrested just inside the doorway, he stared, and she resisted the violent urge to turn away. She *longed* for him. She wanted that strength holding her, touching her, and his mouth giving her pleasure. It was most certainly her mature female body signaling its readiness to procreate with a virile male. It was a perfectly natural reaction.

That did not make it *right*. He was her most virulent public detractor, who made light of the suffering of others simply to amuse his fellow lords who despised Lady Justice too. Her intellect was screaming at her to run, but there was such a desperate ache in her chest, and she knew it was not her mature body or any other sort of thin excuse that attached her feet now to the floor. It was *he*. This man. Only this man.

Because he had carried her up a mountain and ridden a carriage horse and eaten raw mushrooms and barely slept in days in order to ensure her safety. Because he had been considerate of the Archers even when they doubted his word. Because he had offered Davie Wallace an entire farm though he might have offered him much less. Because he had wrested a tiny peasant girl from unspeakable circumstances despite the inconvenience and sheer insanity of abducting a child from her own family while being pursued by people who already thought he was a thief and a murderer. Because even now he was staring at her across the parlor as though he intended to rescue her from those pursuers.

And because he was an arrogant, privileged, haughty aristocrat who thought far too highly of his own consequence, but he was still Colin, *her* Colin, and she had always adored him, even when she had hated him.

"What is it?" He shut the door without taking his gaze from her. "Has something happened?"

"Why did you go without me?"

"You were asleep. Haste was essential."

"Will the duke help us?"

"Yes," he said, not coming forward. "You are obviously distressed. Tell me what is wrong."

"I—" she said, then her lips snapped shut of their own accord. With the same torrent of need that always drove her pen to write impassioned speeches, she forced her lips open. "I was thinking of you. I was thinking of you kissing me. Of how I wanted it to go on and on. And of how I want you to kiss me again."

He did not move. "You said it was a mistake. You told me to stop."

"I *want* it to be a mistake."

"Emily." His voice was stripped. "This is killing me."

Killing him?

"What is?" she said.

"*You*. Are you so thoroughly unaware—so naïve—that you cannot see it?"

"I am not naïve." Not as he assumed. "I am confused. I didn't know it was possible for me to kill anyone. Most especially not you. Until two days ago I thought you hated me."

"I do," he said upon a rasp. "I did. No. That is—*no*. No. Never. Never you. Rather, myself."

"You hated yourself for wanting to kiss me?"

"*No*." He looked up, away, and his throat worked. "My God, Emily—"

"Colin—"

"*Nothing* is as it should be." He ran a hand through his hair, mussing the dark locks and gripping his head. "I don't know what's happening to me. I just spent an hour with Loch Irvine and I haven't any idea what we spoke of. None. I cannot think, and my hands are shaking so hard I could barely hold the reins as I rode here. It's a miracle I made it back alive."

"You haven't slept in days. You are exhausted."

"I want you."

The air clogged in her windpipe.

"I want you, Emily." His eyes were so dark, fevered, and awash in vulnerability.

"It's—it is only a—a *distraction*, you said," she whispered. "Isn't it?"

"Not any longer. Oh, God—it never was." His breaths were hard, fast. "I thought I could control it. I thought I—" The muscles in his jaw flexed. "I was wrong. Despite your very clearly stated feelings, I cannot—*cannot* control it. And now—" His hands fisted at his side, the knuckles white. "This is unendurable. I should not have kissed you. I beg your pardon for it."

"But we now know something because of it. And kn-knowledge is always a good thing."

"That depends on the particular knowledge." He looked entirely uncertain. "What do we know now?"

"That I want you to do it again! Didn't you even hear what I said a *minute* ago? Why doesn't anyone ever listen to m—"

It took him less than an instant to cross the room and even less time to attach their mouths and to coax her lips apart with his. She parted them willingly, eagerly, welcoming his heat and his hands, and the shocking, perfect intimacy of his tongue stroking hers. Then his mouth was on her neck, her neck arching, his body pressing hers to the wall. She moaned and his hands swept from beneath her arms down her sides, rising again to surround the sides of her breasts.

"I listen," he uttered against her throat, his teeth against her skin making her wild. "Say that you want me too and I'll listen for as long as you wish."

"Only—*ohh*." He caressed her and she reached for air, found it, barely. "Only if I say what you wish?"

He pressed his lips to her ear, held her tightly and abruptly very still.

"Always," he said with raw vehemence. "Whatever you say. However you say it. When you speak, I will always listen."

A sob broke from her chest with a harsh, sudden jolt. A scream climbed up her throat after it, bubbling to burst out, a geyser of guilt and futile regret that he caught with his lips and silenced. She choked on the smothered sound and fought to breathe. He kissed her cheek, her jaw, her mouth again.

She clutched at his shoulders. "I do want you. I do."

"Emily," he said with guttural force, capturing her mouth beneath his. Hands wrapping about her waist, he held her tightly and they kissed without restraint, without pause, their mouths hungry, ravenous, as though they had years of kisses stored away now fighting to be given and taken. She sank her fingers into his hair and opened her mouth to him and pulled him closer, then closer still. She wanted it. She wanted it all, *him*, every touch and caress of his hands and mouth and body—his teeth and lips and breaths and flavor—every bit of this man she had believed for years was as cool and passionless as the façade he showed the world. The hunger to have him everywhere on her, *inside her*, was spectacular, unbearable, a pulsing, insistent thing that made her press her body to his. The more they touched, the more she wanted his touching. The pressure of his arousal against hers was at once sublime satisfaction and urgent need.

As though from a great distance voices came, women's voices, and cool air swirling about her arms and washing over her cheeks.

Then he was putting her off of him, separating them, moving away from her, and the parlor door was swinging wide.

Beside the innkeeper, Mrs. Sybil Charney stood in the opening.

It was no doubt a testament to Colin's years of rigid self-discipline that he managed a perfectly reasonable if rather deep "How do you do?" in response to Mrs. Charney's sugary "My lord!" uttered upon a curtsy.

Then it was her turn, and it was most certainly a testament to her utter lack of experience kissing men in parlors—kissing *him*—that the only thing that rushed into her mind was the last place she had seen Sybil Charney, and the last thing she had seen Sybil Charney doing. All that came to her tongue was, "Oh."

"Lady Emily," Mrs. Charney said with another dainty curtsy. "What a delightful surprise to encounter you here." Knowing eyes slewed between them, her lips sliding into a grin. "Are you traveling"—her brows arched delicately—"together?"

"Yes," he said the moment she said, "No."

He glanced at her and then swiftly away.

"Ma'am," Mrs. Tarry said to her new guest, "You'll wish to freshen up after yer journey. I'll show ye to the Olympe de Gouges."

"That will be fine," Mrs. Charney said, her gaze sliding over Colin and then lingering on Zenobia's hair that was certainly disordered; she could feel exactly where his hands had in fact disordered it. "I will see you at dinner," she said with a sweet smile. "I have been sadly bereft of company on this journey. What an enjoyable visit I look forward to this evening."

That she had been far from bereft of company when Zenobia had seen her by that lean-to did nothing to calm the violent heat in her cheeks as Mrs. Tarry shut the door. Colin walked to it and stood facing it, his shoulders rigid. Finally he lifted a hand and ran it over his face, and then turned to her.

"Timely interruption," he said. "Forgive me."

"For not locking the door when you entered the room?"

"For exposing you to that," he said in a low voice. "And for the violence of my—for touching you as I did."

"I wanted you to touch me like that. You didn't do anything I did not do too."

Sparks were playing again in his gaze that had fallen to her lips. "Emily, I—"

"I have done it before, Colin."

His eyes snapped up to hers. "It?"

"I was curious."

Hesitant surprise shifted his features. "What are you saying?"

She folded her damp hands. "I did not care for the idea of someday dying a virgin without knowing everything I could about the experience of being a woman. Childbirth and motherhood were not to be mine. But I wanted to at least experience sexual pleasure with a man. I wanted to understand that ingredient of the stew for which women relinquish their independence so eagerly." She set her shoulders back a bit. "And, actually, I simply wanted it. I felt desire—I saw it— and I wished to feel its depth. It is difficult to be around my friends with their husbands and not occasionally sense the sensuality in the room. I wanted to understand it. So I did it."

He was blinking, again and again, the lush black lashes about his eyes shading the shock in the midnight blue now.

"I . . . I see," he said so quietly that she saw the words move his lips rather than heard the sound of them.

"I have dashed your notions of propriety and feminine modesty all to pieces," she said, a cloying sourness filling her stomach. "I am not ashamed of it. But you are ashamed for me, aren't you? You think I should be ashamed."

He was not looking at her now, rather at a place on the floor in front of her. He did not reply.

"Colin—"

"I—I need air." He swung around, pulled the door open with a swift, clean movement, and went out.

She remained standing in the middle of the room, her face hot and hands cold with anger and hurt and disappointment so acute, so painful, that for several minutes she could not move. But she had not needed this to prove that he and she were fundamentally different. In their world, his standards reigned. It was the reason she gathered knowledge as she did and wrote about what she learned. It was the reason she was who she was. And, for all his vows that he would listen, she was a woman whose words he would never truly hear.

Closing her eyes, she drew in a long breath and released it slowly. Then she went to the bell pull and rang for her dinner.

Chapter 19

Some Other Truths

He had never felt such fury, such violent, hard, twisted rage that if a man stepped into his path at this moment he would tear him apart before asking his business. He was a half mile along the road, swallowed in darkness illumined by the crescent moon and the stars, before he trusted himself enough to slow his pace.

Propriety.

Feminine modesty.

Ashamed.

Every word was like a red-hot brand dead center of his chest.

Shame: one emotion he understood well, too well, the emotion that had made him study through endless hours when he was a child, that had driven him to excel at every task his tutor put before him and during those hellish months at school. Shame: the emotion that had made him a strong horseman, expert driver, accurate shot, more than competent fencer, fine boxer, and successful at the hunt and every other sport a boy could master. Shame: the emotion that had bound him to the earl's side as he had ridden across Egremoor, listening and learning and asking questions about the craft of farming and the skill of leading other men when he had wanted to be almost anywhere else—when he wanted most to be with the only person in the world who had never once made him feel ashamed of what he was.

The only living person.

He wanted to feel ashamed of her now. He wanted to rail at her father for the loose rein he had kept on his daughter that had allowed her to do what a woman of her birth and breeding should not. He wanted to accuse her of being spoiled and two-faced, the maidenly spinster who was a thorough sham.

But he felt none of that. Her lusty nature was a dream he hadn't even had the courage to conjure. It was a miracle. For God's sake, he would *celebrate* it if he weren't so sick to his stomach.

Boots skidding to a halt, he doubled over, pressing his palms into his knees and dragging air into his lungs.

Here was proof—the proof that only now he realized he had been awaiting—the final proof that she had never intended to marry him. *Never.* She had told him so. But he hadn't believed her. Not really. Not entirely. And yet years ago she had decided without doubt that she would not marry him.

While he had not.

Not consciously.

It was the most irresponsible thing he had ever done, the *only* irresponsible thing: failing to honor the promise that two comrades in arms had made to each other a continent and a lifetime ago, binding their children at birth to an arrangement more typical of medieval lords than modern men. He had consistently refused to even address the issue; he had never made it clear to either Vale or the earl that he would not marry her. And he didn't know why he had not. Because he was too much of a coward to refuse the earl's demands outright? Because he did not wish to hurt her—though in avoiding it so dishonorably he would have done exactly that if she had actually been waiting for him? Because pretending she simply did not exist was easier than . . . than *this*? Knowing her again. Caring for her. *Needing her.*

While she had moved on long ago, unconcerned, oblivious to the lies he had been telling himself for years, uninterested in whether she ever saw him again or not.

The Scottish night was cold and clear. He heard the men's voices before he saw their black silhouettes. Two men, walking up the road toward him.

It was too late to run. Too late to hide. He stood in the center of the road and he waited, and watched them come.

MRS. CHARNEY CAST HER playful glances throughout dinner. But the presence of two other guests defeated the busybody's attempts to wheedle information from her. Zenobia concentrated her attention on the elderly gentlewomen, encouraging them to share details about their journey. By the time they said good-night she was certain she knew everything there was to know about every inn along the west-east road across Scotland. They had heard nothing of the imposter earl, which was reassuring. When Mrs. Charney mentioned that her coachman had gotten news of the thieves days ago in Luss, Zenobia felt green about the gills.

She could not help but wonder that if she and Mrs. Charney were men instead of women, would she ask her now about disporting with the coachman? Perhaps she would jibe her, chuckling and raising a salacious brow, nodding as if she knew exactly what had gone on behind that lean-to.

Men were curious creatures.

If she were a man, she would ask outright. She would want to know what had pleased them both so extraordinarily well that they had been entirely oblivious to the scratchy grass and damp ground and the woman standing a dozen yards away staring in fascination. But if she were a man, of course, she probably would not now want to learn the details of it so she could do it to the Earl of Egremoor.

In her imagination only. The potential for making that dream into reality had swiftly, harshly become moot.

She set down her teacup. "I will turn in—"

"Oh, no you don't," Mrs. Charney said with a glimmering grin, and blocked the doorway. "You shan't escape me. I vow to never tell another living soul, of course. But you must give me at least a little something to chew on."

"Mrs. Charney, I have had an unbelievably long day, and am drooping. I can offer you nothing chewable at this time."

"Nothing?" She pouted. "Dear me, Lady Emily, I had imagined you more interestingly unconventional than this. Especially after what I saw earlier." Her smile was pure delight.

"I am unconventional, it is true. But not unconventional enough to share with a stranger my personal business. If you will excuse me—"

"So it *was* personal?" she said, thrusting out a staying hand swathed in lace. "How positively delicious!"

Zenobia screwed up her brow and at that moment the door behind Mrs. Charney opened, and there was Colin.

Mrs. Charney pivoted, her frothy skirts swirling about the earl's ankles. She dropped a curtsy that put her face perilously close to the level where it had hovered by her coachman at the lean-to.

"My lord," she cooed. "We were just speaking of you."

"No, we were *not*," Zenobia said as his gaze came quickly to her. "She was asking questions and I was not answering them. Now, if both of you would move out of the doorway, I would like to go to—"

"Mrs. Charney," he said in a gorgeously smooth baritone, "would you be so kind as to allow Lady Emily and me a moment's privacy before she retires?" He smiled gallantly, almost intimately, as though he were certain she would comply, at once taking the woman into his confidence and ejecting her completely from it.

Mrs. Charney's lashes batted several star-struck times.

"Of *course*, my lord." And then with a frilly twirl of

skirts she was gone, and Colin was closing the door. He did not lock it. While she knew that was for the best, she hated him a little bit for it.

"Where have you been?" she said.

"Drinking whiskey with the veterans of Waterloo with whom you made friends earlier today. They were full of your praises."

"Was that only today? It seems a lifetime ago already." A lifetime during which she had found her sister and lost him—again.

"Doesn't it?" he said mildly.

"And you were drinking whiskey?" *With vagabonds?*

He nodded. "Excellent whiskey. There is apparently a distillery on Loch Irvine's property."

"Oh."

"That response was unusually cloquent for you," he said.

"I've just said I had a long day."

"Who was he?"

"He?"

"The man you gave yourself to. Or *men*," he added upon a jerk of his Adam's apple.

Nausea welled up in her chest. "Are you drunk?"

"Not in the least."

"I did not give myself to him. I shared sexual relations with him, briefly, temporarily. Throughout and afterward I retained full possession of myself." She knew she was saying too much, speaking in Lady Justice's voice, and that she must not. But he looked confused, as though he did not— *could not*—comprehend the words. It was painful, and she wanted it to stop. "My maidenhead is not me, Colin. It never was. My mind and heart and my *entire* body are."

"All right," he said slowly. "I understand."

"Do you?"

"I am trying to." He drew a deep breath. "Who was he?"

"You don't honestly expect me to tell you, do you?"

"Yes," he growled. "Yes, I do."

"Lord Abernathy."

Stunned astonishment washed over his face. *"Abernathy?"*

"He is attractive and unmarried. And I knew from gossip that he would be willing. He has a reputation for seducing maidens who subsequently fall in love with him, which led me to assume that all of those maidens must be very foolish or that he is very good at it. I decided the latter explanation was more likely, so I asked him. He promised secrecy, and to my knowledge he has kept to that. I have told no one, not even Clarice. Except you now."

He looked as though he might be ill. Then murderous intensity came into his eyes.

It reignited her anger.

"Oh, good grief, Colin. Must you be so thoroughly tedious? I am not married or a nun. I haven't broken any vows. It's not as though *you* are a virgin, after all." Her brows perked. "Are you?"

"For God's sake, how could you have been so careless—"

"Of my reputation? In truth, it wouldn't matter if he told anyone. No one would believe it of me. There are some small advantages to everybody thinking I am a recluse."

"Careless of your *safety*," he bit out. "He might have hurt you."

His words were cold rain upon her indignation. And unexpected.

"I know," she said. "But he did not."

He came forward until he stood very close and his gaze was all over her. "Was he—did he treat you well?"

Her throat clogged. This she had not expected either. "Yes. Quite well. I enjoyed it. When he offered to meet again—"

"Again?"

"Don't be such an angry bull. He only asked once, and I declined. Without regret. It had been difficult to conceal it from both his household and mine. He said he would be happy to hire a room at an inn but I didn't like the possibility of being accidentally seen by someone who might know me."

His nostrils flared. "Didn't you?"

"And timing is always tricky, of course."

"Timing?"

"Just as you, I am not keen on having a child out of wedlock. My family would suffer for it. My youngest sisters are not yet wed and it could hurt their prospects. But the reason I told you the truth about it was to make it clear that you needn't apologize to me. I am no innocent to be despoiled by a passionate kiss." She lifted her eyes. "Although, admittedly, that time—with him—did not feel like this."

"This?"

"Kissing you. Touching you. Being touched by you. Standing before you when you look at me like this."

His chest rose upon a hard inhalation. "Didn't it?"

"There was pleasure, but there was no . . ."

"No what?"

"Fever. Need. Desperation for more that leaves me feeling like another person altogether."

"Do you want to be that other person, the person who feels those things?"

She gazed into his beautiful midnight eyes and she shook her head. "No."

She had not lifted a hand and yet he looked as though she had struck him. She backed away from him. Then she went around him and out of the parlor.

Sybil Charney was lingering in the corridor before a door marked "Olympe de Gouges" in crisp cursive.

"Mrs. Charney, have you been waiting here to discover whether I left Lord Egremoor alone or snuck away with him to my bedchamber?"

"Absolutely not! Well, perhaps I was. Lady Emily, you are a fantastic tease!"

"Not really. Sometimes I wish I were. But that is not how I think people should behave with each other. Teasing is dishonest." She went to her door. Mrs. Charney stood watching her.

Zenobia returned to her. "Are you continuing on

tomorrow? That is, are you leaving early in the morning to go wherever it is you are going on this journey?"

"I have no fixed plans," she said with a lovely twinkle of her eyes. "I am on holiday, darling Lady Emily, from my wretched husband. I know! I know I should not speak ill of him. But he is such a miserable person, and I am positively reveling in your little romance that I have stumbled upon, you see, so I feel that I can confide in you. Also, you won't tell anyone."

"Because I don't have any acquaintance that you share in London?"

"No, darling. Because you have *morals*."

"You have seen me kissing a man to whom I am not married or even betrothed. How do you then conclude that I have morals?"

"There is a lot more to morality than illicit kisses, darling," Mrs. Charney said with a tick of her fingertip toward Zenobia's nose. "Anyway, at present I can do whatever I please. What are your plans for tomorrow? More trysts with that gorgeous man?"

"I have an appointment at the castle at dawn. But I have no transportation. May I borrow your carriage? And, er, your coachman?"

"Lady *Emily*. Have you an assignation with the duke? How positively frisky you are! Two lovers at once. Who would have thought it of you?"

"An assignation? No! I only—"

"And you wish to keep it a secret from his lordship. He is so spectacularly honorable, of course, he would never understand a dalliance on the side. Pity." She shook her head. Then her eyes brightened. "Though, you know, men are jealous creatures. If Lord Egremoor heard of your peccadillo through some back channel, he might be inspired to offer for you. I would be happy to drop the word into his ear, innocently, of course, as though I had absolutely no idea what I was divulging. I'm very good at that sort of thing."

"No, truly, Mrs. Charney. The last thing I wish is to inspire him to propose marriage to me." *Again*. "I—"

"Do call me Sybil." She made a pretty moue of her lips. "Though I don't think we can be very good friends if you truly would not want a handsome earl to propose to you. What an odd creature you would be, to be sure! But darling Lady Emily, whatever your business is with Loch Irvine, I will be delighted to take you in my carriage to the castle to-morrow at dawn. I insist that you introduce me to him before you go off and do whatever it is you plan to do with him. I have been dying to meet him, whatever they're saying about devils and such. I hear he is a great big handsome bear of a man. And I do like my men big." She smiled like a cat.

"My meeting is not with the duke, but with someone, I believe, who is employed at the castle. But if I do become acquainted with him, I promise to make the introduction."

"Splendid!"

"Thank you, Sybil. You are very kind to help me."

Her brows flew upward. "Kind?"

"Yes. You needn't help me. I haven't paid you any attention in London, and you haven't made any effort to know me beyond our introduction because I am not fashionable. But you have just offered to assist me, and that is a kindness on your part. I am grateful for it."

"Oh." Her cheeks were spots of rosy chagrin. "Of course."

Zenobia said good-night and went into her bedchamber. Glorious white silk nightclothes embroidered with exotic lilies and trimmed in delicate lace had been laid across the bed. Twisting her arms to unfasten Miss Sophie's gown and undergarments, she removed them and put them carefully in the clothes press. She saw no reason to soil multiple garments simply to sleep. So she left the night shift on a chair and drew the silky dressing gown over her shoulders and cinched it about the waist.

But standing beside the luxurious bed she could not imagine sleeping. Despite her weariness, she could not even bring herself to lie down.

Slinging her cloak over the dressing gown, she pulled it tight across her breasts and went to request that tea be brought to her room an hour before dawn—quietly. Colin must not hear her depart. She supposed Sybil would be careful not to be heard too; it was clear enough that she was proficient at executing secret assignations.

Silence had fallen in the inn for the night and she padded on bared feet to the ground floor. In the large, neat kitchen she found Rebecca and made her request. Returning up the stairs, she came to the landing. Fingers wrapped around the door handle, Colin stood before a door upon which the word SAPPHO was painted in roman block capitals.

"Do you know," he said, turning his face to her, "in nearly thirty-two years I have only ever apologized to one person, and that was a matter of honor. And yet today I apologized to you at least three times. Perhaps four." A lock of hair had fallen over his brow, and the candle on the table in the corridor cast his cheeks into stark angles. She wanted to brush the hair from his eyes and wrap her arms around him and hold him.

"I did not ask you to apologize," she said. "I did not ask you for anything."

"I think, actually, that you asked me to kiss you. But perhaps that was my hopeful imagination playing tricks on me. As you said, I haven't slept much recently."

"It cannot be." She gripped the stair railing. "Nothing can happen between us. It is simply not . . . possible."

He saw her fingers wound about the railing as though he were feeling the smooth, polished wood himself, as though his veins were distended in his own hand as he clutched it. But it was her hand, her veins, her intensity, her beauty. And she was telling him that it could not be his.

"I adored you," she whispered across the space between them. "With all the trust that a little girl can hold in her heart as easily as she holds a flower in the palm of her hand—I adored you. But I am no longer a little girl, and you have changed."

Beneath his ribs he felt such pain he could barely endure it, as though a great axe had smashed down upon the granite mass of his chest and cleaved it apart.

Releasing the railing, she came toward him, the hem of her cloak brushing the floor with a *hush-hush*, bringing with her the aromas of rosemary and bread that had been baked for the morning. She had been in the kitchen, perhaps, wearing a cloak and, beneath it, a garment of some shimmery ivory fabric that whispered against her legs. She halted before him and her eyes were like a forest at night. If she allowed him the time, he could count every one of the silvery-golden hairs that had escaped the hastily tied ribbon.

"What if I weren't that man," he said, "the man you believe me to be now? What if instead I were the man you imagine I could have become?"

"I think if that were so," she said, "I would be frightened."

"Frightened?"

The emerald green was full of feeling. "The man you are now makes me want you—more than I understand. I am afraid that if I felt anything more for you, I would—"

He grasped her arm, swung her against his chest, and kissed her.

Chapter 20

A Thorough Loss of Control

He kissed her deeply. She opened her lush lips and let him inside her and he tasted and tasted and tasted again until he was drunk, finally. They clung to each other, his hands covering her waist and hips, feeling her, her fingers pulling at his shoulders, pulling him as close as she could.

"Let me be that man," he said against her skin, "the man who frightens you because he makes you feel what you have not felt before. Let me be him."

She kissed him. Drinking from his lips, she cupped his face in her hands and pressed her lithe body to his.

He kicked open the door to his bedchamber and pulled her inside. He lifted her as easily as if she were a feather, her garment gathering at her hips as he pressed her back against the closed door and made her straddle him. His body was hard and powerful, his hands on her bare skin grasping her thighs and forcing her to him, making her feel his arousal.

"You drive me mad," he said against her throat, his voice rough and wonderfully urgent.

Thrills of disbelief rolled in her. And now that she was here, now that she was finally allowing herself him, she wanted every part of him at once. With her hands she pushed his coat from his shoulders and felt the bone and muscles that inspired her lust so thoroughly. She bore down on his arousal, hungry, aching with hunger, and kissed him open-mouthed as his hands clasped her buttocks and ground her against him. She felt the sweet, urgent tension, the marvel of pleasure rising and throbbing. Her mouth needed him, her tongue, to taste him and touch him and feel him. She bent her head and spread her lips over his neck, and his body shuddered. He smelled of whiskey and soap and him, and she licked his skin, hungry for his flavor, hungry to know him. She was wet against the fabric of his breeches, making love to him through his clothing, hot and open and shaking and ready for him to be undressed and inside her—*so ready.* Thrusting to him, she moaned.

Beneath her hands, his muscles were hardening, his shoulders and neck like rock. But quite suddenly she could wait no longer. She surged against him.

"Emily," he groaned, gripping her hips hard. "*Stop.* You must—"

"*Now.*" It rose in her and she whimpered. "Please, Colin." She bit his lower lip and gyrated her hips, reaching to unfasten his breeches. "Now. I—"

"*Emily.*"

He clamped her to him and her body convulsed, a hard, deep jolt that shuddered to her throat with a cry that mingled with his groan. She rode him, finding her pleasure deeper and gasping as it filled her.

When she covered his lips with hers, his breaths were trembling, like his arms locked to hold her so tightly to him. He kissed her. She surrounded his face with her hands and tasted every bit of his mouth, his tongue and teeth and lips.

"That was"—he said between her kisses—"not exactly

what I hoped." His voice was deliciously deep and thoroughly unsteady.

She was boneless, and radiating warmth everywhere inside and out as though she were a cake directly from the oven. Draping her arms over his partially undressed shoulders, she buried her nose against his neck and heaved in an enormous breath.

"It was divine," she sighed and found that she had to explore the hot, perfect place behind his ear with her lips. His quick intake of breath and hands tightening around her hips were precious bits of miracle. "Perfect," she whispered, sinking her fingers into his hair and breathing him in.

"Do you—do you understand what just happened?" he said.

"Do I understand that the bed is two yards away yet neither of us could wait to get there? Yes." His skin was hot beneath her lips. "I think it was all of that riding."

"I feel like I'm sixteen again," he said, then in an odd voice, quieter: "Rather, twenty-one."

"Given the precipitate nature of boys in all things, sixteen I think I understand," she murmured against his neck. "Why twenty-one?"

His hands tightened on her hips.

"Why twenty-one?" she repeated.

He said nothing and she pulled back a bit so she could look into his eyes.

"Colin?"

"I visited Willows Hall for the last time when I was twenty-one."

"For my parents' Christmas party, the party to which they invited everybody in the world. The house was overrun with society."

"You remember," he said quietly, surprised.

"I remember because I was miserable that entire fortnight. I could not find even an empty nook in which to hide. But I wonder that you recall it. You were not there more than a day."

"Long enough to—" He bent his head.

She scraped her fingertips lightly over his cheek. Her palm cupped his jaw and urged his face up. "To what?"

"Emily," he said upon a warning growl.

"Colin, you must tell me now. I am all curiosity."

"For the party," he said slowly, "your mother had dressed you in a new gown, suited to a lady rather than a girl. You hated it."

"I did. It was my first grown-up party dress. The stays I was obliged to wear were the height of ridiculous French fashion and wretchedly tight. But how do you know that I hated it?"

"I could see it in your scowl at that party. Your eyes have always been beacons of your every emotion."

The tenderness in his voice made her heart do a little jerk. *Foolishness.* He did not know her every emotion. He never would.

"You did not speak to me at that party," she said. "You did not speak to me the entire twenty-four hours you were on the estate on that occasion." He barely had for years before that, not directly.

"You looked exactly as your mother wished you to in that gown: like a woman."

"Yet I felt as comfortable as a modiste's dress stand."

"It was the first time I saw your breasts."

She frowned. "You had been to Willows Hall only six months earlier for—"

"Your skin. Your flesh. With so little covering—with almost nothing covering your breasts," he said huskily. "The first time."

"Probably the only time. I don't think I have worn such a silly gown since. The bodice was nearly nonexistent."

"Listen to me, Emily," he said quietly.

Leaning back in his arms, she closed her lips.

"It was a revelation," he said.

"That I had breasts? I suppose I see how that could be, men being generally preoccupied by women's breasts, after all. Why are you comparing it to this moment?"

"Straight to the point, always with you."

"It makes everything easier," she said, untying his neckcloth.

"A man in my position—a man mustn't ever lose control of himself."

"Lose control? But—*oh*. I understand. Like we did just now." She tilted her head to lay her lips lightly upon his. "You needn't be chagrined to have lost control." She brushed her lips over his until he met the caress. This—kissing him—was so easy, so good, so real. "I helped you," she said. "I encouraged it."

"You did not help the night of that party."

Air slipped sickly through her lips. "Did someone else?"

"If by someone else you mean my own hand, yes." He was again breathing hard and he blinked as though he were just waking up. "Good God, this is the most difficult thing I have ever said to anyone in my entire life."

"That *cannot* be true."

"Yet it is. Emily, that night I barely made it to privacy on time to save myself from public disgrace."

"I was oblivious! Actually, I didn't even know men did that sort of thing. Not then."

"You shouldn't have. And it was not intentional. I was a grown man, yet I lost control of myself."

"Because of *me*." She could not believe it. "Because from across a room you saw my breasts in that gown."

He nodded.

"*My* breasts? Are you certain?"

"Emily," he said, looking away.

"Had that happened before? In that manner, without—without—"

"Stimulation? No."

"What about after? Because of"—she swallowed dryly—"any other woman?"

"No." A tentative smile lifted the corner of his beautiful lips. "You always made me do what no one else could." Then the smile faded. "You are—you have always been—the exception."

"Colin," she said, and her voice trembled a little. "Make love to me now. I want you to lose control again, and this time I want to feel it happen inside of me."

"How is it that you speak about this as about everything else, with such unashamed ease?"

"Why should I be ashamed to feel the desire that is natural to my body? And why should I not speak about it? Because I am a woman?"

"Because I don't want you to speak about it to any man except me." Naked honesty shone in his dark eyes.

She kissed him on his lips, then on his throat, then along the uncompromising line of his jaw. He carried her to the bed and set her on her feet beside it and unfastened the sash of her dressing gown. It fell open but his gaze was on her face as he stroked a strand of hair from before her eyes.

"You are beautiful," he whispered.

"I am not. Especially not among the women of your acquaintance. Constance is beautiful, spectacularly so. And Kitty is gorgeous and elegant. And my sisters, all of them, each one prettier than the next. I have always been a pigeon among doves."

His smile was gently tolerant. "You have no idea what you're talking about."

"I particularly dislike it when men say that to women."

"Your perception of yourself is inaccurate."

"You mustn't think that I mind my lack of beauty. I never cared about frills and furbelows anyway." She spread her hands on his chest. "That is—I did mind it, when I was young and I knew little more than my parents' beauty and my mother's preoccupation with dressing up her daughters like dolls. But I eventually came to know people who did not privilege beauty like my parents did and I left off feeling inadequate. More importantly," she added, smoothing her palms over his chest, "my lack of beauty has not prohibited me from attracting a man who wishes to give me pleasure."

"Interesting theory."

"Don't laugh. It is really the only reason I can think of for a woman to be beautiful." All ten of her fingertips pressed into his chest. "It attracts men."

His throat was dry. "Men?"

"Man." With one fingertip she traced a spiral over his ribs. "Are you about to say something foolish?"

"I will now try not to."

"Then I will." She lifted to him eyes dark with desire. "I like that you found me attractive all those years ago. But I am far happier that you find me attractive now, when we can actually do something about it. Now, about that pleasure . . ." She shrugged the dressing gown off her shoulders and it slid to the floor in a shimmery puddle. She stood before him naked and unashamed to be so, looking directly into his eyes, and it was the most erotic thing he had ever seen.

"You needn't say anything," she said softly. "I will probably talk incessantly throughout this, what we are about to do. But you needn't talk at all, if you don't wish to."

The nerves in his stomach bunched.

"I want to taste you—everywhere," he said, hunger like the chimes of bells upon his tongue. "I want to touch every part of your body, caress every plane and crevice of your skin. I want to hear your breaths catching against my neck and feel your heart beating too swiftly against my chest. I want your scent on me, and I want you to use me exactly as you wish. Whatever you want of me tonight, I am yours."

A flush of pink had spread across her breasts and throat and cheeks, and her nipples had grown tight. Her sweet lips parted but, astonishingly, she said nothing.

"Does that plan appeal to you?" he said.

She nodded.

"Then I have only one further proviso."

"Another?" Her voice was husky.

"I must be allowed to tell you how beautiful you are without you silencing me."

Awareness came into her eyes, and then distress. "I would *never* try to silence you. I am—oh, Colin—"

He kissed her, taking her into his arms and molding her body to his. She tugged at his clothing, dragging his coat off his shoulders and freeing the long hems of his shirt from his breeches. Sweeping it off, he tossed the soiled linen aside. Then her hands came upon his skin, trailing across his arms and chest and waist, and it was torture, perfect torture to not immediately throw her onto her back and sink himself into her.

One hand stealing up to the back of his neck, she kissed his throat, and her other hand slid over his abdomen to cover his cock.

"Are you—" Her voice seemed to catch. "When will you be ready again?"

He curved his hands down her back. Her skin was fine, thin over her bones, like milk. He forced himself to hold her lightly, loosely. His nose and mouth and head were full of her already, yet still he could scoop her up and consume her in one swallow. He had never understood the peculiar, intense sensitivity of his senses, never known why he had been given this curse.

A curse no longer.

"Whenever you need me," he said.

"Whenever—?" Her eyes shot up to meet his. "Now?"

He smiled, every other muscle in his body in full restraint.

"Good Lord, Colin!" She laughed. "What are you waiting for?" She grasped his arm and pulled. She was a little thing, but he allowed her to draw him onto the bed. He could not tell her the truth: that in fact he had been waiting for this since that night of her parents' party years ago, that he had denied himself this again and again and again until he finally believed he did not want it, and that now he was terrified. If he allowed those words to begin flowing, he would never be able to stanch them.

So he busied his mouth. Spreading her on the mattress, his eyes consuming her pink and milk and silvery-gold beauty illumined by firelight, finally he tasted her. She gasped when his mouth closed over one rosy nipple. It tasted like black currants. She tasted like currants everywhere, sweet and tart and fresh, just like her speech—currants between his teeth and on his tongue. And she felt like silk in his hands and against his cheek. Silk and currants. He got dizzy inhaling.

Wiggling beneath him, she lifted her back from the mattress and whimpered. Her breasts were soft and snugly peaked and perfect in his mouth and hands.

"Oh, Colin—this is—this—" Her eyes were squeezed shut, her lips wide, gulping in air, her hands plucking at the bed linen. She released the coverlet and clutched his waist. "Please consummate this. *Now*. I fear I am on the verge of— *unh!*" She moaned and jerked against his hand. "Re—" She gasped, undulating her hips to his caress even as she pushed at the waistband of his breeches. "Remove these and get inside me." And then she was laughing. "How many times must I tell you to *get on the horse*?" she exclaimed and convulsed in laughter.

He nudged her knees apart, and urged his cock into her. Her laughter ceased abruptly. Her eyes flew open. Then her lips. A groan of pure feminine pleasure spilled from her. Pressing forward, he felt her flesh give way to him. Deeper. And then he was embedded, surrounded by her, locked inside her hot, wet body, her belly flat against his and her thighs cradling his hips. She was tight, so tight, and he was *inside her* and the world was spinning around him, careening.

"Oh," she whispered. A tear fell from the corner of her eye, shimmering a tiny silvery path into her hair. Her fingertips made craters in his shoulders.

"Am I hurting you?" he said—he thought he said he said in the back of his throat. She could not be weeping. *She must not be weeping*.

"No," she barely whispered. "No. No." Now her breasts rose against his chest, hard, harder breaths, one after another. Their bodies were entirely motionless, yet within hers she was working him.

"Emily," he uttered, fighting against the tightening of his ballocks.

"If I move," she mouthed, her delicate, strong muscles massaging him. "If you move—"

"This will swiftly be over."

"Could we remain like this? Just like this? Until the—the urgency passes?"

He almost laughed. He didn't dare. He could barely breathe. "You *must* cease what you are doing," he whispered.

Her lips curved into a devilish grin. He wanted to bite it.

"I don't wish to cease doing it," she hummed, tightening her muscles to his cock again, sending the world spiraling anew, into one place, one nexus, the very center of him. "I enjoy making every tendon in your neck and chest thoroughly distressed," she said.

He drove into her. Capturing her mouth beneath his, he kissed her and took her, hard, faster with each thrust, until they were both gasping, straining. It was a wild, entwined seeking of skin and muscle and heat that forced them deeper and then deeper together. Then, swiftly, they were coming. She cried out his name many times. Her voice was music, sweet and pure and heady and gritty and sounding of sex, of what he was doing to her, of what she was doing to him, everything inside him funneling, tearing, spewing into her. She took him, dragging him in, wrapping herself around him, every part of him inside all of her, and she emptied him with her hands and the taut, glorious pull of her body.

There were stars before his eyes—actual stars.

Gulping air, he touched her, stroked her, eased her through it, through her final, softer moans and then her sighs.

One of her arms dropped to the mattress and her eyes were closed, but her lips were smiling and her fingers were in his hair and her thighs were around his hips.

"I have decided," she said languidly, "that I prefer riding with you in this manner."

He laughed and buried his nose in the silky crook of her neck. Inhaling the air that caressed her skin, he intoxicated himself on the sweet musk of her sweat and some scent of herbs or flowers that clung to her. Absently, it seemed, her fingertips stroked the back of his neck.

They said nothing for some time, their breathing slowing and the dampness of his body growing cool.

When he lifted his head her eyes were open, sleepy but clear. She smiled, simply.

"If I climb off of you," he said, "will you leap up and leave?"

"I won't leave or even leap up." Her fingertips walked along his shoulder and then down his chest. "I will instead wrap myself around you and learn what it is like to lie motionless against a man's body."

His throat was too thick. "A man's body?"

Her gaze slipped away from his.

"Your body," she whispered. "You." And then: "Only you."

He understood. She was making a concession to his jealousy, but she didn't like doing it.

He drew away, kissing her shoulder, and then the swell of her breast, and rolled onto his back. Tugging the bedclothes over them, she turned onto her side, tucking her hands around his arm and her cheek against his shoulder, and curling up so her knees abutted his hip. Possibly she said something then, whispered against his skin. But he was already asleep, or partially asleep, and she would never have said what he thought he'd heard anyway.

"The night is young," she whispered into his ear, sliding her fingertips over his extraordinarily hard pectoral muscles to his equally extraordinary abdominal muscles. "Wake up."

Colin's eyelids flickered but the even cadence of his breathing did not alter.

She put her tongue in his ear.

He woke up.

She traced the edge of his ear with the tip of her tongue, then nibbled on the lobe.

"Nibbleable, indeed," she murmured, and shifted her teeth to his jaw.

"Mm," he mumbled. His chest rose, drawing in a waking inhalation. "What did you say?"

He was beautiful, like a magnificent Greek statue, all noble bones and virile muscles and taut skin and dark hair distributed in ideal places. And the part of him that was hard already now, that had been hard inside her and driven her wild when he moved in her . . . She stroked her hand along it and got an immediate response.

"Actually," he murmured, shifting a bit, "I don't care what you said as long as you continue doing that."

She ceased doing it.

After a moment of stillness he said, "I cannot say what I wish to say now without sounding like a cad."

His eyes opened and for a moment she was lost, foundering, helpless.

She despised the feeling. *Despised it.*

He shifted onto his side. Then he took her hand, lifted it to his lips, and placed a soft kiss on her knuckles.

"It is not difficult," he said quietly, "when a man of my wealth and position has need, to find—" He squeezed her hand.

"Oh, say it," she said. "It is not difficult for a man of your wealth and position to find women eager to populate his bed."

His lips flirted with a smile. "I would not have used the word *populate*."

"I daresay."

"I love what you say, Emily," he said quite soberly, turning her heart over. "I would rather hear your voice than anyone else's. You needn't touch me to please me." The corner of his mouth ticked up. "Don't misunderstand me: I do also very much enjoy your touch. Very, very much." His smile grew. "In truth, it comes in only second to your v—"

She kissed him on the mouth. His hand came up behind her neck and he pulled her to him. She learned what it was, then, to hold a man skin to skin, breasts to chest, to feel the taut, hot, smooth-and-scratchiness of his body, and enjoy his mouth without haste or purpose other than these kisses. She could kiss him forever.

But she did have other purpose. One other purpose. Her curiosity had become a preoccupation.

"I want to share with you . . . something." Her face was hot, which was ridiculous. But her blush had nothing to do with the specific request she was about to make—rather, with her reason for requesting it.

"Something?" A smile lifted one side of his mouth.

She urged his shoulders back to the mattress and crawled over him, lodging her thighs to either side of his. His eyes were sleepy, contented, black in the flickering firelight. His hand shifted to her leg to stroke her skin.

"What are you doing?" he murmured.

"Something I once saw." She laid her hands on the flat, hard plane of his belly and drew the bed linens down.

"Emily?"

"Something I have never done before." Leaning forward, she brushed her lips over his. "I want to do it with you." She kissed him again, lightly, barely grazing his lips. "With only you." She slipped her hand down to surround his arousal and she looked into his eyes. "I want to take you inside my mouth."

His cock twitched in her hand.

"Where exactly did you once see *that*?" he said hoarsely. "Do not tell me you have been to a brothel." His palm came up to cover his face. "My God, you have been to a brothel, haven't you?" He gasped and flinched, his body responding to her touch. Grabbing her wrist, he plucked her fingers away. "If that libertine took you to a brothel, I will murder—"

"No." She tugged free. "I have never been to a brothel, although I don't understand why you can now comfortably reveal that you have visited one, but I cannot have."

"You don't *understand*? What in the blazes is wrong with you that—"

She jerked back from him. "Nothing is wrong with me, of course. I only—"

He seized her shoulders and pulled her down to him and took her mouth with his until she responded, sinking her hands into his hair and pressing herself to him. He was fully aroused and she shifted herself against him and moaned.

"*Colin.*"

"I want to be inside your mouth," he whispered harshly against her lips. "I want to be inside every part of you. I am aching again already to be inside you and I will do anything you wish to make it so, and hate myself for it. You are a *lady*, not a prostitute. I should not use you so, but if you wish it, I will, because I am weak—*weak* with need for you."

She laid her hand on his chest and felt the hard, uneven rhythm of his heartbeats. She kissed him softly, trailing the tip of her tongue over his lower lip.

"I am made of the same parts, the same flesh, the same desire as any woman," she said softly, touching her lips to his chin, then his throat. "The only difference between those women and me is coin on the table, and that I do this because I wish to." Trailing her fingertips down his waist, she set her lips to the swell of muscle over his throbbing heart and found his nipple with her tongue. His moan and the surge of his cock against her hip shot stunning heat through her.

"So unless you intend to pay me for this," she said, tasting the salt on his skin, "you mustn't stand in judgment on either of us for it. And, Colin . . ." Slipping her hand over his erection, she licked her lips and waited until he met her gaze. "You are the strongest person I have ever known."

"You cannot know what this is doing to me," he whispered.

"Now," she said, "let me make you lose control again." Gently sliding her hand down his cock, she drew back the foreskin and took him into her mouth.

He tasted hot and sweet and salty and musky at once, and silky, and she was shocked by the response in her own body to her tongue's discoveries, the quickening and aching.

But she didn't really know how to do it.

So she asked him.

Jaw locked, eyes closed, he replied that she was doing splendidly without instruction.

"I want it to be perfect for you," she said.

Face averted, he was breathing hard, the muscles in his chest and arms all gloriously strained.

"You need"—he gasped—"you need only touch me"—a moan broke from his chest—"for it to be perfect. *Emily*—"

"Zenobia," she murmured, and licked the hot length of him.

Back arching, he bucked into her mouth. Then he was grabbing her, dragging her up his body with his strong hands and spreading her thighs. He sank into her and she filled herself with him and felt his pleasure release in hard, wrenching jerks deep inside of her. Hands clamped about her hips, he held her tightly to him, until he threw back his head and his groan filled the room. Bending to him, she kissed him and her hair fell over his cheeks. She moved on him, his hands guiding her, and she took her pleasure on him until she was whimpering and desperate for more. Then his fingers were inside her, pushing in, up, harder, making her writhe and beg him to never cease.

He kissed her after that—everywhere, just as he had promised—on her lips, the tender lobes of her ears, her chin and throat and the slender bone that ran the length of her shoulder to her arms that were at once soft and determined as she pulled him to her breast. He lingered on her breasts, drawing rich sighs from her as she wound her fingers into his hair and wished for his hands never to leave her waist, then never to leave her breasts, and then her nipples that were almost sore now from caresses.

He urged her onto her side and kissed her shoulders, the dip of her waist, the long, graceful line of her spine, and the round fullness of her buttocks. Stroking her between her legs, stirring her swollen flesh anew, he lifted her hips from the mattress and slipped his fingers inside her again and caressed her until she moaned. Then he laid her on her back, parted her thighs, and kissed her there.

She came against his tongue in rolling, frantic waves of hard pleasure. When it was over, she could not find enough air, yet still he kissed her—the lengths of her thighs and her neck and her trembling belly and her fingertips, and again her sex. As he kissed her, he touched her, tenderly, as though he were memorizing her skin and the angles of her tendons and the curves of her flesh with his fingertips. Ragged and delirious with exhaustion, she allowed it, but she would have anyway even fully awake and alert. She thought perhaps that she would never again truly want anything in the world except his touch, his kiss, anywhere on her that he wished.

They lay facing each other, close but not touching, the bedclothes only haphazardly covering them, alternately dozing and staring into each other's eyes with the eyes of a gorgeous, full euphoria that filled them up and made them unable to say words worthy of the perfection of this moment. There was such pleasure—in what they had done, what they felt now, and what they knew would happen if they touched again. It was ecstasy and they both knew it and neither could utter a syllable.

Now she understood that what she had said to him earlier, that a woman did not give herself in the act of sex, was nonsense. It was frightening and astonishing and alarming. She had given herself to him. He would never own her, not in any way that mattered to the world. But she had given him part of her, nevertheless.

She slept. When she roused, she found his dark gaze upon her, sober and full of thought.

As though he had been waiting to do so, he curved his palm around her face, and her body responded with a pang of pleasure. He rose over her, placed his lips upon hers, and kissed her with tenderness that stunned her. Then he pulled her against him, she twined her arms about him, and they made love again.

It was slow and tender, unrushed, as unlike what had come before as he was unlike the man she had believed him to be. They touched, endlessly, and his gentleness did not surprise her. He had always had gentle beauty in him, only encased now in a steely suit of armor—just as within her she had always had defiant fire, even when swathed in lace and French corsets. That he had seen that, known that, even when she had thought him indifferent to her, even when he had acted indifferently to her, created an echoing ache deep within her.

Afterward, she awoke to see him placing a spear of wood upon the fire. Wearing only his breeches, he crouched before the hearth, the flickering golden flames illumining his skin and casting shadows along the contours of his muscles.

As though he felt her attention, he turned his head. A smile of pleased conspiracy slid across his lips and the dimple appeared.

"Come here," he said.

She could not. She was sitting on the bed, holding the sheet over her breasts, staring, and everything inside her was needy again, and tangled with her heart and head.

His brow creased. "What is it?"

"If only we could remain like this forever."

"How, like this?"

"Undressed."

He chuckled. "I rather like you undressed too."

"I meant undressed as . . . no rules," she said. "No restrictions. No expectations." No insurmountable differences. No secrets. "No disappointments."

"Disappointments?"

"Oh . . ." She swallowed bumpily. "For instance, shirts. You will no doubt don a shirt again, but that will be a disappointment to me. For I am now discovering that I quite like watching you build up a fire while shirtless."

He smiled. "Do you?"

"I like being near your shirtlessness even more so," she said.

"Then come here," he repeated.

She climbed off the bed and went to him. He kissed her brow and the bridge of her nose and she ran her hands along his shoulders. He smelled of wood smoke and fire-warmed skin and their lovemaking. Leaning her cheek against the muscle in his arm, she trailed her fingertips over his chest, making swirls in the soft dark hair and feeling the blaze heat her skin as his hands did.

"I must tell you something," he said.

"Oh?"

"Some months ago I studied Loch Irvine's activities."

She looked up into his eyes. "What activities?"

"Shipping activities. And other matters."

"Whatever for? Do you believe he is the Devil's Duke?" She was holding her breath. He would tell her now.

"No. No longer, that is. But I began studying him because of the girls that went missing from Edinburgh last year. Then other details came to light. We believe—"

"We?"

He paused a moment. "I have sometimes been tasked with projects that require discretion and the freedom of movement that I enjoyed until recently. They are matters best kept out of the public eye."

"What sort of matters?"

He was stroking back her hair and nuzzling her temple. "At this moment I cannot remember a one."

"Colin."

"Powerful men have called on me and my friends for aid, and we have given them that aid with the assurance that their secrets will not be revealed."

"Which powerful men? What sorts of secrets?"

"Dukes. Princes. Kings. An Italian bishop with ties to Spanish royalty once lost track of his niece to whom he was guardian. She had run away to England. Finding herself in desperate straits she had taken employment in a household."

"Why didn't she go home?"

"She had no money and she feared to ruin her family. She was young, alone, in a foreign land. When we reunited her with her uncle, he told her that his greatest fear had been that she would be hurt. But he had come to us because he also feared for her reputation, and his own. The King had told him of our discretion. He knew we would not reveal the story to anyone."

"Who is 'we'?"

"My friends and I. A club. You know the sort, I suspect: quantities of brandy consumed and very little else accomplished." His smile was humble, almost self-deprecating. There was nothing in it of the man she had met in the cemetery in London, none of the arrogance or aggression. And yet he was telling her only a partial truth.

"It sounds as if you did accomplish more than drinking brandy."

"Yes," he admitted. "Frequently during the war. But since its end, less often."

"If you did this all in secret, why are you telling me?"

He looked down into her face. "I think I need you to know."

"So that I can feel certain of your discretion? That you will keep this tryst secret?"

Firelight glinted in the shadows of his eyes. "So that you will come to trust me again. And because I cannot lie to you."

She could no longer meet his gaze. Instead she followed the patterns her fingertips drew on his flesh. He was not the man she had met in that cemetery. Everything he had done to keep her safe, Pip, the Archers, Davie, all of it had been for the good of others. This could not be the alteration of a week, nor the Highlands having their brazen way with him. This was simply the man that he was.

She drew him down to her and touched her lips to his neck. Then she kissed his throat, his collarbone, feeling his bold strength beneath her hands, caressing him and taking a last taste of his skin.

This miracle would end here, shortly. Until then, she would pretend for few precious moments more that it needn't.

HER HEART BEAT against his chest, her lips pressed to his neck, and he thought that this might have been his—*she* might have been his—for years already. Yet she called it a tryst. She had no notion of his intentions.

"Emily."

"Zenobia." Her hands were roaming his waist, her touch confident and yet strangely reverent.

He grasped her arms and looked down into her face. "I am sorry for leaving you that first season in London."

A dart formed at the bridge of her nose. "Leaving me?"

"When your father wrote to me, telling me of his plans to bring you to town, I left England."

Her lashes made a single beat. "You were not already abroad? You left town *because* of me?"

"Yes. I did not understand that at the time. But, yes."

"You found the prospect of marrying me so repugnant that you left the *country*?"

"I found the prospect terrifying."

"Despite my breasts that you admired?" Her voice smiled, but it did not loosen the tightness in his throat.

"In those years, I ceased visiting Willows Hall because . . ." His tongue was failing him. "When our families would meet, I could hardly bear to be in the same room with you."

Her hands slipped off of him and she backed away.

"By your own admission you desired me," she said. "But you did not speak to me. So I can only think that you were ashamed of me, of my unconventionality, my unwillingness to be guided by my mother."

"No. Never." Air would not come. "I believed it was weakness."

"Desiring me? *Speaking* to me?"

"Caring for you. Depending upon you."

"You thought it was a weakness to care for me?" She shook her head. And then, abruptly, comprehension came into her eyes. "Before, you mean. Years earlier. Caring for me then."

He nodded.

"We were children," she said. "We were *friends*."

"You were my crutch."

"Your father convinced you of that."

"He was right."

"He was a cold-hearted authoritarian, Colin, with an inflated sense of righteousness."

"To govern people, a man must learn to control his emotions." He spoke the words like a child reciting a reader, as he had never actually been able to recite anything when he was a child. "Passion has no place in leading others."

For a moment she stared at him without expression. Then she turned away and took up her clothing.

"Emily," he said, moving to her but unable to bring himself to touch her. "I was wrong about you. About me. With you in my arms, I am strong."

The pain in her chest was spreading, swallowing pleasure and affection, even regret.

"Colin, I cannot—"

His hands surrounded her shoulders and he turned her to him. Palm shooting up, she pressed it against his chest, but he held her fast.

"You cannot what?" he said. "Care for me?"

She cared for him so much that she could not endure it. But he was wrong, dreadfully wrong. The passion in her writing inspired people.

"Do not push me away," he said, grasping her hand. "Let us leave the past where it belongs. Let us begin anew."

No words would come to her, nothing safe.

"Allow me to begin." He bent his head and kissed her cheek. "How do you do? I am Colin." Another kiss dropped softly upon her neck. "Colin Percival Gray, Viscount Gray, the Earl of Egremoor." Softly his lips strafed the depression beneath her ear, urging warmth through her. "There is nothing else of note about me, except that for the first thirteen years of my life I could not speak until a slip of a daring girl forced the words out of me." He kissed her lips so tenderly. "Now," he murmured. "What is your name?"

She twined her arms about his neck and kissed him, allowed him to kiss her, to wrap her in his arms and to take what he wished from her—part of what he wished—the part she needn't hide from him—the only part of herself that she could give.

Chapter 21

An Unexpected Discovery

*B*right-eyed and perky, Sybil accepted her attractive coachman's hand in the misty gray before dawn and he assisted her into the carriage. Then it was Zenobia's turn. He winked at her and squeezed her fingers too tightly. She wanted to chastise him, but she needed his discretion and she pinned her lips together.

Bruised lips. Whisker-abraded skin. Sore body. Everywhere she felt raw and ragged and delectably exercised and used. She hoped that when Colin woke up he felt that way too. She had tried her best to ensure it.

True to Sybil's whispered promise, her carriage was sprung on silent clouds. Sybil's husband adored riding and driving and kept the finest carriages, horses, and grooms. He especially liked riding his wife, she said upon a pretty scowl and then her fingertips shot up to cover her mouth.

"Oh, dear, darling Emily, I positively should *not* have said that to you. But, I suppose once a woman has heard another woman making wanton love to a man, there really isn't anything they cannot share with each other. Is there?" Sybil smiled cheerily. "You mustn't mind it. If a gorgeous earl had wanted to make love to me instead of you, I daresay I would have spent the night shouting and moaning too."

"I hope we did not . . . keep you awake."

"Not in the least! I was already awake." Her gaze shifted to the roof of the carriage.

"Does your husband know? About you and—" She gestured her chin upward.

Sybil's pretty smile wavered a bit. "No. If he did, I would be dead now. Charney has said any number of times that if he discovered me cuckolding him he would put his hands around my neck and strangle me, and then bury me secretly in the woods."

"Sybil! That is horrifying!"

She shrugged. "It is. But I cannot do a thing about it, darling."

"You could cease your liaison."

She released a sigh. "I cannot. Sammy is blackmailing me."

"Your *coachman*?"

Glitter had appeared in the brown eyes. "Mostly for money, of course, but occasionally other favors. He says that if I refuse he will tell Charney. As I don't wish to be strangled, I must simply live with the situation."

"But—are you—does he—" The hastily drunk tea was curdling in her stomach. What Colin had said about prostitutes . . . "Does he force you to perform sexual acts?"

"Oh, no, darling! *That* is the saving grace of the whole thing. And he is so deliciously rustic, I daresay he will never go soft about the middle like Charney did the moment the marriage contract was signed. And he likes doing it in places where we might get caught. It's delightfully naughty." She gave a saucy grin.

Zenobia slumped against the squabs. There was so much she did not understand about men and women.

Sybil drew the blind aside and dawn filled the interior. "I daresay we shall arrive at the castle any—"

The carriage jolted to a halt, hurling them forward. Zenobia broke the impact with her arm as she seized Sybil with her other hand and pulled her back to the seat.

Two gunshots sounded, clear and crisp across the mists. The carriage jerked once, then shuddered into stillness.

Sybil's mouth popped open. Zenobia clamped a hand over it.

"No," she hissed, then pushed the other woman onto the floor and flung the carriage rug over her. "Don't speak. Don't move. Don't do anything until you are certain all is safe."

"But what will you—?"

"Hush." She twitched the blanket over Sybil's curls and grasped the door handle.

In the rising mists, nothing stirred. The glen was spectacularly beautiful. A river ran along the valley flanked by dark conifers on one side and glimmering white and gray birches on the other, and the hills rose in steep green-and-rusty-red glory high above the trees.

"Your jewels, madam," a voice quite like any she had heard in London drawing rooms said not five yards away. "And do make haste. My friend has already reloaded his pistol, you see, and he has a shockingly quick finger on the trigger."

She swiveled her head and there they were: two mounted men, one quite small, with long, pale straight locks poking out from beneath his hat, and the other taller in the saddle, with dark hair, a fine, square jaw, and eyes so much like Colin's that she gaped.

"It's you," she said. "The imposters."

The tall man's eyes narrowed. "I prefer your lordship," he drawled. "Now, madam, do supply me with your jewels and money."

"I haven't any jewels. Because of you—because I have been mistaken for him, I believe—I have been fleeing pursuers all week. I had to leave everything behind in Balloch."

"Your companion, of course, must carry a wallet," he said with impressive nonchalance. "Do poke your head back inside the vehicle and inform him that both Mr. Swift and I have pistols trained on the doorway and we will shoot him if he shows any unwise courage."

"I believe you. I know you shot and killed a woman in Dumbarton. But there isn't anyone else in the carriage."

He lifted a skeptical brow, so much like Colin often did that her stomach felt queasy.

"Madam, I'll thank you to—"

"Lower your weapons." Colin's voice rang across the mists. Atop a gray horse, he stood shrouded in shadows.

But the thieves did not heed his command.

The first shot smacked against the wall of the carriage. She ducked. Sybil shrieked.

Colin shouted, "Get inside!"

Zenobia dove to the floor, and the second shot ricocheted off the carriage roof. Her head came up, and she was staring down the barrel of a pistol one foot away.

"Take it!" Sybil whined. "Sammy insists I carry it but I don't know how to shoot!"

Zenobia snatched the pistol as another shot sounded without, and hoof beats. Hand shaking, she cocked the dainty weapon and peeked through the window.

"You don't happen to have a pair of spectacles too, do you?" she whispered.

"Can't you *see*?"

Not well at this distance in this light. But somewhere out there two men were pointing pistols at Colin. If need be, she could fly.

Dropping to the floor in the tight space between Sybil and the bench, she poked the nose of the pistol out the door and saw the small man riding close to the edge of the thicket. Squinting, she gripped her pistol hand in her other to steady it, and pulled the trigger.

Her hands leaped and a burst of stinging smoke filled the carriage. She coughed and waved it away. The little man was clutching his shoulder and pointing his pistol dead aim at the wide-open doorway.

A crack sounded from within the trees, the little man's shoulder jerked, and he fell backward off his horse. Colin appeared between the trees and rode into a patch of clearing mist. The imposter earl was on the ground not twenty feet away, struggling to his knees, no pistol in sight. Dismounting, Colin moved to him.

"Well, well," the thief mumbled, spitting blood, and he lurched to his feet. "That was a neat trick, making my horse r—"

Colin hit him.

Then he hit him again with great force and ease, as though he spent every day driving his fist into other men's faces. The imposter wavered. Colin hit him yet again. Finally the thief collapsed on the ground.

On shaking legs Zenobia stumbled out of the carriage. Atop it, Sybil's coachman slumped over the bench.

She went toward the little man lying motionless in the grass. Nearly white in the nascent light, his face was lax. He was young, no more than a youth, with finely chiseled features, pale lashes, and smooth skin.

"We killed him," she whispered.

"I killed him," Colin said, unbinding his neckcloth. "Your shot wounded him only." He shoved the imposter earl on his side and wound the linen about his wrists, then looked over at her. "Where did you find a pistol?"

A groan punctuated the stillness of the morning into which only the burble of the river, the chirps of birds, and the snuffle of horses sounded. Atop the carriage, the coachman stirred.

"Sammy!" Sybil tumbled out. Frilly skirts every which way, she climbed up onto the box. "My darling!"

"I will need your help to put him in the carriage," Colin said.

Zenobia went to him. "How did you—"

"You were gone. I searched the inn and then the outbuildings." His voice was flat. "This coach had disappeared and you had told me your destination was Kallin."

She lifted the unconscious man's feet but Colin did most of the work of hauling him inside. Then he tied the inn's gray horse to the rear of the carriage.

"Can you ride?" He gestured to the small thief's mount now grazing by the river.

"Of course."

"The castle is still a distance away. The village is closer," he said and led the imposter earl's horse to the carriage to tie it beside the gray. "Are you all right?"

"Shaken, only." She had shared the most powerful intimacies with him hours earlier, and yet she did not recognize this man. This was the real Peregrine, she suspected, the man of few words and sober intent.

The small thief's horse was far from fresh and it was easy to ride. Colin took the box beside Sybil and her wounded coachman, and they left the dead man and drove through shadows cast by the rising morning.

They entered an inn yard cluttered with horses and carts. The stable mistress, Zion, was leading a heavily saddled horse into the building. Colin halted the carriage and descended, offering his hand to Sybil to follow him.

"Who is the law in this village?" he said to the stable mistress.

"His Grace."

"Send word to him immediately that the thief who calls himself the Earl of Egremoor is apprehended. He is in this carriage, unconscious. I need help to move him to a chamber that can be locked."

She nodded, quite as if men delivered unconscious thieves into her keeping all the time. "One of the storage rooms will do."

"Mrs. Charney's coachman has been shot. If anyone here can tend to him, make it so before he loses further blood," he said, taking hold of the horse she was leading. "Whose are these animals and vehicles?"

"They've just arrived from the south. They have been riding through the night and are all at breakfast."

"Quickly now," he said to Zion. "He will be easier to imprison while he is still unconscious."

She hurried into the inn.

Zenobia led the small thief's horse into the stable. When she emerged, a young woman was atop the carriage, tending to the coachman's wound. Sybil sat on the other side of him, a lace kerchief pressed to her nose. Colin was untying the other horse from the carriage.

"Do you think our pursuers have caught up with us?" she said, watching his hands as he drew the reins over the animal's ears.

"It could be," he said, leading it into the stable, and she went with him. "You will tell me why you intended to go to the duke's castle this morning," he said with utter calm.

"Not your earl's voice, exactly," she said. "But close."

"I don't find that amusing. Not at present." He halted. His eyes seemed everywhere but on her face, and overly bright. "What was your intention?"

"I had an appointment at the castle at dawn."

"With Loch Irvine?"

"I don't know who with."

His gaze snapped to her eyes, disbelieving.

She touched his arm. "Believe me. I did not know. It might have been he, but it could have been anybody."

"What was the purpose of it?"

She withdrew her hand. "I cannot tell you."

He stared into her eyes for what seemed eons. "All right."

"What is?"

"I cannot force information from you. If you don't wish to tell me, I must accept that." His voice had grown cooler with each word. Turning from her, he started away.

"Colin, the imposter earl—he seemed to believe that I was in the carriage with a man."

"Did he?"

"I don't think it was accidental, that robbery. I think they intended us as their victims. You and me."

"I see."

"Why else would they have been there, in the glen so close to the duke's castle, so enclosed and difficult to escape swiftly, at that hour? I think they saw me leave the inn this morning and followed the carriage."

"Perhaps."

"For pity's sake, don't you wonder *why*? What would be the benefit to them of harming us? While everybody has been chasing us they cannot have been chasing them too. The real thieves had absolutely no reason to attack us. We have been their perfect alibi."

"If that is the case, they have made a mistake." His features were entirely unexpressive. "But now they are finished. You needn't analyze their motives and actions any longer."

"What is *wrong* with you?" she exclaimed. "Where did the man I left in that bedchamber this morning go?"

His eyes did a peculiar retreat. "I daresay he is still on the bank of Irvine River, watching a man he has shot bleed to death in the grass."

"Oh." She grabbed him and went to her toes to press her cheek against his. "I am sorry. I am so sorry." She turned her lips against his skin and held him close.

After a moment, his arms encircled her waist.

"You did what had to be done," she whispered. "You mustn't dwell on it."

"He is not the first," he said, and drew back to look into her eyes. "Does that distress you?"

"I don't distress easily."

A tentative smile played with the corner of his lips, but it faded swiftly.

"It does not get any easier," he said. "Some men say it does. But I have not found that to be the case."

"Perhaps because you are a very exceptional sort of man."

"I'm glad to hear you say that." But even as his voice smiled his eyes remained troubled.

"It is at an end now."

His fingertips slipped along the side of her face. "It could have been you," he said roughly. "I could not allow that."

She pressed her lips to his. Then he was gathering her up against him, bending his head, and kissing her in earnest.

Heavy footsteps sounded inside the stable. Colin released her. As the three men came into view, it occurred to Zenobia that until now she had not seen a man other than Colin and Sybil's coachman in Glen Village.

"Good day, sir, ma'am," the man in the front said. Gray-haired and wiry, he had well-weathered skin and weary bags beneath his eyes.

"How may I help you?" Colin said, moving between her and the men. The two others were younger, both thickset, and their faces were not friendly.

"I'm Callum Gibbs, constable down at Dumbarton."

"You are quite a distance from home, Mr. Gibbs."

"Aye. Chasin' a murderer. I'd hoped ye'd be able to give me some answers."

"When His Grace of Loch Irvine arrives I will be glad to tell you the particulars of the attempted robbery this morning."

"There's the trouble o' it, sir. They tell me His Grace rode out last night."

"That is unfortunate. I recommend that you bid one of these men ride to the nearest magistrate and alert him that the robbers have been caught."

"I hear ye left one o' them in the glen," Mr. Gibbs said with a tilt of his grizzled head.

"I did. Mr. Gibbs, I am the actual Earl of Egremoor. The man locked in the storeroom of this inn is an imposter who has been using my name to cozen gullible people into relaxing their vigilance long enough to rob them. I have now delivered this criminal to you in a neatly wrapped package. Your troubles, and mine, are at an end."

"Aye, sir. But the man ye tied up, he's sayin' *he's* the earl and ye're the imposter. And some of the men who've ridden with me these past few days—they say the lady there"—he gestured—"was with ye when ye diverted a herd to block the road. And there's a missin' boat to be accounted for down at Tarbet, and a carriage horse here in this very stable that belongs to a fine French lady down the loch."

"That Frenchwoman was my traveling companion before we were obliged to flee for our lives," she said, "and that is my horse."

Mr. Gibbs nodded thoughtfully. "I think ye'd best tell that to the boys."

"No," Colin said. "She has suffered sufficient discomfort already because of those villains. I—"

"Colin," she said. "I will speak to them. In a few minutes," she said to the constable, "all of this will be settled and his lordship and I can be on our way."

The men followed them into the inn, where another dozen men were gathered around tables, glasses of ale and whiskey strewn about liberally. At least half of them stared with undisguised hostility as they entered the room.

"Bring the thief," Colin said. Despite his lack of neckcloth, open shirt collar, and the shadow of whiskers across his jaw, he looked every bit the earl. She hadn't any idea how they all did not see that clearly.

But when the imposter came into the room, hands bound behind his back, led by the constable's two companions, she understood how the men of Dumbarton could doubt. Nearly Colin's height, with dark hair cropped fashionably à la Brutus, a perfectly tailored coat, gleaming Hessians, and a neckcloth tied in an intricate pattern though now stained with blood from his own nose, he looked even more like an English nobleman than the actual nobleman in the room. But his most disturbing feature was his eyes: dark blue and, except for the mocking gleam in them, exactly like Colin's.

"Ah," he drawled like a dandy making his bows at Almack's. "There he is: my imitator. How utterly flattering."

"Who are you?" Colin said.

"More to the point, old chap, who are *you*?" He glanced about the room at the men from Dumbarton, all of them filthy from days on the road, and at the women of Glen

Village. "Can anyone tell me why this villain is free as a hawk while I am trussed like a capon?"

Several men started speaking at once. The constable of Dumbarton watched, bemusement scoring his wan face.

Zenobia found Rebecca in the cluster of women at the kitchen door. "Do you know the young woman with bright red hair who works at the teashop?" she whispered. "The Englishwoman?"

"Yes, milady."

"Fetch her now. Quickly."

The maidservant darted around a newcomer standing at the doorway and was gone.

"We've brought the body, Mr. Gibbs," the newcomer said.

"Nobody'll be bringin' a corpse into my house," Mrs. Tarry exclaimed. "All o' ye, outside!"

The men piled into the yard. The day had risen bright, the sun already drying the earth, only bits of snow clinging tenaciously here and there to shadowed spots. The smaller thief had been laid out in the center of the yard, a cloth draped over his face. Colin was studying the imposter earl.

The constable climbed up onto the step of Sybil's carriage from which the horses had been unhitched, and his assistants hauled the imposter up beside him.

"As I'd rather be escortin' only one man down the loch today," the constable said, "'tis time we made sense o' matters. Now, sir," he said to the imposter, "can ye tell us the name o' yer companion here?" He gestured to the body.

"My good fellow," the imposter said with a haughty sniff, looking down his nose at the constable. "That man is not my companion. He is my valet. It's a dreadful shame I've lost him. He tied the most devilishly clever Mathematical, and his Oriental is the talk of London."

"What do you wish to accomplish by this charade?" Colin spoke to him as though there were not twenty other people around them, in a voice that was not elevated in volume yet carried clearly across the yard. "Even if you somehow manage to convince these people that you are me, where will you go from here? My employees, tenants, and neighbors have known me my entire life, as well as every member of the peerage. You cannot hope to reap any benefit from continuing to borrow the title beyond manipulating travelers. But that cannot possibly serve you for long. Someone would be bound to capture you again. What do you hope to gain from seeing me condemned for your crimes?"

"And the lady condemned as well," the imposter said in an entirely altered voice, shifting his gaze to her, "You mustn't forget dear Emily, your longtime accomplice in crime."

Colin's face went slack. Zenobia gaped.

"Take your eyes off of her," Colin said in a deadly calm, "or—bound or not—I will pound you into the ground again."

The thief's gaze slid away from her.

"He knows something," she said.

The imposter pursed his lips. "I know more than you could possibly imagine, my sweet."

Rebecca ran into the crowd. "She's gone, milady!"

"Gone?"

"She took her horse and rode out last night."

After the Duke of Loch Irvine.

"Who?" Colin said.

Zenobia shook her head.

"You cannot tell me this either?" he said, his eyes hard.

"Ah," the thief drawled. "Your father would be so pleased to see how well you have your woman in hand."

"What do ye know of his father, sir?" the constable said.

His eyes upon Colin were ablaze. "I daresay I know as much about the dear old departed earl as you do." He paused. "Brother."

Chapter 22

The Imposter

A murmur arose from the crowd.

"Tell me your name," Colin said, his jaw like stone.

"Eamon Wells at your service, *my lord*," the other man said through tight teeth, then executed a florid bow. "I might have been Gray too, but dear old Dad didn't like to sully the official family tree with common blood, however much he enjoyed cavorting with my mother."

Colin's face paled.

"You . . ." he said and seemed to struggle to breathe. "You are . . ."

"Your bastard younger brother? Why yes, as it happens. And, let me tell you, I am positively delighted to finally make your acquaintance. Father said if I ever came closer than fifty miles of you he would see me thrashed to within an inch of my life. What fond memories I have of him. Suffice it to say, I was thrilled to hear of his death. I have longed to finally see the son who got everything. Lucky chap."

Sybil burst from the inn's door in a froth of skirts.

"Darling Lady Emily! Why didn't you tell me this was

happening? I just heard it from that serving girl. Who are all of these *people*?" She halted before the crowd of Scotsmen and looked up at Eamon. "Good gracious, he *does* look like you, my lord. Why, the two of you could be brothers."

"As I was saying," Eamon drawled.

"Sybil—"

Sybil spun around. "Constable—oh, which of you *is* the constable?"

"I am, ma'am."

"Constable, I am Mrs. Robert Charney of the Charneys of Riding Crescent, and, being a regular patron of the same fashionable venues and homes which are frequented by the Earl of Egremoor, I can tell you that *this* man"—she pointed to Eamon—"is an imposter. And as it is a capital offense to impersonate a lord of the realm, I suggest that you take him along directly to whomever you must—the duke or whatnot—and have him hanged."

"'Tis a fine idea," came from the crowd like the growl of an animal.

"Now, Aillig, I know ye be hurting," Mr. Gibbs said from his place on the carriage beside Eamon. "But 'tis just now settled. As His Grace of Loch Irvine has gone off to Edinburgh, I'll be taking Mr. Wells down to Inveraray to His Grace of Argyll."

"He's a clever one," another man said. "Stealin' his own brother's name. He'll be loose afore ye've put him in Argyll's keeping."

"We could try him right here and now," Aillig said, "and hang him quick. Then he wouldna hurt another soul."

"Aillig, there'll be no talk o' hanging till he's had a correct trial."

"You are too kind, Mr. Gibbs," Eamon said. "But dragging me across these godforsaken mountains only to put me into the hands of a judge who will most certainly drop the gavel on me is remarkably shortsighted. These men are all eager to return home. Why don't we take care of matters now and spare ourselves time and effort?"

"Now, sir, dinna be jesting," the constable said. "Ye'll have a fair chance to defend yerself in court."

"Mr. Wells," Zenobia said. "A moment ago you were trying to have Lord Egremoor condemned for your crimes, and now you are encouraging these men to hang you? I don't understand."

"You wouldn't, would you?" he said with hooded eyes, and his gaze passed swiftly over his half brother's face, then away to the trees across the yard. "Why, there's a fine hanging branch, gentlemen. Who's brought a rope?"

Hoof beats pounded up the road and a single horseman clattered into the yard. Slowing swiftly, he rode directly up to the carriage.

"Broderick?" Mr. Gibbs exclaimed. "I sent ye to Edinburgh after the duke, man."

"I've news from Tyndrum," he panted and glanced at Eamon. "Yesterday eve the highwaymen attacked a carriage heading east. Two ladies and a lad aboard. The driver sped off quick as a hare. But one of the ladies and the outrider were shot. Killed."

The men who had been drinking whiskey roared. Other men started talking. The constable raised his voice but no one was listening.

"Colin?" Zenobia said.

He was staring at Eamon, his features immobile.

"Mr. Gibbs," she said, "you must halt this."

"There'll be no hanging!" Mr. Gibbs shouted, but weakly, as though he'd no hope of being heeded.

"Shall we hear what that lord of the realm has to say about it?" Eamon taunted, but there was a brittleness to his insouciance now, and his eyes shone peculiarly bright.

"He murdered my wife," Aillig cried above the noise, stepping forward with a coil of rope. "Now he's murdered two more innocent souls. 'Tis time he met justice. And I've your justice here, Wells." He thrust the rope upward. "With my Betsy's name written on it."

"Is it really?" he said as though asking the time of day in

Hyde Park. "You know, I did not actually pull the trigger. That boy Swift did. But I've done other deplorable deeds in my life, so if it will give you comfort I don't mind taking the blame for your wife's death."

"Nobody'll be hangin' anybody today," Mr. Gibbs called out but even his henchmen ignored him now. Pulling Eamon down from the carriage they dragged him toward a tree. The women of Glen Village were shouting at the men to stop. The Earl of Egremoor stood silently watching, his eyes entirely remote.

Zenobia ran after the crowd, pushing through them, her heart a mess of splintering panic. When the initial shock of his father's lie faded, Colin would regret allowing this to happen. It would kill him.

Someone brought a horse from the stable and led it beneath a thick jutting branch of an oak bordering the yard. Eamon was no longer grinning. His face was drawn and as stark as his brother's. He was terrified, finally, but his lips were tight and he did not fight the men who were hauling him onto the horse's back. The old earl's pride showed in his stiff features, and she suspected he must truly have known his father. He was too much like him—too much like Colin.

"This is wrong." She pushed against the tide of the crowd. "Colin, you must stop them from doing this."

He stared at the men looping the rope around the branch.

"Colin, I beg of you," she said. "With a word you can end this. You must speak to them, now, before it is too late."

Then she saw it—the hot, hard gleam of helplessness in his eyes—and she realized quite suddenly that he could not speak.

She ran to the crowd.

"Listen to me! Lord Egremoor does not want this."

No one heard her. The men were singing, chanting some horrible song of war as they bound Eamon's wrists in another length of rope. Throwing her foot onto the lowest tree branch, she hoisted herself up, climbing swiftly to the branch where they had slung the noose, her skirts tangling and hands slippery on the bark.

"Stop!" she cried. "Cease this! His lordship does not want it."

The shouts ebbed. A few of the men looked to the earl for confirmation, but he said nothing, did nothing, made no indication that they should stop. The constable was shaking his head.

"Come down off there, lass," he said, "or ye'll get yerself hurt."

"No! You *must* believe me. Lord Egremoor wishes this man to have a fair trial, with a suitable judge and a jury and due process of the law. It is the law he holds dear—dearer than anything."

Shoving Eamon's head down, they were draping the noose over it.

"Lass," another man said, "'tis clear his lordship's of a different mind."

"Please! Wait an hour to do this—thirty minutes, for pity's sake."

"Pull her down off there," cried a man who was clearly drunk. "'Tis no place for a woman."

"Aye, there be only one woman with the courage to hang a bastard who's done wrong to simple folk like Betsy Kendrick," said another. "The finest woman: Lady Justice!"

Her stomach leaped, then twisted.

"For Lady Justice!" another shouted.

"If she were here, she'd give ye an earful o' justice, lad," someone said to the prisoner. "Alas, ye'll have to settle for a neck-full."

They laughed.

"This is not justice!" she cried.

"With all due respect to ye, miss, how's a lady who goes calling at a duke's castle to know a thing about justice for poor men like us?"

"Because—because *I* am Lady Justice."

Only the men directly beneath the branch heard her.

"'Tis no' a thing to be pretending, miss," one of them said gravely.

"I am not pretending. I am Lady Justice!"

Quiet descended. In the trees across the yard birds chirped, and the breeze blew cold and crisp beneath the open sky. Not a man or woman made a sound.

"Well," Eamon said from his backward seat on the horse. "Convenient revelation, wouldn't you say, brother? I for one don't believe her." His voice slurred oddly now. "Gentlemen, slap this poor beast out from under me and have it done with."

"Send to Ardlui for my coachman and my friend. They will vouch for me." She spoke swiftly, holding each man's gaze, one after another. "Lord Egremoor can tell you the very month that I moved to London to reside in my family's house there. Since that month, I have been writing about the causes that inspire me, and those causes that others bring to my attention through their letters—*your* letters. I have received hundreds of letters from Scotland alone, from farmers and tradesmen and peddlers and sailors. I have learned from what you have written to me, and I have told the world about your troubles, hoping for change to come through it. I have penned each of those pamphlets with my own hand, and the words have come from my heart. I am she. I am Lady Justice."

Finally she had to look at Colin. He stood completely still, his eyes overbright.

The moment his thoughts carried him to the realization that she knew his secret—had known since the cemetery—she saw the change in his eyes: the sudden, sharp shock.

And then anger.

She dragged her attention to the men below her.

"Miss—"

"Not *miss*," she snapped. "*My lady*. I am the daughter of an earl. I am the most read female alive in Britain today. And I am horrified by what you are doing here, ignoring the law of both England and Scotland, ancient law that demands a man be given a fair trial, instead allowing fury and grief"—she looked at Aillig—"and drink to overcome you and make you act like beasts. If you are so hungry to hang an imposter today, hang me. For I could not be more ashamed of what my words have wrought here, of the use you are putting them to. Show the world that you have learned nothing from what I have written of compassion and generosity for others, and execute me without trial for having fooled you all into believing that I would ever condone this sort of horror."

She looked over the gaping men and women.

"Go ahead," she said. "Who among you has the courage to put the noose around *my* neck?"

Colin broke the crowd's paralysis. Crossing the yard, he came toward the tree. The men parted for him so he could reach his brother.

"Remove the rope." He took hold of the horse's bridle. "There will be no hanging today. Not of highway robbers nor of Britain's favorite pamphleteer."

A man drew the noose from around Eamon's neck and passed it to the constable.

"Mr. Gibbs, where is the nearest secure jail cell other than Castle Kallin?"

"Inveraray, my lord."

"Bind Mr. Wells well and take him to Inveraray and incarcerate him," Colin said. "I will join you shortly and write to the Duke of Argyll of the situation." He passed the horse's lead to another man. Then he moved to stand beneath her. She lowered herself to sit on the branch, and reached for his shoulders. He lifted her down and released her.

"Gentlemen," he said, turning to the remaining men standing about uncomfortably. "Mr. Wells will be punished for his crimes. You may return home in the comfort that justice will be done. Mr. Kendrick, your wife's murderer is dead. I am profoundly sorry for your loss. But you can do nothing more than grieve her now."

Without another word, he left her among the Scotsmen and the women of Glen Village standing beneath the massive oak, and went into the inn.

Chapter 23

The Origins of a Lady

*L*ater, in Gallic fashion, Clarice philosophized roundly on the timing of her arrival in Glen Village at that precise moment, with Jonah and the carriage and a borrowed pair. Fate had compelled her *petite Emilie* to divulge her *grand secret* in this manner, before they could appear and put a stop to the violent fury of *les paysans*. It was better *comme ça*, she insisted, that the world—and the earl—should know the truth about her *chère*, so that they could all celebrate her greatness.

At first the people gathered in the Solstice Inn did not celebrate, despite Clarice and Jonah's testimony. Some were in awe, others openly skeptical. They barraged her with questions, demanding that she prove her authorship of Lady Justice's pamphlets, including a tract on the Clearances that Mrs. Tarry produced, which Zenobia was obliged to recite from memory.

Ale and whiskey flowed freely with conversation and some debate, however, and within an hour everybody seemed to have accepted her revelation. The announcement had succeeded in jarring the men from their vengeful mission, for over the course of days on the road they had become as exhausted and desperate as she. All were glad to have a satisfying end to it. It confirmed what she had known for a sennight: Scots were wonderful people, full of both passion and compassion, easily roused to offense yet just as easily forgiving.

Colin had not reappeared.

After looking in on Sybil to ensure that Sammy was recovering, and being assured that he was *the veriest darling of a patient*, she went in search of the Earl of Egremoor.

She found him in the stable, saddling the inn's gray horse. She remained on the other side of the stall's half door and he did not acknowledge her presence.

"Are you leaving now?" she said.

"Momentarily."

"Why are you doing that? Where is the stable hand?"

"I sent her to Edinburgh to apprise Loch Irvine of matters here." His voice was curt. He slipped a bridle over the horse's muzzle and fit the bit between its teeth.

"I am sorry about your father. I am sorry that he kept the secret from you."

"Yes," he said without turning from his task. "It seems that you were justified after all in thinking him a prize bastard. Rather, father of a bastard." He took up a saddle blanket and settled it atop the gray's back. "I will now make a request of you, and I should like you to agree to it without argument and without lying."

"What is it?"

"Yesterday Loch Irvine sent a fast rider to Egremoor. Two men in my employ, Grimm and Cooper, will arrive here within the next several days. I must go to Inveraray now and—and see to matters. I want you to wait here for Grimm and Cooper, and to travel with them to London."

"But—"

"I am not offering this as an option. I am telling you that this is what you will do."

"You said it was a request."

In profile, his face looked like stone. He lifted the saddle and placed it over the blanket, then buckled the girth.

"Will you return home?" she said. "After Inveraray?"

"Now that I needn't search for Penny Baker?" he clipped.

"Yes."

With a jerk of his hand he tightened the buckle and the horse sidestepped. He set his palm on the animal's neck and bent his head. "Did you invent her?"

"No. She was real."

He lifted his chin and stared at the opposite wall. "Was?"

"I discovered—yesterday, here—that she passed away."

"I see," he said, his voice never more like his father's.

She folded her hands before her. "You will see to Pip's welfare, I assume."

"I will."

"You have done well by her, Colin."

"Remarkable as it may seem to you, I don't care to hear praise from the kingdom's favorite pamphleteer at this particular moment," he bit out.

"Colin—"

"You *lied* to me." Finally he turned to her. "For weeks."

"And you lied to everyone. For years."

"A fact which makes you unhappy now only because you were wrong about the man you cheerfully eviscerated in public. As to the accusation of lying, madam, I can only reply that your hypocrisy clearly knows no bounds."

"You should have *known*," she cried.

"I should have known?"

"Why did you never discover Lady Justice's identity, Colin—you, who are so experienced in ferreting out people's secrets—who have made it your mission to do precisely that?"

"*Why?*" he snapped. "Because I thought I was looking for a *man*."

"Your prejudice became your failure. But I don't actually think it was that. Lady Justice's identity was right before you all along. I discovered Wyn Yale's part in it, after all, and I haven't even the skills of finding people that you do. I think you did not want to face your nemesis. I think you knew she was right, and that if you learned who she was you would have to cease pretending it was a game."

"How did you discover Yale?"

"One of my staff happened to be on Dover Street and saw him leave your club. After that I hired a detective from Bow Street. He followed Wyn when he left London. Later Diantha told me details of their journey that revealed much more than she realized. It was as simple as that."

"From *that* you extrapolated the club's mission?"

"Of course not. There were other clues. When Viola Carlyle returned to England after years missing, I happened to visit Savege Park. Wyn had brought her there. And long before that, when Kitty and I were stranded in the snow on a journey to my parents' home, Wyn and Leam were obviously hiding some intrigue they would not divulge. Clarice was certain they were spies. Has Leam been part of it too?"

He nodded, but slowly, as though even now he did not wish to divulge the truth.

"And small details," she said, "comments Kitty has made over the years, other things Diantha has said to me offhandedly. The accumulation of bits and pieces of information happened gradually. But it was not until I asked for Peregrine's help and you did not reject me instantly that I suspected your club's true purpose. When I canceled that request yet you set out to find Penny anyway, I thought at first your pride made you do it. But I have come to understand that is not the case. When you took Pip, I think I finally understood fully."

"This is impossible. How could you have known while I did not?"

"You might have at any time put a watcher on Brittle & Sons and followed people who came and went from there. Yet you did not, *for five years*. Either you merely found Lady Justice a mildly amusing distraction from your regular

concerns, or you did not actually want to know her identity.
I suspect the latter."

His eyes were like black ice on the surface of a lake.
"Who was Penny Baker?"

"A decoy. I was not actually searching for her—rather,
for Amarantha. Amy was missing for months, without news.
She had sailed from the West Indies in search of Penny. I
gave you Penny's name so that you would not attach my
family to Lady Justice's request for assistance. I hoped that
in finding Penny, you would bring me closer to Amy."

"Amarantha was *missing*? Is she—"

"She is well. I met with her yesterday. She left here last
night."

"For God's sake, why didn't you just tell me your worries
about Amarantha? As yourself? To *me*. You should have."

"Because you have been so devoted to my family of late?
No, of course not." She set her shoulders back and that tiny
gesture of defiance dug into Colin's gut. "I did not want to
ask you for anything."

"That is nonsensical. You did so anyway, even after you
knew me."

"You didn't know it was me asking. And I was desperate.
My parents, Amy's friends, no one knew where she was, but
no one was looking for her. I needed help."

He dragged his hand over his face, trying to wipe it all
away, but it clung like mud, heavy and suffocating.

"I care about your sisters." For years they had been the
closest he had to siblings. Now he knew better, and the suffocation made him dizzy.

"No, Colin." Her emerald eyes flashed, color staining
her cheeks. "You care about honor and doing what you have
been bred to do. But I'm not certain that you actually care
about people."

His head was a morass of confusion. He cared about
her, more than he knew what to do with. He cared about
his friends—Leam, Jinan, Constance, Wyn. Yet when the
director and King asked him to, he had manipulated them.

Anger was washing through him now in waves, hot pressure building again behind his throat and pounding in his blood, pressing at him, urgent and hideously desperate. And he was confused because it felt like desire, like lust, and like pain all at once—like *longing* he had not known in years. Decades. With a single mocking word—*brother*—the remnants of the edifice of the earl's control over him had crumbled. And the wound that had opened his chest the night before, splitting his ribs apart, was bleeding. Nothing he said now to her was stanching it.

"What of you," he ground out, "holed up in a house alone, hiding behind locked doors and false names?"

"You are correct. I am alone." Her voice had become nearly serene. "I have dear friends that I cherish, but none with whom I can share this crusade. I am a quiet person by nature, and I do like solitude and, admittedly, anonymity. But for a purpose. No one would listen to my message as Emily Vale, a member of the privileged class. As Lady Justice I can speak with sincerity. I have so much to say, Colin. I want to change the world. For *people*. For actual individuals, like the soldiers with whom you drank whiskey, poor men who have no recourse to justice under the law. I want to make Britain a better place for everyone, not only for the rich and wellborn whom you secretly wait upon."

"After you suspected the true purpose of the club," he managed to press between his lips, "you did not break off your public correspondence with me. You continued replying. For two years. Why?"

"It served my purpose," she said.

"What purpose was that? To humiliate me? Do you intend now to reveal me too?"

"No. I—"

"I understand. You used Peregrine as a straw man."

"And you used Lady Justice to denigrate the causes that you disapprove of," she shot back.

"Is it real, Emily?" curled off his tongue. "Are you honest

in your convictions? Or, now that you have tasted fame, do you simply write what your readers want to hear?"

"I believe in everything I write. The people of Britain listen to Lady Justice not because I wield power over them, but because they feel the honesty in my convictions. The *passion*. And they like it. The printing of my first pamphlet was fifty copies. Now it is fifty-five thousand. People are longing for someone to speak out against injustices. They want their grievances to be heard."

"The Domestic Felicity Act," he said. "Do you actually despise marriage?"

She could not lie to him, not another lie. But abruptly nerves spun in her mouth. "N-not as such."

"Then why your virulence about it?" he said, now severe again. "Your own parents have been happily wed for years. Your friends as well. Have all of those women sunk themselves so deeply, so unwittingly in the—what did you call it?—the *stew* that they are blind to its perils?"

"No. Of course not. Supporting that reform has nothing to do with my friends or my mother. It is—it is—"

His eyes were hard. "It is what?"

"I am doing it for *her*," she blurted out and felt as though every last piece of her heart were lying on the ground before him. "And for women like her."

He frowned. "Her?"

"Because of what he did to her, sending her away." Tears rose in her throat. She swallowed them back. "No man should be able to separate a mother from her child. No man. Not even a great lord."

Understanding rolled into his eyes like thunder, and then, swiftly, disbelief.

"You cannot possibly remember my mother," he said in an entirely altered tone. "You were too young."

"Too young to know *her*."

"I don't understand."

"Colin, *you* are the reason for this." Her voice was shaking. "I became Lady Justice because of you."

His lips were parted, his eyes confounded as though he had not heard her.

"From the time I could speak," she said, "I was someone else's voice. Your voice. From the moment I learned how to form words on my tongue, I was learning how to form words for you as well. You taught me how to speak for others. When you no longer needed me to speak for you, I found people who did." A tear slid down her cheek.

"Emily." His chest was moving in brutal inhalations that she could hear in the silence.

"So many people in this kingdom have no voice, Colin. So many people are suffering with no one to speak for them to men like you. The law gives you and your friends the benefit of the doubt, the privileges, the wealth, the power. I love England. But I want to help make it a place in which people who are not born into titles and wealth can live with equal dignity as we do."

"Would you have a mob dictate to Parliament?" he said in disbelief. "Would you have a revolution, like the French, with battles in the streets and innocent people dying as their homes burn, and every last man with a drop of noble blood executed as traitors?"

"Of course not. I would have the men who rule actually *hear* the voices of women and simple laborers and the desperately poor, and take those into consideration when they determine what is best for Britain. I would have them privilege their humanity over their purses, and compassion over financial gain and social prestige."

"What you are saying is impossible. Men of wealth and power must guide those who haven't the wisdom or experience to rule themselves."

"You sound like your father."

"If I do, it is because he was right."

"How can you not see that a man who does not truly listen to those who are weaker than he, who does not *trust* them, is using his power not for the good of all but for himself alone?"

"Emily." The word came as a whisper. "If my mother had obeyed my father, she would not have died on that road."

"Oh, Colin. Is that what you have been telling yourself all these years? That it was *her* fault that she was on that road that day when he sent her away, that she was to blame for thieves taking her life?"

He said nothing.

"No," she said with sudden, horrible certainty. "You have blamed yourself. All these years you have believed that you were at fault for her death. Haven't you?"

"The other day you said that I was not just any boy. And you were correct." His eyes had lost all light. "I was the boy whose silence killed his mother. I was to blame for her death."

"You were not. He was. Sending her away to punish you did not make you speak."

"No," he said. "That did not."

The truth, then, hit her with all the force of the silent years between them.

"He blamed me," she uttered. "After you spoke, each time he saw me it reminded him of what he had done to her, and he hated me. Didn't he? That was why he told you that caring for me was a weakness. He did not know how to cure you, but he tried again and again by punishing both of you. But he was wrong. When you lost her each time he sent her away, you did not speak, yet—"

"When I feared losing you, I did."

For a moment there was no sound between them.

"You were a child," she said. "He should not have burdened you with that."

"He did not burden me. You were my responsibility."

"I was careless and I should not have gone to the cliffs that day."

"You cared. You were the only person alive who cared about me like that, Emily—with affection and joy. You were just a little girl," he said upon an exhalation of laughter, "yet you were my lifeline . . . to *life*. Afterward, after it changed,

I worked hard to forget that, to pretend that was not true. I was terrified of going back. I was finally what I was expected to be, what I *wanted* to be, and I wanted to forget everything that had come before, all the weakness and dependence and shame. But every time I saw you, that was impossible. I would remember it all as though I were reliving it. On all those holidays when I did not speak to you, it was not because I did not wish to speak to you. It was because I *could* not."

"I was so angry with you for abandoning me—for so long." Her eyes sparkled with tears, but there was defiant strength in the emeralds, an honest bravery he had never known. "But still I worshipped you—*for years*," she said. "I watched you with others, watched you converse, even tease, and I thought there could be no greater hero, a warrior who had battled his demon and won."

"I was no warrior. I was a desperate man clinging to the side of a cliff by my fingertips."

As he watched, something new entered her eyes. Despair.

"We are so different, you and I," she said in a hush. "Oceans apart."

He shook his head, not understanding.

"Where I see courage in the face of suffering," she said, swallowing back her tears, "he taught you to see weakness. Where I see vulnerability crying out for compassion, he taught you to see failure."

"He taught me how to be strong."

"No. He taught you how not to feel. And you were so hungry for his approval that you believed his lies."

A spike of hard iron poked at his chest. "You cannot possibly understand," he said too thinly, shame lapping again, and fear.

"I understand that you wanted him to be proud of you. That you strove to be like him."

"He was a great man."

"A great man is not measured by the strength of his pedigree, but by the depth of his heart. Perhaps your father was a great man in the ways of power and authority that the world values. But he did not have your heart. And he taught you the wrong lessons."

It was too much, and his father's lie made it all a lie now.

"And what lesson did you learn from your parents?" he heard himself snap. "To fear speaking out except from the safety of anonymity? Here's a home truth, Emily Vale: you hide behind the names of invented heroes because you haven't the courage to show the world who you truly are. *You.* Peculiar, socially awkward, not as pretty as your sisters, with radical beliefs that your friends might condemn and a penchant for insulting with the sharpest tongue on earth every man who crosses you."

Her face fell wide open with astonishment.

"Yes," he said. "*That* is you. That is the woman you have become, unvarnished. It hurts to be obliged to stare your imperfections in the face and acknowledge them, doesn't it? But you—living alone, rarely seeing anybody but a handful of servants, and rejecting everyone who does not perceive the world precisely as you do—you have cleverly contrived to exist so that you needn't ever confront your flaws. In this battle you fight against the ills of humanity you have enclosed yourself in armor so thoroughly that you needn't ever feel the sting of disapproval."

"That is not—"

"You want the world to kneel at your feet in admiration, without suffering any discomfort for having spoken your mind. I have no doubt that is exactly why you corresponded with a stranger all these years, why you did not simply ignore the taunting. You cannot bear to be criticized for your imperfections. You wanted—*needed*—to prove me wrong. Well, let me tell you, Lady *Justice*, that is one valuable lesson my father did teach me. Every shortcoming of my character was held to the light—painfully so—until I overcame it. If he refused to allow me any weakness it was because he knew that the world would seize upon that weakness and use it to hurt the people in my care. I am a lord of this realm, with responsibilities not only for my lands but for all of England. I haven't the luxury of tucking myself away in safe seclusion and sitting in self-satisfied judgment on everybody else."

Her eyes were like fire. "You know nothing about me," she said. "Nothing."

"I know you wish that were true."

Silence echoed between them.

He took the horse's reins and walked to the stall door, and she moved back from it as he opened it. She was blinking repeatedly, staring at nothing, not him, and he champed on the sour, metallic taste in his mouth, the flavor of blood and shame, and led his mount toward the stable's entrance.

"I will post a letter to your father today," he said.

"To tell him about Lady Justice?" she said behind him. "No, please. I wish to tell them myself."

The horse's hooves scuffed on the floor as he paused. "To instruct him to have the banns published."

"Banns?" Surprise filled her eyes. "What banns?"

Cold panic swept from his belly up beneath his ribs. Abruptly his head felt heavy again, clouded, like it had in the inn yard.

"For our wedding," he forced over his thick tongue.

"*Our* wedding?"

His throat was nearly closed. "I did not take my oldest friend to bed without the intention of making her my wife. Whoever she has turned out to be in the meantime makes no difference to that."

"It *should*." Her face had paled; her eyes and parted lips were three rich spots of dark against white. "You haven't understood a thing I have said, have you? Still, after all of this, you cannot see the truth."

He could not draw breaths.

"Colin . . ."

He waited.

Then, with the slightest shake of her head and the pained flicker of her lashes, she drove the spike all the way in.

He pulled air into his lungs, the world red and black and a clamor of syllables from which he could drag no whole words. He turned away from her, heaving in air, forcing it over his throat, focusing his vision on his hand gripping the horse's rein. His lips moved and speech fell out like spitting dirt.

"So be it." He walked away.

"Colin," she called. "I beg of you, don't do this. I could not bear it if you hated me again."

He met her gaze a final time.

"I do not hate you. I am giving you your autonomy, as you wish. It was my wish as well, of course. The day I buried my father, I ordered the trees cut down."

SYBIL AND CLARICE found her there, standing in the stable, ten minutes later.

"But where is his lordship, *ma chère*? I thought him here with you, celebrating the true meeting of hearts, *enfin*."

She felt numb. All over. In her stomach and lips and everywhere. "He left."

Sybil's and Clarice's eyes popped open like a pair of waking birds.

"Did you let him *go*?" Sybil exclaimed.

"What do you mean, did I let him go? He is not a dog tied to a leash to be let loose only as his master pleases."

"Of course he isn't, darling Emily," Sybil cooed, draping a palm over her numb hand. "Or shall I be the first to call you Lady Egremoor?"

She snatched away her hand. "You should call me nothing of the sort."

Sybil blinked. Clarice blinked.

"But, *ma chère* . . . Did you not explain—"

"Of course I explained." Until there were no more words left to use.

"Oh! Naturally, you would rather accept his offer in more accommodating circumstances," Sybil said, glancing about at hay and buckets. "A woman would not like to have *this* as her memory of receiving a marriage proposal."

"I should think that if a woman admires a man, it wouldn't matter in the least where he proposed to her."

"There you are entirely mistaken, darling. When my father told me that Charney intended to propose, I instructed him as to precisely how I wished it to be done."

"But you don't admire your husband, do you? And that is a tragedy, and I am so sorry for you, Sybil. I wish I could turn back time to the moment you accepted him and make it right for you." Tears were gathering at the backs of her eyes with horrible, prickly pressure.

Sybil's mouth opened in a little O. "Darling, after all of that, did you actually fail to capture him?"

"Ma petite," Clarice said with pinched lips, "he is not the honorable man, to have left you now. You are better without him, as you have always said."

"That is not true." She backed away from them. "That is—I don't know if it's true. I cannot marry him, but I don't know if it is for the better. But I can assure you, however incompatible we are, he is honorable. Wonderfully so."

"But he has—" Clarice's gaze darted to Sybil and her next words were uttered quickly. "He has not been the gentleman with you."

"Dearest Madame Roche," Sybil said, "I know perfectly well what passed between them in this inn." She released a sigh worthy of Clarice. "The truth of it, darling Emily, is that men are beasts."

Cheeks hot, she looked between their sympathetic faces and the final thread of her frayed temper snapped.

"Men are not beasts," she said, her voice coming from somewhere deep inside her. "Every woman I have encountered since setting out from Balloch has told me of her worries about his intentions—Mrs. Archer, Abigail Boyd, you," she said to Sybil. "No one ever considered that *I* was the one with the dishonorable intentions. Everybody assumed that he is the 'catch,' the one to be captured if only I could hold him off long enough to coerce an offer from him."

"But he *is* a catch, darling," Sybil said. "He is rich,

handsome, and titled. There are scores of ladies in London alone who would jump through flaming hoops for the chance to ensnare that man."

"How in the world did we come to this place where marriage is constructed so that finding the person with whom to spend a lifetime—*intimately connected*—becomes a game?" she exclaimed. "Then it is considered a triumph when, by dangling temptation before a man and then forcing him to bridle his passionate nature, a woman somehow manages to win that game, as though she has snagged a dangerous beast and brought him to heel? It is positively grotesque."

"*Ma chère—*"

"*No*, Clarice. That language makes me ill. A man is not a wild creature to be caught and tamed. If a man is dangerous it is not because he is a beast; rather the opposite." Her voice wobbled now, but she didn't care. "Pip had it right, bless her heart! A man is all the beauty and majesty and complicated essence of an angel, powerful and protective and furious and compassionate and wise. He is equally as foolish and confused and fallible and a slave to the basest carnal desires as Adam was in Paradise. He is magnificent. He is *real*. To speak of a man as though he is the prize at the end of a hunt is to make him into an object to acquire, stuff full of sawdust, and hang on the wall like a stag's head. I have spent years—*years*—fighting against that very notion of women. How on earth could considering a man in that same light be acceptable?"

The final word, shouted from the depth of her belly, sank into the straw as Clarice and Sybil gaped.

"Well," Sybil said, turning to Clarice, "she certainly *is* in love with him."

Clarice nodded. *"Bien sûr."*

Zenobia swallowed over the clotted misery in her throat. Then she strode past them and out of the stable.

Chapter 24

A Great Man

Colin made the journey to Inveraray and the Duke of Argyll's castle swiftly, remaining there only one night. The duke himself was not at home, and Colin had little to say to his half brother except that if Swift had truly done the murders, he would do what he could to soften the punishment for the robberies.

He would not demand justice for the misuse of his name. If his father were alive, he would have his illegitimate son beaten for that crime. Colin would not.

From the corner of the cell that Colin had ensured would remain empty of other prisoners—a luxury in the crowded jail—Eamon grumbled his thanks and bade him adieu. Instead of leaving, Colin asked the guard to open the cell, took a seat across the tiny room from his father's son, and asked questions.

Eamon answered them readily; he was not ashamed of his breeding or rearing, only acutely jealous, it seemed, of the public recognition of his blood that had been denied to him. The earl had seen to his comfort and his mother's. She had been a maid at Maryport Court. When shortly after the countess's death she got with child, the earl moved her to a house in Yorkshire, where he occasionally visited them. Eamon had been provided with tutors that had prepared him for a career as a clerk, and he had lived modestly. But he'd had an unfortunate loss at the track, which had put him deeply in debt. When he met Swift at Newmarket, it had been natural to ally with the young thief and turn his education and intelligence to robbing the rich and idle, one of which he had always longed to be.

He said the last with a defiant eye, as though he wanted Colin to condemn him, as though he expected it. Colin did not oblige. He asked instead why he had borrowed his name.

"I thought you might someday come to Scotland, yes," Eamon said quite soberly. "It seemed like a lark, peculiarly. Until Swift shot the woman."

"You wanted me to catch you, didn't you? When he killed Aillig Kendrick's wife, you realized that you had gone too far and you counted on this, on my—"

"Compassion? I know what it is to be an only son too, brother." Then his face relaxed. "When I heard that your traveling companion resembled Swift, I—"

"Not a word about her. Not a single word or I will send for Argyll and instruct him to fit the noose around your neck himself."

The stranger that resembled portraits of the earl from thirty years ago regarded him carefully. Then he nodded.

Colin departed, and rode north to the Boyds' farm. Davie had gone, fulfilling his obligations. In the lad's absence, Colin made arrangements with young Meghan. Then he took Pip aside and explained matters to her. She begged to be allowed to accompany the newlyweds to Egremoor, and to live on their farm. When he glanced up from her pleading eyes, the entire Boyd family was watching him with hopeful faces.

He could not deny them. That Pip looked as much like Gray blood ran in her veins as Eamon did was likely a coincidence, unless his father's profligacy had not halted with Eamon's mother. But it could not be helped. If at Egremoor she was mistaken for his own child, so be it. He could protect her.

Collecting his wallet from Murdo, whose apologies were swallowed in scowls and red-faced shame, he left the Boyd family with a promise to pass along their fond greetings to Lady Emily. It was the only outright lie he had told anyone in months.

He would not be seeing Emily. He would not be corresponding with her. He had every confidence that his life would go along as planned, that he would fulfill his responsibilities to his people and his fellow peers, and that he would excel at it. But he had no confidence whatsoever that he could ever again see her and not end up on his knees begging her to reconsider, even knowing that she would certainly refuse him as many times as he begged.

At the village of Luss, in a soaking drizzle he rode away from the lake and guided his borrowed horse into the rainy hills, and then down the slope to the tavern where he and Emily had briefly, unsuccessfully sought shelter.

Tethering the gray at the door, he shook his coat free of rain and stepped inside. Three men sat at a table, laborers by their thick shoulders, meaty hands, and clothing. Two others stood at the bar, an aproned man behind it with his mitt on the tap. He was not the same tavernkeep that had greeted them before, and the kitchen was quiet.

On the wall close by the bar was the broadsheet he had noticed the previous week when he'd swiftly taken stock of the place. *One of hers.* At that time, he had curled his lip. Now he had the most foolish urge to tear it off the wall and memorize every word, every letter, then to buy it from the tavernkeep for any price he demanded, and carry it someplace ridiculously sentimental—in his waistcoat by his breast bone, or some such thing.

Apparently, all along she had been correct: the idiocy of men, and of him in particular, knew no bounds.

Speaking quietly, he commanded an ale, drank it, set coin upon the bar, and only then asked after his horse.

"'Tis an honor, milord," the tavernkeep said. "I've a cousin did a bit o' masonry on the great house—the Court, he called it. Said he never knew a better man than the Earl o' Egremoor. He said you gave every one o' them a brace o' hens on Boxing Day, though they were Scots to a man."

"Your cousin spoke of my father. He passed away last month."

"Ye've my sympathy, milord. My cousin said he was a great man."

Distant. Demanding. *Fallible*.

"Yes," Colin said. "He was."

In the stable, Goliath greeted him with a nicker. Colin ran his hand along the animal's sleek black hide, and then made him ready to ride. The roof leaked, and where half of it had fallen away entirely, the rain simply fell onto the stable floor.

"Two days," he said to his horse as he drew him from the stall laid with moldy straw, "and you will be in comfort, where an animal like you belongs."

"Earl of Egremoor, eh?" came a voice from the doorway. The three laborers from the tavern stood in the rain falling through the roof, burly shoulders bunched, hands fisted, eyes full of fury. The man in front spat on the wet ground. "A man who uses a great man's name to take advantage of those who've got nothin', he's no' a man. He's a villain."

Colin did not bother arguing the point. He could not. His throat had closed, all access to words denied.

Dropping Goliath's reins, he went forward to face his punishment. Sins of the father, and all that.

Somewhere in the midst of the fight, revelation struck him.

Later—he knew not how much later, except that his horse had not yet wandered off, *excellent breeding*, and the tavernkeep had not yet wondered why the Solstice's gray was still tethered to the post at the door—on his hands and knees, rain pounding his back that they had stripped and scourged, with blood and water running from his chin and the tip of his nose and a dozen other places on his body, he recalled their words—words that his clogged vocal cords had envied.

A man who uses a great man's name.

It hurt like hell, every bone beaten, every muscle pummeled, fury battering at him. But not toward the men who had left him like this. Nor toward her.

Toward his father, who had made him both strong and weak. Toward the director of the club, who had trusted him, depended upon him, and whom he had striven to please. The two men he had admired most in his life. Both of them gone within months, one to disease, the other to betrayal.

Clarity, he thought, came so unexpectedly.

He had not gone to the cemetery in London that night in order to silence the man behind the pamphlets, the man who commanded the attention and admiration of Britain. He had gone in search of something to fill the void. *Someone.* Without the men who had held him to impossible standards, for the first time in eighteen years he had not known who he was.

Now. Finally. He knew what made a great man.

Rain drove down onto his flayed back, running from his battered jaw, slipping between his lips and making sparkling crimson puddles before his eyes, and he felt real. Thoroughly real. In agony, struggling for air beneath broken ribs, bruised, bloody, acutely awake to every sensation, every color, every texture and flavor and sound. It was how he felt with her. *Alive.*

For the first time in decades, he felt like himself.

Chapter 25

A Broadsheet

*S*he was miserable. She pretended not to be. Shauna and Clarice and Franklin cast her sympathetic glances every time they encountered her in the house. She refused to gratify their cloying concern. If a woman could not battle her way past heartbreak to contentment again, then womankind deserved every disparagement mankind had heaped upon her for millennia.

Which was all well and good in theory. In reality, she did not want to get out of bed in the morning.

But she did. She stared out at the world from her parlor window and could not see anything in her heart and head. Not clearly. They were both a muddle.

Walking out the back door of her house and to the mews, she instructed Jonah to harness the gig, took up her cloak and umbrella, and without telling anyone drove herself to the London docks. She had often donated funds to Valerie Ashford's project for sailors who had been impressed into the navy and were now free of it, which placed them in more desirable work situations. Never once had she visited the place.

When she arrived at the bustling office she was told that Lady Ashford was not in. But the clerk seemed thrilled to see her. Gesturing to a sailor sitting before a desk, he told her that everything she required could be found in the folder, and hurried away.

Zenobia looked down at the folder upon the desk, then at the sailor's browned face, and had no idea what to say.

"'Ow d'you do, miss?"

"I am . . ." Not *well*. Not with the ache beneath her ribs and thorough confusion over what she was doing in this place among burly, weathered, scarred seamen, and entirely uncertain that this was not the height of arrogance to imagine *she* could do any good here simply because she wished to. *Needed* to. "All right," she said, using Colin's phrase.

A little tendril of peace slipped into her chest.

She looked the sailor in the eye. "What is your name?"

"Vince, mum."

He reminded her of Davie Wallace, young and big and strong, clear blue eyes in a face that was dark from sun. Creases scored his skin, creases, she supposed, from staring at endless seas. Too many creases for a man of his age.

"What do you like to do, Vince?"

"I likes the idea of gettin' outta this 'ell—er, that is, miss"—he clutched his cap between tar-stained fingers—"I'd like to leave Lunnon behind. And ships. I'd be glad to never see open water again for the rest of me days." He laughed awkwardly. "Me granddad and mum 'ad a farm near Welling. Then one day 'e brung me to the market 'ere and the crew nabbed me."

"When did that happen?"

"Mm. Ten years past. Or twelve."

He could not be more than twenty years old now.

"What can you do?" she said.

"Do, miss?"

"What are your skills?"

His brows steepled. "I can row."

She stared into his eyes and thought of the sheep farm Colin had offered to Davie. With Meghan, the young Scot could learn a new trade. Colin had never doubted it. At the moment he had been desperate for help, but he never would have offered Davie a farm on his own estate if he had not believed the youth could succeed.

"There is a list here." Her fingers fumbled on the paper as she pulled it beneath her eyes and a teardrop struck the lens of her new spectacles. She swiped it away. "How about cabinet making? Lord Dare has offered to fund all expenses for an apprentice to an excellent furniture maker in Somerset."

Vince's nose screwed up. "More *wood*, miss?"

There was an incredible lightness growing inside her now, a strange, airy levity. "I suppose not." She ran her fingertip down the page. "Here is a promising post. Lord Chance is expanding his thoroughbred farm and is in need of several stable hands. I happen to know that Dashbourne is more than half a day's journey from London and"—she smiled—"it is entirely landlocked."

"What d'you reckon, miss?" He spread his callous palms upward. "Could these 'andle fine 'orses?"

"I don't know that you will be handling actual horses. I suspect you'll be doing quite a lot of shoveling straw and mucking out stalls. At least at first."

He grinned. "It's better than tar."

A half dozen interviews later, fingers tight around the reins as she drove home, she heard not the sounds of traffic, only a question.

What do you reckon, miss?

She understood why she had abandoned her name. No one had ever cared what Emily Vale thought or said. Everyone had believed her peculiar and overly fond of solitude. Then the one person in the world who thought her special, extraordinary, left her. It was the easiest thing after that to adopt other names, exalted names, to leave Emily in the past. No one wanted her anyway.

Colin had accused her of enjoying Lady Justice's fame,

and he was not wrong. The world cared what Lady Justice said. The world listened to her.

The world listened to her.

He had told her that she was hiding. He had given her honesty—painful and ugly honesty. But he had not hidden the truth from her, not any truth that mattered. In return she had refused to listen to him. She had refused to hear him. And she had given him nothing that had not already been easy for her to give.

Entering her house, she removed her cloak and went to the parlor. Drawing out a sheet of paper and dipping a quill into the inkpot, she wrote.

PARLIAMENT WAS IN session and Colin's stomach was in knots. He suspected all newly summoned lords felt this way. If they didn't, they were scoundrels.

Bruises still livid around his eye and his lip split in one place, he ignored the curious glances of his fellow peers as they climbed out of carriages before the Palace of Westminster and he handed Goliath over to a waiting boy. Standing before the doors of government, he drew in a lungful of cold London air.

"You'll be well." Leam Blackwood's voice came at his shoulder, then his hand clapped him on the back. "You were bred for this place, Colin. Every drop of blood in you is meant to be here. But I'll tell you a secret, lad." He leaned close. "If you're lucky enough to sit behind one of the old lords wearing a wig, you can nap." Smacking him on the shoulder, he went up the stairs and into the building.

On the corner, a hawker was selling broadsheets.

"Lady Justice's latest, milords!" he called.

Colin drew a coin from his pocket. Folding the broadsheet and tucking it beneath his arm, he returned to the entrance of the most powerful hall on earth, and went inside.

Within the House of Lords Chamber, men were milling about, talking, and taking their seats along the rows that flanked either side. Colin made his way to his seat, greeting friends and accepting condolences on his father's death, and congratulations. He was Parliament's newest peer.

Settling in the place that his father had vacated after thirty-seven years, he allowed the sounds of murmured conversations, feet scuffling on polished boards, and the squeaking of benches that were hundreds of years old to sink beneath his skin. Then he withdrew the broadsheet, unfolded it, and read her words.

My Dear Fellow Subjects,

I have recently learned a Truth that I wish to share with you: A man can be powerful, wealthy, privileged, even arrogant, yet still bend himself down to the level of the lowliest child to act with kindness, compassion, and heroism. I have witnessed it.

I have been wrong, my friends. In the past, cynicism and old hurt threaded through my disparagements of great men. Some men of position and wealth do serve England for their own gain. But some do so because they wish to help others and to make the world a better place. Whether it is always apparent to observers, the fact is that they serve from a place of both Honor and Love—love of their families, their lands, and England.

The People of this great nation and its Rulers have much to teach each other. Both sides should listen.

In this same manner, a wife and her husband must coexist. In sharing and celebrating their partnership, they must trust each other, depend upon each other, support each other, and raise each other up—in equal measure. For where there is Love there must always be Respect.

For Respect to flourish, however, Equality must first exist. I ask you: How can a man with a single slice of bread look upon a rich man's feast day after day, yet not come to resent him for that bounty? And how can a feasting lord look upon a pauper's crust and not feel contempt, even judge that pauper deficient in some manner? Is not a well-fed man a happier man, and a better contributor to Society? Is not an equal sharing of resources a pathway toward equal respect?

In much the same way, to withhold from wives the same rights and privileges in marriage as their husbands is to sow Anger, Resentment, Fear, and Weakness into the fertile soil of this most blessed union. Instead, allowing wives equal rights and privileges as their husbands is to empower women to love and serve with Strength, Vigor, and Honesty.

Dear fellow subjects, I have witnessed the intimate bond between Love and Respect: I have seen it in my parents' marriage and in the marriages of my dearest friends. Now I have also felt it in my heart. And I have learned that without the one, the other cannot survive. Entwined together, however, they can conquer the worst of life's challenges.

In learning this lesson, I have come to understand that I can no longer hide in anonymity. In doing so, I only contribute to the mistrust between the People of this kingdom and its Rulers, who should instead be united, bonded, as spouses are bonded, in Love and Respect. In remaining anonymous, I am also a hypocrite. For how can I claim that women's voices are worthy of being heard when I have hidden my own so effectively behind this crusade that even those I love most dearly do not know me?

Therefore, today I sign off sincerely,

—Emily Vale, "Lady Justice"

He hardly knew where he was. The mumbles and chatter about him buzzed in his ears but he heard nothing clearly.

Even those I love most dearly do not know me.

She had written this to everyone in Britain. To imagine that she referred to him now, *that she loved him*, was certainly to be as arrogant as she accused. Yet the idiot organ in his chest would not heed the caution he should feel. And it told him that if by miracle she did love him, he did not deserve it.

Looking up from the page, he forced his eyes to focus on the reality around him. Throughout the chamber, lords were relaxing into their accustomed places that marked the centuries of their families' privilege and authority, and then the Lord Chancellor was addressing the assembly. Colin's throat was tight, a hard shambles of raw desire and desperation. He belonged here. He *deserved* to be here. He had studied and worked and paid his dues to take his place among these men. To make himself worthy of this chamber, he had suffered. He fully intended to live up to that preparation.

He might as well begin now.

". . . following debate in committee," the Lord Chancellor was intoning. Colin's heart beat furiously fast. But to all the other men present, this was just a typical day. Clutched in his hand, the broadsheet felt like fire.

The Lord Chancellor paused, then opened his mouth again.

Colin stood up. "My lord."

"Lord Egremoor," the Lord Chancellor said.

Colin wet his lips, drew air into his lungs, and the words slid over his tongue with clean, strong clarity.

"My lords, I motion to introduce for debate the Domestic Felicity Act."

The chamber resounded with heavy silence.

Then it erupted into chaos.

It was some minutes before the Lord Chancellor's remonstrations were even audible above the commotion. Men had leaped up from their chairs. Others were shouting to the men beside them. Others were murmuring to their companions and nodding. Not one man in the place had ever imagined the Earl of Egremoor's successor would do something like this.

It suited him. Now he knew a little of what she must feel every time one of her pamphlets stirred England into a furor.

Finally the Lord Chancellor managed to quiet the chamber. Men settled back into their seats. Colin remained standing.

"Lord Egremoor," the Lord Chancellor said. "Do proceed."

"Thank you, my lord." He drew another deep breath. "My lords, I have little doubt that half of you now think me mad. Another quarter of you imagine that, as a stripling in this august assembly, I do not yet fully understand how matters function here. And the final quarter of you suspect me simply skirt-smitten." He brandished the broadsheet. Chuckles sounded throughout the chamber, and a number of outraged harrumphs.

"The first three quarters of you would be wrong. I am perfectly sane, and those of you who were well acquainted with my father will believe my assurance that he taught me from the day I was born precisely what would someday be expected of me here. The final quarter of you, however," he said, "are correct. I am in fact smitten—smitten with a woman who has taught me that my duty to England—my duty to this kingdom that I love—is first and foremost to the least of my fellow citizens and then, only after that, to you gentlemen here. If this kingdom were ruled by the people who most fervently love *every person* in it, she would be standing here instead of many of us."

Murmurs of approval and some of discontent circulated throughout the chamber. Across the chamber, the Earl of Blackwood caught his eye.

A man is only as noble as his honesty.

Colin cleared his throat.

"Several of you knew me when we were children, during my brief sojourn at school." He glanced about, seeing the men whom he had once fought with fists and nails and feet, seeing them as though it was another life, another boy he was remembering. "Even you do not know the truth I have held closely." He mapped out each word, each phrase while brittle anticipation crackled across the chamber.

"For the first thirteen years of my life, I could not speak. I did not speak. Not a word. Not a sound. No one ever understood why, not even I. No physician could diagnose it except to conclude that I was an idiot, a simpleton, and urge my father to swiftly produce more heirs."

A rustle murmured across the rows of men.

"When finally I spoke," he continued, "it was from terrible need. Not for myself. A friend—a person smaller and weaker than me in body only—a friend needed help, and at that moment, finally, words came to my tongue. My lords, I tell you this now, which I have never told a soul, the secret my father guarded close to our family because he could not bear the shame of it—I tell you this because I want you to understand that I know what it is to lack the ability to make myself heard. And I know that throughout this kingdom, people smaller than us—people without noble blood, vast patrimonies, and fine educations—these people need us to speak for them. Their hearts are equally as full of courage and good as ours, and they need us to champion their causes. They need our voices raised on their behalf.

"Therefore, today, in an attempt to bring this kingdom at least one small step closer to the moment when justice becomes reality, I motion to introduce for debate in this chamber an act of government that seeks to liberate the voices of half of our population for the good of Britain: the Domestic Felicity Act."

A fresh volley of complaints and insults echoed throughout the chamber. This time the Lord Chancellor silenced them swiftly.

"To those of you who believe it is a mistake to allow your wives legal authority over their own persons and lives," Colin continued, "I ask you to do this: go home tonight instead of to your clubs and ask your wives what if any privilege they would like that they do not yet enjoy. Then listen to them list the privileges you enjoy each day, the gifts they are in fact so capable of wielding that, if they ever do, what they accomplish with those gifts will put us men to shame. It will not be a weakness on your part to do this. Rather, it will prove your courage, and that you are worthy of the trust that the people of this kingdom have put in us."

More hollers sounded from the men around him, and scattered yet avid applause. Many lords sat with stony faces, furious, disapproving. But not all.

"Someone said to me recently that a great man is not measured by the strength of his privilege, but by the depth of his heart." Colin smiled. "She was right." He bowed. "Thank you, my lords."

HER FAMILY WAS in town.

They had all come—her father, mother, and three unmarried sisters—full of complaints about the horrendous day of travel they had endured in their luxurious carriages and excitement about the prospect of town entertainments even in this dull winter season. But she must tell her parents about Amarantha, and this time she did not mind their company, not as she usually did. It was a Significant Day, after all. None of her family members read anything except fashion magazines, but she was glad to have them in town on this particular day, anyway.

Announcing at breakfast their intention of shopping all day, the Vale ladies departed early for Bond Street. Her father had already gone off to his club. At luncheon she sat in silence with Clarice, whose black eyes upon her were far too keen, and barely managed to nibble a custard. The moment Clarice finally opened her mouth to speak she fled to the parlor.

An hour later, her father strode into the room. Garbed in an unusually sober coat of blue wool with no fewer than five large gold buttons racing up the chest, he sported a puce waistcoat beneath, gold filigree tassels on his boots, and an enameled snuff case the size of Dover that he palmed, flicking it open to reveal a mirror inside the cover.

"Papa," she said, rising from her escritoire and moving to the bell pull. "I missed you at breakfast. Mama and the girls are still at the shops."

He allowed her to relieve him of his walking stick, an affectation he did not need, and he displayed himself upon the sofa.

"You are especially elegant today. Have you been at your club?"

"No, no, m'dear," he sighed. "The club's all at sixes and sevens, what with the *ren-o-vations*, don't you know? Board of regents want to install hot pipes, or some such thing. Say they carry water here and there and all around the place. Dashed inconvenient if the things should burst right inside the walls, I say!"

"I guess it must be welcome to the employees tasked with carrying hot water between the chambers. Thank you, Franklin," she said as he set the tea tray on the table and retreated from the room.

"There's my girl," her father said, accepting a cup from her and dropping sugar into it. "Always thinking of everybody else's comforts."

Not today. Today she had thought only of herself. The embarrassment her family would suffer over what she had done, what people all throughout London were discovering at this very minute, would plunge her into unhappiness. She should tell her father outright. Now. But her tongue was sticking and abruptly she knew a little bit of what it must feel like to be Colin, which made her chest ache so fiercely that she could only nod. She swallowed a gulp of tea.

"If you weren't at your club," she finally managed, "where were you this morning, Papa? Shopping too?"

"I've been up at the Lords, in fact," he said and took a sip of tea. "Most enjoyable few hours I've spent in some time, if I do say so."

"The Lords? Papa, you were at *Westminster* this morning? But you never attend the session." She had no idea if Colin had returned to town yet. He must have plenty to see to on his estate. But Parliament was in session, after all, and she suspected he would be taking his seat soon. She longed to ask her father if Colin had been there, but the last thing she wanted was for him to imagine he had reason to write to urge Colin to propose to her yet again.

"Fine show there, m'dear." Her father chuckled and leaned back on the cushioned sofa. "Fine, fine show. Excellent piece today, by the by. My favorite yet, though I was dashed fond of the one you did about those boys all those years after Ciudad Rodrigo. Poor lads. Know a thing or two about that sort of battle, of course. I was proud as a strutting peacock back when that one showed up in everybody's drawing rooms. Even saw it at the club, by gad! But this one, Emmie—you've taken the cake today, my girl. Why, I've read it three times already and I'm liable to read it three more before the day's over. And dashed if I wasn't pleased as punch at all the stares from this way and that, lords craning their wrinkled old necks to catch a glimpse of me. Knew there was a reason I told Price to brush out this coat for today. Westin's finest gabardine, don't you know? And precisely my shade of blue. Your mother will be delighted it's gotten so many ogles."

"*Papa.*" She could not manage to close her mouth. "What do you mean, you *were* proud? Papa, have you known all along that I am Lady Justice?"

Reaching across the tea table, he chucked her on the chin. "Of course I have."

She threw herself across the table and against his chest. "Oh, Papa!"

"Well, well, I haven't gotten one of these since you were a little thing." He patted her back. "Thought my Emmie had forgotten how to hug her old father. Splendid, I say. Now, watch the trim, m'dear. Mustn't crush the velvet."

She smoothed out his coat, her hands shaking.

"Thank you, Papa. Thank you for believing in me."

"There's my girl." He gave her shoulder a fond squeeze. "Never been a happier father, I daresay."

"But, if you knew, why did you keep throwing suitors at my head?"

His brows flew up. "They weren't for you! I knew you wouldn't accept any of them." He chuckled. "Your mother had hopes for one or two. Why, if that young fellow Yale had taken a fancy to *her* instead of you, I daresay she might've left me to run off with him." He chortled roundly. "But I never suspected my clever girl would give a second glance to any of them."

"You did it to calm Mama's anxiety that I was not married?"

"No, no." He laughed again. "She's busy enough fitting out all your sisters for their weddings. I did it to bring that boy up to scratch, of course. Seemed to me he needed encouragement."

"That boy?" she said thinly.

"I should've known you'd accomplish the thing yourself. My cleverest daughter." He chucked her on the chin once more and went to the door.

Accomplish the thing *herself*?

"Papa, why—" He paused and her tongue stalled. She forced the words across it. "Why did the old earl wish so fervently for—for the marriage? He did not like me above half."

"Well now, I don't know that's true. How could anybody not like my girl?" he said with a handsome smile. "But I suppose he wanted it for Amelia's sake. She was as fond of you as a body could be. Used to say she'd keep you at Maryport Court year-round if we let her." He gave a sorrowful wag of his head. "Terrible tragedy. Eirnin always blamed himself, of course." He brightened. "But no need to dawdle in ancient history, m'dear! Dashed good show today, I say. I ought to take my seat more often." And then he was gone and she was staring at the closed door.

She barely had time to right her thoughts before the door opened again and Franklin entered bearing the silver letter dish and a single letter.

"My lady." He held it forth.

"But the post hasn't yet been delivered, has it?"

"This arrived by special messenger." He pushed it under her chin. She accepted it and he left her alone.

She stared at the letter in mingled dread and eagerness. This was the beginning. She often received mail from strangers; Brittle & Sons sent correspondence addressed to Lady Justice in weekly bundles. Now that Britain would know her real name, readers would inevitably send mail to her house. It felt like an invasion.

But it must be endured. If she were to live up to the courage others expected of her—*that he demanded of her*—she must swiftly learn to be brave.

This letter was not, however, from a stranger. It bore the return address of the London residence of Mr. Wyn Yale.

My lady,

I am all admiration—this time in thorough sincerity. Were I standing before you now, you would see a man full of grateful humility as well. If I had known that you had repaid what you believed to be your debt to me not only the one time I knew of, but twice and so generously, I would have thanked you then. I do so now with profound gratitude. My worthiest compliments to you.

Additional compliments for pulling the wool over Gray's eyes for so many years. I wish I could have seen his face the moment he learned the truth. I shall simply have to imagine it and feel glee in knowing that you pierced that controlled façade when nothing I ever did could.

W. Yale

She could not smile. There was no satisfaction in this when she saw before her only Colin's eyes filled with betrayal as he had stared at her across the yard of the Solstice Inn.

From the doorway, Franklin cleared his throat.

"My lady, another letter has just arrived, also via private messenger."

The note was in Kitty Blackwood's hand.

> *Lady Justice!!!! Of course you are she, brilliant woman!! I am in thorough awe—indeed, all of London is. All of Britain! And were that not sufficient to make this an extraordinary day, Leam and Alex have just returned from Westminster with the most astonishing story. I am trapped with an infant at my breast, but the moment he has finished his meal, Serena and I will be upon your doorstep demanding entrance and* EVERY DETAIL. *Did it happen in Scotland? Leam said that Colin traveled there lately too. You must tell me everything!*
>
> *I send this note in advance because I cannot wait another minute to express my joy and admiration.*
>
>   *Kitty*

When she looked up, Franklin again stood in the doorway.

"Have you been standing there this whole time?" she said with agitated inanity. *The most astonishing story?*

"No, my lady. Lady Fitzwarren's page brought this." He handed her another letter. "And Ladies Rowdon, March, and Macintyre have arrived. Separately, it appears."

"Arrived where?"

"Here, my lady."

"For what?" She slit open the paper.

He lifted his brows. "They are paying calls, my lady."

"Calls? But I don't know them. Lady March a little. But not the others. Not well, at least."

"Everyone, however, now knows *you*."

"Oh." She was not prepared for this.

"Monsieur Franklin, take them to the drawing room! I shall come anon," Clarice exclaimed with a wave of a scented kerchief as she glided forward. "*Ma petite*, I will entertain them all—all of the peoples who like to be near to the celebrities—and you may rest here *dans la solitude, si cela te plaît.*"

"I am a celebrity," she said, her heart pounding and fingers slippery on the paper. "I never wanted this attention." She wished she were back in the Highlands on a snowy mountain slope, with the silence of sunset, and Colin. Despite all the danger and exhaustion and empty stomach, she missed their adventure. She missed *him*. And it was pure foolishness but she wished she could share this all with him now.

"Of course you did not, *ma chère*. You only wanted to help the peoples." Clarice smiled lovingly then swept away to the drawing room.

She unfolded Lady Fitzwarren's note.

They all tried: Eleanor of Aquitaine, Elizabeth I, and countless other Stateswomen in History. Yet through careful argumentation and sheer force of will you *have succeeded. And what a magnificent success! You might have convinced Fitzhugh or another reform-minded Whig to propose the Domestic Felicity Act for debate. But to have it brought to the floor by Egremoor—and so passionately—is a thorough coup, my dear. Well done! The Tories are in a tumult, half of them furious he has departed from his father's alliances so dramatically, and the other half thoroughly intrigued. It is a grand moment for Parliament, and a grand moment for the women of England. A grand moment, indeed! You, Lady Justice, are a national treasure.*

Fondly,
Mellicent Fitzwarren

The page shook in her hands. She could hardly believe it. *Colin* had introduced her bill in Parliament? It was unheard of—a peer acting so contrary to his family's political allegiances.

And so passionately.

She lifted her eyes from the letter and peered about the room. Everything looked familiar, exactly as it always did. Here she was, as usual on a Tuesday afternoon, in her parlor, a blank sheet of paper laid out on her writing desk, her favorite pen beside it, sharpened, with a fresh bottle of ink. Bless Franklin for preparing her writing materials as though it were any normal day. And Shauna, for this morning laying out her favorite dark blue gown that she liked to wear when she wrote. And Jonah for popping his head in during her breakfast that morning to ask whether she would need her saddle horse or carriage readied today, just as he always did. Bless them all for behaving as though it were a perfectly normal day.

In fact, everything had changed. *Everything.*

Her heart ached so fiercely and beat so swiftly, she could not be still. Leaving the parlor, she went to her bedchamber and paced. Finally she halted before the mirror. She looked the same. She was both Emily Vale and Lady Justice, as she had been for years.

She should call on him. It was absurd to bow to the convention that dictated a lady should not call at a bachelor's residence. He had done a magnificent thing. An astonishing thing. She should go to his house and congratulate him. And then perhaps plaster her lips to his and strip him of clothing and demand that he take her to bed. It was all so much easier when they weren't wearing any clothes.

Yes. Excellent plan. She would do that. Just as soon as she could make her knees cease shaking.

"Ahem, my lady?" At the door, Franklin held in his arms a large package wrapped in brown paper. "This just arrived for you. It is quite heavy."

"Set it down here, please." She clasped her hands tightly

together to control their quivering. He placed the package on the dressing table and departed.

She touched the surface; it was hard, a box of some sort, and about fifteen inches square. Twine bound the wrapping. She pried the knots loose and opened the paper.

Fashioned of intricately inlaid wood of two tones, golden and brown, the polished lid depicted two trees, the beautifully sculpted branches thoroughly entwined, like a pair of lovers embracing. Running her fingertips over the silky surface, she found the latch. Within the compartment were elegant sections lined in green satin containing sheets of finely pressed paper, a gold pen, a perfect quill, a glass inkbottle skirted in gold, and atop it all a card with one line written in a familiar hand:

> *In the hope that you will use this to write speeches to be read aloud in the Lords.*
>
> C.P.G.

Her knees were useless. She sank to the floor, gripping the card with both trembling hands.

He was asking her to be his voice again.

Forcing her legs to function, she crawled to the desk. Grabbing a pen and paper as she climbed onto the chair, she opened the inkwell, and it chimed from her trembles.

"What is it?" From the doorway, Shauna stared at the box.

"A—a gift from Lord Egremoor."

Shauna's brow puckered. "What're you doin'?"

"I am writing to him." She set the pen tip to paper. "To thank him." And pour out her heart? She hardly knew. She had never written this sort of letter before. The feather quivered violently.

"*Writin'* to him?" Shauna said. "When he's waitin' downstairs in the parlor?"

She swiveled around.

Shauna nodded.

Dropping the pen, she flew down the stairs.

At the parlor doorway, she halted. Colin stood in the middle of the room. He seemed to release a heavy breath, and he was not perfect. A bruise mottled the skin around his left eye and his hair was tousled and his eyes were as beautifully full of midnight as she had ever seen.

He bowed with sublime elegance. "My lady," he said, and the sound of his voice coated everything inside her with happiness.

Dipping her head, she curtsied. "My lord."

His gaze shifted past her shoulder, and the pleasure drained from his features.

"Wh-what?" she uttered.

He nodded toward the doorway. All five members of her staff were crowded in the aperture.

"Clearly they do not want me here," he said soberly. "Perhaps because they know you do not."

"That's not it at all, milord!" Shauna exclaimed.

"Why are you all looking like that?" she said.

"You see, my lady," Franklin replied, "none of us have ever seen you curtsy before. We didn't know you knew how."

She burst into laughter. Colin smiled and her heart melted, just like that, a puddle in her chest.

"Go away," she said. "All of you."

"You'll tell us what happens?" Shauna said.

She made a shooing motion and they went, Franklin closing the door behind them. She pivoted to Colin. He had gone to one knee. In his hand he extended a single red rose. Its stem was entirely free of thorns.

"Forgive me," he said.

The late-afternoon sunshine cut across him clearly now, illumining wounds on his knuckles, his brow, and his lower lip.

"Colin! What happened?"

"A few men from Balloch, it seems, had not heard the news that the earl had been apprehended. The other earl," he clarified.

"They did this to you? But, how—"

"It's of no consequence. Nothing is of consequence except that you are good and wise and damnably tenacious and sweet and strong and brave, and beautiful no matter what you believe, and I have missed you every moment since I walked away from you."

"I am not sweet. I have been told that my tongue is sharp."

"A blade to cut through to the truth. Zenobia—"

"No."

His chest seemed to constrict. "No . . . don't speak?"

"No, don't call me Zenobia."

Tentative relief glimmered in his eyes. "Pocahontas—"

"Not Pocahontas."

He smiled. "Lady Justice—"

"Emily," she said, the word hitching in her throat. "Please call me Emily."

"Emily, will you marry me?"

Air was abruptly a memory.

"I want you, Emily," he said steadily now, with such certainty. "I am so"—his throat jerked—*"proud* of the woman you have become. That sounds idiotic, I realize. But how could I not be proud? Your convictions are noble and you are unafraid to suffer the consequences of living by them. You are my hero, Emily Vale. You always were. I want you in my life, every day, every night, every moment. I understand that you cannot abide the institution of marriage. If you must stand by that, then I will accept it. I won't like it, but I will accept it if you will be with me. If I were required to give up *speaking* in order to be with you, I would do so." His heart was in his eyes, thoroughly open. "Give me another chance, I beg of you."

"You cannot give up speaking." Her voice shook. "I heard about your speech to the Lords today."

"You gave me the words. You needn't fight alone any longer. Let me fight with you."

"The writing box, the two woods, they are from our trees, aren't they?"

"A bit green still. The artist nearly refused to make it. But

I promised him that if this one cracks he can make another once the woods have matured." He smiled crookedly. "That seemed symbolically appropriate."

Her chest felt too full to contain all the feelings. "You are not asking me to marry you now because you made extraordinarily decadent love to me and you feel honor bound?"

"No." A wicked gleam lit the midnight blue. "Although certainly the prospect of making extraordinarily decadent love to you for the rest of our lives is one deciding factor."

"Be serious. *Oh*—I cannot believe I've just had to say those words to *you*."

"I am serious. Entirely. I want you in my bed. And by my side. And wherever you wish to be as long as I can be nearby. Marry me."

"And this is not about the property and your mother's jewels?"

His brow knit. "They already belong to you."

"Already?"

"I thought you knew."

"Not that. I—I—well, I have been out of town." She almost laughed but abruptly he looked so sober again.

"Upon my father's death they were yours," he said. "My mother thought of you as the daughter she never had. And I think my father did as well, in his own way."

"Yet I have hated him all these years."

"While you should have only hated me."

"Colin—"

"I tried to convince myself that it was better to leave the past behind. For years. But I cannot walk away from your friendship. Never again."

"What of our differences? Have you decided they are not insurmountable when we aren't wearing any clothes?"

"I have been a blind fool."

"Yes, I know."

"I am in love with you."

Euphoria, it seemed, could expand beyond the limits of flesh. She was bursting with it, and her face was damp with tears. "You are a fool because you are in love with me, or you are in love with me because you are a fool?"

"I need you, Emily. I need you. After we parted in Scotland I could not breathe. Through my own stubborn blindness I had lost you, and I could not actually draw breaths. Lady Justice's latest pamphlet has given me hope. Can I have breached that heart so full of good for others? Am *I* inside?"

"You always were," she whispered, entirely overcome. She went to him, to her knees, and took his hands. They were strong and she clasped them tightly, and his bruised face was the most beautiful thing in the world. "I don't want you kneeling before me. I want to look directly into your eyes. And I don't want to be a goddess or a queen or even a lady. Not any longer. I want to be just a person with you, an equal, like we were once upon a time when neither of us knew we weren't supposed to be. Please, Colin, let us be equals now."

"If your staff weren't on the other side of that door, I would show you at this very moment just how equal I want to be with you."

She laughed and kissed his battered knuckles, then laid his hands up and kissed his palms. "I understand now," she said. "I understand who you are. Forgive me for misunderstanding. Forgive me for my fear."

"There is nothing to forgive."

"Then accept my thanks for having the courage to tell me what I did not wish to hear—what I needed to hear."

His smile twisted. "Not courage. I believed that I could say anything I wished, however hurtful. At that moment I honestly did not fathom you could refuse me. But you did. You actually live according to your principles, even when—"

"Even when my heart is breaking." She twined her hands in his lapels. "Now you have mended it." She smiled. "My hero, again."

He bent his brow to hers. "I love you, Emily," he said softly, tenderly, for her.

"I've got my best friend back." She curved her hand around his face and kissed his cheek, then his jaw, then beside his mouth. He turned his mouth to hers and kissed her with a sweetness that made her sigh against his lips.

"You know," she said, her fingers playing in his hair at his nape, "I never thought to marry. It would be a significant shock to me."

"Not to me," he said with a smile. "I have always known that you were mine, a gift, that it was my privilege to care for you. I am sorry it took me so long to actually do so."

"With these cuts and bruises, it is I that will be taking care of you now, it seems."

"Rabble-rouser turned nursemaid. Can you stand the idea of it?"

"I can be both at once, of course. And perhaps if you lounge about without your shirt while I very slowly dress your wounds it will not prove too taxing."

He wrapped her in his arms and the kiss he gave her was eloquent proof of his feelings on the matter.

She placed her palm on his cheek, her fingertips tracing the outline of the bruise on his eye.

"Colin," she murmured against his lips, "I do not intend to retire Lady Justice."

"I would not wish you to." He kissed her throat and then the sensitive place beneath her ear.

"Even now that everybody knows who I am?"

"Especially now that everybody knows. My days of secrecy and subterfuge are over. It is time now to put to use a decade's worth of work on behalf of others."

She leaned back and regarded him in surprise. "I think I have just understood why you became Peregrine."

A glimmer lit his eyes. "I have spent a dozen years doing favors for men of power and influence and keeping their secrets."

"*Colin*. Do you mean to *blackmail* your fellow peers into accepting reforms?"

"Blackmail is an ignoble word. I prefer to think of it as collecting on debts."

She stroked his dimple with a fingertip. "How clever you have been."

"This is not, by the way, carte blanche support of every mad reform you have ever advocated."

"Mm." She kissed the dimple. "I will convince you."

"Some of them are as unbalanced as old Murdo." His hands moved up her waist. "I do have the welfare of the people of this kingdom to consider."

"You are a pompous elitist and you still need educating."

"And how do you propose to do that?"

"With rational argumentation, of course. And perhaps other sorts of encouragement."

"Other—" His voice choked as her hand encouraged. *"Emily."*

"How I want to climb all over you right now." She kissed his neck and stroked again. "I never realized how arousing disagreement could be."

He laughed. "You positively glory in disagreement. You adored quarreling with Peregrine."

"I despised Peregrine." She pressed her body against his and he pulled her snugly to him. She returned to nibbling his jaw. "You read my responses to your letters."

"The responses in which you wrote of your bed, your feminine breast, and enjoying the benefits of marriage outside of the wedded state? Yes, I read those."

"Choosing the details he likes best and plucking them out of context so he can ignore all the rest," she said breathlessly. "How utterly like a man."

"I *am* a man."

"For which I am grateful." Her hands crossed his ribs and he flinched. "Oh, no! You should not be on your knees like this, not injured as you are."

"And yet I feel no pain. None whatsoever."

"Colin. I love you."

Hands around her face, fingers sinking into her hair, he captured her mouth beneath his and kissed her with astonishing thoroughness.

"You look dazed," he said as he drew back, his eyes hooded and his smile thoroughly confident.

"I think I am dazed," she said a little drunkenly. "It seems you have ruined me, after all. Lady Justice reduced to the state of a sighing maiden will not go over well with my readers."

"I feel certain that whatever you choose to reveal to the public about yourself, they will still adore you as much as I do," he murmured, pressing kisses onto the corner of her mouth, then her throat.

"Would you object to taking me up to my bedchamber now so that I can ravish you?" she said.

"You have not yet said you will marry me," he whispered at her ear.

"I haven't?"

His kiss stirred the tender skin on her neck. She was all need, all love, and all his.

"Not yet," he murmured. "Emily, if the Domestic Felicity Act does not pass—"

"It *will* pass."

"—will you wish to retain your independence? Will you refuse me?"

"Come upstairs with me now"—his fingers caressed and she gasped against his lips—"and I promise to give the question sincere atten—"

The rest of her reply was subsumed in a moan that, later, the members of her household swore they absolutely did not hear, despite their ears pressed to the parlor door. But Colin, who seemed to know precisely how most effectively to argue his point, eventually had her response. From the beauty of his smile, she suspected it suited him well.

Epilogue

Very Happily

"*P*allas."

The carriage rumbled over the cobbles, nearly drowning out Diantha Yale's suggestion.

"But she has already been Athena," Kitty replied. "Pallas is another name for Athena. It would be redundant."

"Then Sappho," Diantha offered. "How would Sappho suit?"

Despite her not inconsiderable experience in the sensual arts by now, in her corner of the carriage Emily nevertheless blushed. The name Sappho inevitably reminded her of the bedchamber at the Solstice Inn in which she had first experimented in those sensual arts on her lover and nemesis with utter abandon. It was not, of course, the particulars of that abandonment that made her blush, but the eventual outcome of it. That her friends were already accustomed to her arrangement with the Earl of Egremoor did not make any aspect of it easier *for her* to negotiate.

In the opposite seat, Viola Seton caught her eye and grinned, as though she knew what Emily was thinking.

Emily snatched her gaze away and peered out the window,

regretting that she had agreed that Colin should go ahead to the party with Leam, Wyn, Jinan, and Constance. Tonight, in a private ceremony in an antechamber during the party, His Majesty would personally thank the former agents of the Falcon Club. Before that, the five of them had wanted to retire the office at 14½ Dover Street together with one final toast.

She could not begrudge him it. She could not begrudge him anything. Her pique was from nerves alone.

"I have an idea," Kitty said. "Molly Brown. She was a famous pirate."

Viola scowled prettily. "Famous, yes. Good at it, no. I suggest Nefertiti. She was a queen."

"You are fond of Egyptians, of course," Diantha said with candid eyes.

The carriage crept through traffic toward the magnificent mass of Carlton House. Diantha, Kitty, and Viola continued to debate, but Emily had attention only for the man standing with his friends before the building, watching for her.

"We'll think of something, I'm certain," Kitty said as a footman let down the step.

Colin extended a hand and Emily placed hers, gloved in thin kidskin, upon his palm. He lifted it to his lips and set a kiss upon it so softly that it left no mark on her glove and yet she felt it to her toes. There were, she had discovered, many advantages to having a lover who was both a consummate gentleman and an expert at hiding from prying eyes that which he did not wish seen.

"My lady," he said with a smile. "I have missed you."

They had been apart for only two hours. But he had said the same words to her so often over the past weeks that she suspected he said it to remind himself that he *could*—that the past that had ruled him no longer held any power.

Tucking her fingers into the crook of his arm, she went forward with him inside. The house was ablaze with sparkling chandeliers, music, and laughter. The King was currently flush in the pockets and lavishly celebrating it. All of London was in high good spirits.

To Emily's horror, they were also all *here*. It was the first time Lady Justice was venturing into society since she had revealed her identity, and Kitty and Constance had told her that no one dared miss the occasion.

In the past weeks, from across Britain people had written to her. Some excoriated her, claiming that she was an aberration of femininity and a blot upon society, England, Britain, and for that matter all of womankind. But most applauded her, thanking her, begging favors, suggesting new reforms, even proposing marriage, and many advising her on how to proceed with Peregrine on the one hand and Lord Egremoor on the other.

A number of them urged her to continue to insist that the former secretary of the Falcon Club reveal himself publicly, and that when he did she should make him into some sort of exalted servant—possibly her secretary, for irony. When she suggested this to Colin, he rolled his eyes and without comment returned to reading the newspaper.

Others, however, recommended that she accept the Earl of Egremoor's suit, which Sybil Charney had made common gossip in every drawing room and public house from Glasgow to London. *To help matters along, darling*, Sybil had written to her in effusively curling script, *for I knew you would never do the thing if left to yourself!* When informed of the now massively public nature of his proposal, Colin lifted a brow, colored only slightly in the cheeks, then proceeded to attempt to influence her decision by kissing her while offering rational grounds regarding the benefits of becoming a countess: the ready ear of influential statesmen, plenty of funds to pursue reform programs, an extensive estate upon which to put her revolutionary ideas into actual practice, and of course him.

He was, in short, no help whatsoever.

Given all, she was now understandably apprehensive. And the gown that her mother had insisted she wear was encrusted with sequins, and the stays were far too tight about her ribs.

"If I swoon from suffocation," she mumbled to her handsome escort, "will you carry me up a mountain again?"

He squeezed her fingers. "Always," he murmured reassuringly. "But you won't swoon."

"My temperament is better suited to modest gatherings." She strained to see the faces of people through her spectacles, which had fogged up. "Gatherings of two people or fewer."

"I promise to host just such a gathering on your behalf as soon as we are home tonight," he said with a benign eye on the crowd. But the dimple dented his cheek.

"You are trying to distract me."

"Is it effective?"

"A little." They were moving forward in the line to be formally introduced. Dozens of eyes followed her progress, monocles raised to study the flesh-and-blood woman behind the pamphlets.

"I never wanted this," she whispered. "This notoriety."

"You are not notorious. You are famous. There is a difference."

Ahead of them at the door to the grand drawing room, the majordomo announced, "Mr. Frederick Saint-André Sterling and Lady Constance Sterling!" Candlelight glinted off the hilt of Saint's dress sword and sparkled in Constance's diamonds, blinding Emily momentarily. Then, abruptly, there was no one in front of her. She was entirely exposed, standing before hundreds of people packed into the most exalted place in London, with her hand trembling fiercely in her best friend's steady grasp.

He bent his head to her and whispered conversationally, "What was that—that the others were speaking of when you arrived?"

"Oh." Her voice wobbled. "Now that Zenobia is no longer fresh, they are trying to decide on a new name for me."

"Aha," he said with easy aplomb. Then, with a crooked smile that entirely dashed away her nerves, he added huskily, "And here I thought you already had one."

The majordomo cleared his throat.

***

Lady Justice
The Parlor Downstairs

> Dear Lady,
>
> I have prepared the festivities that I promised earlier. If she can tear herself away from her work, I await only the guest of honor—the lady of my heart.
>
> In eager anticipation,
> Your consort, Peregrine

The Earl of Egremoor
The Master Bedchamber

> Dear Colin,
>
> That is the best letter I have ever received. In approximately ten seconds, when I deliver this reply to you in person, I will show you exactly how much I adore it—adore you—adore us!
>
> With all of my love,
> Your Emily

A Note on Women's Rights & Historical Inspiration

Human rights are difficult to pin down because their definition, indeed their very existence, depends on emotions as much as on reason.

— Lynn Hunt, *Inventing Human Rights* (2007)

The eighteenth century was an era of extraordinary change and upheaval. On either side of the Atlantic Ocean revolutionaries of all sorts—politicians, playwrights, poets, pamphleteers, novelists, soldiers, sailors, laborers, slaves, and people from all avenues of life cried out for liberty from laws that hurt them, fought for freedom from rulers who governed arbitrarily and to the vast benefit of the wealthy, and left an indelible mark on the world. The language of universal "human rights" that Thomas Jefferson included in the *Declaration of Independence* and that was repeated in the French Revolution's *Declaration of the Rights of Man and of the Citizen* remains the foundation of all democracies today. It means that *every* human being has a fundamental, natural right to a voice in the public realm—that is, the right to be able to contribute to making the laws that rule every individual in society on an equal basis.

But there was a catch. Historian Lynn Hunt sums it up: "those who so confidently declared rights to be universal in the late eighteenth century turned out to have something much less all-inclusive in mind. . . . they considered children, the insane, the imprisoned, or foreigners to be incapable or unworthy of full participation in the political process . . . But they also excluded those without property, slaves, free blacks, in some cases religious minorities, and always and everywhere, women."

In the early 1800s, under English common law a husband had virtually complete control over his wife's property, any income from it, her income, her children, and her actions. He could abuse their common property, her property, their children, and her body and mind, yet suffer no penalty for it under the law. One might argue that a woman could simply choose not to marry, but that argument would be anachronistic. The reality was that there were few viable life options for women to pursue other than marriage, which made marriage inevitable for most Englishwomen.

Plenty of women and men did not like the inequity built into the laws that governed marriage on both sides of the Atlantic. While my Domestic Felicity Act is fictional, in pressuring Parliament to ensure equal rights for women in marriage, Lady Justice is only a few years ahead of her time. Activists had already been demanding equality of the sexes for decades. Across the Channel, Olympe de Gouges's *The Declaration of the Rights of Women* (quoted in the epigraph to this novel) was a direct response to her countrymen's document *The Declaration of the Rights of Man and of the Citizen* (1789). To women like this popular French playwright, the limited definition of "human rights" set out in that official declaration of the revolutionary government was not acceptable. But to many, her claims were too extreme; among the thousands who became enmeshed in the vicious partisan squabbles of competing factions of the French revolutionary government, her life abruptly ended on the guillotine.

Fearing a popular uprising on their side of the Channel, and certain of the natural authority carried in bloodlines and noble family names, most of the men who ruled England rejected the reform ideas of French revolutionaries. Nevertheless, there were reformers of all sorts in Britain, including those who fought for women's rights. But it wasn't until the middle of the century that protofeminists began fighting for equality within marriage with especial fervor. It was a tough, tough fight. Custom, grounded in religious law as well as notions of work and the nuclear family in the industrial Victorian era, dictated that a husband should be the principal breadwinner and overlord of his household. Most people also believed that men were best suited to rule the nation. The roots of this patriarchal model of both the family and the state were not only centuries but *millennia* old by the 1800s, based on beliefs that included the intellectual, mental, spiritual, and physical inferiority of females, which—the argument went—made rational thought impossible for women.

That wasn't all. One of the biggest roadblocks that activists for equal rights faced in the nineteenth century was the prevailing notion that government should play no role in legislating the private relationship between a married man and woman. Political theory demanded the separation of the public (politics and law) and private (family) realms. This made it incredibly difficult for activists to argue that government should in fact intervene in the domestic realm when it came to ensuring a woman's rights and safety. In making their case, then, these protofeminists needed not only to overcome historical social custom but also to change powerful beliefs about the very *purpose* of government.

Despite the uphill battle, throughout the nineteenth century activists challenged laws on divorce, married women's property, child custody, wife abuse, and a husband's "conjugal rights." Under English common law, at marriage a woman legally became part of her husband; she had no legal rights of her own, and no recourse to justice if her husband squandered the family's money or property, abused their children, or abused her. Divorce was nearly impossible until Parliament passed the divorce act in 1857, and only then if the husband was "physically cruel, incestuous, or bestial *in addition to* being adulterous" (Mary Lyndon Shanley, *Feminism, Marriage and the Law in Victorian England, 1850–1895*, italics mine). In short, throughout the century, inequity in marriage in England persisted, despite reformers' efforts.

I modeled Lady Justice's critiques of the unjust circumstances of marriage for women (which also appear in her correspondence with Peregrine in my novel *The Rogue*) on the writings of protofeminists of the era. One of the most fascinating pieces by a nineteenth-century pamphleteer, entitled *Remarks upon the Law of Marriage and Divorce; Suggested by the Hon. Mrs. Norton's Letter to the Queen*, depicts marriage as a prison in some horrible fairytale of yore.

These huge and mighty Giants of the Law have long maintained and upheld . . . an ancient but most nefarious custom, by which all damsels travelling by a certain well-frequented road [that is, marriage], (which few, except those immured in nunneries, can possibly avoid), are despoiled of their money, goods, and chattels, of their jewels and ornaments, nay even of their garments, and condemned to prison for life. A curious part of this custom is, that each of these unhappy creatures is allowed to select a Gaoler of her own, . . . who then becomes the absolute master of her person as well as of the property of which she had been plundered, and of all other property that may accrue to her during her imprisonment, and even of her earnings in prison. The Giants of the Law will compel her, by force if necessary, to obey her Gaoler, and they maintain that she is also bound to love and honour him, though he may be the most odious and the basest of mankind. However infamous may be his treatment of her—however horrible his cruelties to her or her children—though he may turn out to be a gamester, a sot, a brutally licentious profligate, a burglar, a high-wayman, or an assassin, the Law Giants will scarcely ever permit her to get rid of her tyrant altogether.

In the 1856 edition, an editor's footnote indicates how the laws were once so strict that if a wife did in fact manage to escape a cruel husband, it was *illegal* for another man to invite her into his house unless she was in danger of dying. For centuries, the editor notes, very few exceptions were made to this law: "*three* cases only in which a stranger was allowed to carry her behind him on horseback" without afterward being condemned as a criminal for his humanitarian act. That image—of a woman fleeing danger, seeking the aid of a stranger, and later forgiven for that in court only because *she sat behind him* on the horse—stuck with me. And so in that editor's outraged footnote, dear reader, you have an example of how historical research can inspire an author's imagination.

Wives eventually gained many legal rights, but in bits and pieces (rather than in one swooping piece of legislation), with great effort, and at enormous cost in both social and financial terms to the activists. Benchmark legislation included allowing married women rights over their own property, a woman's right to sue for divorce on the same grounds as her husband, the right to claim custody of her children in cases of divorce or separation, and other acts addressing specific aspects of the laws that governed marriage.

I must include here a brief word on parliamentary procedure. The process by which a bill was introduced into the Parliament of the United Kingdom, and debated, was determined by specific rules and customs. A member of Parliament could not typically introduce a bill on the spur of the moment. To propose a bill for consideration in the Lords, a peer was obliged to essentially sign up weeks in advance, in a sort of first-come-first-served system that required those scions of society to actually wait in line until the relevant government office opened, sometimes for hours before dawn. I have streamlined that parliamentary procedure for the sake of the story. I hope that, like viewers of courtroom dramas today, the gentle reader will forgive me for compressing the legal process in favor of dramatic effect. (Shakespeare and Dumas intentionally and frequently fiddled with historical accuracy in order to tell a story, so I'm most humbly taking my cue from the greats in this.) The reality of it was that debate over controversial bills in both the House of Lords and the Commons could be fabulously dramatic, with MPs shouting and verbally abusing each other and even weeping on the floor of Parliament on occasion.

Regarding Scotland—oh, Scotland! I trekked Emily and Colin's route several times to learn the landscape, scents, sounds, textures, and flavors—to learn them as well as I reasonably could from a distance of two hundred years. And I fell in love with it. The beauty of Loch Lomond and the Central Highlands is extraordinary, gentle at turns and wild at others. For the book, on occasion I moved a building or hill from here to there as the need suited (for instance, the church of Saint Andrew is actually elsewhere along the loch and is named for another saint). But for the most part the landscape and architecture is just as I saw and experienced it, and as history books and images from the early nineteenth century taught me.

Inspiration for the writing box fashioned from the wood of Colin and Emily's trees came from a delightful visit to the Metropolitan Museum of Art in New York City. During the time I was writing *The Rogue*, I spent several hours in the Arms and Armor exhibition rooms gazing longingly at swords (that I was not, alas, allowed to touch). With my remaining time that day, I decided to steal away to the European Decorative Arts rooms, where I had the great fortune to come upon a gorgeously crafted writing box. I stood before it rapt, staring at it and writing in my imagination the final scene of *The Earl*.

I share these and other details about the inspirations for

my books in my e-newsletter, which you can subscribe to via my website, www.KatharineAshe.com. My website also has lots of information about the other books in my Falcon Club and Devil's Duke series in which Emily and Colin appear, including the full story of Emily's relationship with Wyn Yale in *When a Scot Loves a Lady* and *How a Lady Weds a Rogue.*

Thank-Yous

But if I was fearless, could I be your reckless friend?
And if I was helpless, could you be the one comes rushin' in?
— Cyndi Lauper, "Fearless"

I am neither an antiquarian, who studies history for history's own sake, nor a presentist, who interprets the past chiefly through the lens of our era's preoccupations. At heart I am an historian, which just means that I love people and stories and I want to understand *why* people did, felt, and believed what they did, felt, and believed in the past as much as I do in the present. It also means that I don't mind *in the least little bit* taking inspiration from a modern source to help me write an historical novel. After six years of planning this novel, by the time I finally started writing it I knew a lot about Lady Justice, Emily Vale, Peregrine, and Colin Gray; they had already appeared in four of my novels. But it was not until I heard Cyndi Lauper perform "Fearless" in a live concert, and my heart turned inside out, that I really knew Emily—*entirely*, from the hour of her birth to the moment she tells Colin she cannot be with him. For Cyndi's courage to sing messages of both female strength and feminine vulnerability I thank her.

And so I have finally come to the end of my Falcon Club series. Like Emily and Colin along their route through Scotland, I have many people to thank for helping me on this journey.

Many thanks to Maya Rodale for allowing me to begin this story with the *London Weekly*, which she invented for her fabulous Writing Girls series. To Sarah Lyons and Eric Selinger, generous and creative writers and thinkers, and advocates for the romance genre, I give thanks for their scholarship that has inspired not only my teaching but also my fiction. Copious thanks to Shauna George, who suggested Hyde Park; to clever Marcia Abercrombie for the existence of Eamon and Mr. Swift; to Anne Brophy and Georgie C. Brophy for assistance with names; to Laurie LaBean for honest advice on Emily's decisions; to Dr. Charles Miller and Celia Wolff for wise counsel on horse behavior; to Teresa More and Dr. Sandie Blaise, for their invaluable assistance with French; to Mary Brophy Marcus and Georgann Brophy for essential help, under insane pressure at that; to the wonderful folks at the Washington Duke Inn for the best snowed-in writer's retreat I have ever had; and to my beta readers Celia, Donna, Georgie, Marcia, Mary, Meg, Nita, and Sonja I owe piles of gratitude. Those who have helped me with this story are blameless for any deviation from accuracy in this novel—whether intentional or unintentional—and are only to be praised with parades of gratitude and great rejoicing.

To the people I've met in Scotland on my journeys to research this series. Scotland is a magical place, but the people are what make it truly special. I am a stranger there and yet they always make me feel entirely at home. For their warm, wonderful hospitality, I thank them.

To the Princesses, and particularly to Susan Knight, who gave me four perfect words to put upon Colin's tongue, I declare my thanks and affection. Thanks to Abby, Christine, Helen, and Lucy, my "happy place" on campus during the semester I finished this book, women who make me proud to be a graduate of Duke University. For The Lady

Authors—Caroline Linden, Miranda Neville, and Maya Rodale—whose professional sisterhood and cherished friendship mean more to me than they know even from my overly effusive expressions of adoration that make them roll their eyes and possibly gag—I am so completely grateful. For my sisters and brother and mother, without whose unfailing support and enthusiasm I would not have the courage to continue in this career, my heart is eternally theirs.

For my agent, Kimberly Whalen, and my editor Lucia Macro, about whom I (*a writer*) haven't even sufficient words of praise, for they are wonderful beyond telling, patient, wise, and so darn good at what they do; I am indebted to them. Thank you, also, to everyone at Avon who produces my books and makes them available to readers with apparent ease (that in reality isn't easy at all, rather, the product of these people's talent and hard work), especially Shawn Nicholls, Caroline Perny, Pamela Jaffee, and Nicole Fischer. And thanks to Thomas Egner for the perfectly perfect covers of my Devil's Duke series, and to Tara Carberry at Trident Media Group, who is fabulous.

To all of my loyal readers, thank you from my heart.

Finally, to my husband, my son, and my Idaho—my sunshine, my moonshine, my starshine, and every sparkle upon the surface of the ocean to me. Thank you for helping me with my novels in so many ways small and large. But mostly thank you for making my life so happy and full of love.

The door with the falcon-shaped knocker at 14½ Dover Street has closed for the last time (probably, but what author ever knows when a series is finished, really?). A diabolical duke, however, is still at large in Scotland, and he is determined not to be undone by a certain lady bent on discovering every one of his secrets. Gabriel and Amarantha's love story, *The Duke*, is coming soon. For more about the Devil's Duke series, my Falcon Club series, and all my books, please visit me at www.KatharineAshe.com or drop me a letter the lovely old-fashioned way at PO Box 51702, Durham, NC 27717. I love hearing from readers.

LK3 1215

THE SMYTHE-SMITH QUARTET BY
#1 *NEW YORK TIMES*
BESTSELLING AUTHOR

JULIA QUINN

JUST LIKE HEAVEN
978-0-06-149190-0

Honoria Smythe-Smith is to play the violin (badly) in the annual musicale performed by the Smythe-Smith quartet. But first she's determined to marry by the end of the season. When her advances are spurned, can Marcus Holroyd, her brother Daniel's best friend, swoop in and steal her heart in time for the musicale?

A NIGHT LIKE THIS
978-0-06-207290-0

Anne Wynter is not who she says she is, but she's managing quite well as a governess to three highborn young ladies. Daniel Smythe-Smith might be in mortal danger, but that's not going to stop the young earl from falling in love. And when he spies a mysterious woman at his family's annual musicale, he vows to pursue her.

THE SUM OF ALL KISSES
978-0-06-207292-4

Hugh Prentice has never had patience for dramatic females, and Lady Sarah Pleinsworth has never been acquainted with the words *shy* or *retiring*. Besides, a reckless duel has left Hugh with a ruined leg, and now he could never court a woman like Sarah, much less dream of marrying her.

THE SECRETS OF SIR RICHARD KENWORTHY
978-0-06-207294-8

Sir Richard Kenworthy has less than a month to find a bride, and when he sees Iris Smythe-Smith hiding behind her cello at her family's infamous musicale, he thinks he might have struck gold. Iris is used to blending into the background, so when Richard courts her, she can't quite believe it's true.

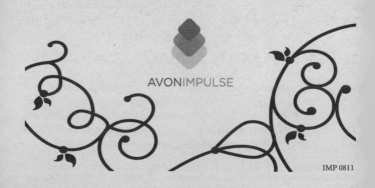

At Avon Books, we know your passion for romance—once you finish one of our novels, you find yourself wanting more.

May we tempt you with . . .

- **Excerpts** from our upcoming releases.

- Entertaining **extras**, including authors' personal photo albums and book lists.

- Behind-the-scenes **scoop** on your favorite characters and series.

- **Sweepstakes** for the chance to win free books, romantic getaways, and other fun prizes.

- Writing **tips** from our authors and editors.

- **Blog** with our authors and find out why they love to write romance.

- **Exclusive content** that's not contained within the pages of our novels.

Join us at
www.avonbooks.com

An Imprint of HarperCollins*Publishers*
www.avonromance.com